LOWER YOUR SIGHTS

Laura Chacón
Founder

Mark London
CEO and Chief Creative Officer

Mark Irwin
VP of Business Development

Chris Fernandez
Publisher

Cecilia Medina
Chief Financial Officer

Kurt Nelson
Director of Sales

Allison Pond
Marketing Director

Giovanna T. Orozco
Production Manager

Miguel A. Zapata
Design Director

Chas! Pangburn
Senior Editor

Lauren Hitzhusen
Senior Editor

James B. Emmett
Senior Editor

Maya Lopez
Marketing Manager

Diana Bermúdez
Graphic Designer

David Reyes
Graphic Designer

Adriana T. Orozco
Interactive Media Designer

Nicolás Zea Arias
Audiovisual Production

Frank Silva
Executive Assistant

Pedro Herrera
Retail Associate

Stephanie Hidalgo
Office Manager

FOR MAD CAVE COMICS, INC. Lower Your Sights
Published by Mad Cave Studios, Inc. 8838 SW 129th St. Miami,
FL 33176. © 2022 Mad Cave Studios, Inc. All rights reserved.

LOWER YOUR SIGHTS

A Benefit Anthology For Ukraine

COVER ARTIST
YEV HAIDAMAKA

PIN-UP ARTISTS

LIANA KANSAS + CHARLOTTE BALOGH + GAB CONTRERAS, JOHN K. SNYDER III, BRYAN SILVERBAX + KOTE CARVAJAL, NICKY NOONS, RYAN ODAGAWA, SEAN VON GORMAN

LOGO DESIGN
TIM DANIEL

BOOK DESIGN
MIGUEL A. ZAPATA

EDITOR
CHAS! PANGBURN

Special thanks to
Tanya Vovk, Lena Rozvadovska, Azad Safarov, Olena Ermolenko, and the rest of the Voices of Children foundation

VOICES OF CHILDREN

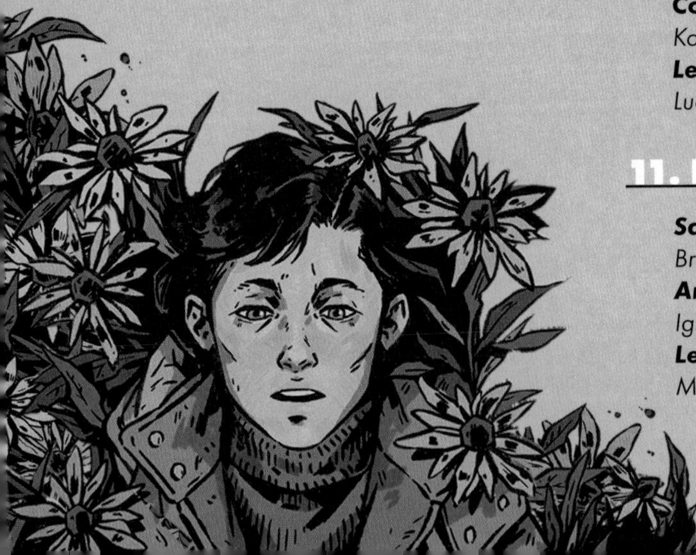

BLOOD, SWEAT, AND INK:
AN INTRODUCTION

Anger, sadness, and frustration are very real and extremely valid emotions toward the horrific events continuing to take place in Ukraine. For some, the constant bombardment of tragic details deeply rattles within your bones and urges you to do something-- anything, really.

Thankfully, I come from a publisher whose entire staff felt that call. Being sequential storytellers, we planned to assist with our weapons of choice: pencils and keyboards.

We quickly set out to create a comic book anthology highlighting *industry greats, indie darlings, rising stars, and, most importantly, numerous Ukrainian creators.* Our goal was to curate a collection of powerful and poignant tales for an anthology where all proceeds would be donated to a Ukrainian foundation. Upon discovering Voices of Children, we quickly realized we found the perfect collaborator for this endeavor.

Voices of Children provides psychological and psychosocial support for children affected by war. Their targeted humanitarian aid also ensures basic necessities, shelter, relocation assistance, educational options, and various forms of rehabilitation. In these dark times, they act as a ray of light to ensure the proper development and support of children.

With our goal and foundation locked in, we got to work. All collaborators were given **one month** to craft their tales. It was a very tight deadline, but everyone knew its reasoning and rose to the challenge. They donated their time and talent pro bono.

It goes without saying that this book would not be possible if it weren't for their contributions. A warm thanks to them all. Every word, pen stroke, and splash of color brings forth layers of emotional resonance that will stay with readers for years to come.

• Thanks must also be given to the entirety of Mad Cave's staff, but specific employees deserve individual call-outs: Allison Pond and Maya Lopez's marketing push ensured the book found its rightful audience, Miguel A. Zapata's excellent design skills cemented a gorgeous book, Giovanna T. Orozco's production management secured all behind-the-scenes processes in a timely manner, and Mark Irwin's insights and infinitely deep Rolodex opened the door to many new collaborators and friends.

• A heartfelt thanks to Lena Rozvadovska, Olena Ermolenko, Azad Safarov, Tanya Vovk, and the rest of the Voices of Children foundation. We sincerely hope we did you proud.

• Tim Daniel's multiple logo variations ensured that each variant cover of this anthology felt beyond appropriate.

• We also thank you—the reader. By supporting this book, you're benefiting the Voices of Children foundation and their efforts. It means the world to us all.

With the above in mind, we invite you to dive into these tales. We did our best to let creators go wherever their heads and hearts took them. Naturally, this brought forth varied tales about history, heartbreak, and hope. We start off with some powerful shorts, transition into historical stories, spice things up with unique takes and fables, and follow up with tales that inspire strength. Most importantly, we close out the book with art pieces and write-ups from numerous Ukrainian illustrators. By the end of the book, you'll rediscover **the power of resiliency and community**.

Just remember: whether you live on the frontline or view things from afar, you can make a difference. ***Together, we can overcome anything.***

- Chas! Pangburn, Editor

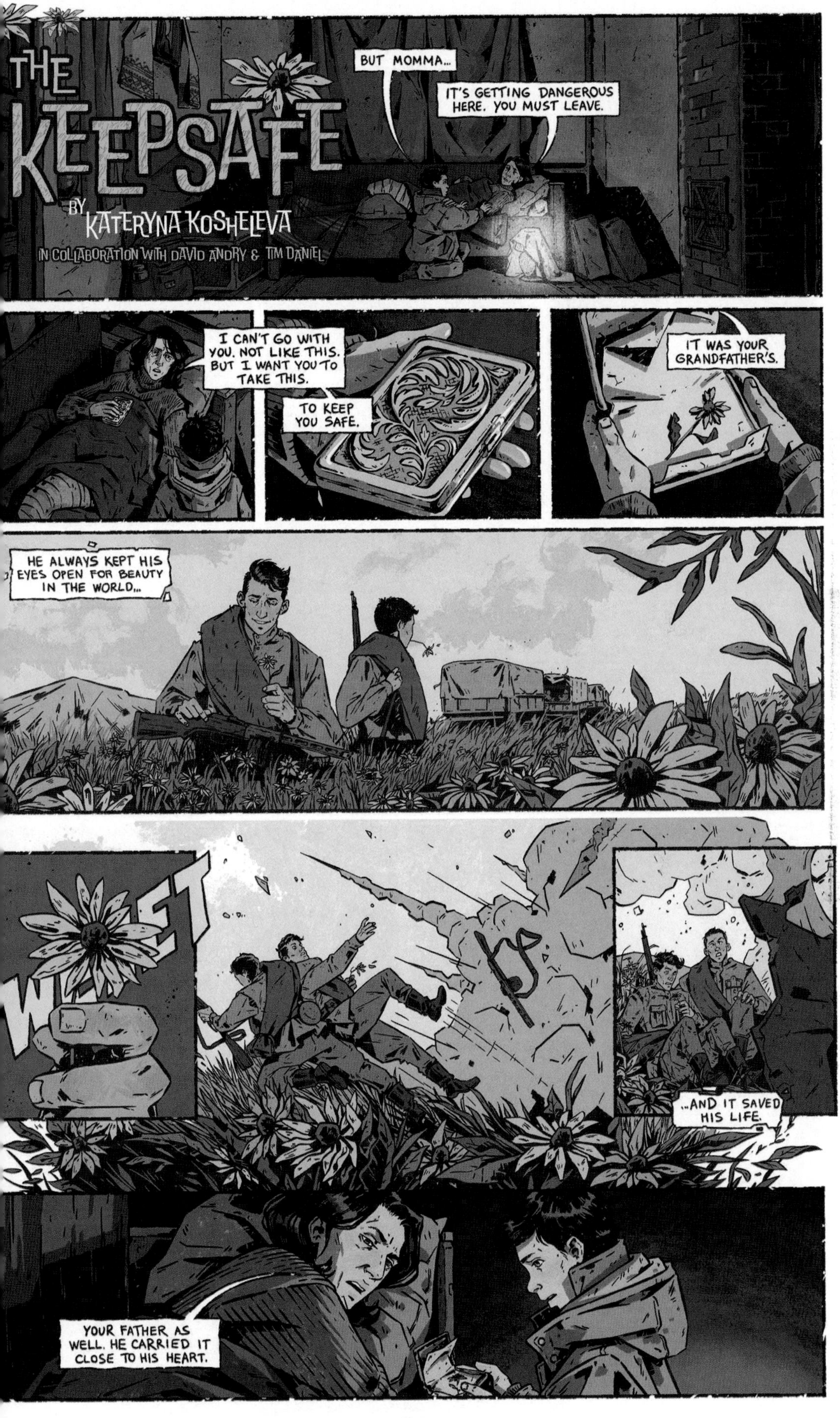
THE KEEPSAFE
BY KATERYNA KOSHELEVA
IN COLLABORATION WITH DAVID ANDRY & TIM DANIEL
BUT MOMMA...
IT'S GETTING DANGEROUS HERE. YOU MUST LEAVE.
I CAN'T GO WITH YOU. NOT LIKE THIS. BUT I WANT YOU TO TAKE THIS.
TO KEEP YOU SAFE.
IT WAS YOUR GRANDFATHER'S.
HE ALWAYS KEPT HIS EYES OPEN FOR BEAUTY IN THE WORLD...
...AND IT SAVED HIS LIFE.
YOUR FATHER AS WELL. HE CARRIED IT CLOSE TO HIS HEART.

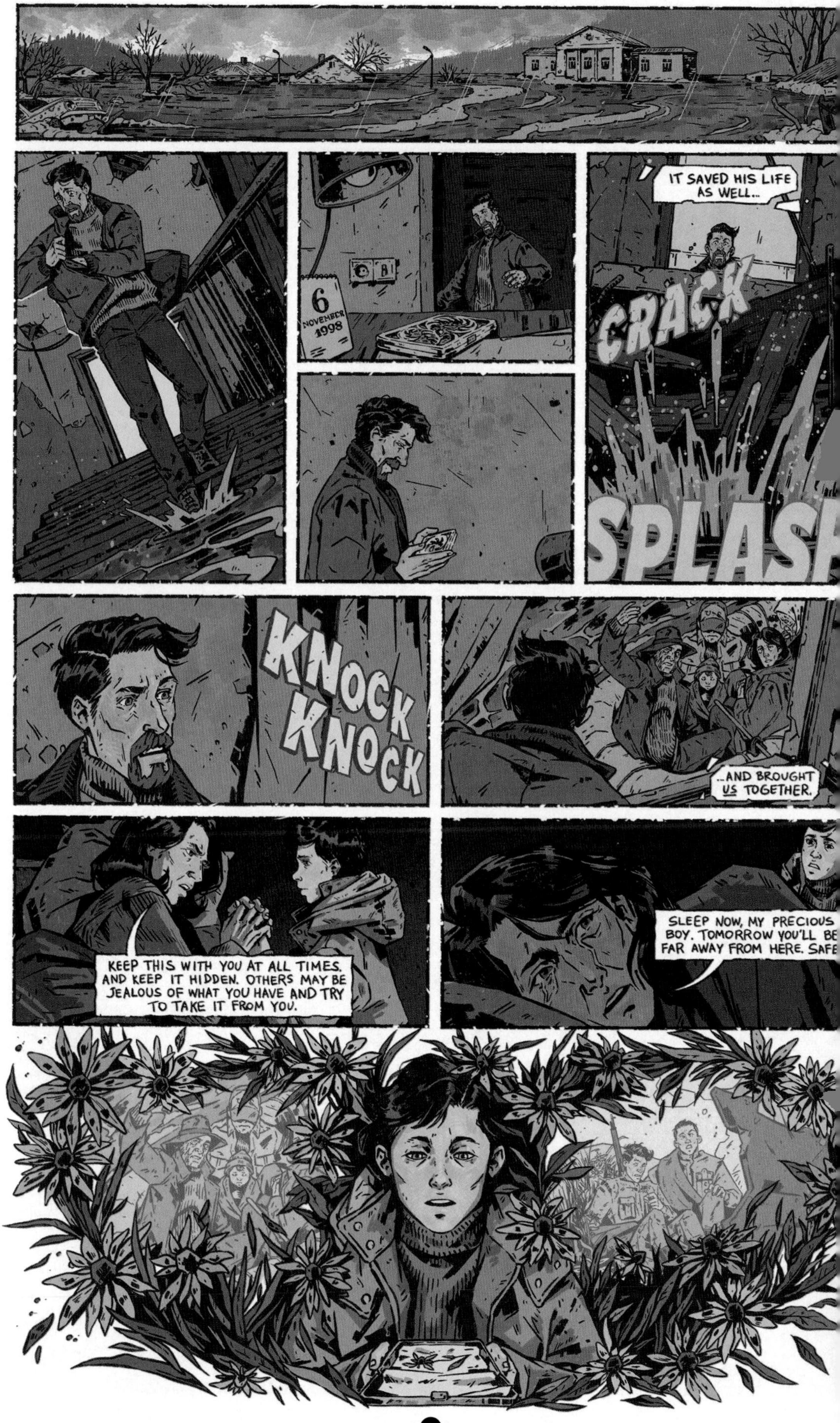
6
NOVEMBER
1998
IT SAVED HIS LIFE AS WELL...
CRACK
SPLASH
KNOCK KNOCK
...AND BROUGHT US TOGETHER.
KEEP THIS WITH YOU AT ALL TIMES. AND KEEP IT HIDDEN. OTHERS MAY BE JEALOUS OF WHAT YOU HAVE AND TRY TO TAKE IT FROM YOU.
SLEEP NOW, MY PRECIOUS BOY. TOMORROW YOU'LL BE FAR AWAY FROM HERE. SAFE

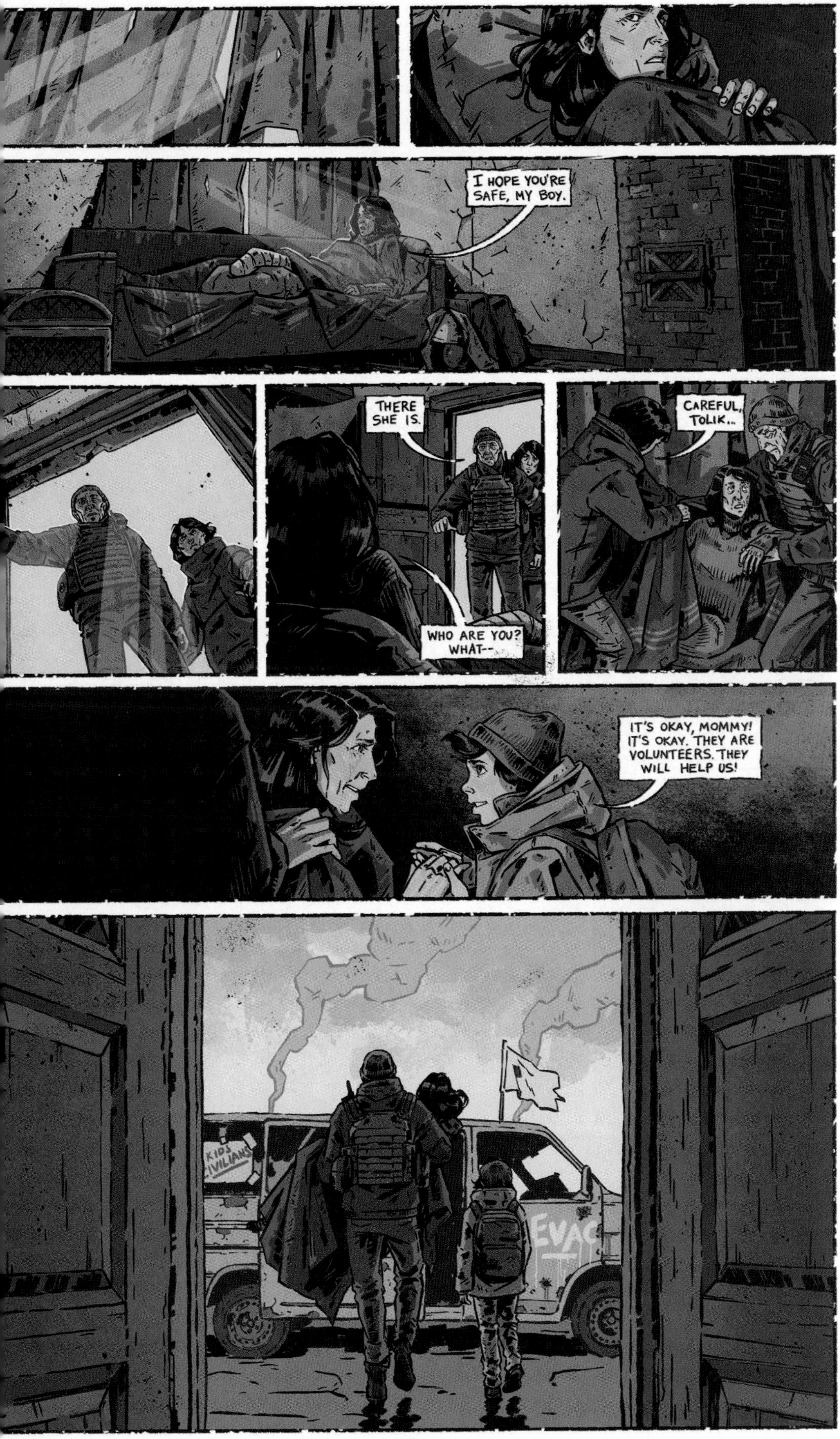
I HOPE YOU'RE SAFE, MY BOY.
THERE SHE IS.
WHO ARE YOU? WHAT--
CAREFUL, TOLIK..
IT'S OKAY, MOMMY! IT'S OKAY. THEY ARE VOLUNTEERS. THEY WILL HELP US!
KIDS CIVILIANS
EVAC

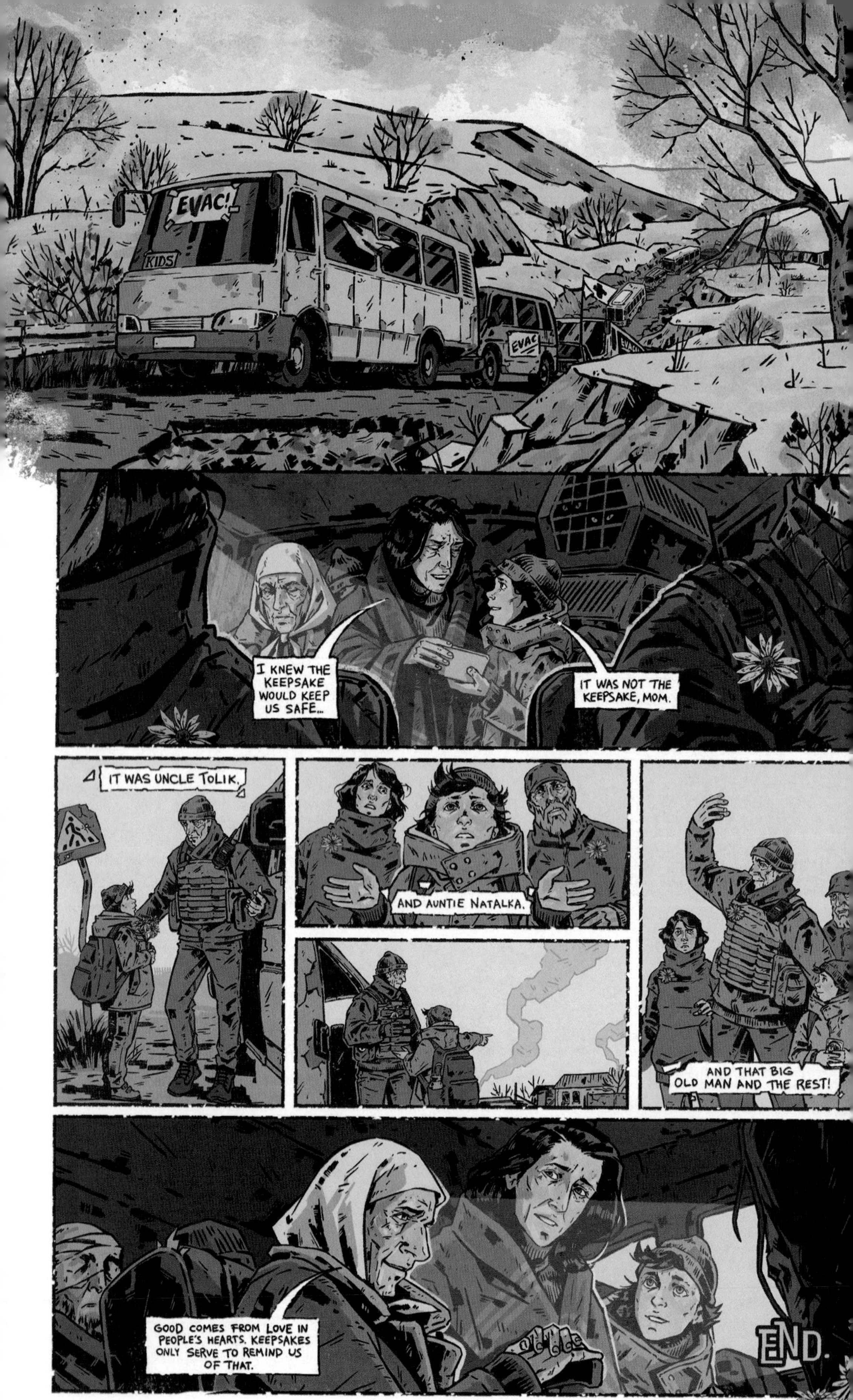
EVAC!
KIDS
EVAC
I KNEW THE KEEPSAKE WOULD KEEP US SAFE...
IT WAS NOT THE KEEPSAKE, MOM.
IT WAS UNCLE TOLIK,
AND AUNTIE NATALKA,
AND THAT BIG OLD MAN AND THE REST!
GOOD COMES FROM LOVE IN PEOPLE'S HEARTS. KEEPSAKES ONLY SERVE TO REMIND US OF THAT.
END.

THE WAIT

STORY AND ART BY: ENNUN ANA IUROV
COLORS BY: ANNA PAPADOPOULOU

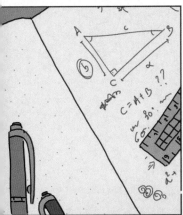

LIVE FOOTAGE

BREAKING ...INE UNDER FIRE * EAST BORDER HAS BEEN ATTACKED AT 10:25 THIS MORNING

HAHAHAHA
LMFAO XD
Today
I just saw the news
R U OK?

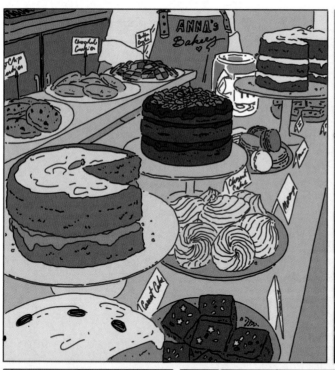

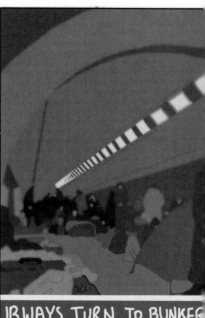

ANNA's Bakery
Carrot Cake
Meringue
BWAYS TURN TO BUNKE
LIVE
I'm trying to find out where Alex is, I haven't heard from him in 5 days. Can you dm me please... r u still in Kyiv?
Maria when you get some internet please dm...
Alex answered me. He's in Poland with his wbv.
Yesterday
Maria...
They said peop
Are u with yo
please....
Toda
Maria plea
the news sa
message @ ma
BOMBS WER
ER KYIV TO

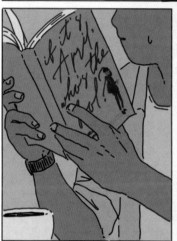

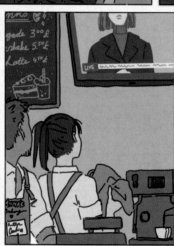

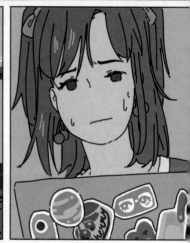

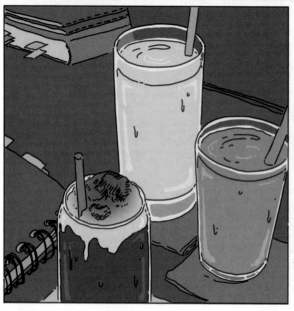

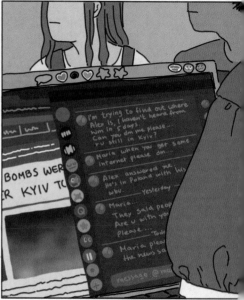

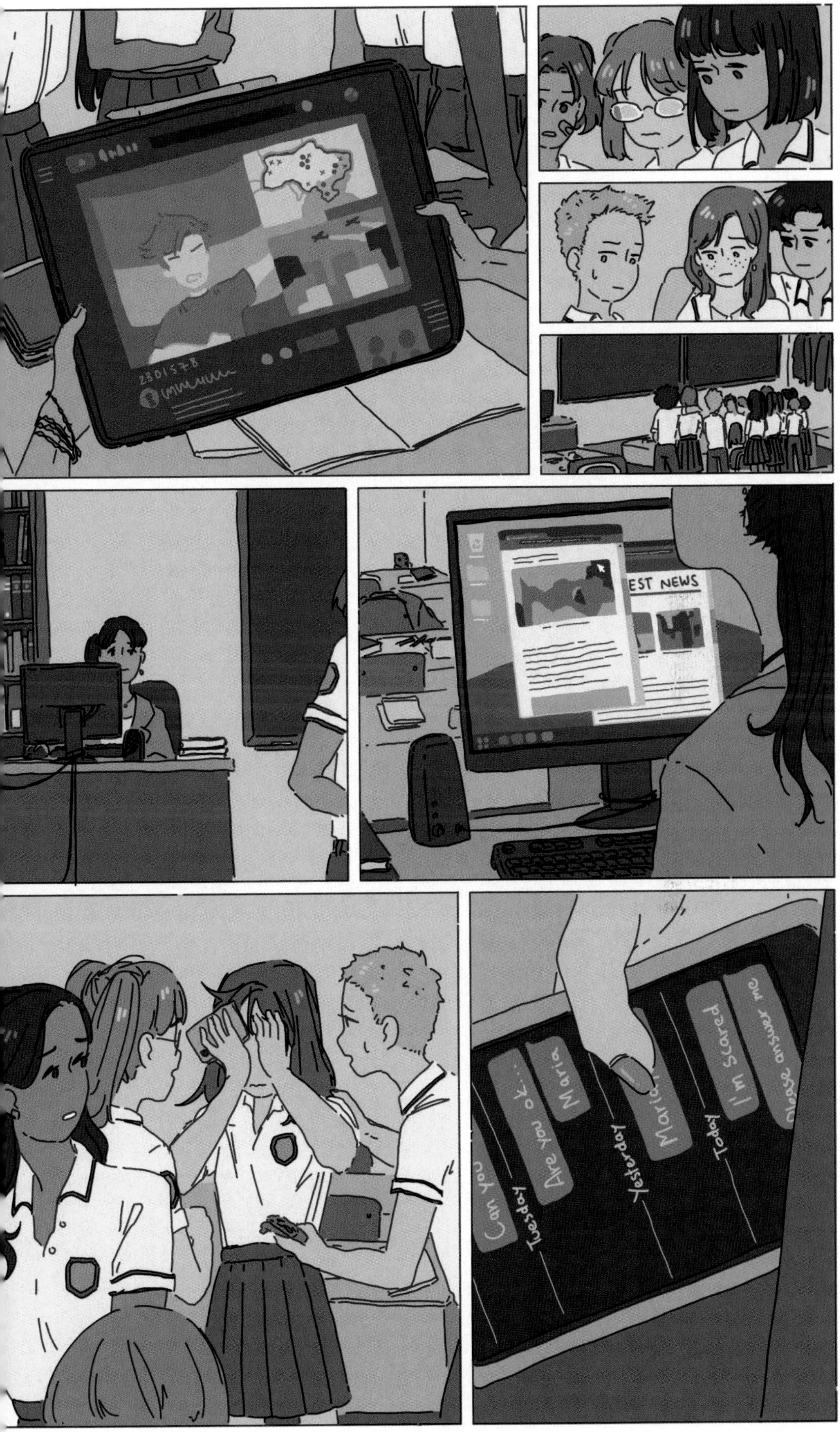
2301578
EST NEWS
Can you
Tuesday
Are you ok...
Maria
Yesterday
Maria
Today
I'm scared
Please answer me

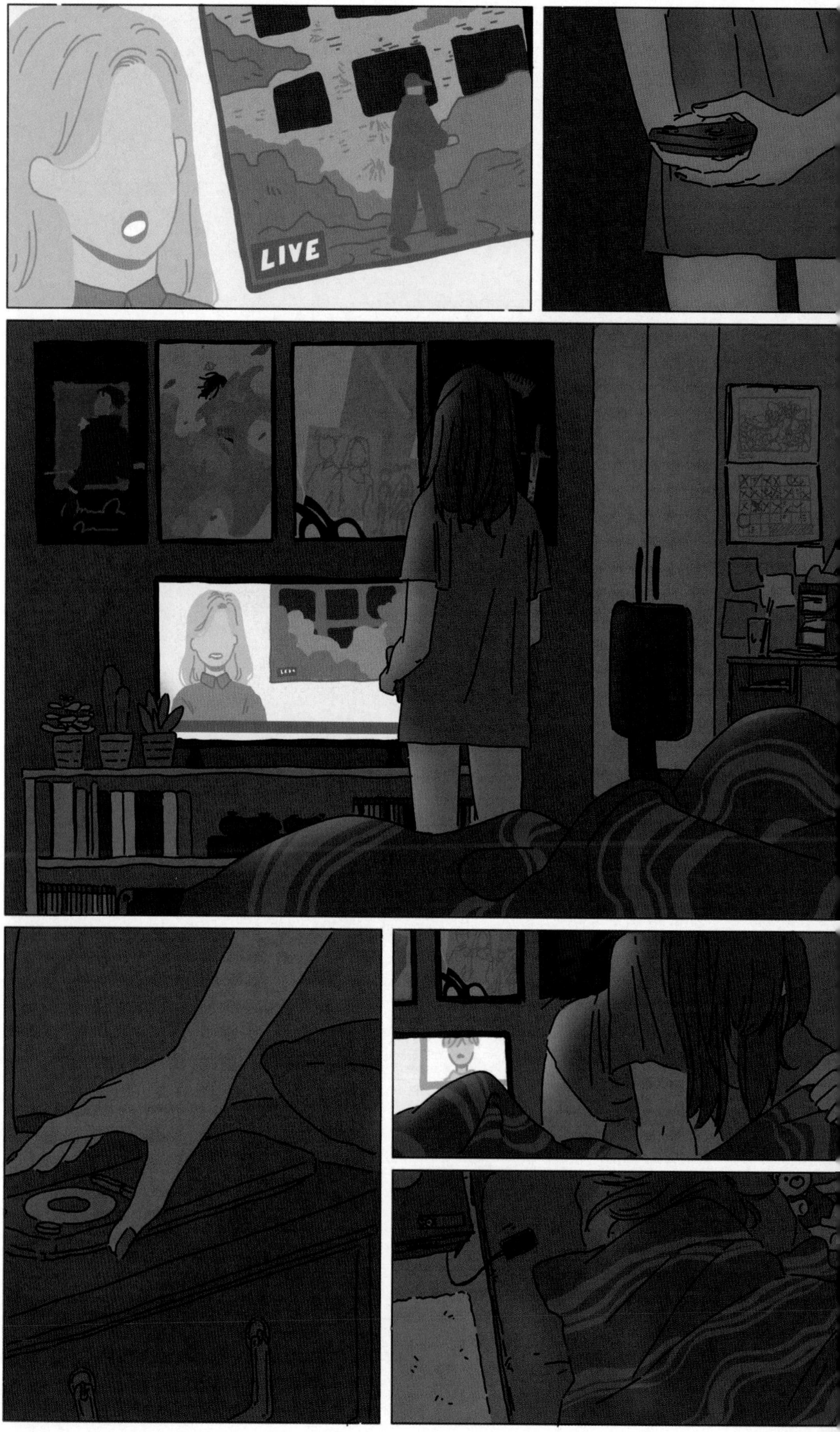
LIVE

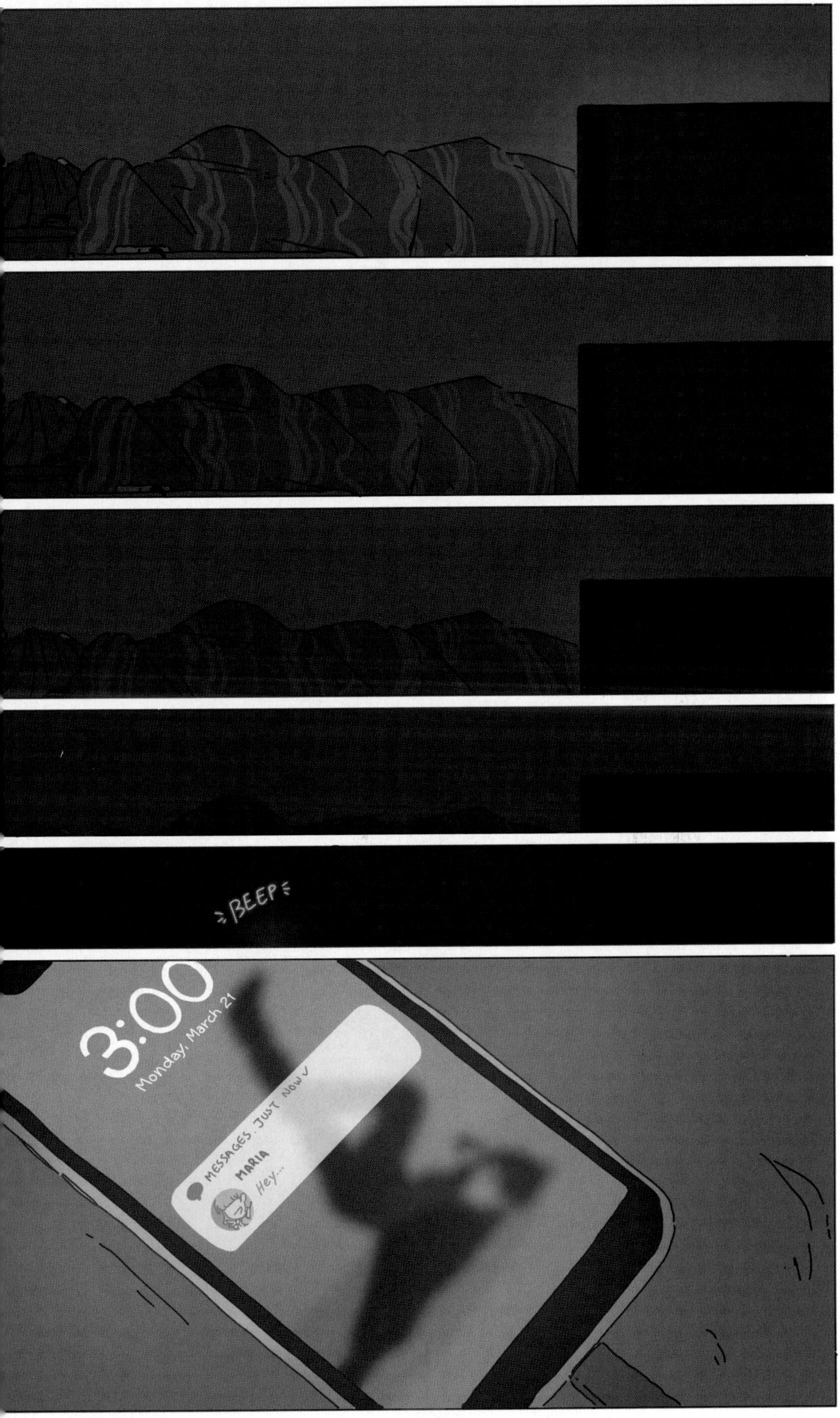
BEEP
3:00
Monday, March 21
MESSAGES . JUST NOW
MARIA
Hey...

Artist: **John K. Snyder III**

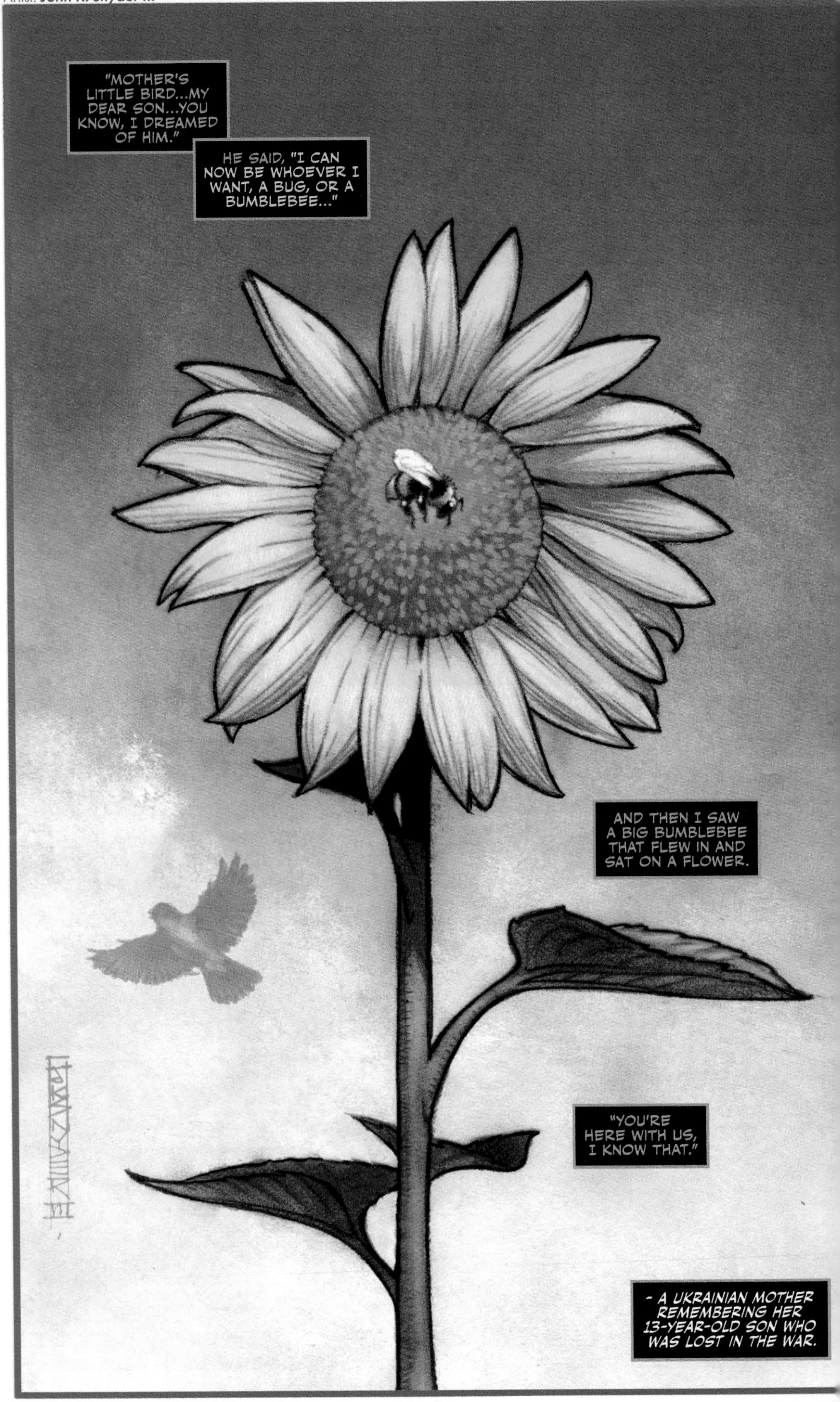

"MOTHER'S LITTLE BIRD...MY DEAR SON...YOU KNOW, I DREAMED OF HIM."
HE SAID, "I CAN NOW BE WHOEVER I WANT, A BUG, OR A BUMBLEBEE..."
AND THEN I SAW A BIG BUMBLEBEE THAT FLEW IN AND SAT ON A FLOWER.
"YOU'RE HERE WITH US, I KNOW THAT."
- A UKRAINIAN MOTHER REMEMBERING HER 13-YEAR-OLD SON WHO WAS LOST IN THE WAR.

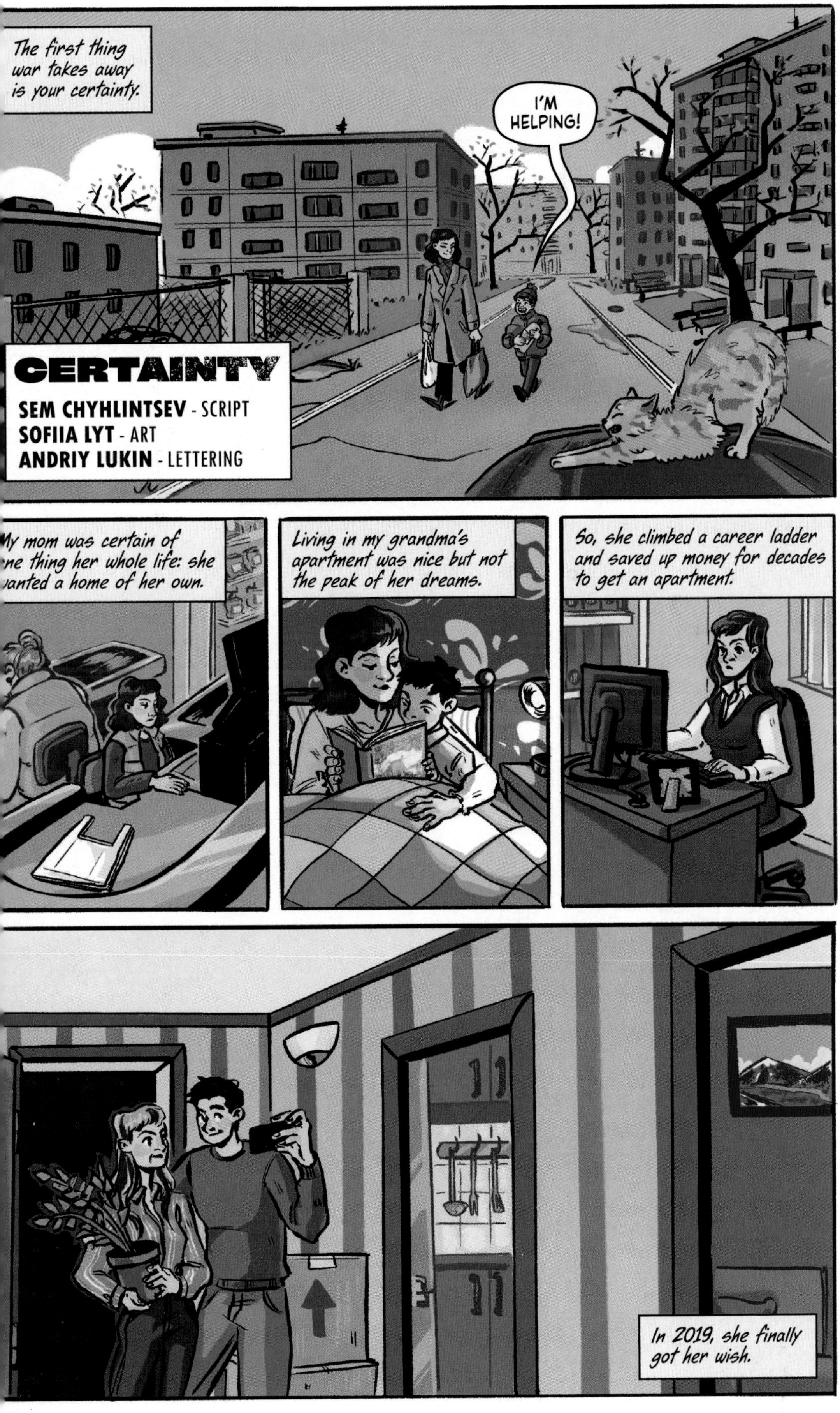
The first thing war takes away is your certainty.
I'M HELPING!
CERTAINTY
SEM CHYHLINTSEV - SCRIPT
SOFIIA LYT - ART
ANDRIY LUKIN - LETTERING
My mom was certain of ne thing her whole life: she vanted a home of her own.
Living in my grandma's apartment was nice but not the peak of her dreams.
So, she climbed a career ladder and saved up money for decades to get an apartment.
In 2019, she finally got her wish.

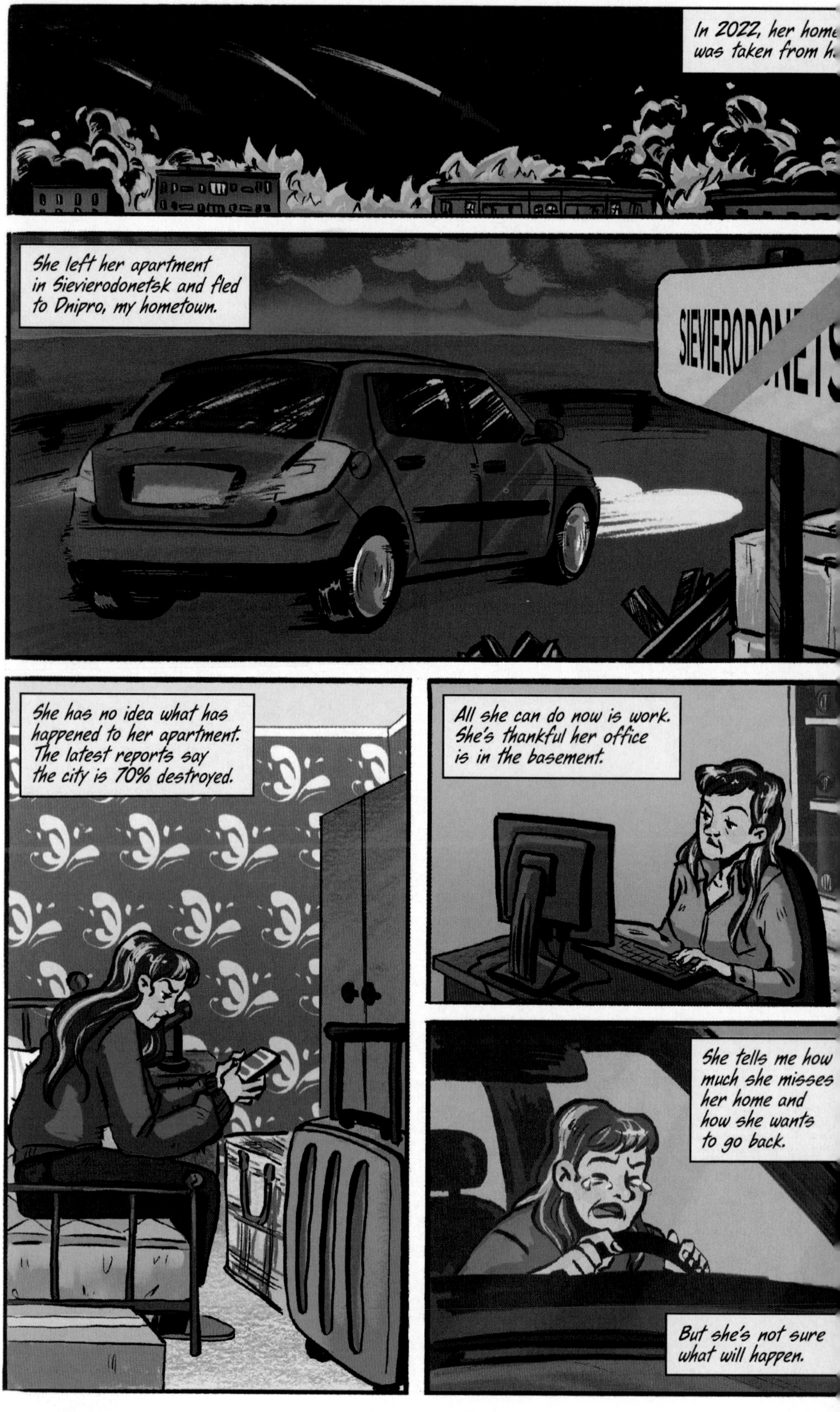
In 2022, her home
was taken from
She left her apartment in Sievierodonetsk and fled to Dnipro, my hometown.
SIEVIERODONETS
She has no idea what has happened to her apartment. The latest reports say the city is 70% destroyed.
All she can do now is work. She's thankful her office is in the basement.
She tells me how much she misses her home and how she wants to go back.
But she's not sure what will happen.

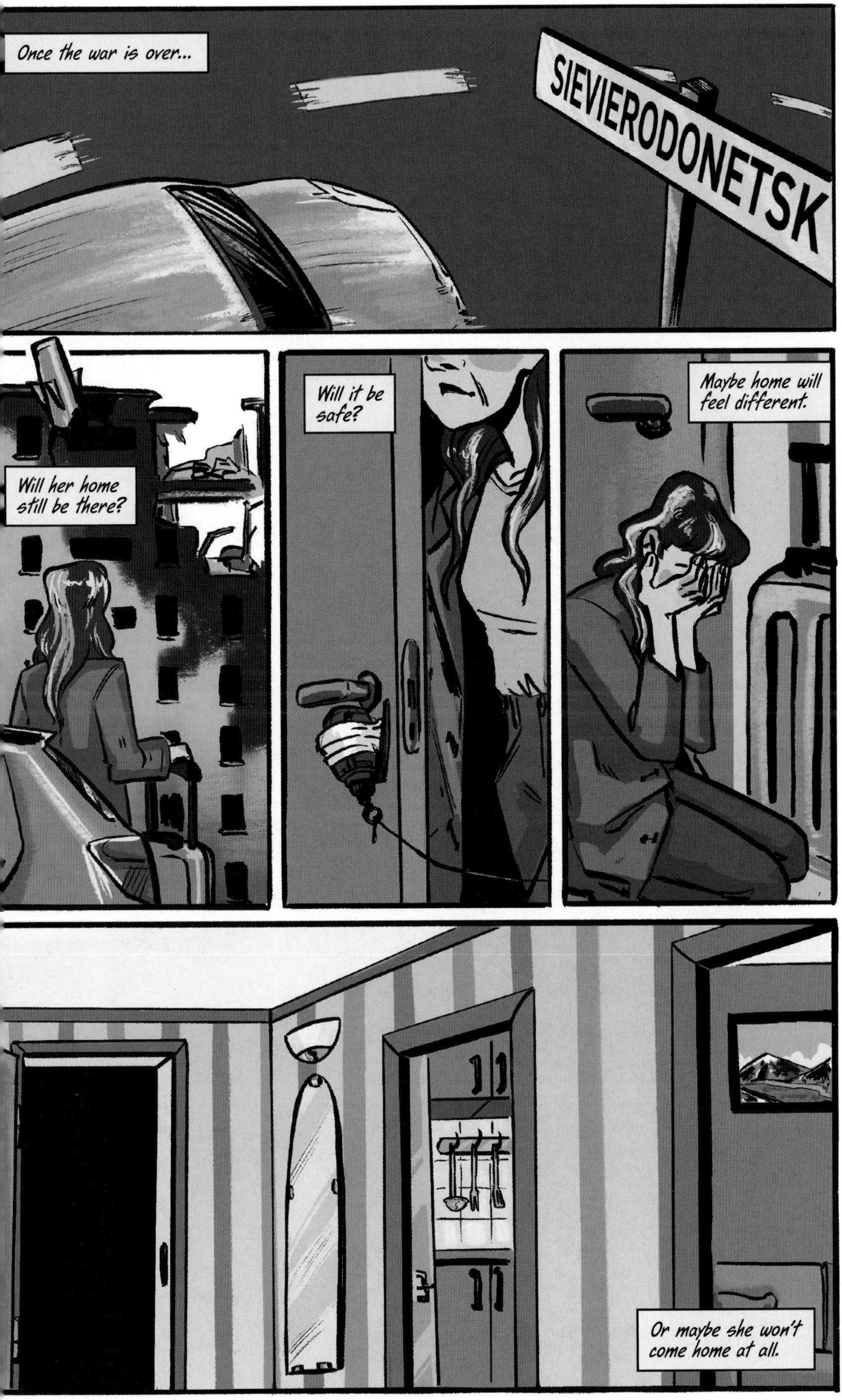
Once the war is over...
SIEVIERODONETSK
Will her home still be there?
Will it be safe?
Maybe home will feel different.
Or maybe she won't come home at all.

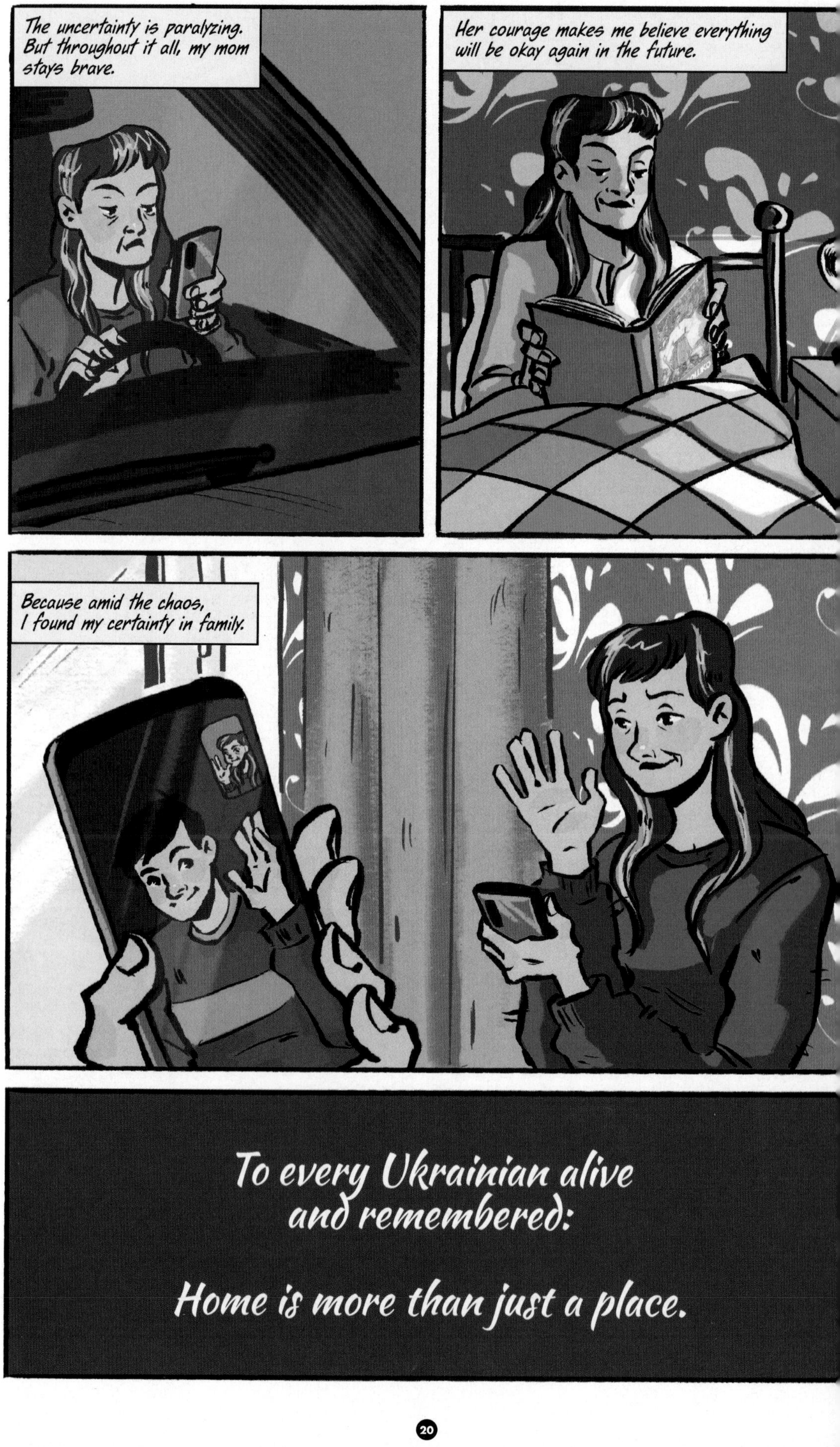
The uncertainty is paralyzing. But throughout it all, my mom stays brave.
Her courage makes me believe everything will be okay again in the future.
Because amid the chaos, I found my certainty in family.

To every Ukrainian alive
and remembered:

Home is more than just a place.

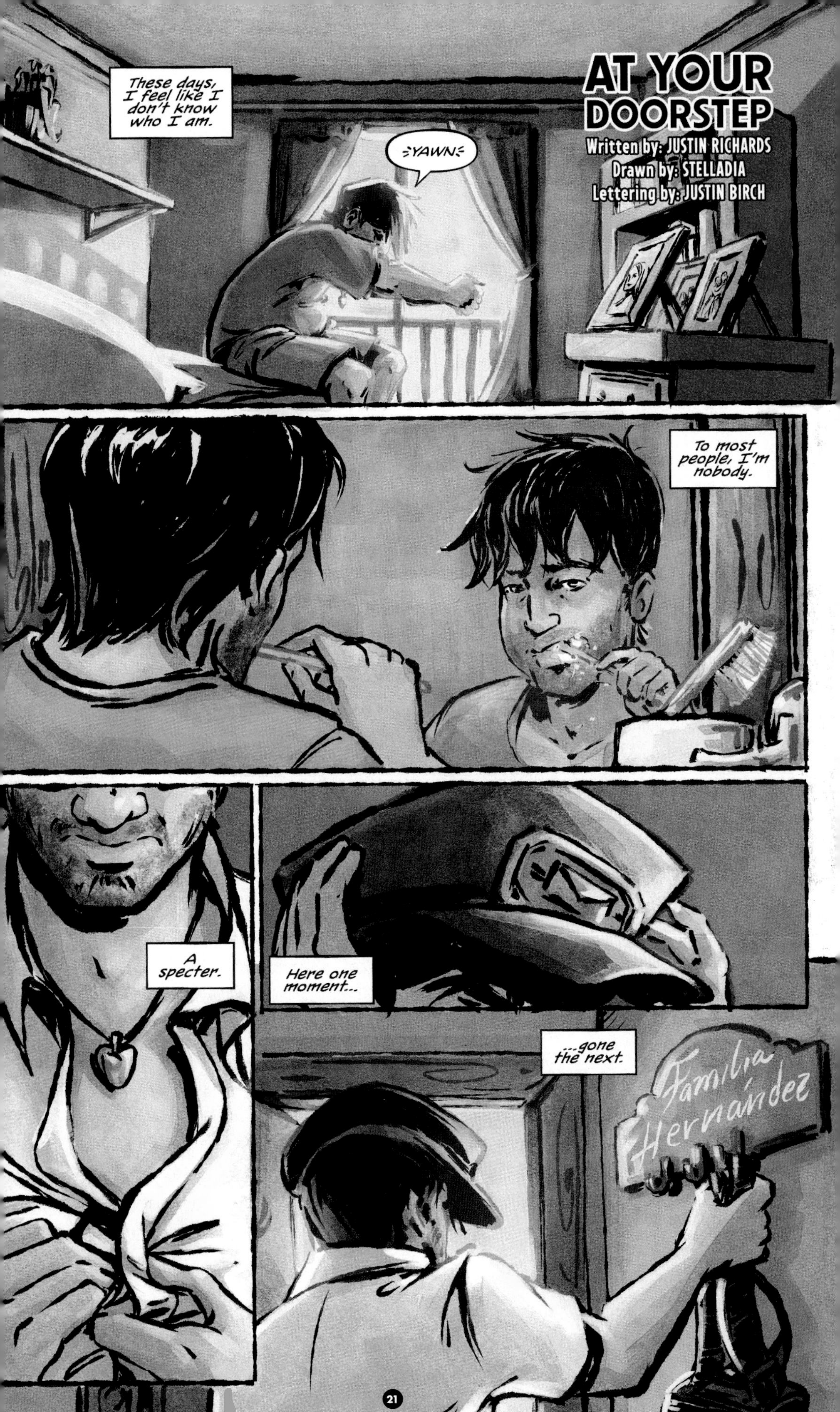

AT YOUR DOORSTEP
Written by: JUSTIN RICHARDS
Drawn by: STELLADIA
Lettering by: JUSTIN BIRCH
These days, I feel like I don't know who I am.
YAWN
To most people, I'm nobody.
A specter.
Here one moment...
...gone the next.
Familia Hernández

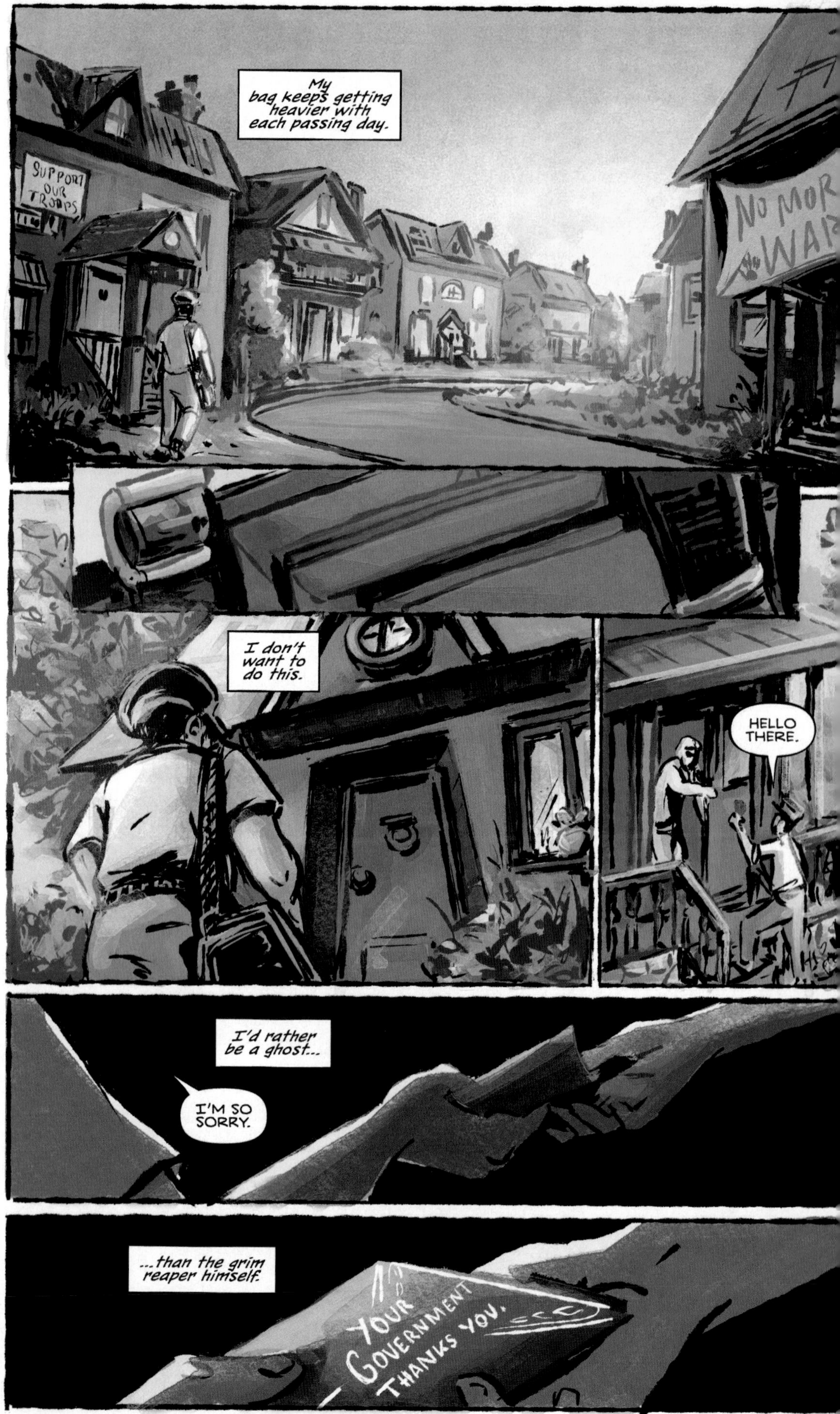

My bag keeps getting heavier with each passing day.
SUPPORT OUR TROOPS
NO MOR
WA
I don't want to do this.
HELLO THERE.
I'd rather be a ghost...
I'M SO SORRY.
...than the grim reaper himself.
YOUR GOVERNMENT THANKS YOU.

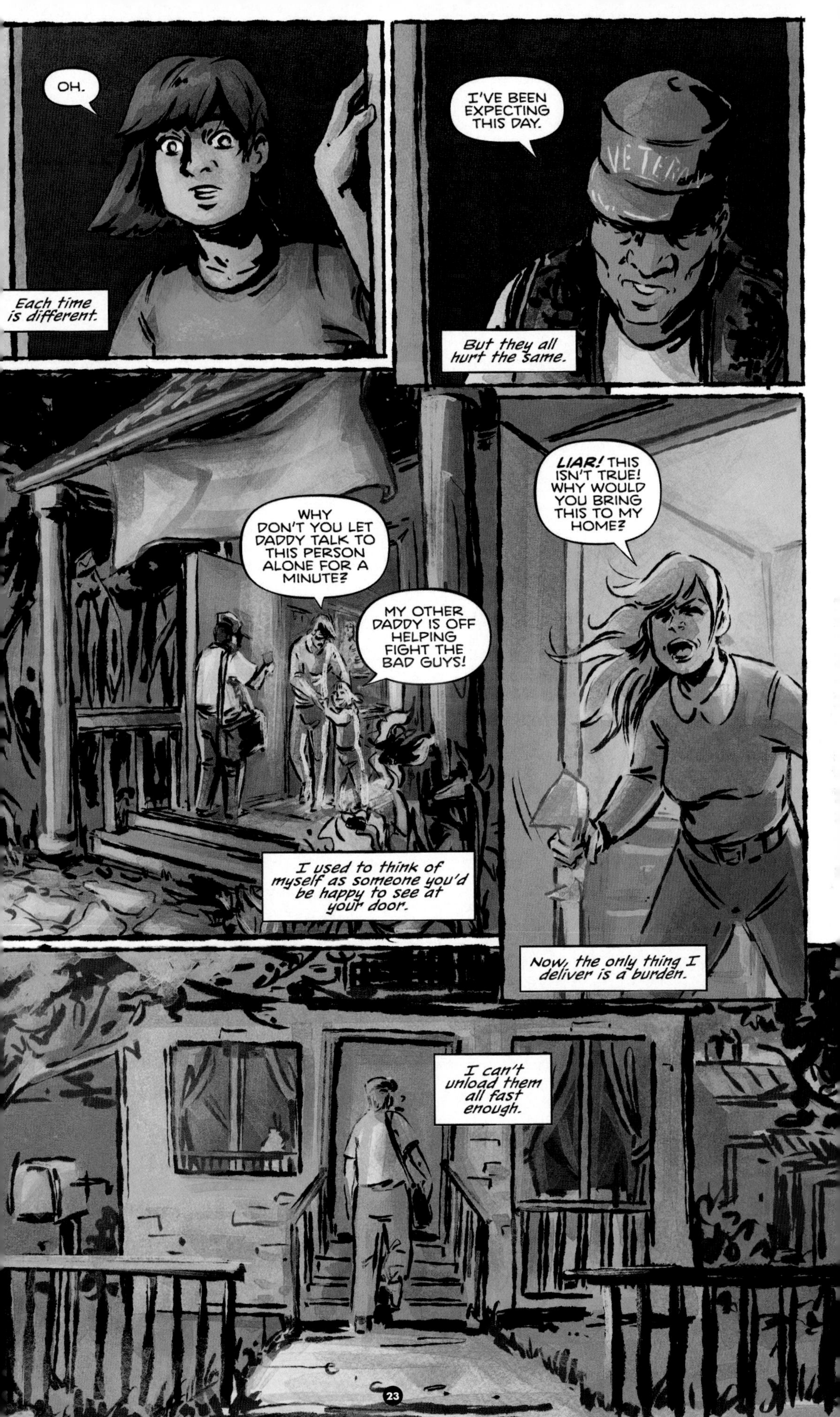
OH.
Each time is different.
I'VE BEEN EXPECTING THIS DAY.
But they all hurt the same.
WHY DON'T YOU LET DADDY TALK TO THIS PERSON ALONE FOR A MINUTE?
MY OTHER DADDY IS OFF HELPING FIGHT THE BAD GUYS!
I used to think of myself as someone you'd be happy to see at your door.
LIAR! THIS ISN'T TRUE! WHY WOULD YOU BRING THIS TO MY HOME?
Now, the only thing I deliver is a burden.
I can't unload them all fast enough.

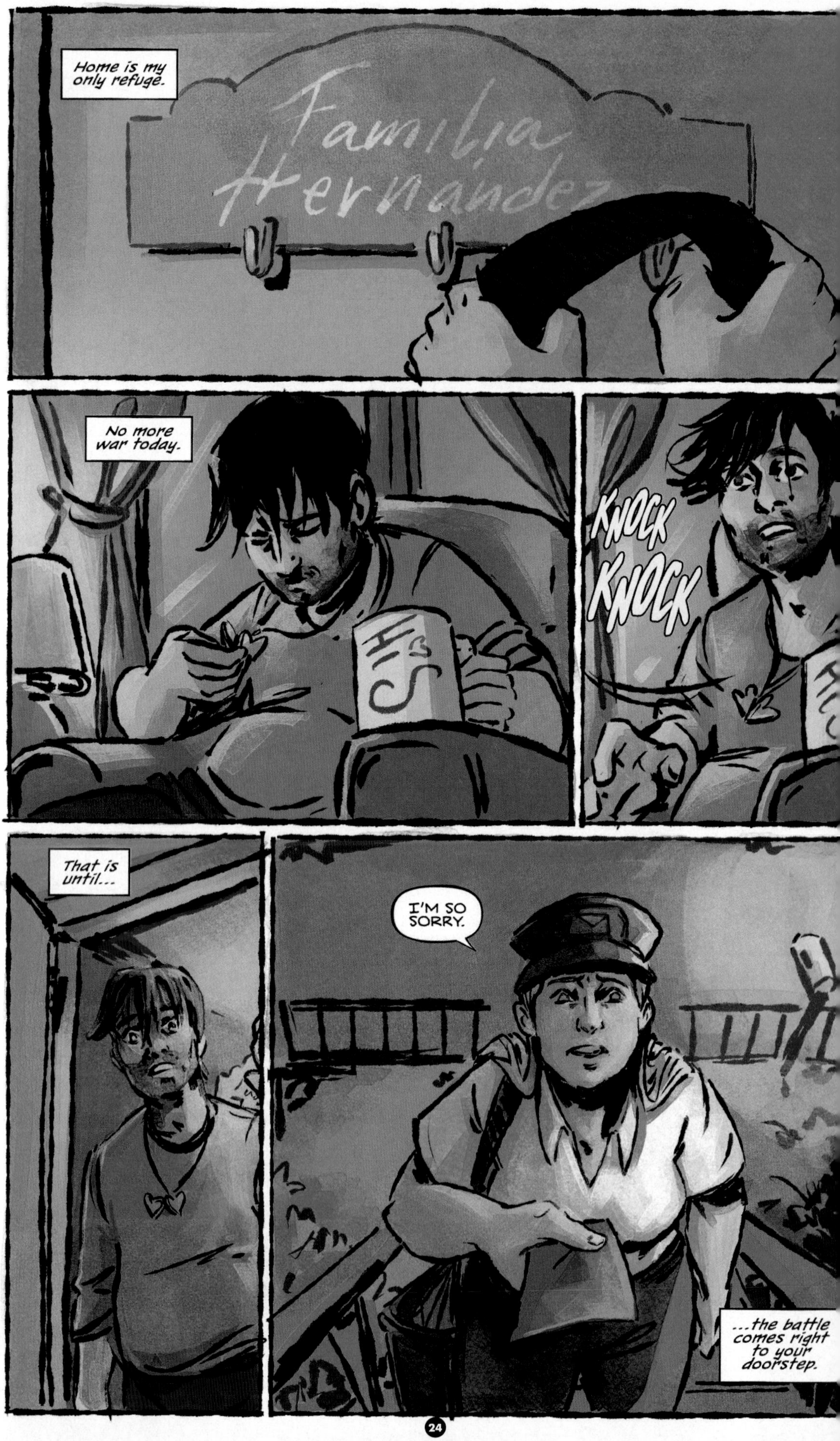
Home is my only refuge.
Familia Hernández
No more war today.
KNOCK KNOCK
That is until...
I'M SO SORRY.
...the battle comes right to your doorstep.

in spite of it by becca Kubrick

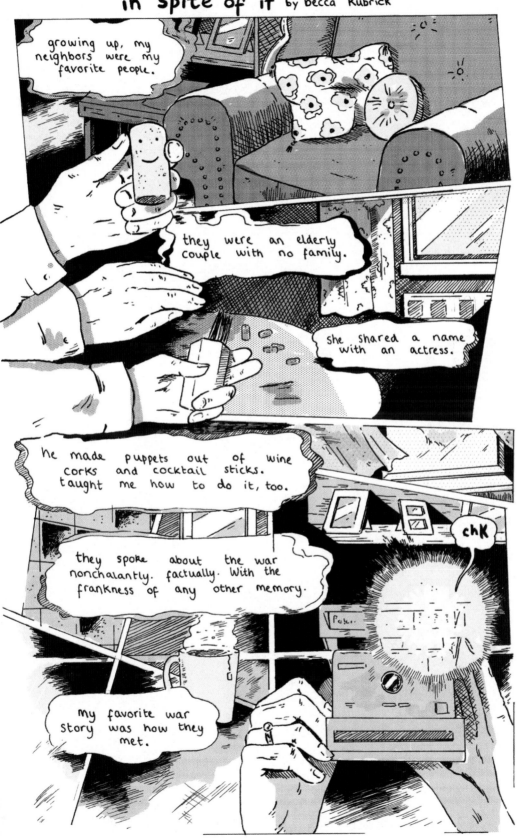

growing up, my neighbors were my favorite people.

they were an elderly couple with no family.

she shared a name with an actress.

he made puppets out of wine corks and cocktail sticks. taught me how to do it, too.

they spoke about the war nonchalantly. factually. With the frankness of any other memory.

My favorite war story was how they met.

chK

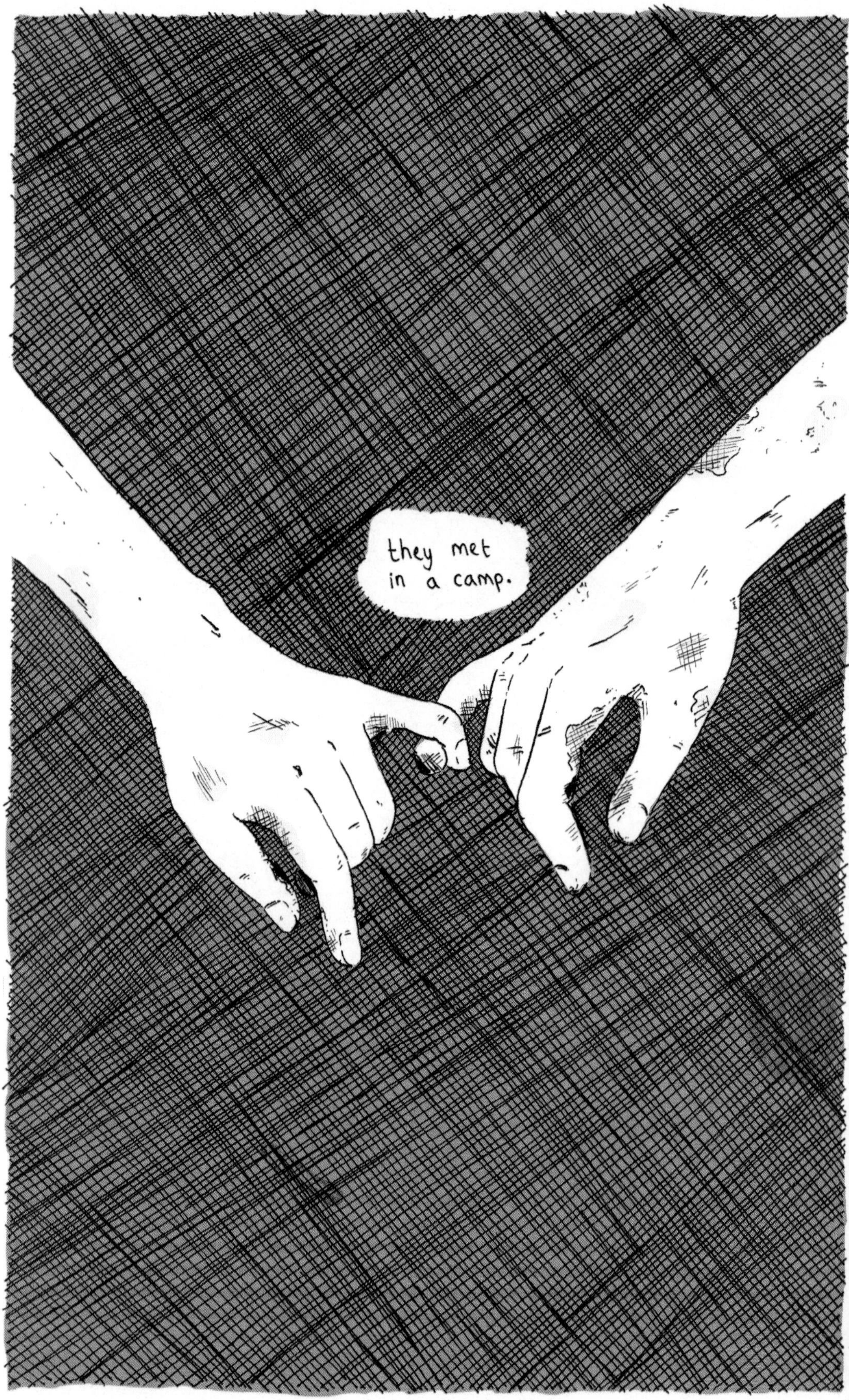
they met in a camp.

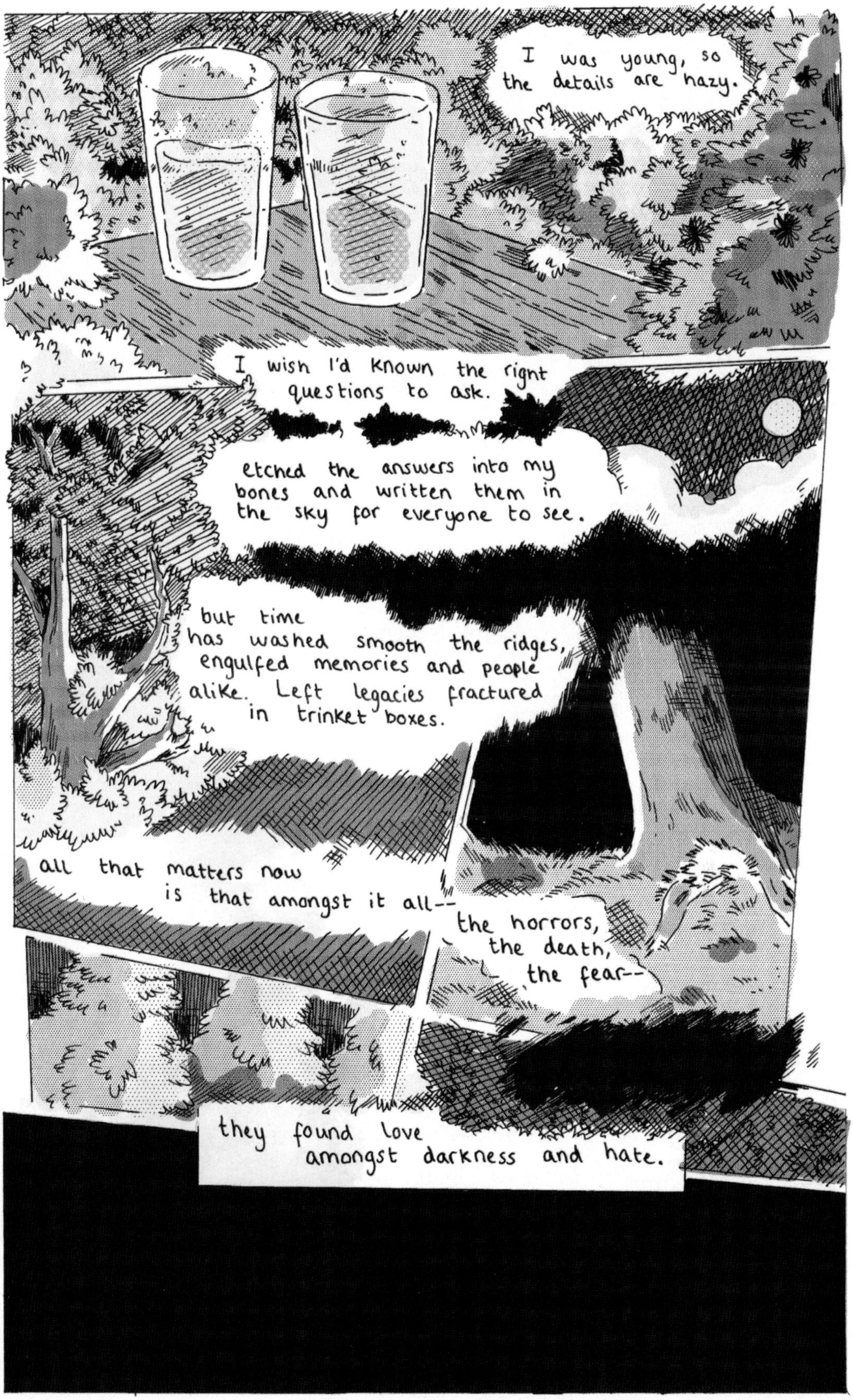
I was young, so the details are hazy.
I wish I'd known the right questions to ask.
etched the answers into my bones and written them in the sky for everyone to see.
but time has washed smooth the ridges, engulfed memories and people alike. Left legacies fractured in trinket boxes.
all that matters now is that amongst it all--
the horrors, the death, the fear--
they found love amongst darkness and hate.

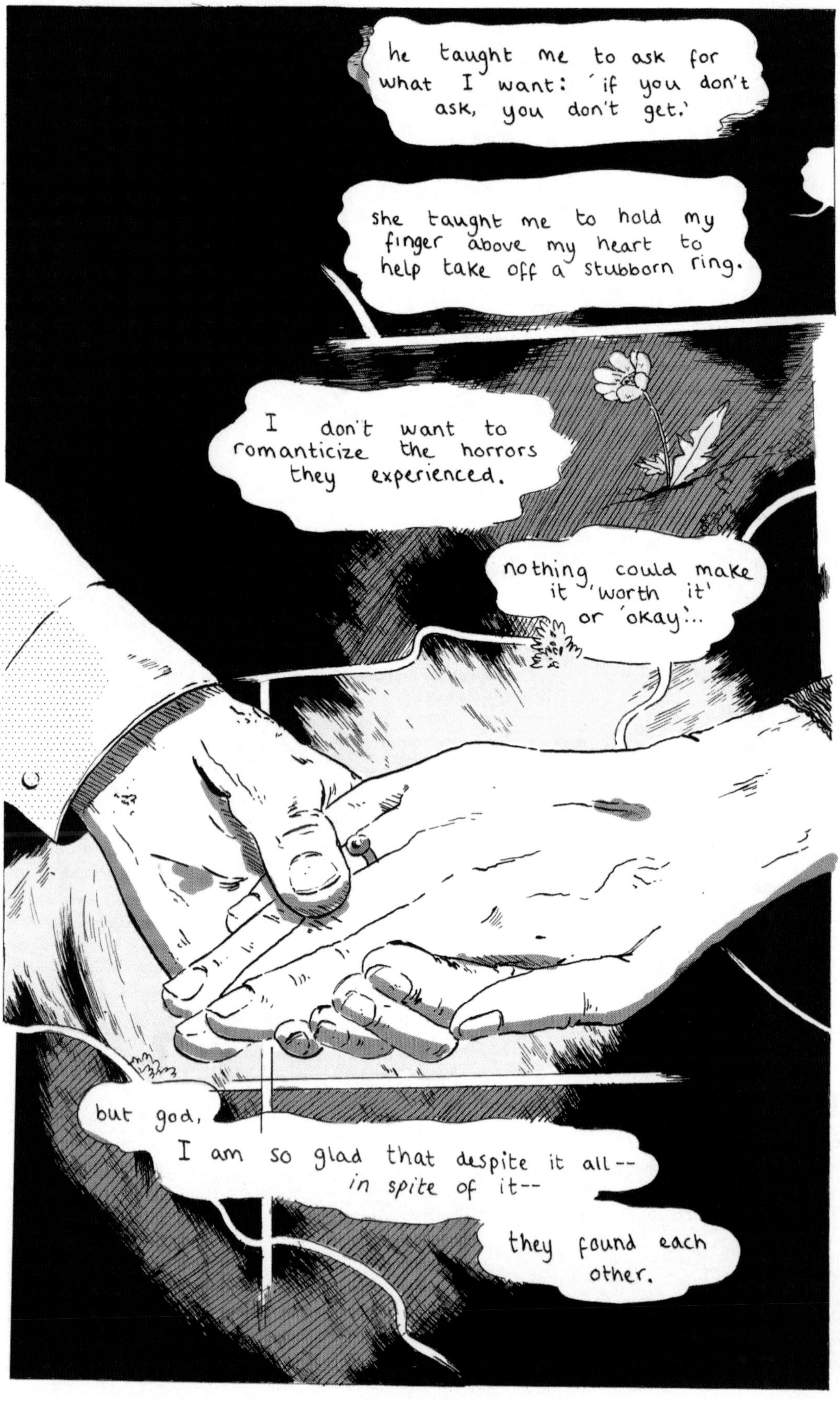
he taught me to ask for what I want: 'if you don't ask, you don't get.'
she taught me to hold my finger above my heart to help take off a stubborn ring.
I don't want to romanticize the horrors they experienced.
nothing could make it 'worth it' or 'okay'...
but god,
I am so glad that despite it all--
in spite of it--
they found each other.

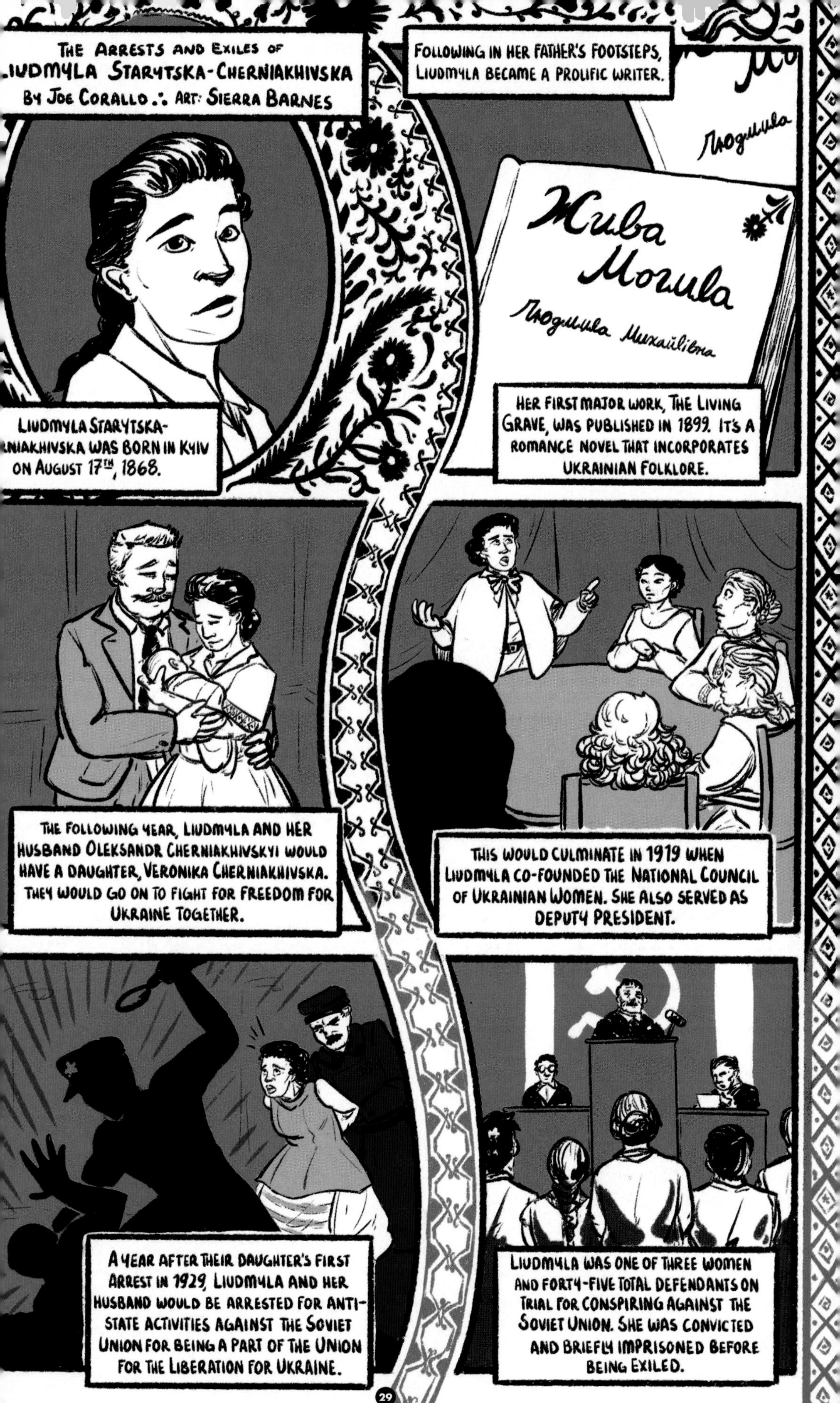

THE ARRESTS AND EXILES OF
LIUDMYLA STARYTSKA-CHERNIAKHIVSKA
BY JOE CORALLO .·. ART: SIERRA BARNES
LIUDMYLA STARYTSKA-
NIAKHIVSKA WAS BORN IN KYIV ON AUGUST 17TH, 1868.
FOLLOWING IN HER FATHER'S FOOTSTEPS, LIUDMYLA BECAME A PROLIFIC WRITER.
Мо
Людмила
Жива Могила
Людмила Михайлівна
HER FIRST MAJOR WORK, THE LIVING GRAVE, WAS PUBLISHED IN 1899. IT'S A ROMANCE NOVEL THAT INCORPORATES UKRAINIAN FOLKLORE.
THE FOLLOWING YEAR, LIUDMYLA AND HER HUSBAND OLEKSANDR CHERNIAKHIVSKYI WOULD HAVE A DAUGHTER, VERONIKA CHERNIAKHIVSKA. THEY WOULD GO ON TO FIGHT FOR FREEDOM FOR UKRAINE TOGETHER.
THIS WOULD CULMINATE IN 1919 WHEN LIUDMYLA CO-FOUNDED THE NATIONAL COUNCIL OF UKRAINIAN WOMEN. SHE ALSO SERVED AS DEPUTY PRESIDENT.
A YEAR AFTER THEIR DAUGHTER'S FIRST ARREST IN 1929, LIUDMYLA AND HER HUSBAND WOULD BE ARRESTED FOR ANTI-STATE ACTIVITIES AGAINST THE SOVIET UNION FOR BEING A PART OF THE UNION FOR THE LIBERATION FOR UKRAINE.
LIUDMYLA WAS ONE OF THREE WOMEN AND FORTY-FIVE TOTAL DEFENDANTS ON TRIAL FOR CONSPIRING AGAINST THE SOVIET UNION. SHE WAS CONVICTED AND BRIEFLY IMPRISONED BEFORE BEING EXILED.

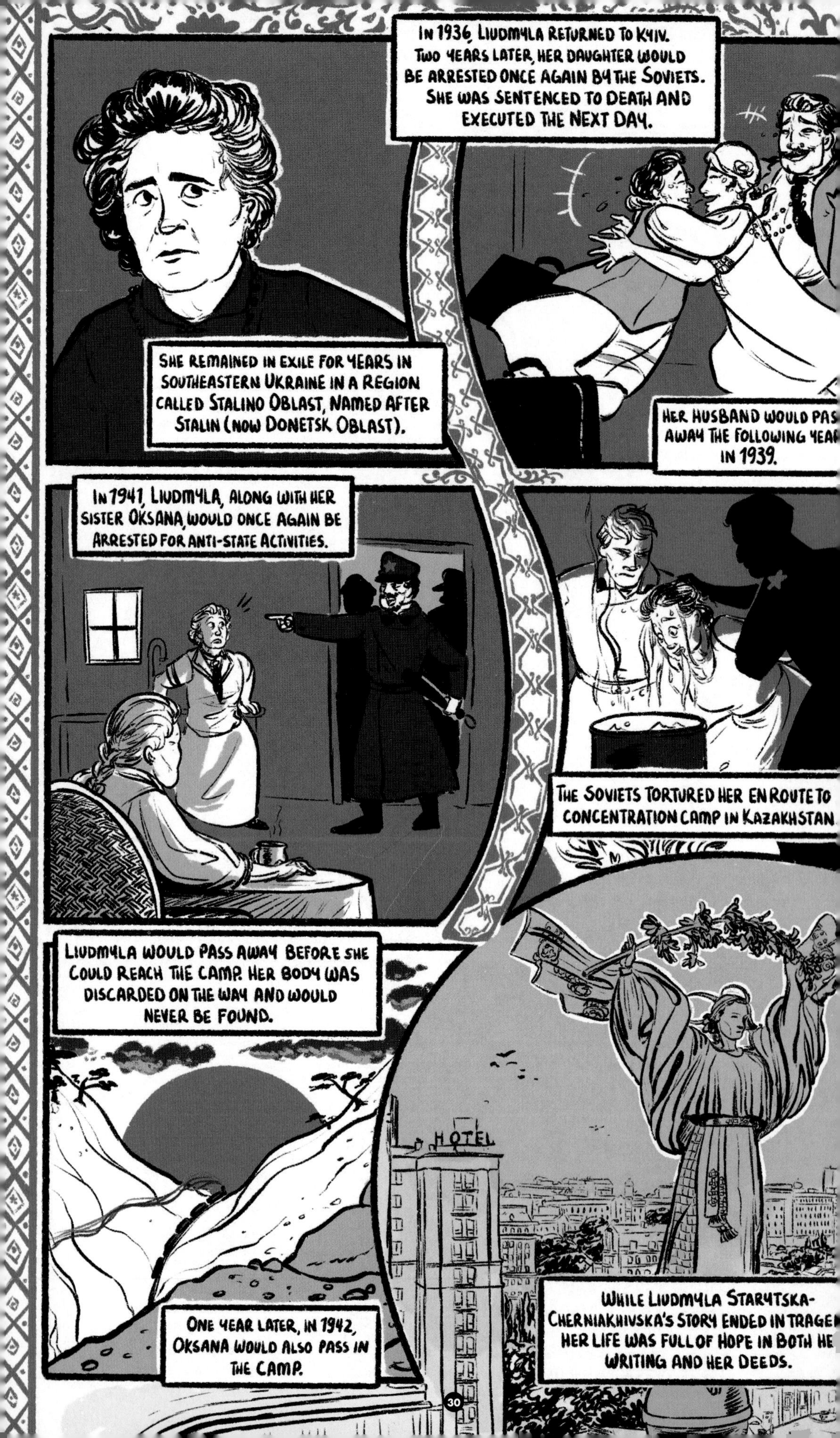
SHE REMAINED IN EXILE FOR YEARS IN SOUTHEASTERN UKRAINE IN A REGION CALLED STALINO OBLAST, NAMED AFTER STALIN (NOW DONETSK OBLAST).
IN 1936, LIUDMYLA RETURNED TO KYIV. TWO YEARS LATER, HER DAUGHTER WOULD BE ARRESTED ONCE AGAIN BY THE SOVIETS. SHE WAS SENTENCED TO DEATH AND EXECUTED THE NEXT DAY.
HER HUSBAND WOULD PAS AWAY THE FOLLOWING YEA IN 1939.
IN 1941, LIUDMYLA, ALONG WITH HER SISTER OKSANA, WOULD ONCE AGAIN BE ARRESTED FOR ANTI-STATE ACTIVITIES.
THE SOVIETS TORTURED HER EN ROUTE TO CONCENTRATION CAMP IN KAZAKHSTAN.
LIUDMYLA WOULD PASS AWAY BEFORE SHE COULD REACH THE CAMP. HER BODY WAS DISCARDED ON THE WAY AND WOULD NEVER BE FOUND.
ONE YEAR LATER, IN 1942, OKSANA WOULD ALSO PASS IN THE CAMP.
HOTEL
WHILE LIUDMYLA STARYTSKA-CHERNIAKHIVSKA'S STORY ENDED IN TRAGE HER LIFE WAS FULL OF HOPE IN BOTH HE WRITING AND HER DEEDS.

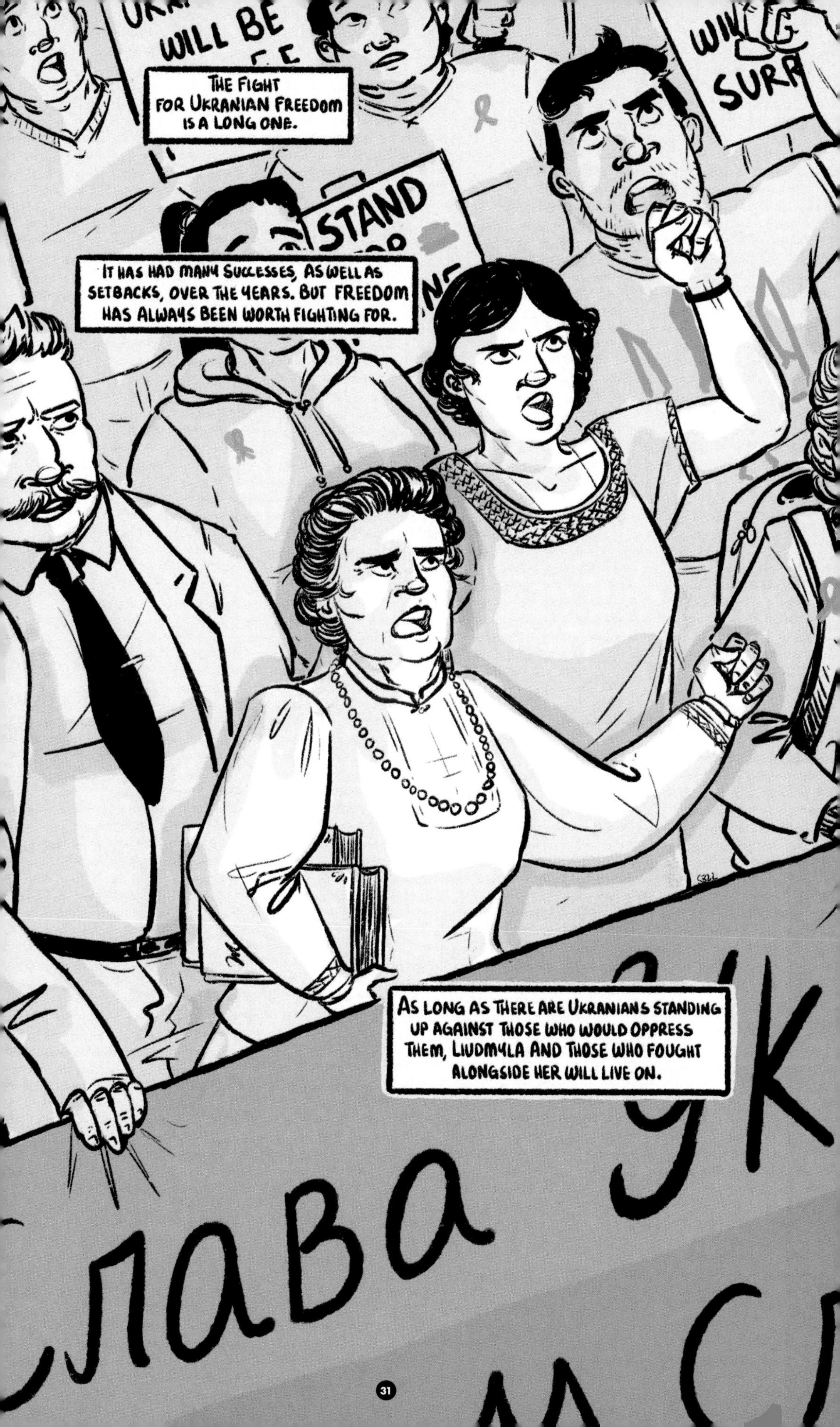
WILL BE
THE FIGHT FOR UKRANIAN FREEDOM IS A LONG ONE.
STAND
IT HAS HAD MANY SUCCESSES, AS WELL AS SETBACKS, OVER THE YEARS. BUT FREEDOM HAS ALWAYS BEEN WORTH FIGHTING FOR.
AS LONG AS THERE ARE UKRANIANS STANDING UP AGAINST THOSE WHO WOULD OPPRESS THEM, LIUDMYLA AND THOSE WHO FOUGHT ALONGSIDE HER WILL LIVE ON.
Слава

heliotropic

THERE ARE STORIES MY GRANDMOTHER WILL NEVER SHARE
PLACES UNTOLD, FAMILY UNMET
AND NIGHTS THAT STAY PRESSED IN THE PAGES OF HER MEMORY
CAUTIOUSLY FOLDED, CAREFULLY SET

WHEN SHE DOES SPEAK, IF SHE WILL, IT IS NOT DETAILS
BUT NAMES
THE SEEDS OF A COLLECTIVE PRESENT TURNED PAST
AND A LIFE SLOWLY, GENTLY, RECLAIMED

THERE IS THE DOG WHO BARKED AT SHADOWS
AND AN ORGAN PLAYER WHO NEVER BOWED
THE PIANO TEACHER WHO LOST HIS WALL
AND HIS STUDENTS WHO REBUILT IT,
BRICK BY STOLEN BRICK
THEY BUILT IT ALL

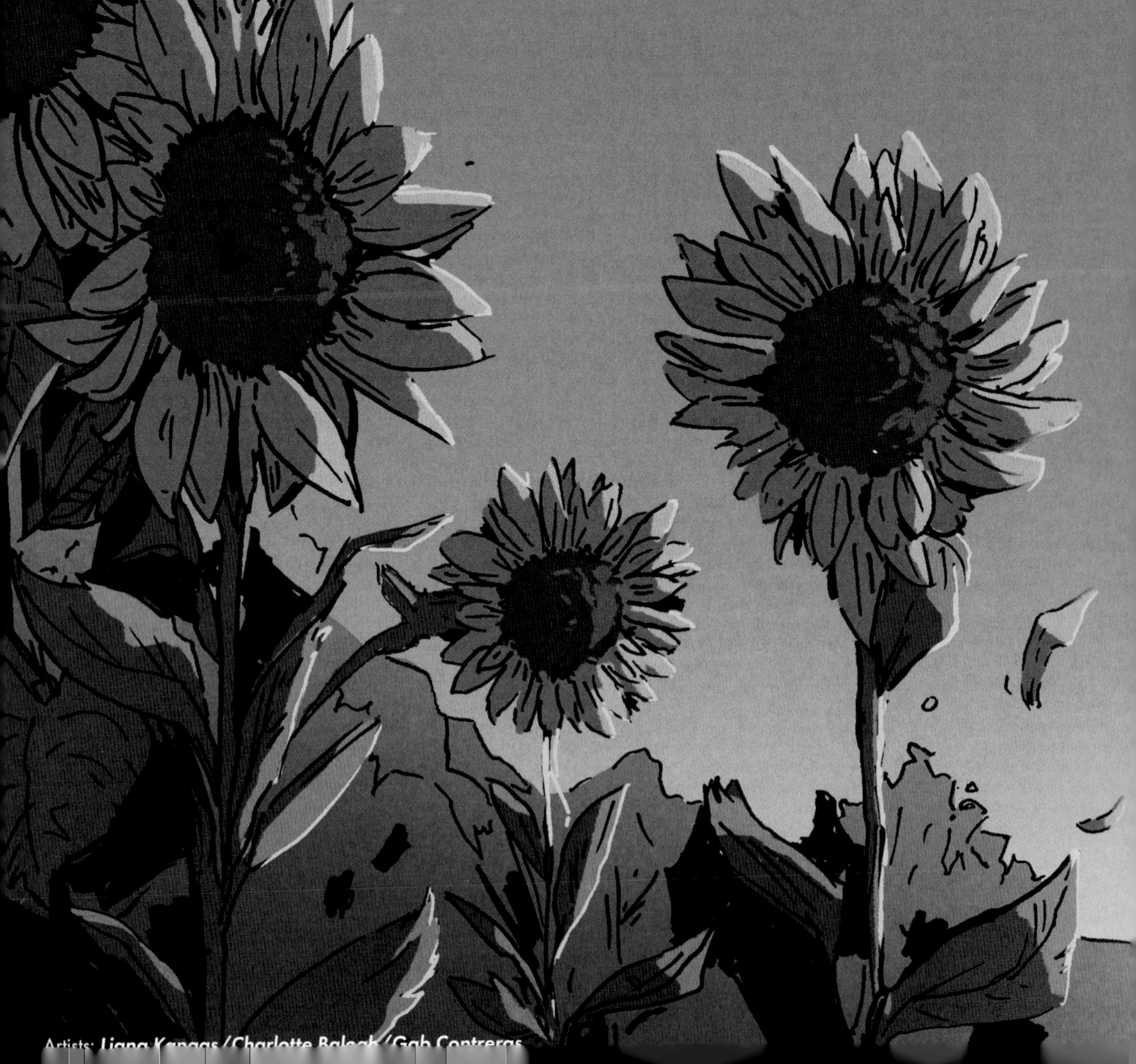

Artists: Liana Kanaas / Charlotte Baleah / Gab Contreras

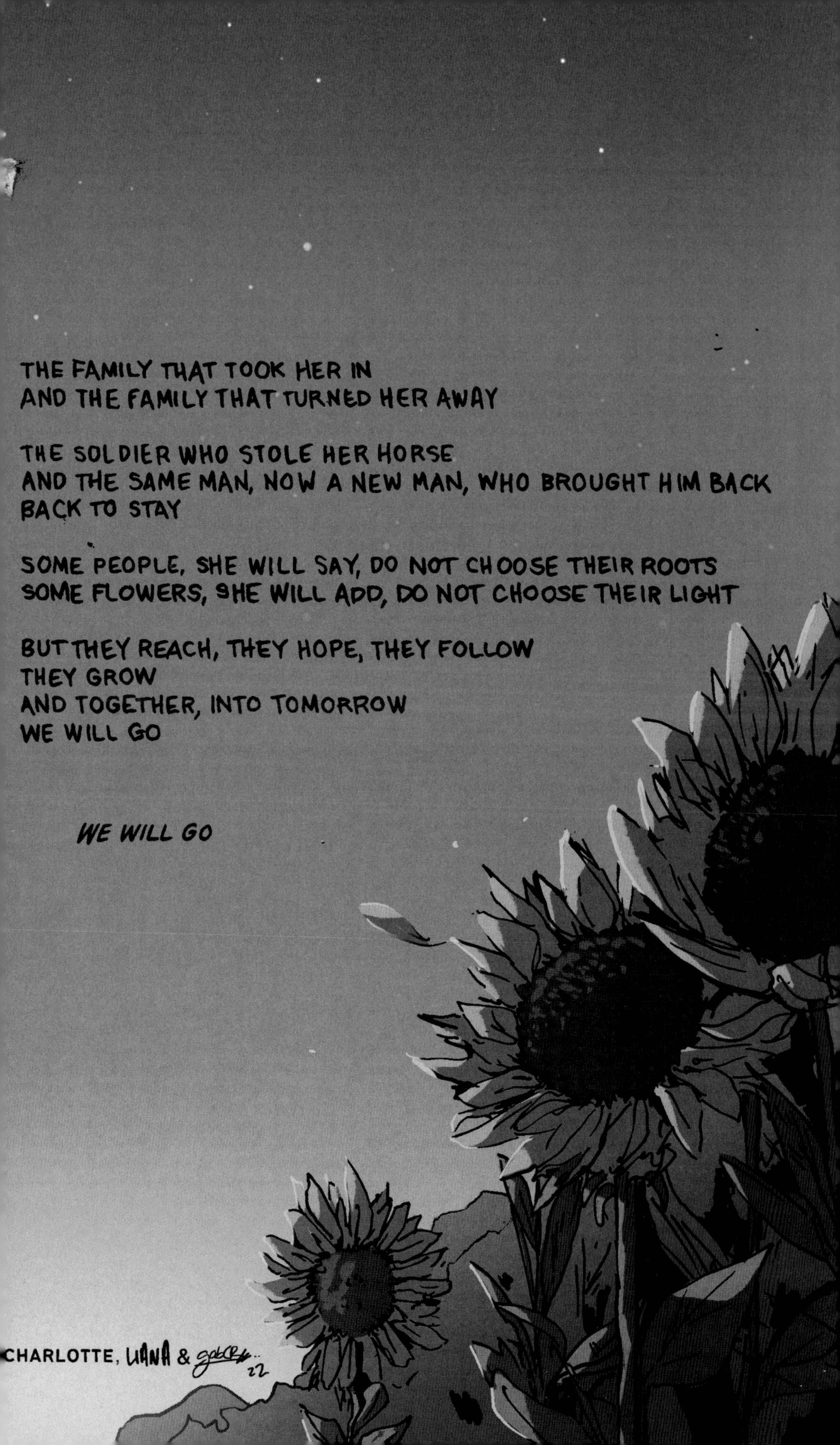
THE FAMILY THAT TOOK HER IN
AND THE FAMILY THAT TURNED HER AWAY
THE SOLDIER WHO STOLE HER HORSE
AND THE SAME MAN, NOW A NEW MAN, WHO BROUGHT HIM BACK
BACK TO STAY
SOME PEOPLE, SHE WILL SAY, DO NOT CHOOSE THEIR ROOTS
SOME FLOWERS, SHE WILL ADD, DO NOT CHOOSE THEIR LIGHT
BUT THEY REACH, THEY HOPE, THEY FOLLOW
THEY GROW
AND TOGETHER, INTO TOMORROW
WE WILL GO
WE WILL GO
CHARLOTTE, LIANA &

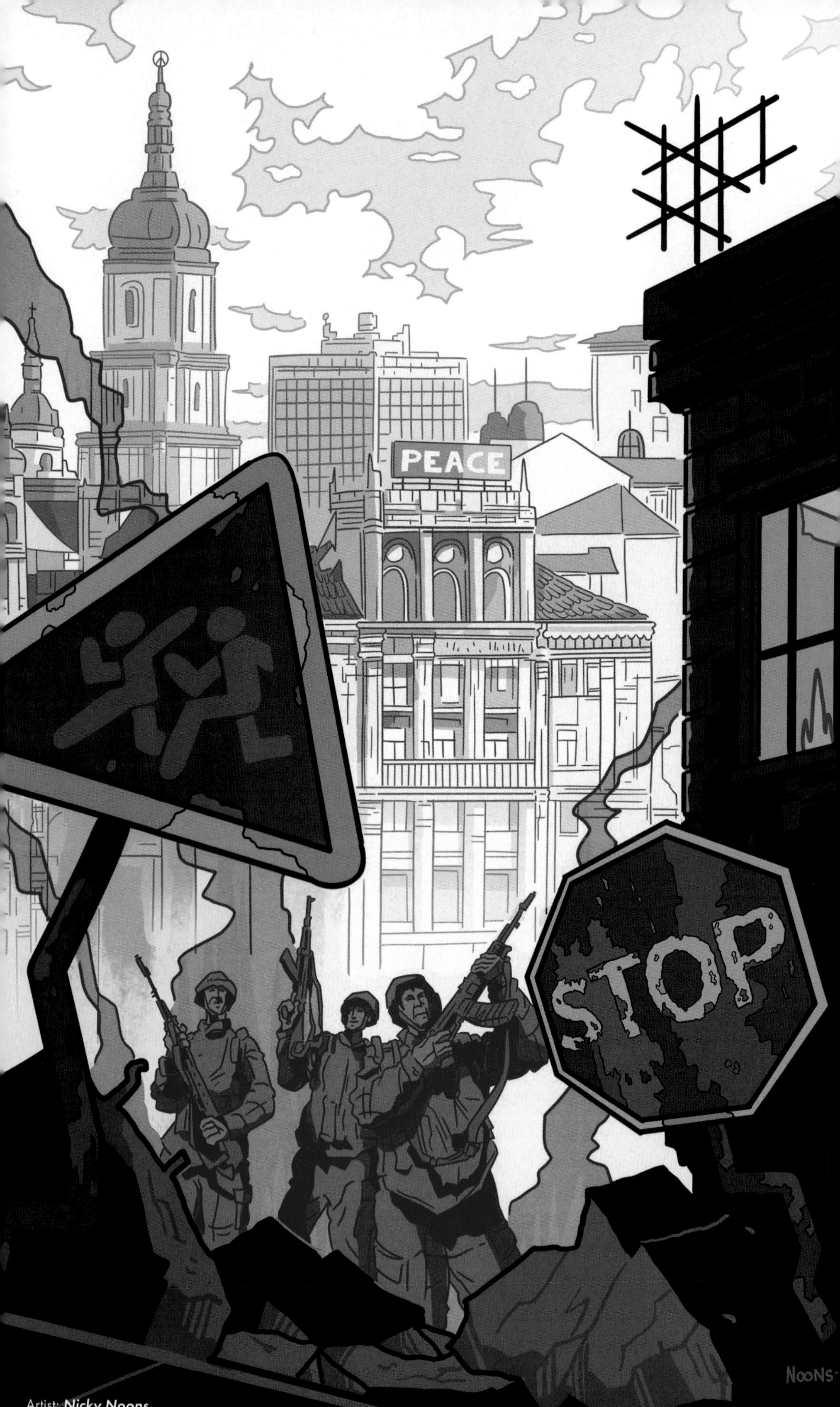
PEACE
STOP
NOONS

Artist: **Nicky Noons**

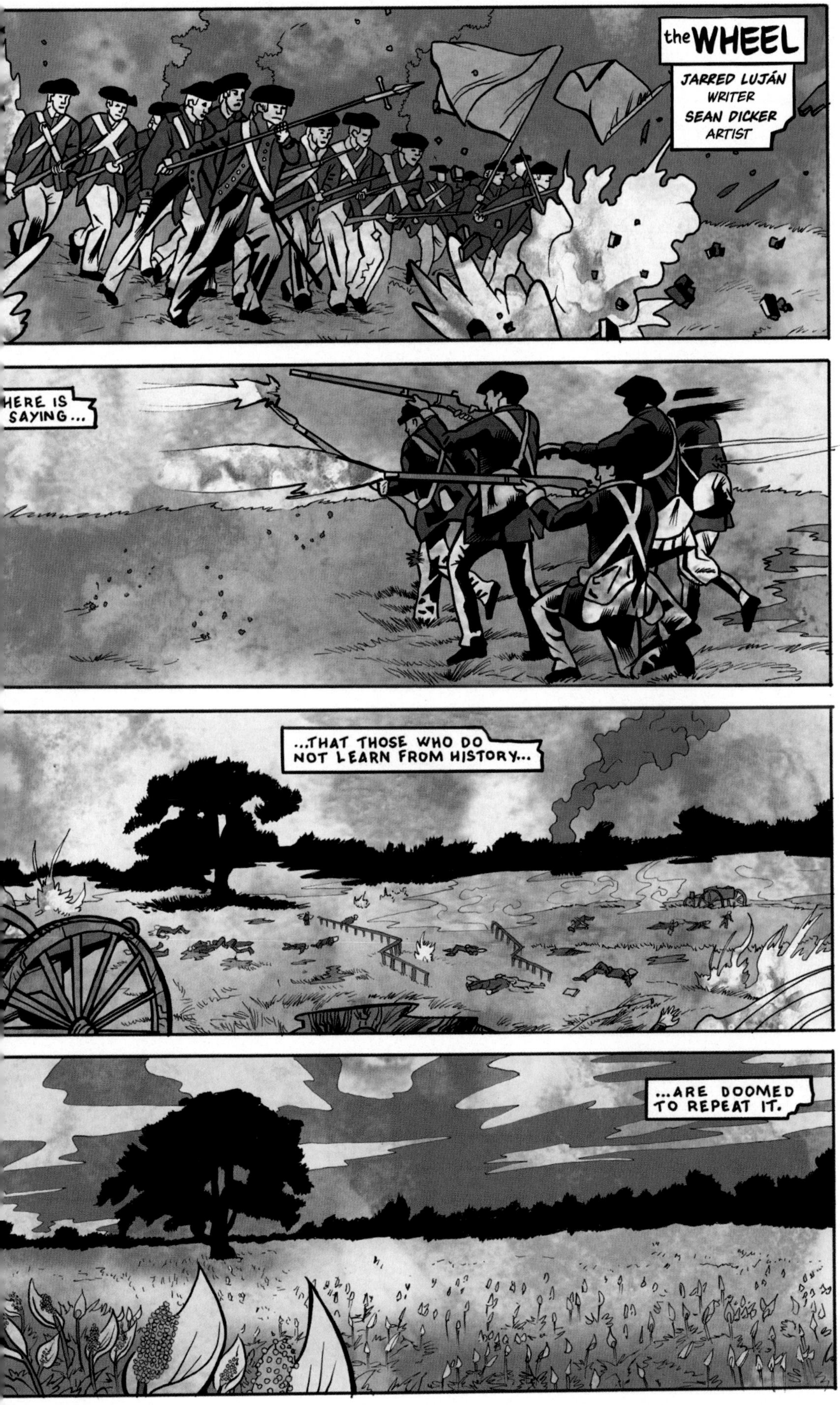

the WHEEL
JARRED LUJÁN WRITER
SEAN DICKER ARTIST
HERE IS SAYING...
...THAT THOSE WHO DO NOT LEARN FROM HISTORY...
...ARE DOOMED TO REPEAT IT.

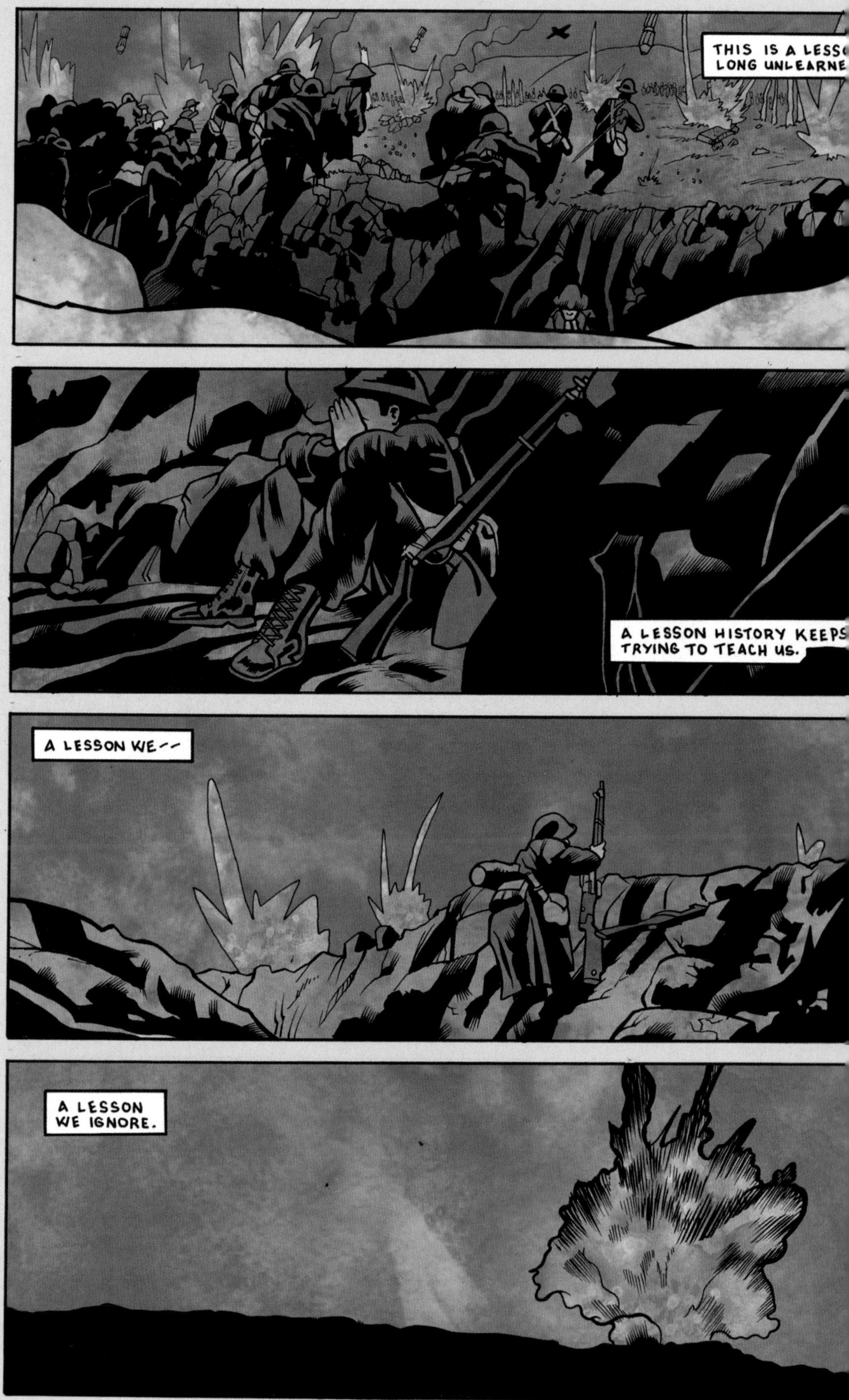
THIS IS A LESS
LONG UNLEARNE
A LESSON HISTORY KEEPS
TRYING TO TEACH US.
A LESSON WE--
A LESSON
WE IGNORE.

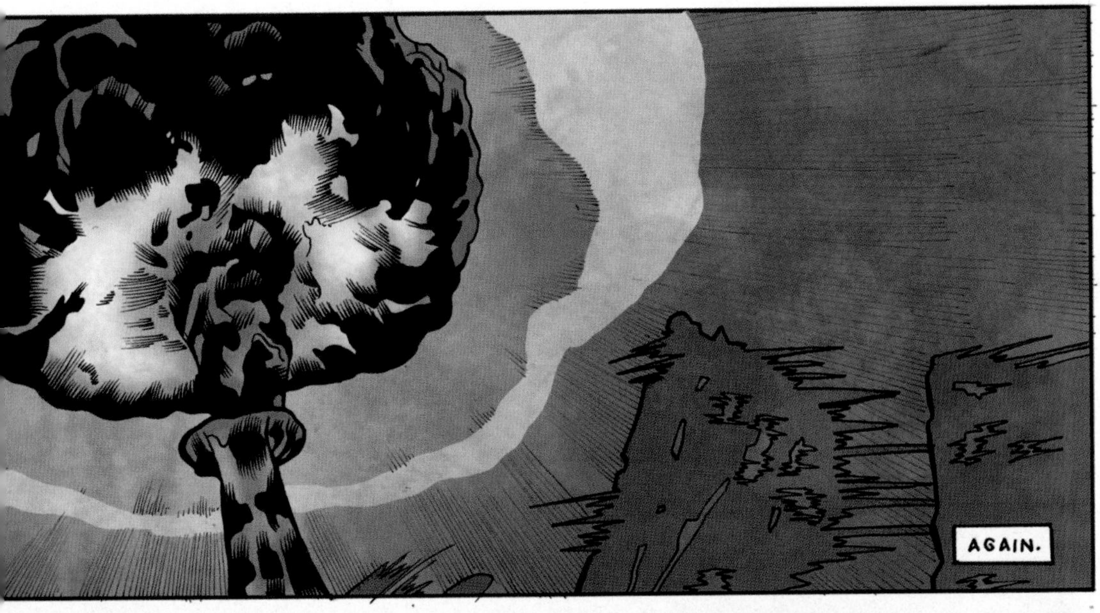
AGAIN.

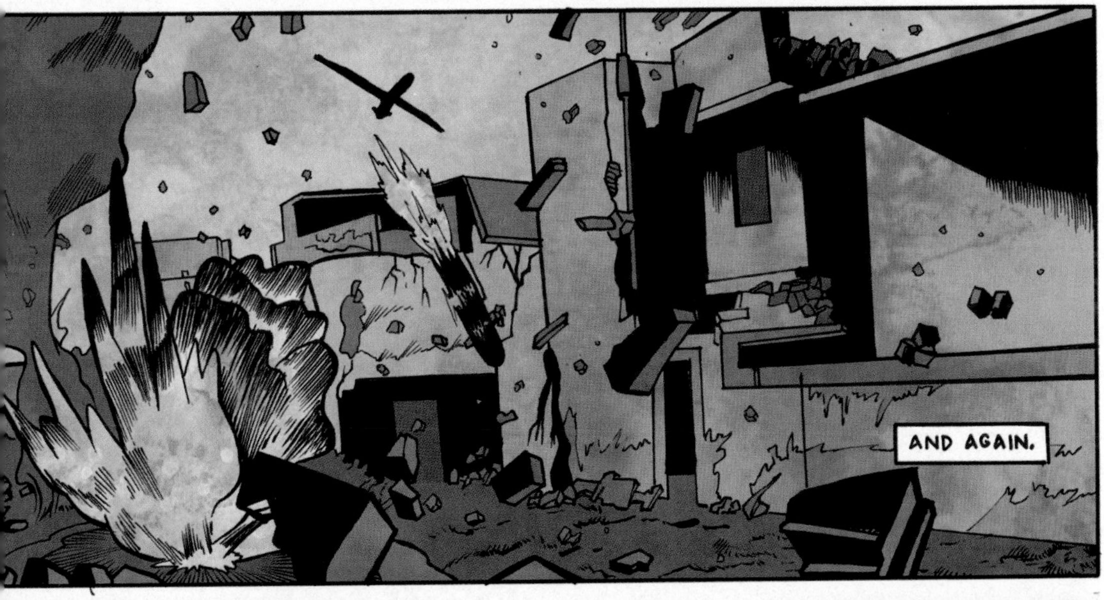
AND AGAIN.

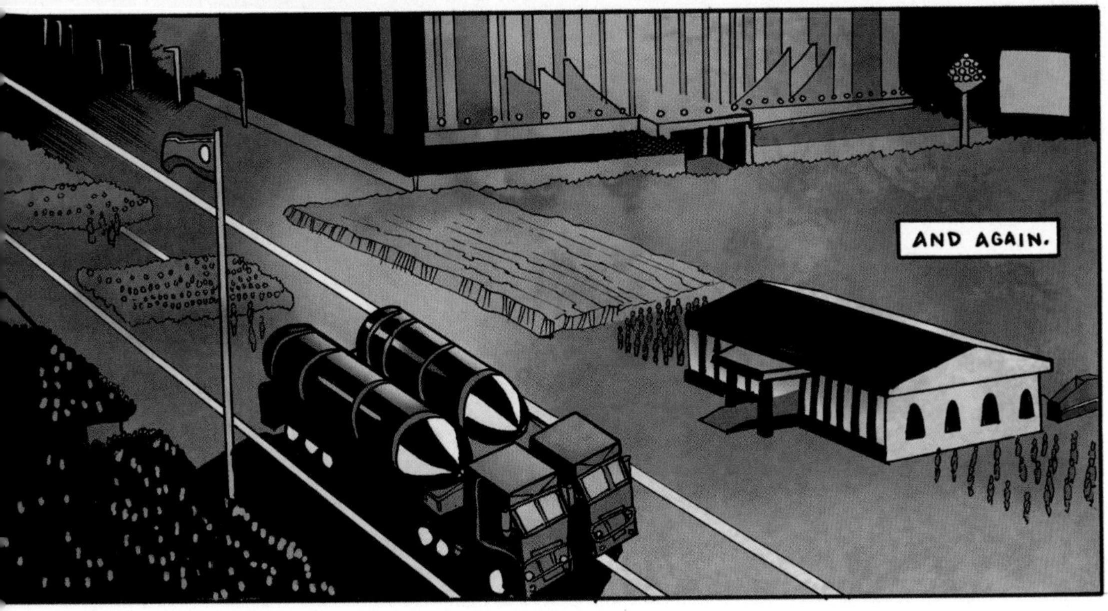
AND AGAIN.

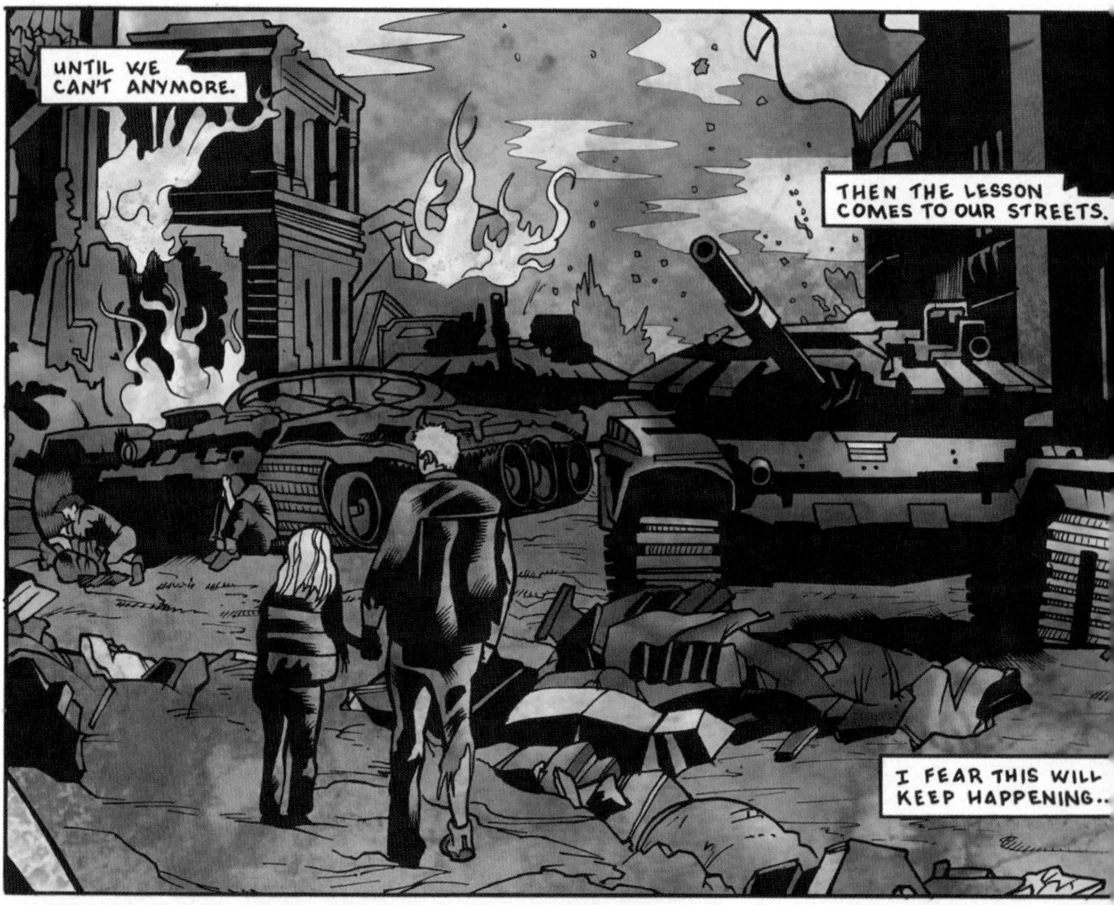
UNTIL WE CAN'T ANYMORE.
THEN THE LESSON COMES TO OUR STREETS.
I FEAR THIS WILL KEEP HAPPENING...

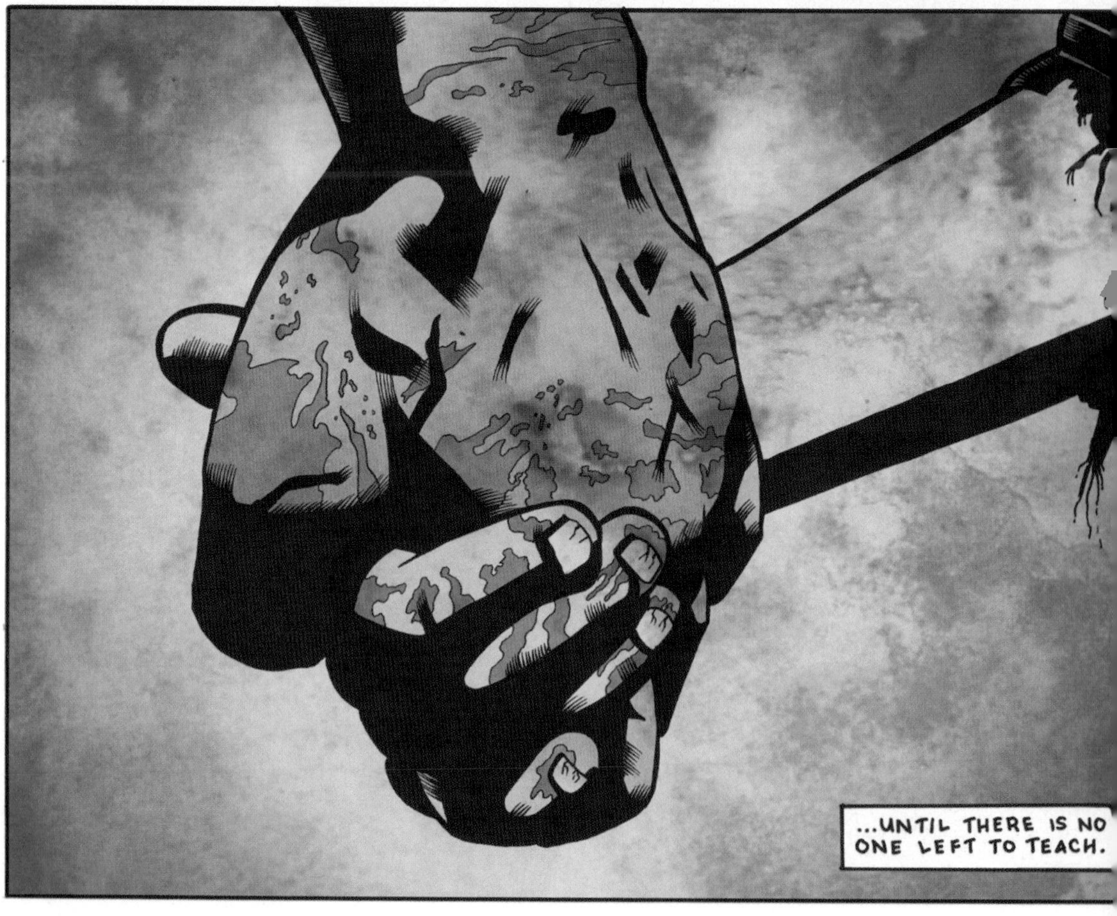
...UNTIL THERE IS NO ONE LEFT TO TEACH.

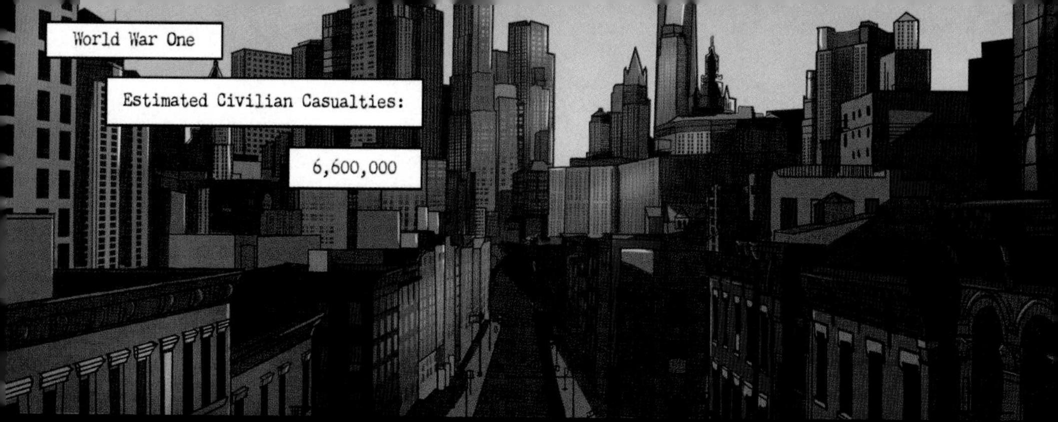
World War One
Estimated Civilian Casualties:
6,600,000

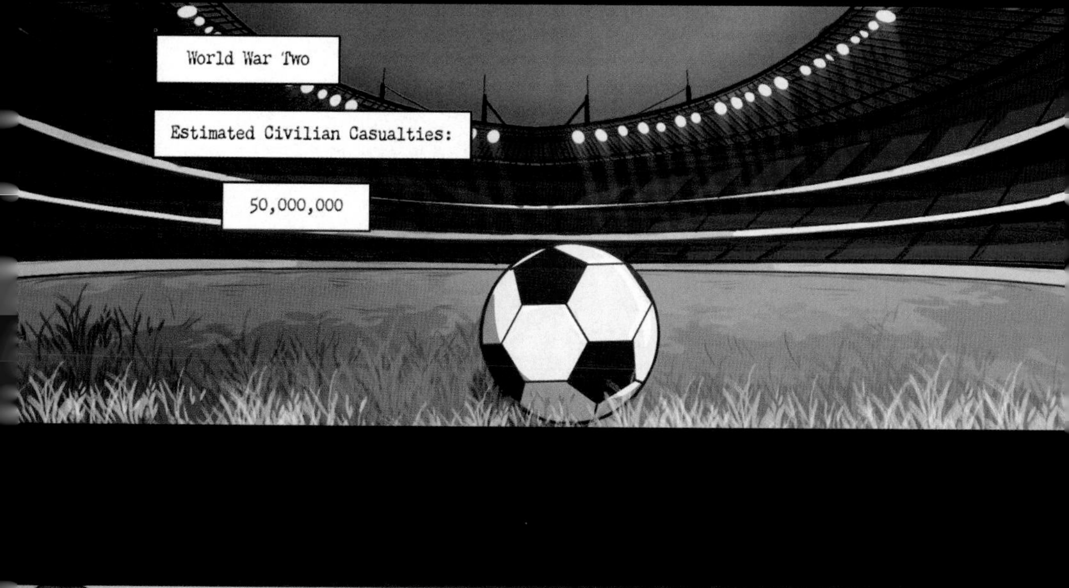
World War Two
Estimated Civilian Casualties:
50,000,000

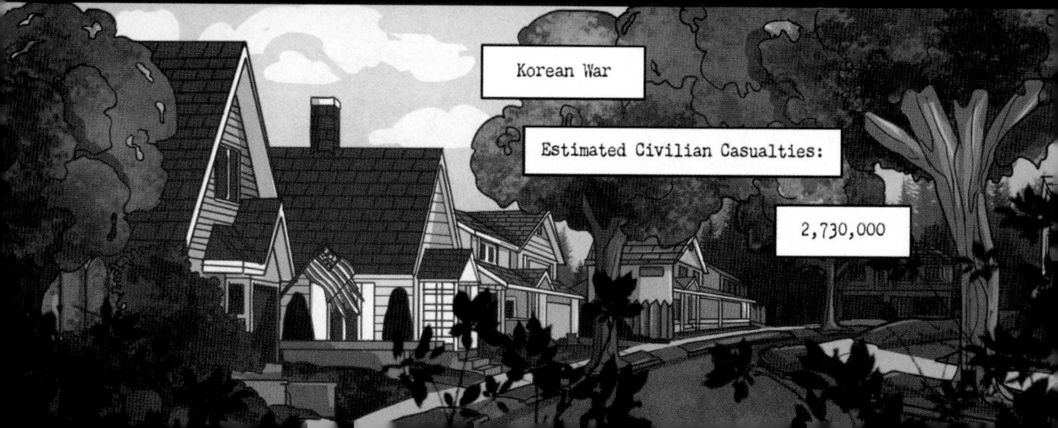
Korean War
Estimated Civilian Casualties:
2,730,000

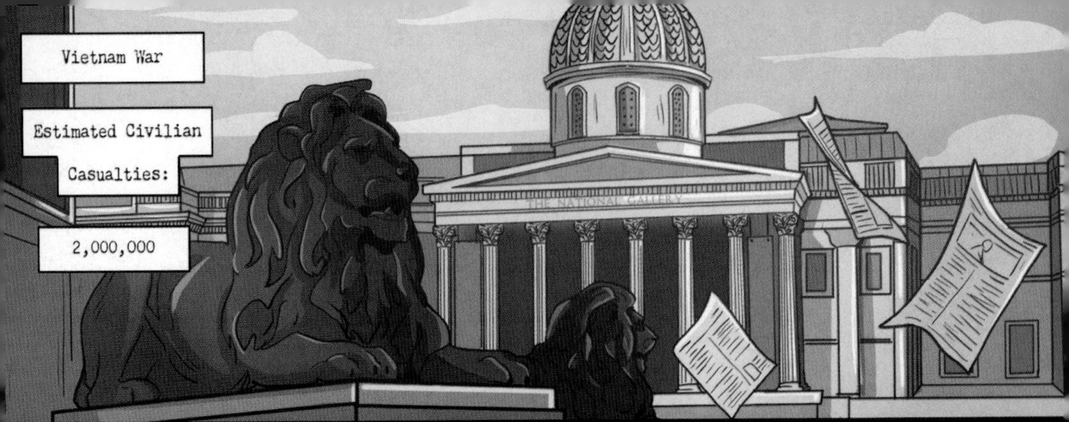
Vietnam War
Estimated Civilian Casualties:
2,000,000
THE NATIONAL GALLERY

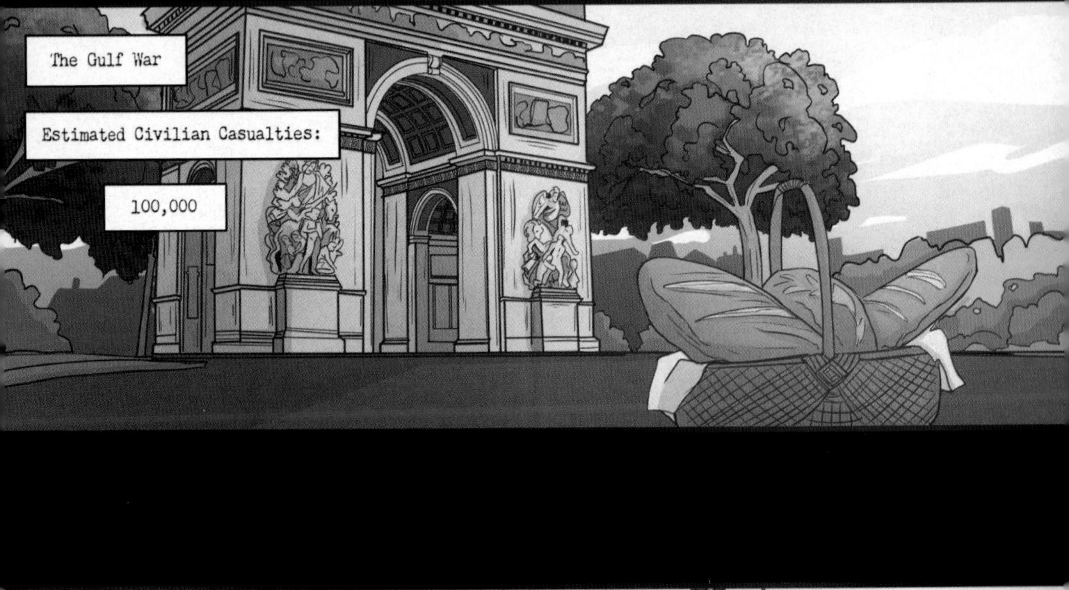
The Gulf War
Estimated Civilian Casualties:
100,000

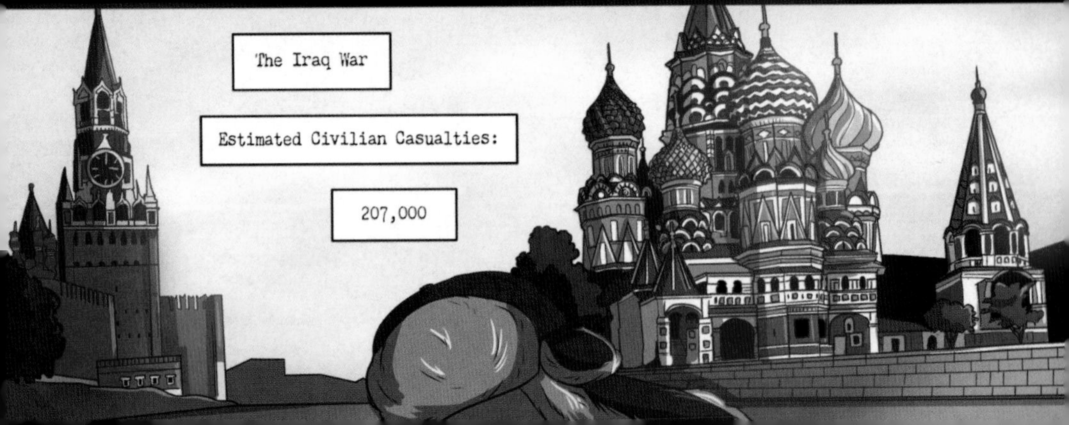
The Iraq War
Estimated Civilian Casualties:
207,000

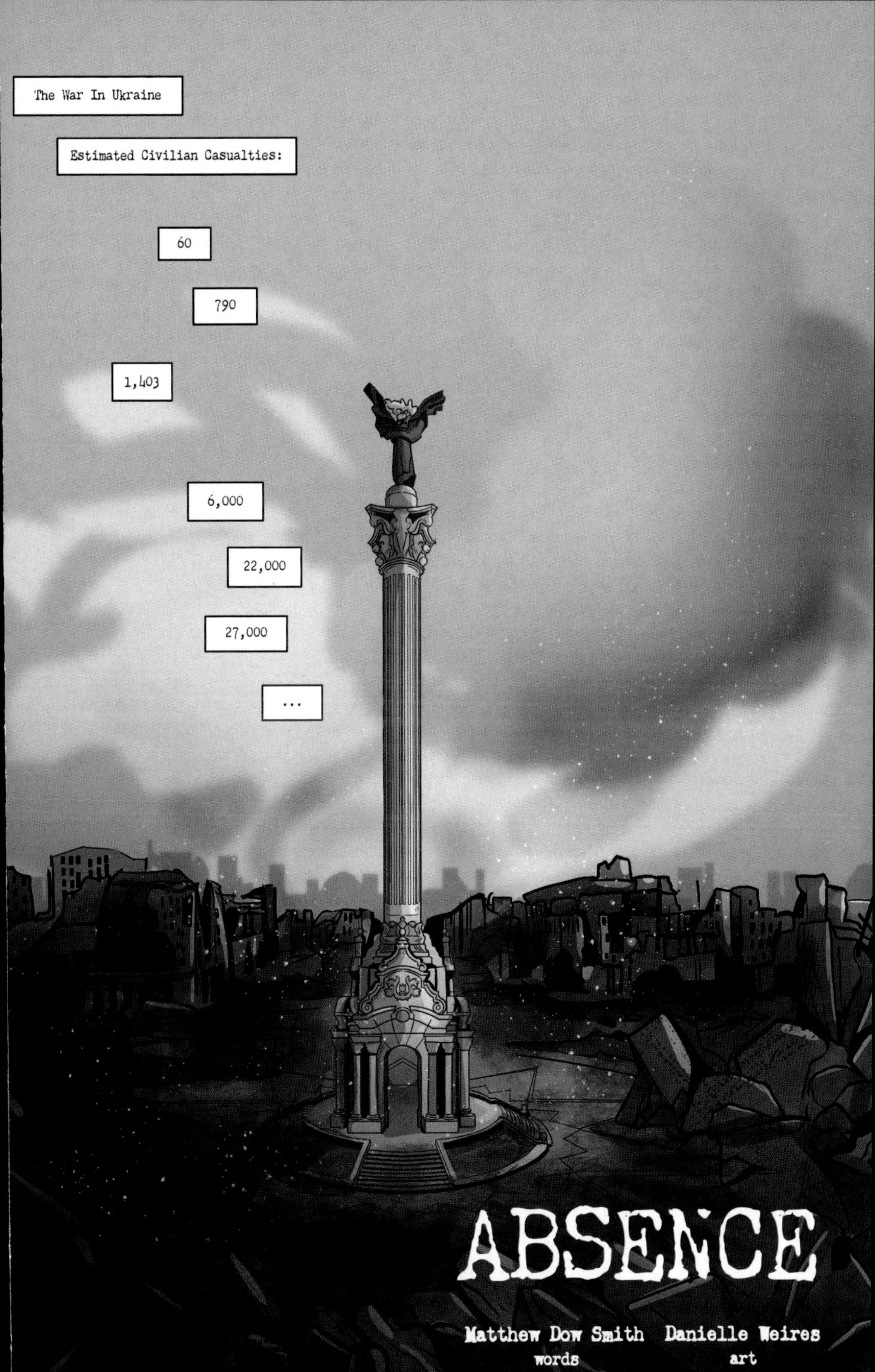

The War In Ukraine
Estimated Civilian Casualties:
60
790
1,403
6,000
22,000
27,000
...
ABSENCE
Matthew Dow Smith
words
Danielle Weires
art

Artist: **Bryan Silver**
Colorist: **Kote Carv**

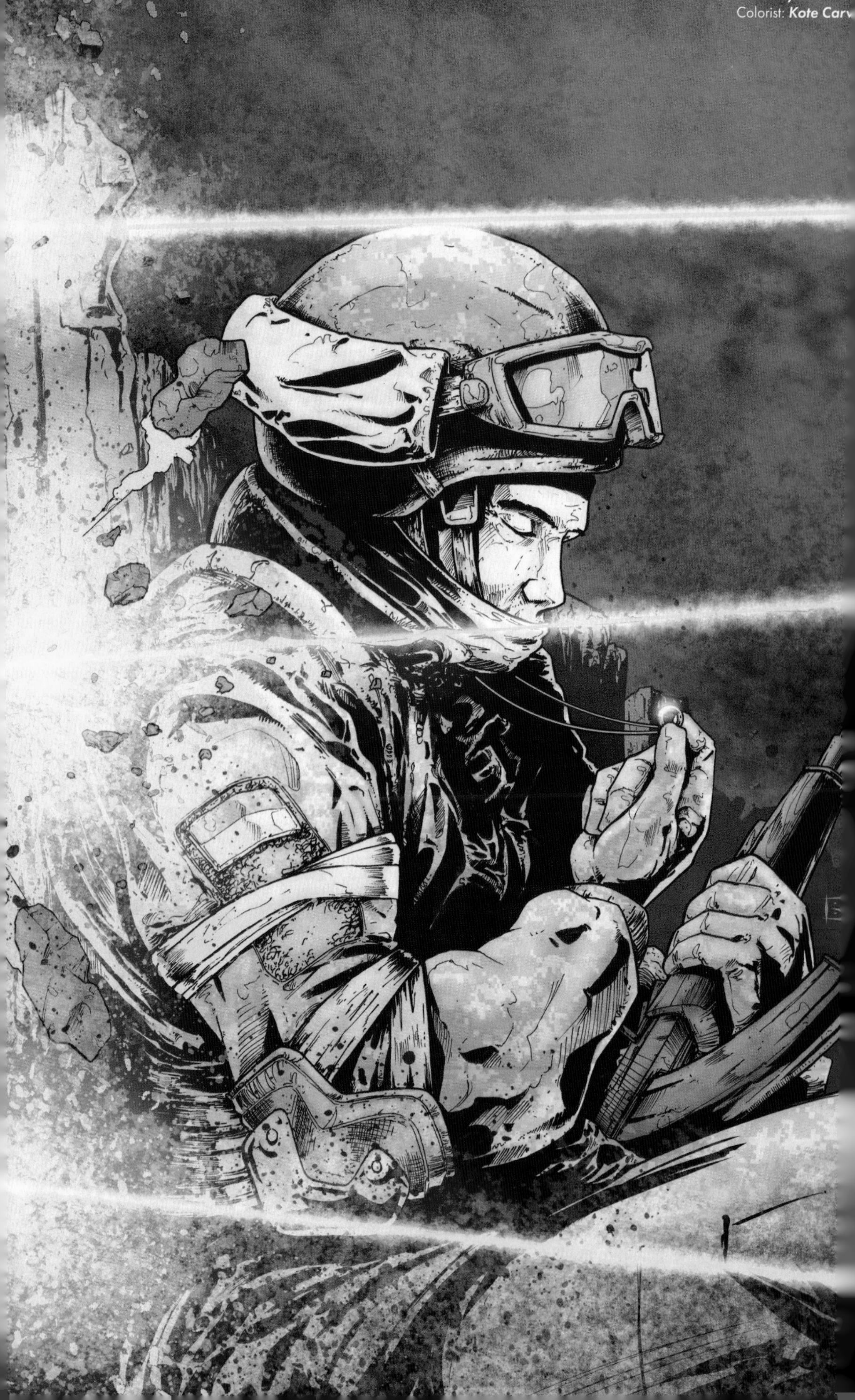

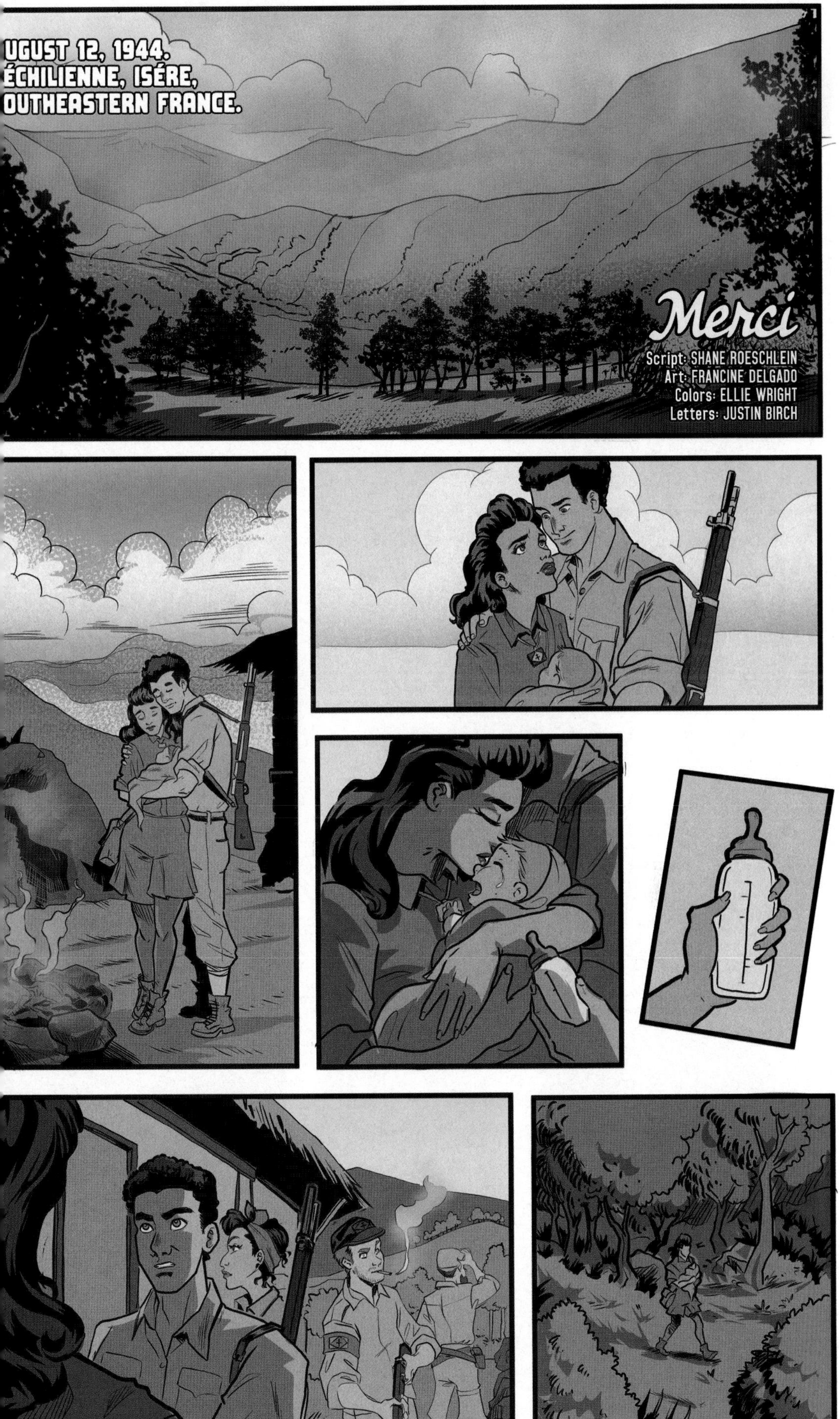

UGUST 12, 1944.
ÉCHILIENNE, ISÉRE,
OUTHEASTERN FRANCE.
Merci
Script: SHANE ROESCHLEIN
Art: FRANCINE DELGADO
Colors: ELLIE WRIGHT
Letters: JUSTIN BIRCH

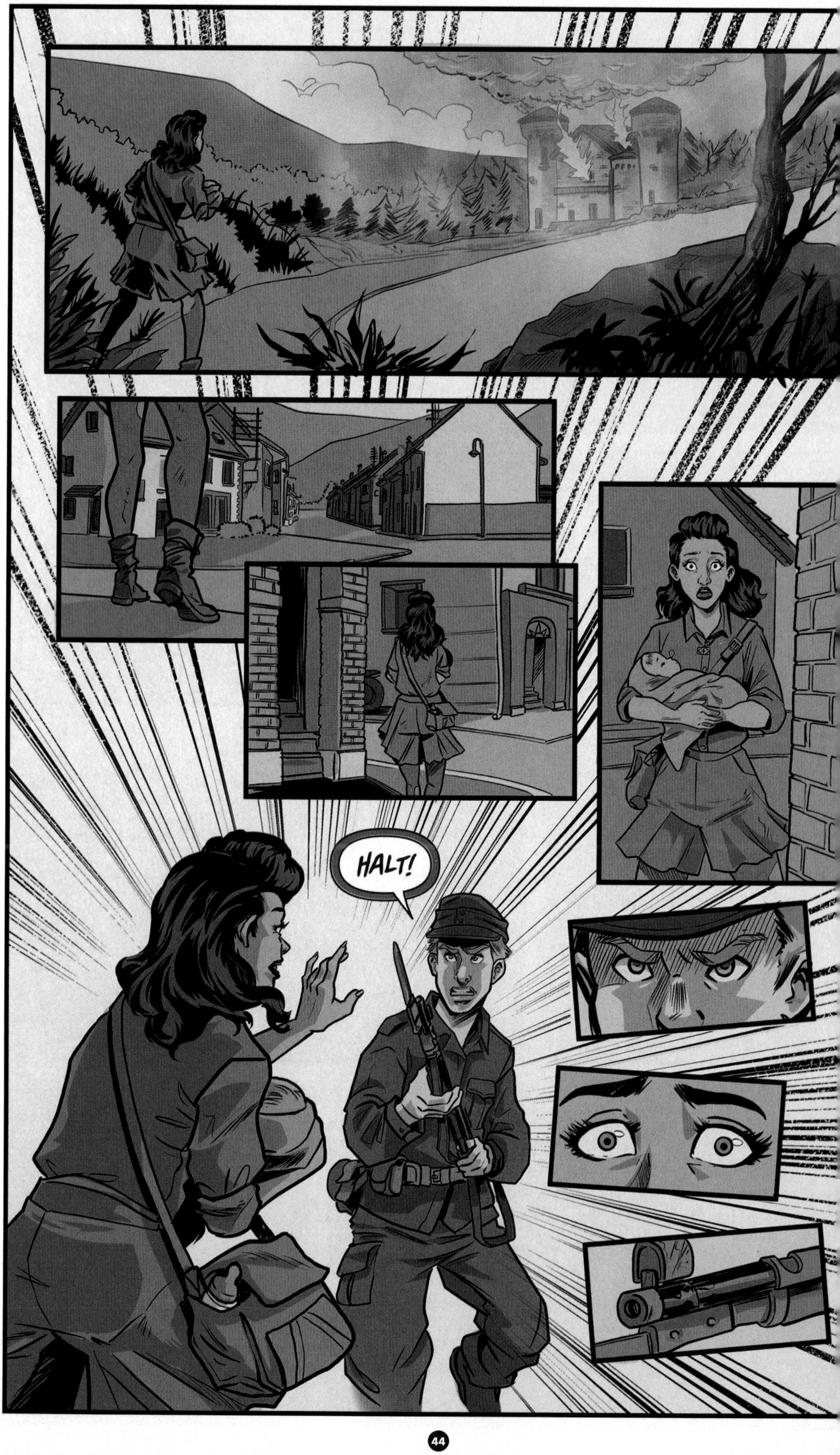
HALT!

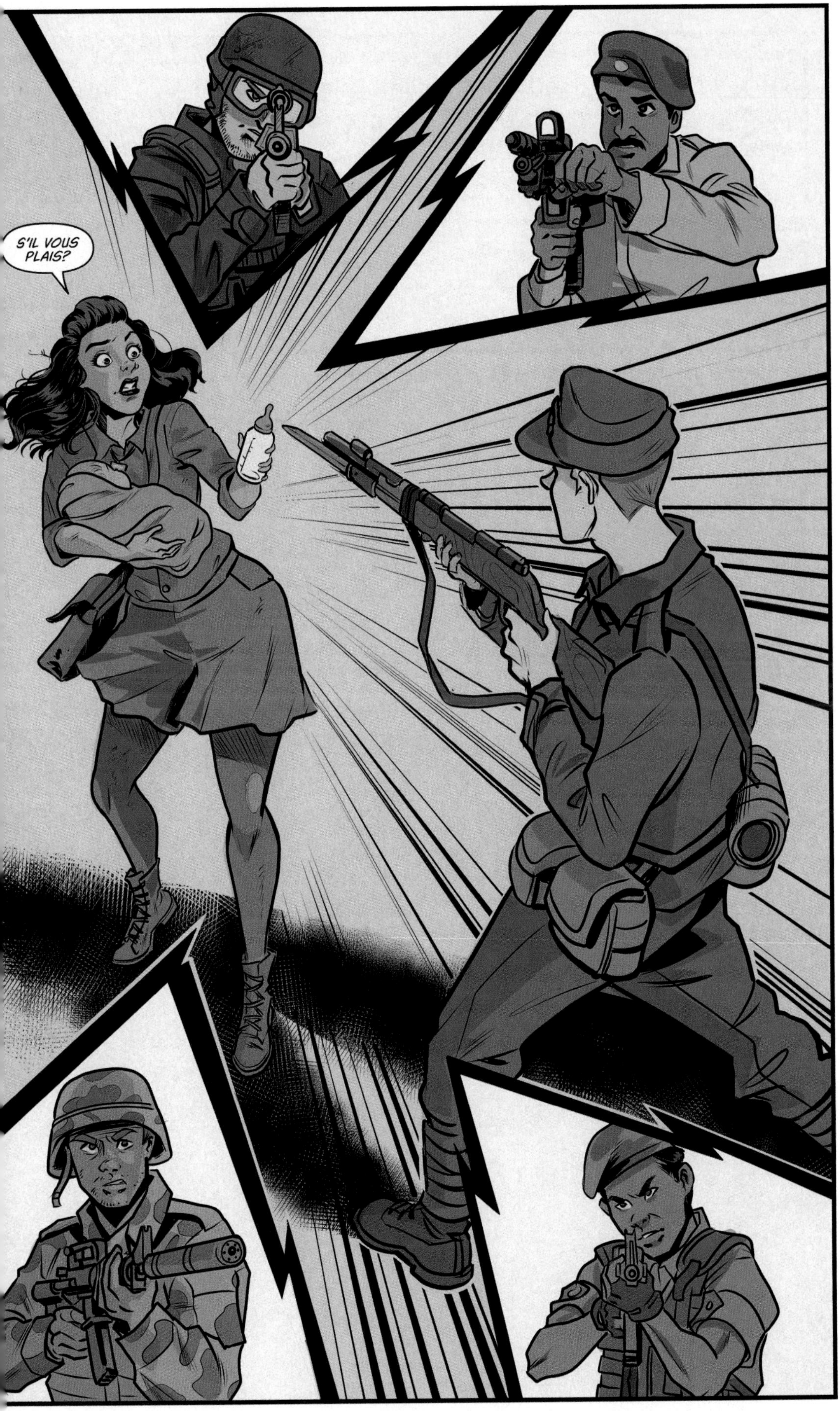
S'IL VOUS PLAIS?

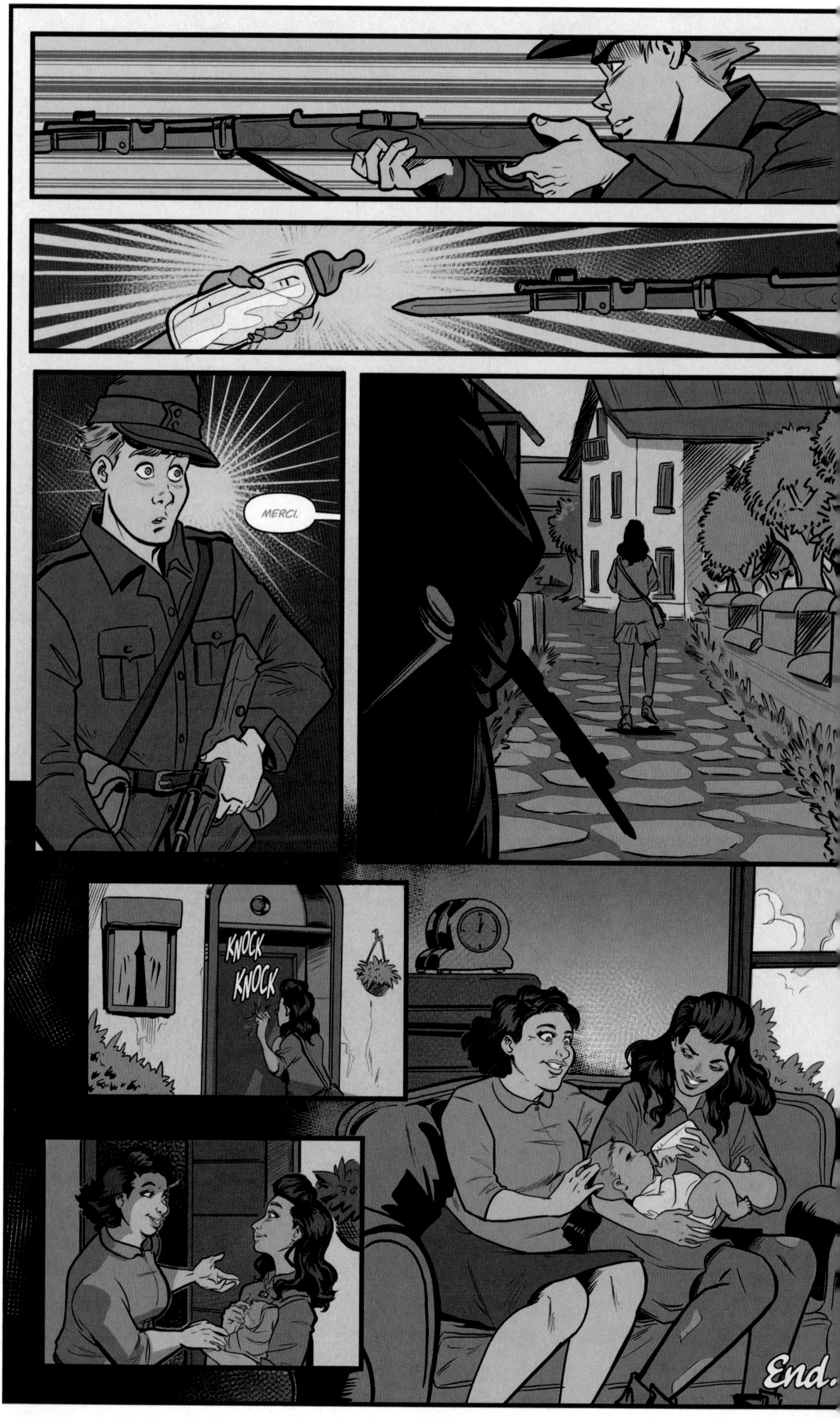
MERCI.
KNOCK
KNOCK
End.

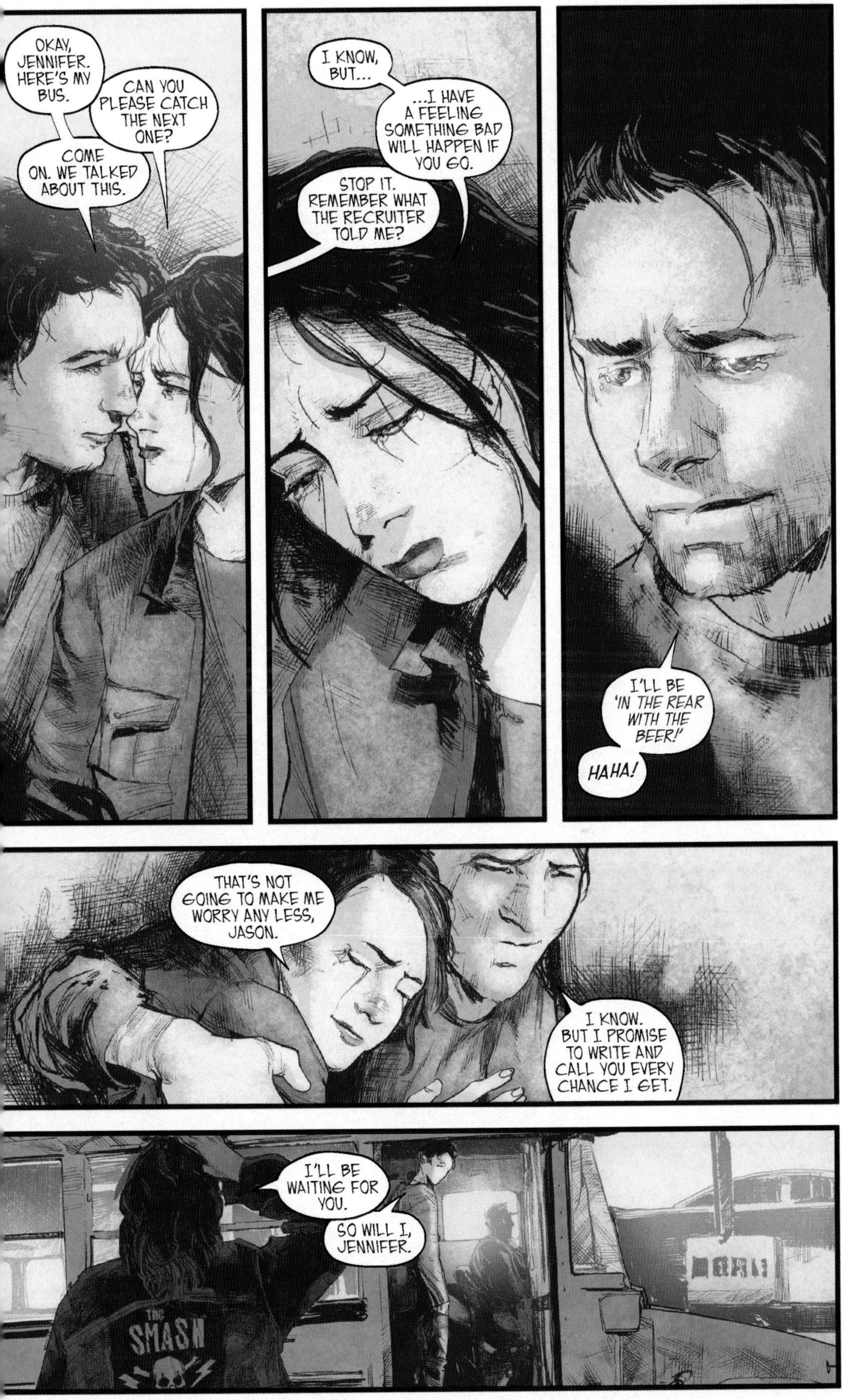
OKAY, JENNIFER. HERE'S MY BUS.
CAN YOU PLEASE CATCH THE NEXT ONE?
COME ON. WE TALKED ABOUT THIS.
I KNOW, BUT...
...I HAVE A FEELING SOMETHING BAD WILL HAPPEN IF YOU GO.
STOP IT. REMEMBER WHAT THE RECRUITER TOLD ME?
I'LL BE 'IN THE REAR WITH THE BEER!'
HAHA!
THAT'S NOT GOING TO MAKE ME WORRY ANY LESS, JASON.
I KNOW. BUT I PROMISE TO WRITE AND CALL YOU EVERY CHANCE I GET.
I'LL BE WAITING FOR YOU.
SO WILL I, JENNIFER.
THE SMASH

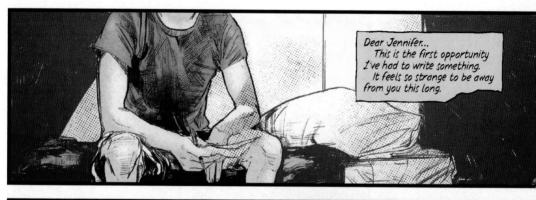

Dear Jennifer...
This is the first opportunity I've had to write something. It feels so strange to be away from you this long.

I'm in my second week of Basic Training. There's always someone screaming!

To say it's been exciting would be an understatement.

You'd be amazed at how quickly I can make a bed now. My hospital corners are at perfect 45-degree angles.

That should scare all of the bad guys away.

And I've never been more hungry in my life!

Don't get me wrong. They're feeding us well. But I think we're burning a day's worth of calories between each meal.

I've put the mailing address at the bottom of this letter. I'm really excited to hear from you!
Love,
Private Hurley.

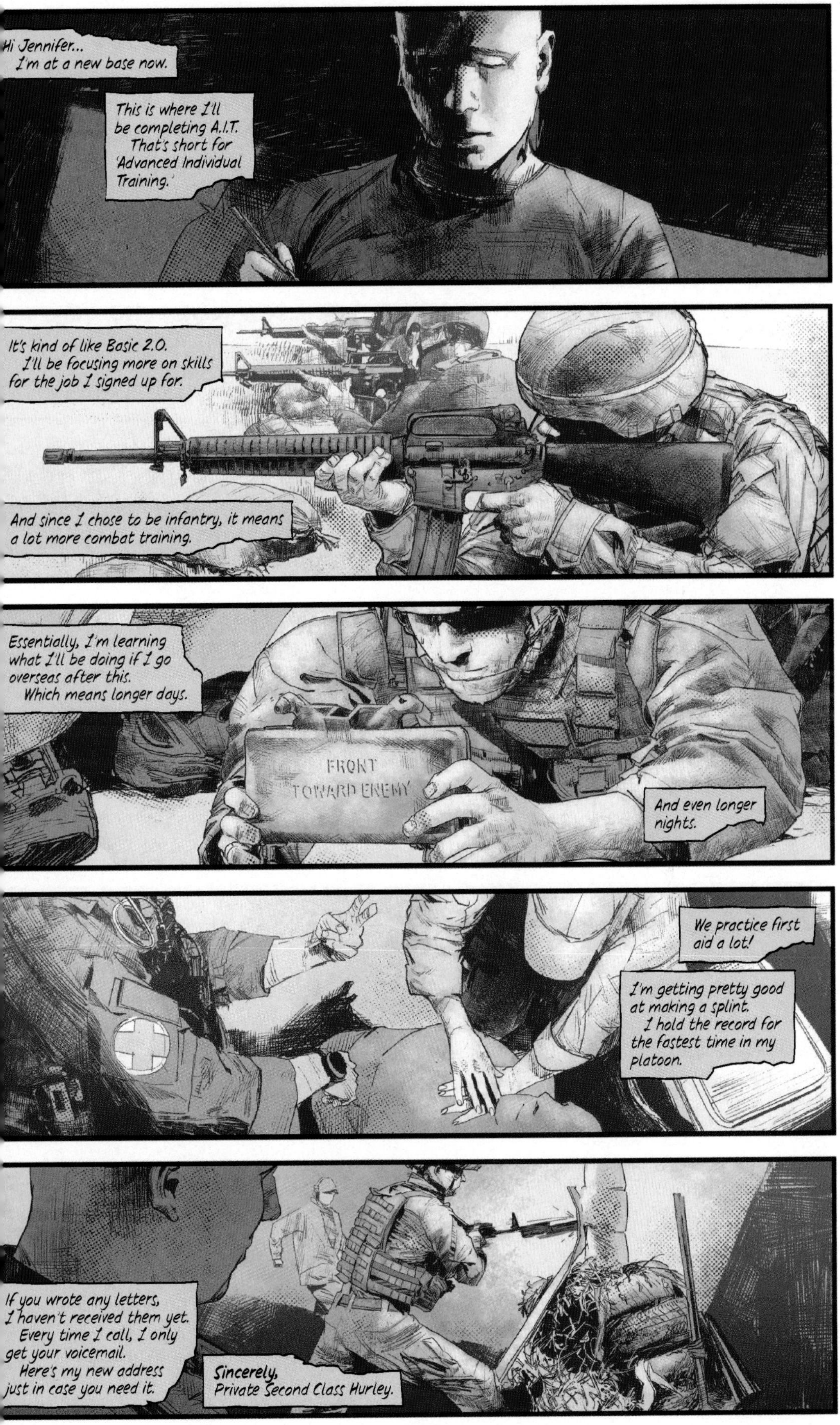
Hi Jennifer...
I'm at a new base now.
This is where I'll be completing A.I.T. That's short for 'Advanced Individual Training.'
It's kind of like Basic 2.0. I'll be focusing more on skills for the job I signed up for.
And since I chose to be infantry, it means a lot more combat training.
Essentially, I'm learning what I'll be doing if I go overseas after this. Which means longer days.
FRONT TOWARD ENEMY
And even longer nights.
We practice first aid a lot!
I'm getting pretty good at making a splint. I hold the record for the fastest time in my platoon.
If you wrote any letters, I haven't received them yet. Every time I call, I only get your voicemail. Here's my new address just in case you need it.
Sincerely,
Private Second Class Hurley.

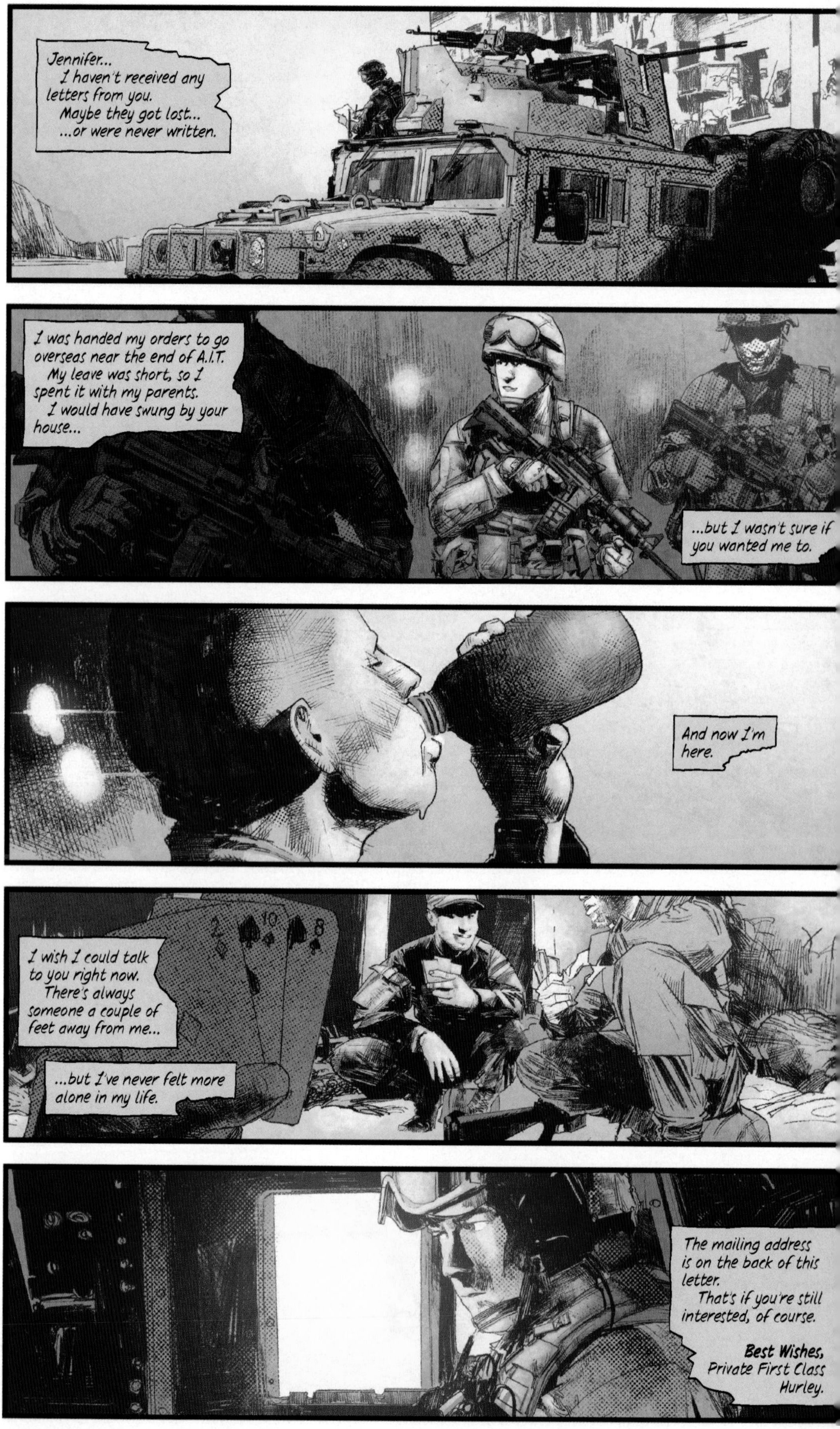
Jennifer...
I haven't received any letters from you.
Maybe they got lost...
...or were never written.
I was handed my orders to go overseas near the end of A.I.T.
My leave was short, so I spent it with my parents.
I would have swung by your house...
...but I wasn't sure if you wanted me to.
And now I'm here.
I wish I could talk to you right now.
There's always someone a couple of feet away from me...
...but I've never felt more alone in my life.
The mailing address is on the back of this letter.
That's if you're still interested, of course.
Best Wishes,
Private First Class
Hurley.

Dear Private First Class Hurley... You and I have never met, but I'm Jennifer's mother.

I wish I could have written to you sooner... ...but the pain has kept me from doing so.

Jennifer passed away before your first letter arrived. She had a brain aneurysm in her sleep.

It happened about a week after you left. During that time, she spoke about you often. She was very worried for you.

I could feel the pain in your words from your last letter. So that's why I'm finally writing to you.

IS THAT FROM THE GIRL YOU NEVER SHUT UP ABOUT?

YEAH.

YOU COULD SAY THAT.

Please be safe.

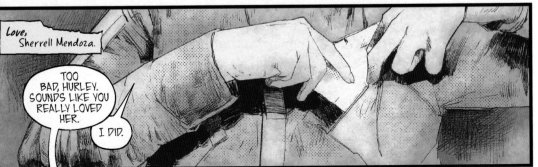

Love,
Sherrell Mendoza.

TOO BAD, HURLEY. SOUNDS LIKE YOU REALLY LOVED HER.

I DID.

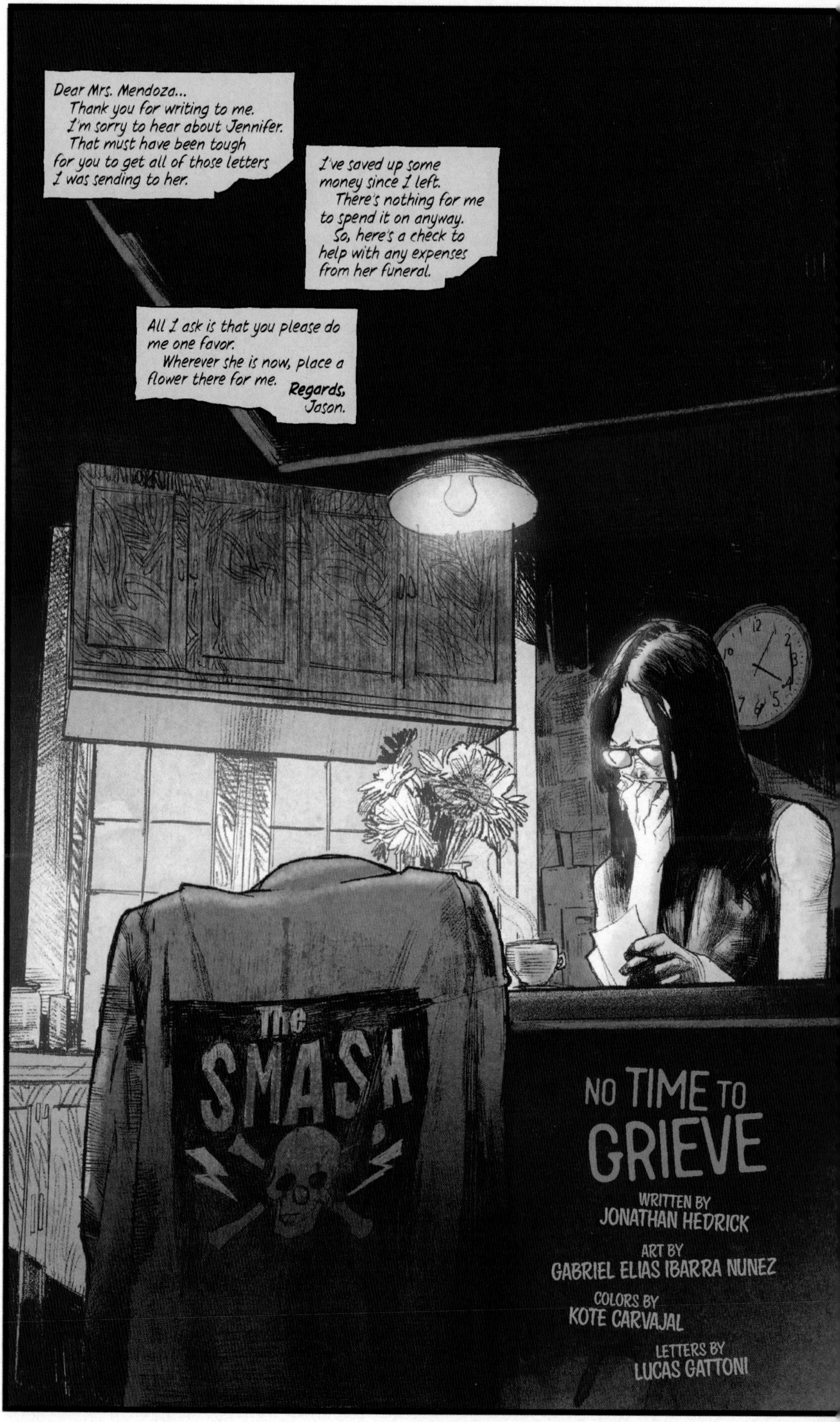

Dear Mrs. Mendoza...
Thank you for writing to me.
I'm sorry to hear about Jennifer.
That must have been tough for you to get all of those letters I was sending to her.
I've saved up some money since I left.
There's nothing for me to spend it on anyway.
So, here's a check to help with any expenses from her funeral.
All I ask is that you please do me one favor.
Wherever she is now, place a flower there for me.
Regards, Jason.
The SMASH
NO TIME TO GRIEVE
WRITTEN BY JONATHAN HEDRICK
ART BY GABRIEL ELIAS IBARRA NUNEZ
COLORS BY KOTE CARVAJAL
LETTERS BY LUCAS GATTONI

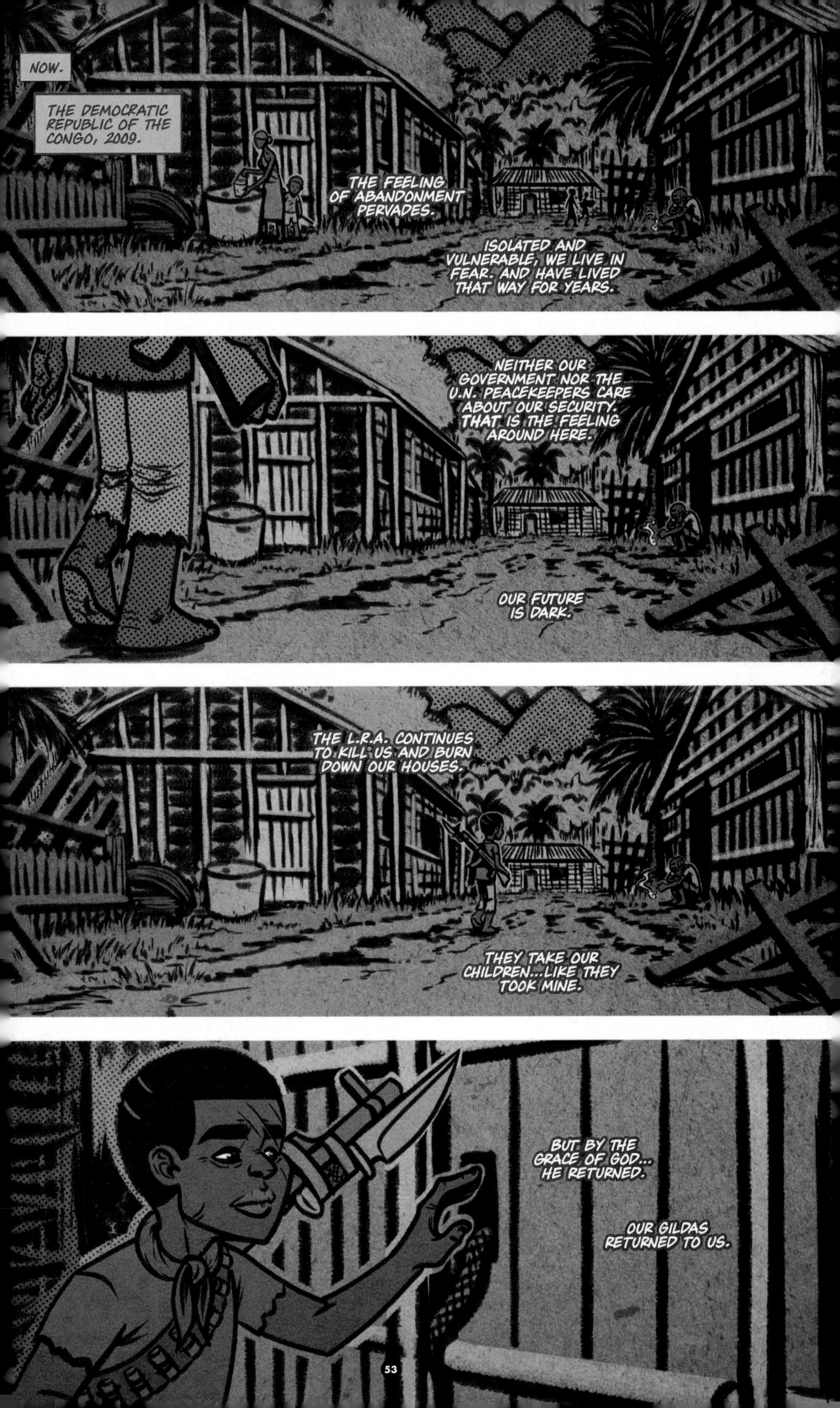

NOW.
THE DEMOCRATIC REPUBLIC OF THE CONGO, 2009.
THE FEELING OF ABANDONMENT PERVADES.
ISOLATED AND VULNERABLE, WE LIVE IN FEAR. AND HAVE LIVED THAT WAY FOR YEARS.
NEITHER OUR GOVERNMENT NOR THE U.N. PEACEKEEPERS CARE ABOUT OUR SECURITY. THAT IS THE FEELING AROUND HERE.
OUR FUTURE IS DARK.
THE L.R.A. CONTINUES TO KILL US AND BURN DOWN OUR HOUSES.
THEY TAKE OUR CHILDREN...LIKE THEY TOOK MINE.
BUT BY THE GRACE OF GOD... HE RETURNED.
OUR GILDAS RETURNED TO US.

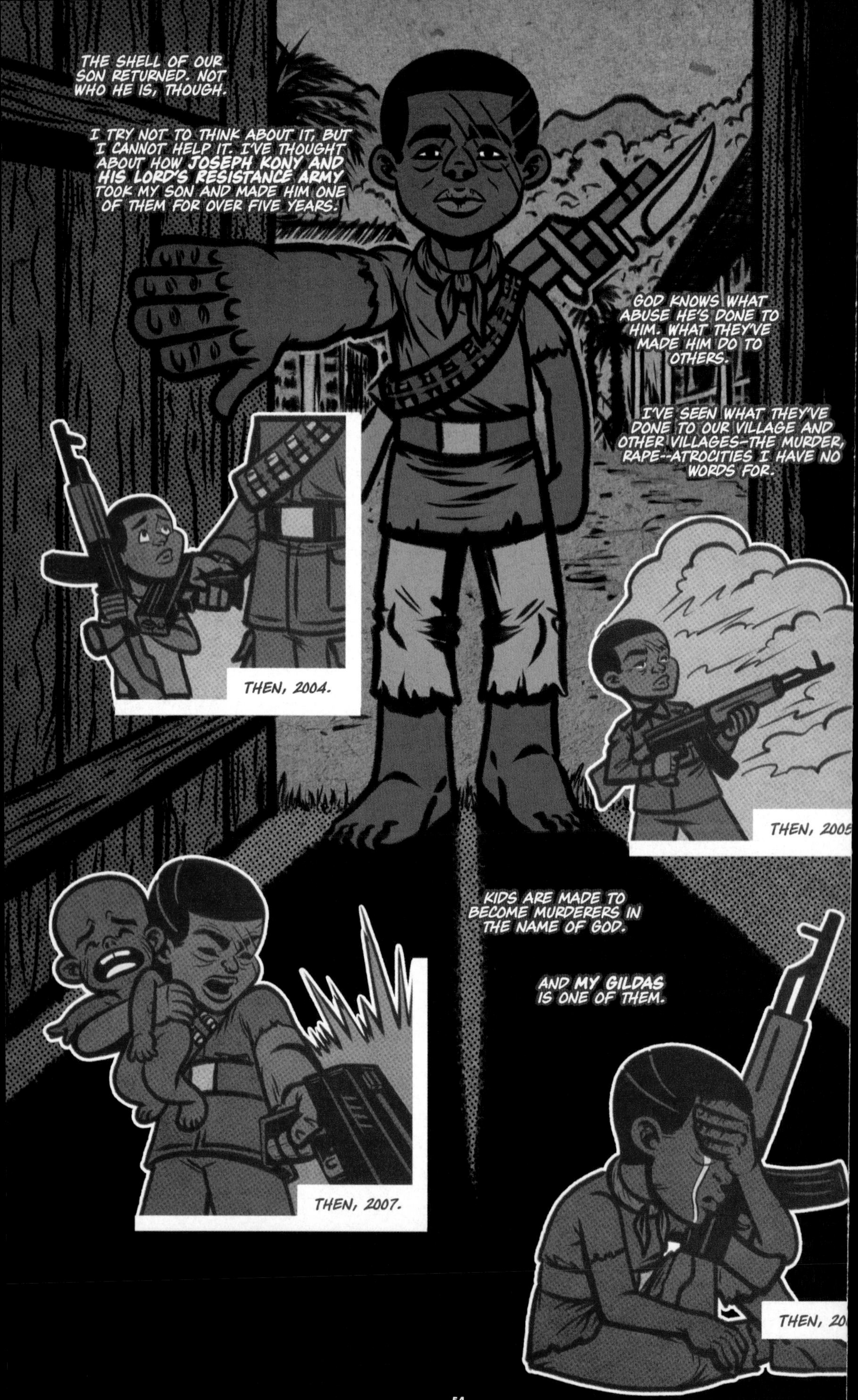
THE SHELL OF OUR SON RETURNED. NOT WHO HE IS, THOUGH.
I TRY NOT TO THINK ABOUT IT, BUT I CANNOT HELP IT. I'VE THOUGHT ABOUT HOW JOSEPH KONY AND HIS LORD'S RESISTANCE ARMY TOOK MY SON AND MADE HIM ONE OF THEM FOR OVER FIVE YEARS.
GOD KNOWS WHAT ABUSE HE'S DONE TO HIM. WHAT THEY'VE MADE HIM DO TO OTHERS.
I'VE SEEN WHAT THEY'VE DONE TO OUR VILLAGE AND OTHER VILLAGES--THE MURDER, RAPE--ATROCITIES I HAVE NO WORDS FOR.
THEN, 2004.
THEN, 2005
KIDS ARE MADE TO BECOME MURDERERS IN THE NAME OF GOD.
AND MY GILDAS IS ONE OF THEM.
THEN, 2007.
THEN, 20

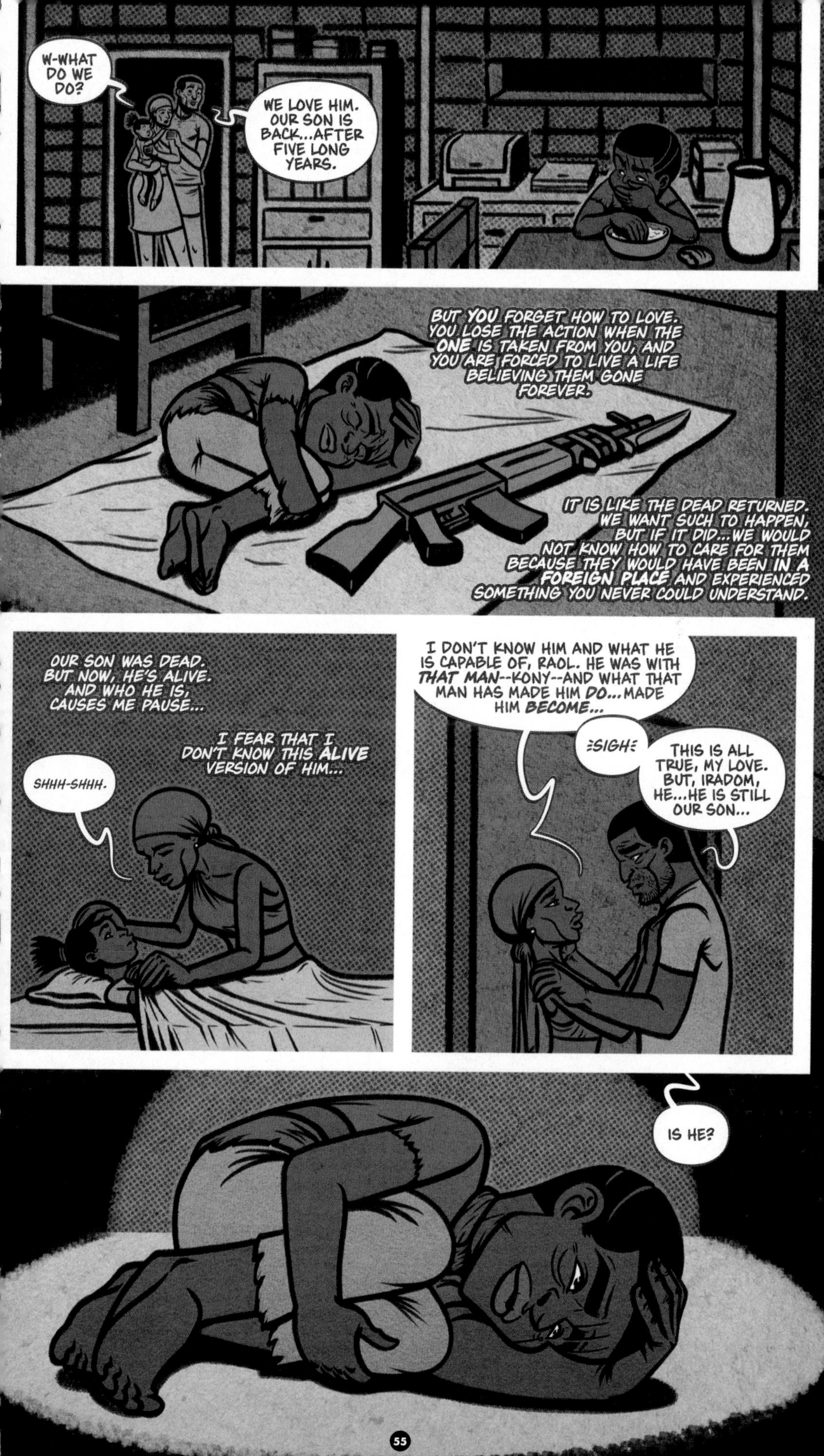
W-WHAT DO WE DO?
WE LOVE HIM. OUR SON IS BACK...AFTER FIVE LONG YEARS.
BUT YOU FORGET HOW TO LOVE. YOU LOSE THE ACTION WHEN THE ONE IS TAKEN FROM YOU, AND YOU ARE FORCED TO LIVE A LIFE BELIEVING THEM GONE FOREVER.
IT IS LIKE THE DEAD RETURNED. WE WANT SUCH TO HAPPEN, BUT IF IT DID...WE WOULD NOT KNOW HOW TO CARE FOR THEM BECAUSE THEY WOULD HAVE BEEN IN A FOREIGN PLACE AND EXPERIENCED SOMETHING YOU NEVER COULD UNDERSTAND.
OUR SON WAS DEAD. BUT NOW, HE'S ALIVE. AND WHO HE IS, CAUSES ME PAUSE...
I FEAR THAT I DON'T KNOW THIS ALIVE VERSION OF HIM...
SHHH-SHHH.
I DON'T KNOW HIM AND WHAT HE IS CAPABLE OF, RAOL. HE WAS WITH THAT MAN--KONY--AND WHAT THAT MAN HAS MADE HIM DO... MADE HIM BECOME...
SIGH
THIS IS ALL TRUE, MY LOVE. BUT, IRADOM, HE...HE IS STILL OUR SON...
IS HE?

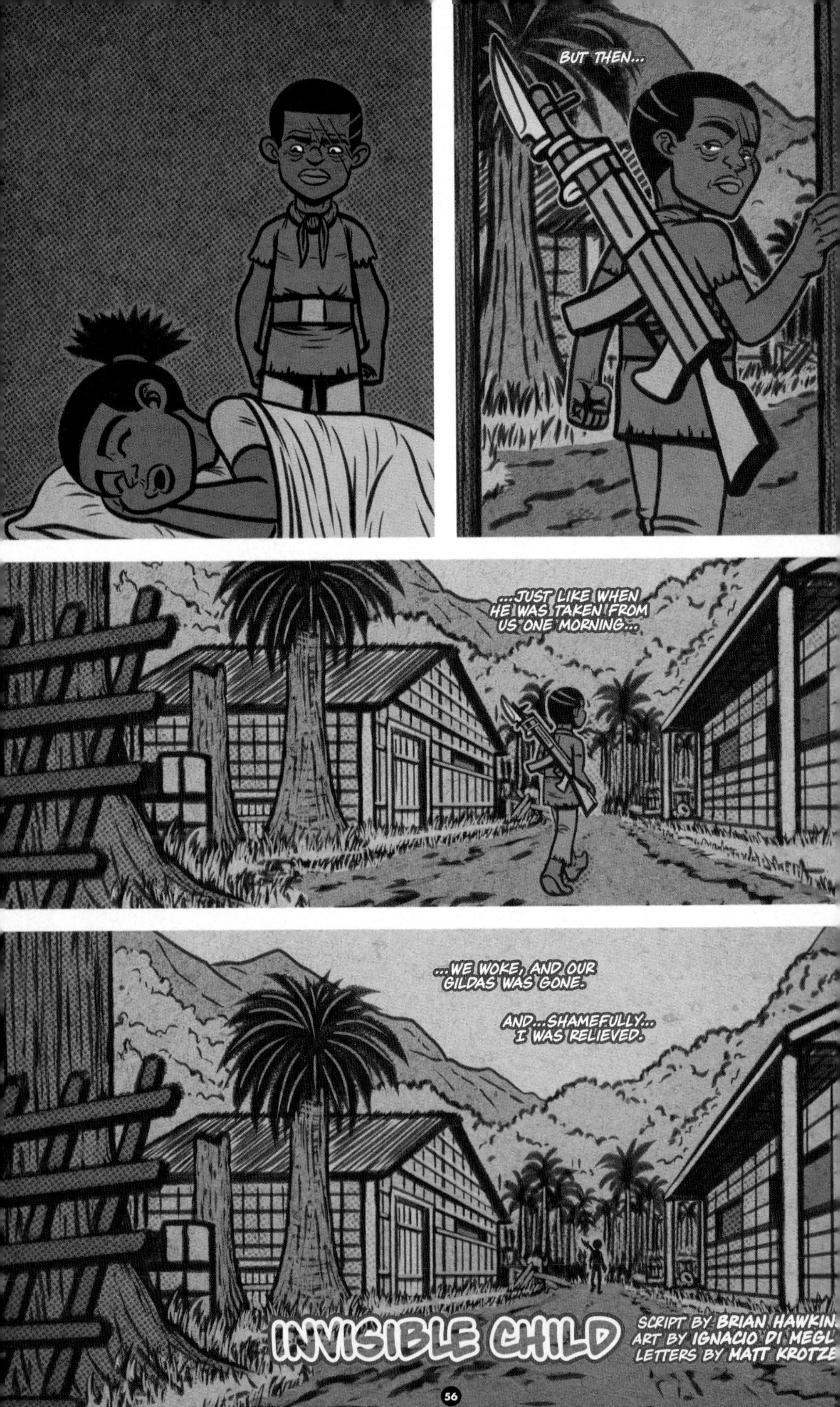
BUT THEN...
...JUST LIKE WHEN HE WAS TAKEN FROM US ONE MORNING...
...WE WOKE, AND OUR GILDAS WAS GONE.
AND...SHAMEFULLY... I WAS RELIEVED.
INVISIBLE CHILD
SCRIPT BY BRIAN HAWKIN
ART BY IGNACIO DI MEGL
LETTERS BY MATT KROTZE

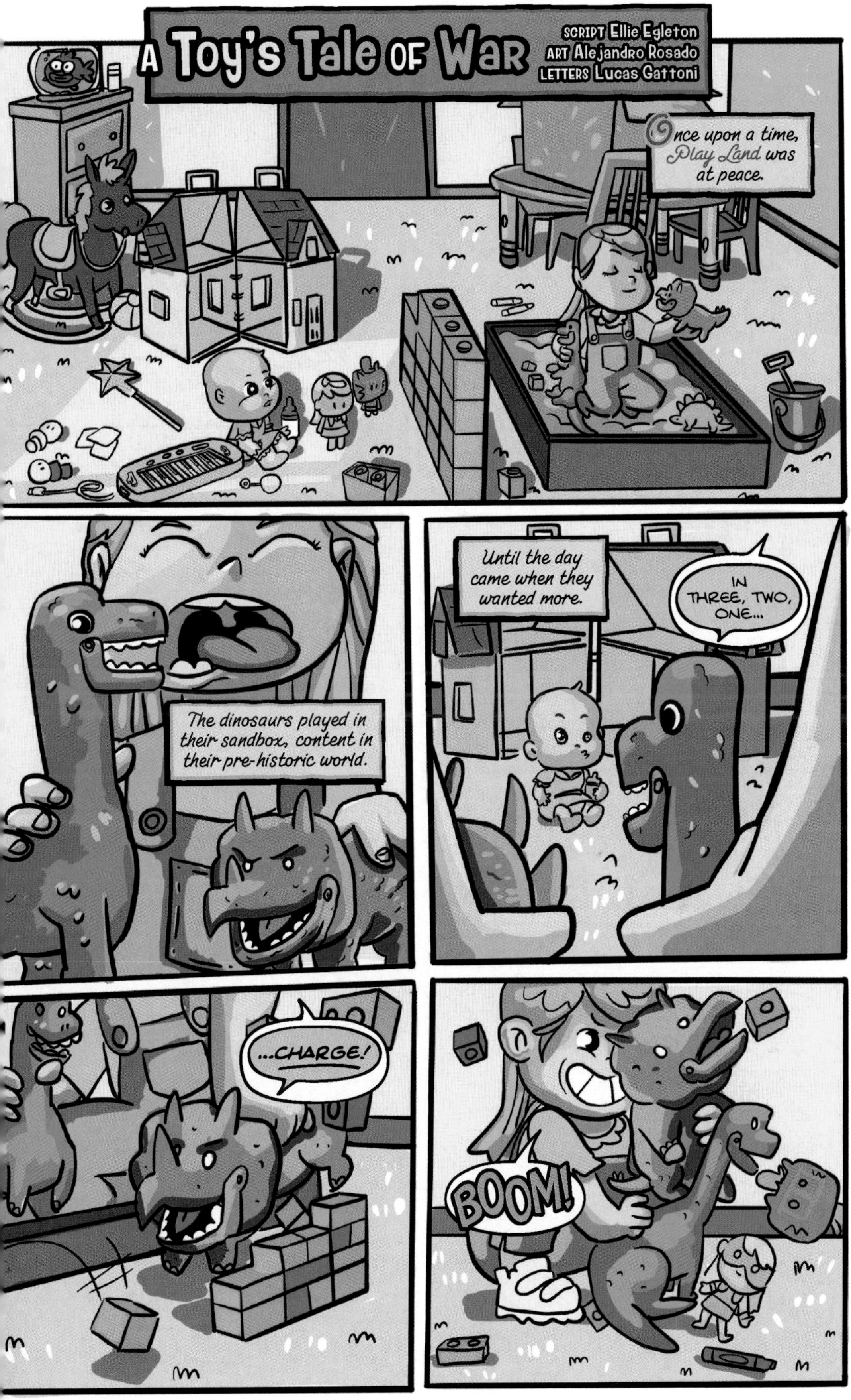
A Toy's Tale of War
SCRIPT Ellie Egleton
ART Alejandro Rosado
LETTERS Lucas Gattoni
Once upon a time, Play Land was at peace.
The dinosaurs played in their sandbox, content in their pre-historic world.
Until the day came when they wanted more.
IN THREE, TWO, ONE...
...CHARGE!
BOOM!

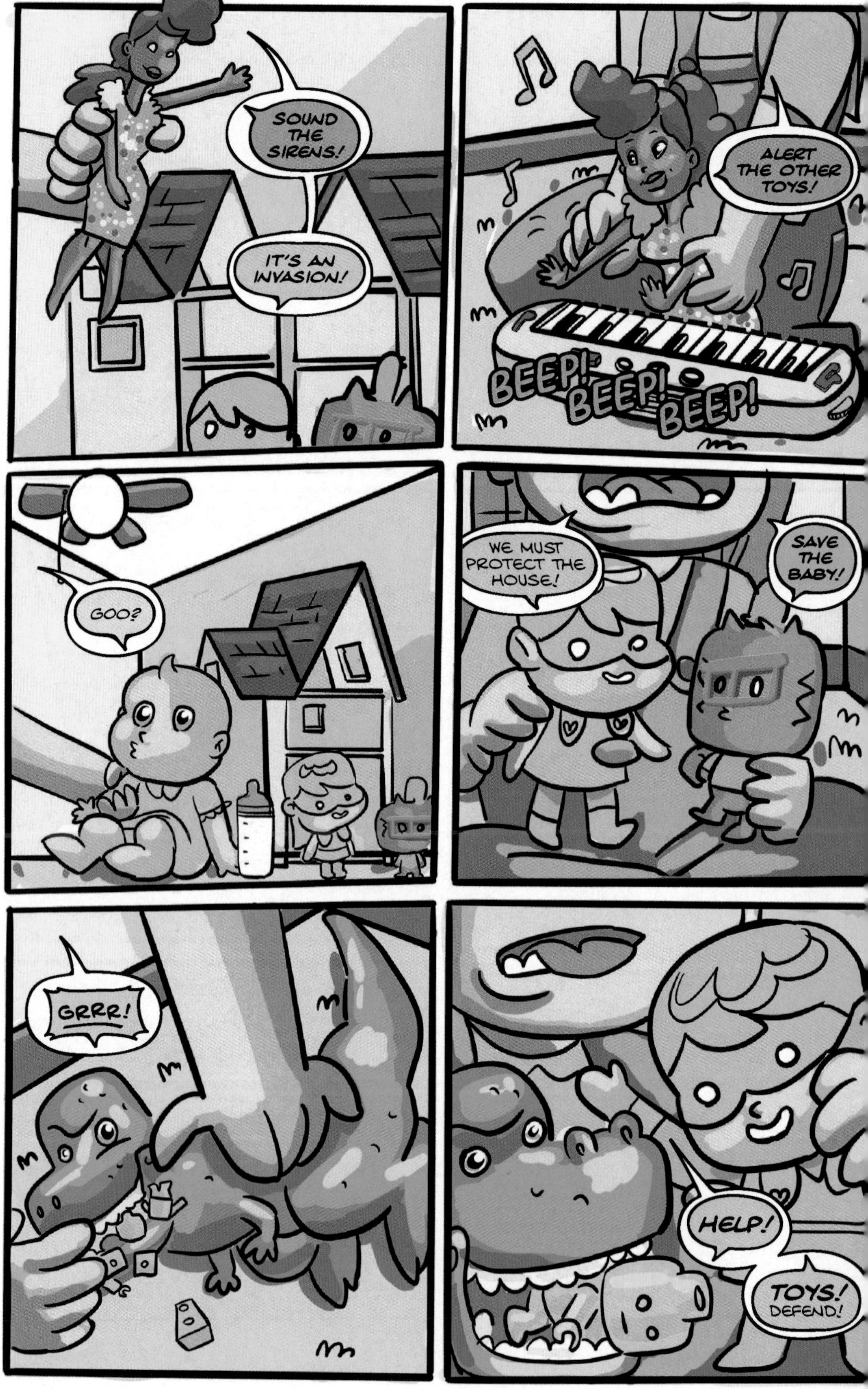
SOUND THE SIRENS!
IT'S AN INVASION!
ALERT THE OTHER TOYS!
BEEP! BEEP! BEEP!
GOO?
WE MUST PROTECT THE HOUSE!
SAVE THE BABY!
GRRR!
HELP!
TOYS! DEFEND!

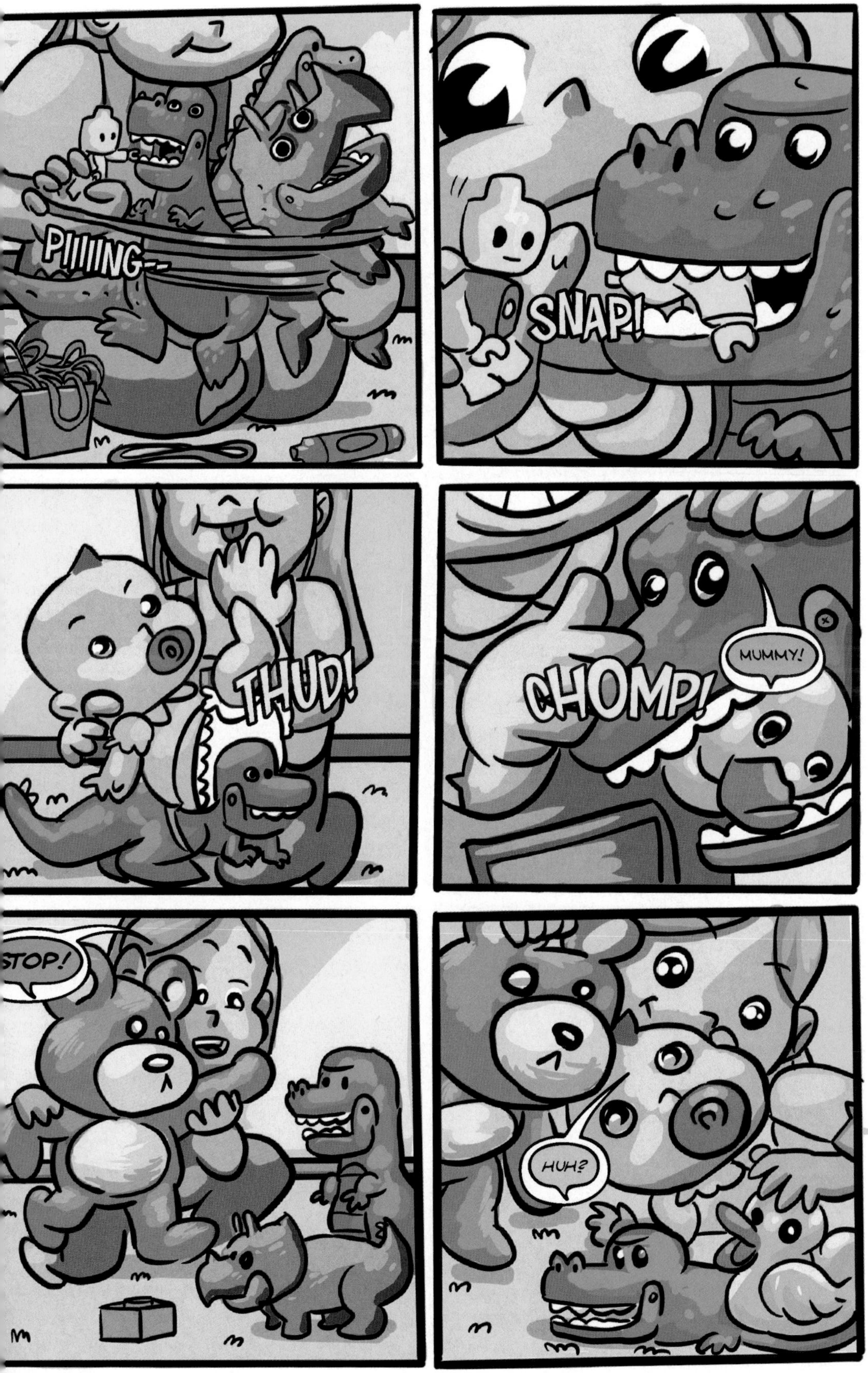
PIIIIING
SNAP!
THUD!
CHOMP!
MUMMY!
STOP!
HUH?

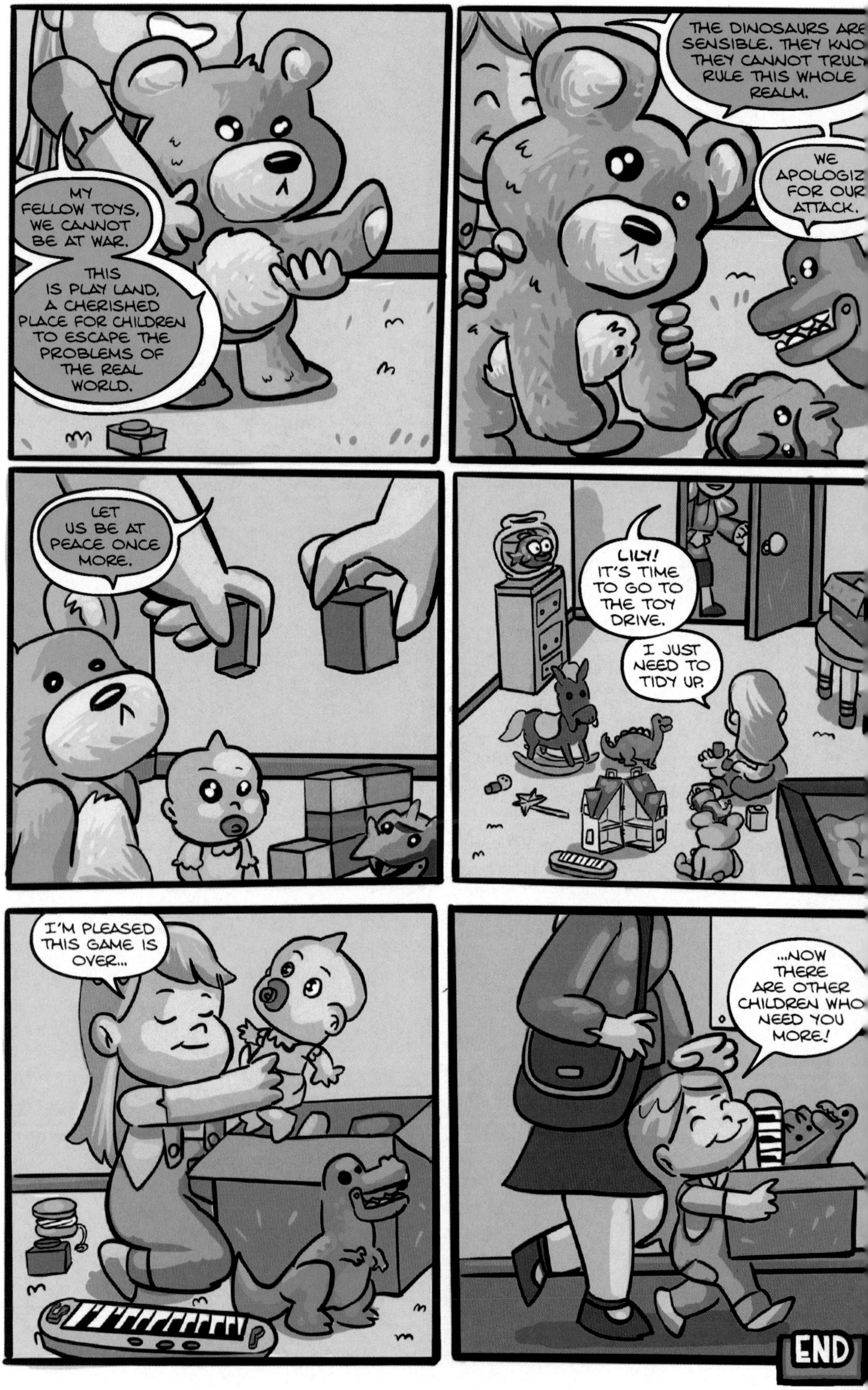
MY FELLOW TOYS, WE CANNOT BE AT WAR.
THIS IS PLAY LAND, A CHERISHED PLACE FOR CHILDREN TO ESCAPE THE PROBLEMS OF THE REAL WORLD.
THE DINOSAURS ARE SENSIBLE. THEY KNO THEY CANNOT TRULY RULE THIS WHOLE REALM.
WE APOLOGIZ FOR OUR ATTACK.
LET US BE AT PEACE ONCE MORE.
LILY! IT'S TIME TO GO TO THE TOY DRIVE.
I JUST NEED TO TIDY UP.
I'M PLEASED THIS GAME IS OVER...
...NOW THERE ARE OTHER CHILDREN WHO NEED YOU MORE!
END

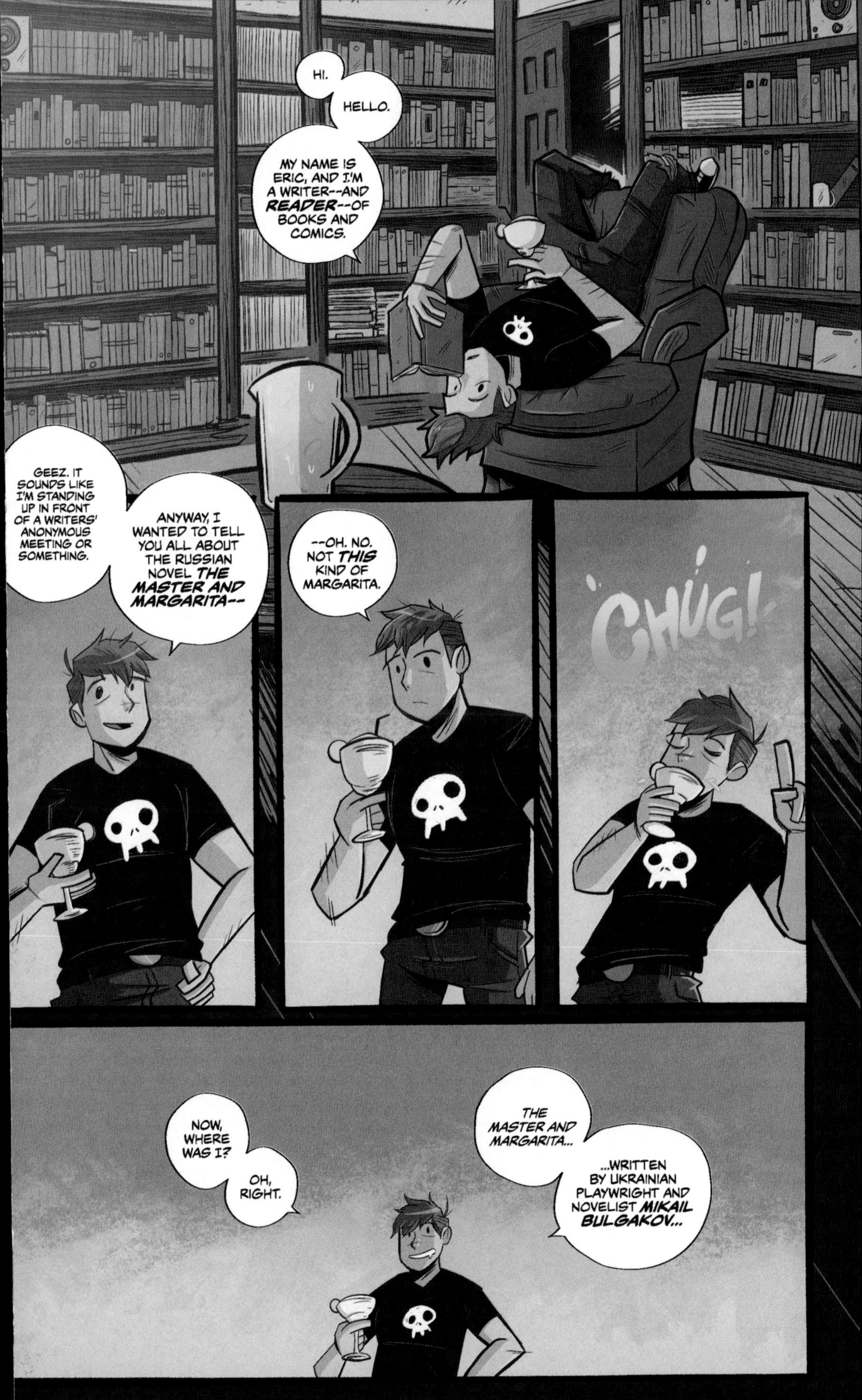
HI.
HELLO.
MY NAME IS ERIC, AND I'M A WRITER--AND READER--OF BOOKS AND COMICS.
GEEZ. IT SOUNDS LIKE I'M STANDING UP IN FRONT OF A WRITERS' ANONYMOUS MEETING OR SOMETHING.
ANYWAY, I WANTED TO TELL YOU ALL ABOUT THE RUSSIAN NOVEL THE MASTER AND MARGARITA--
--OH. NO. NOT THIS KIND OF MARGARITA.
CHUG!
NOW, WHERE WAS I?
OH, RIGHT.
THE MASTER AND MARGARITA...
...WRITTEN BY UKRAINIAN PLAYWRIGHT AND NOVELIST MIKAIL BULGAKOV...

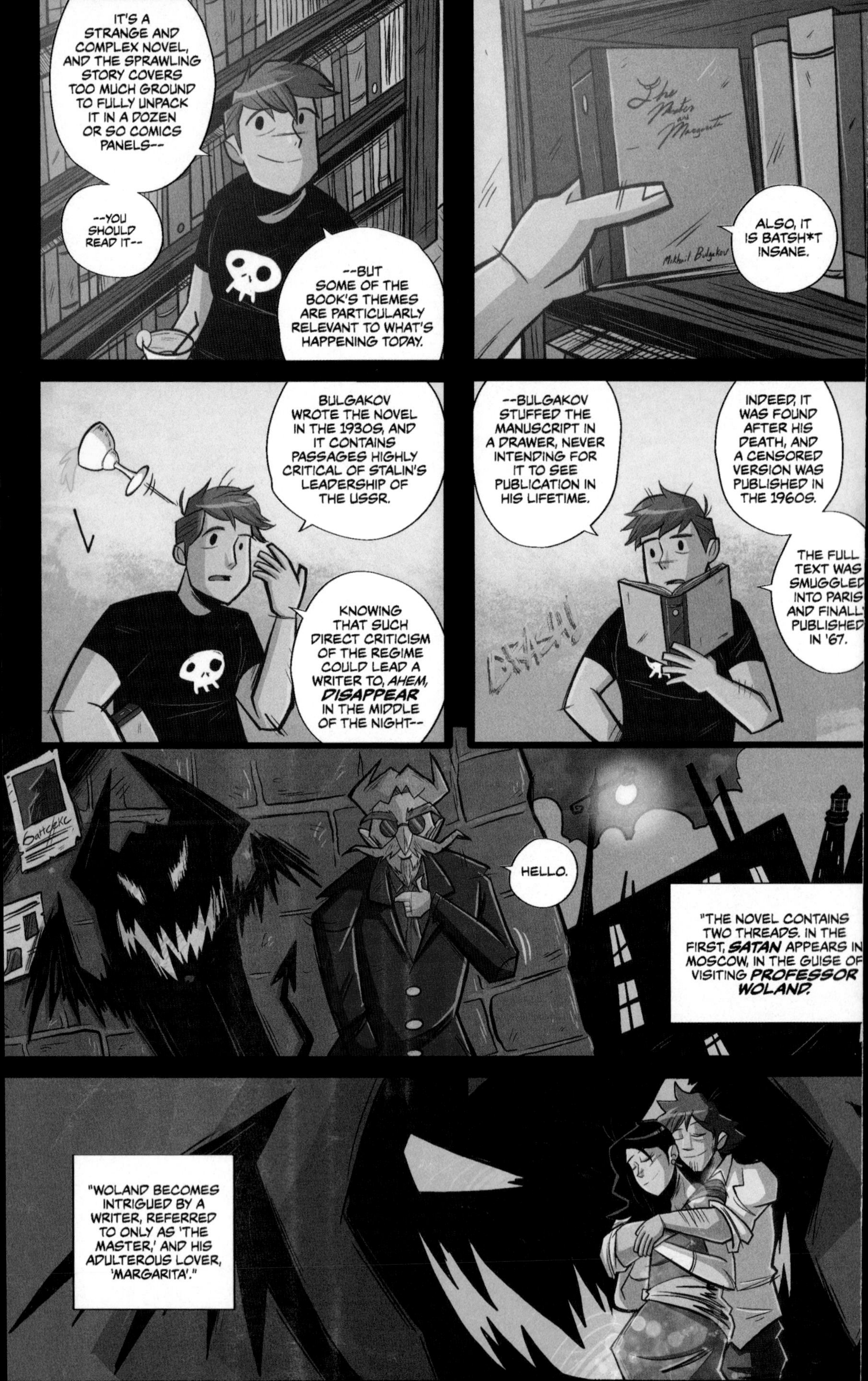

IT'S A STRANGE AND COMPLEX NOVEL, AND THE SPRAWLING STORY COVERS TOO MUCH GROUND TO FULLY UNPACK IT IN A DOZEN OR SO COMICS PANELS--
--YOU SHOULD READ IT--
--BUT SOME OF THE BOOK'S THEMES ARE PARTICULARLY RELEVANT TO WHAT'S HAPPENING TODAY.
The Master and Margarita
Mikhail Bulgakov
ALSO, IT IS BATSH*T INSANE.
BULGAKOV WROTE THE NOVEL IN THE 1930S, AND IT CONTAINS PASSAGES HIGHLY CRITICAL OF STALIN'S LEADERSHIP OF THE USSR.
KNOWING THAT SUCH DIRECT CRITICISM OF THE REGIME COULD LEAD A WRITER TO, *AHEM*, ***DISAPPEAR*** IN THE MIDDLE OF THE NIGHT--
--BULGAKOV STUFFED THE MANUSCRIPT IN A DRAWER, NEVER INTENDING FOR IT TO SEE PUBLICATION IN HIS LIFETIME.
INDEED, IT WAS FOUND AFTER HIS DEATH, AND A CENSORED VERSION WAS PUBLISHED IN THE 1960S.
THE FULL TEXT WAS SMUGGLED INTO PARIS AND FINALLY PUBLISHED IN '67.
CRASH!
HELLO.
"THE NOVEL CONTAINS TWO THREADS. IN THE FIRST, ***SATAN*** APPEARS IN MOSCOW, IN THE GUISE OF VISITING ***PROFESSOR WOLAND.***
"WOLAND BECOMES INTRIGUED BY A WRITER, REFERRED TO ONLY AS 'THE MASTER,' AND HIS ADULTEROUS LOVER, 'MARGARITA'."

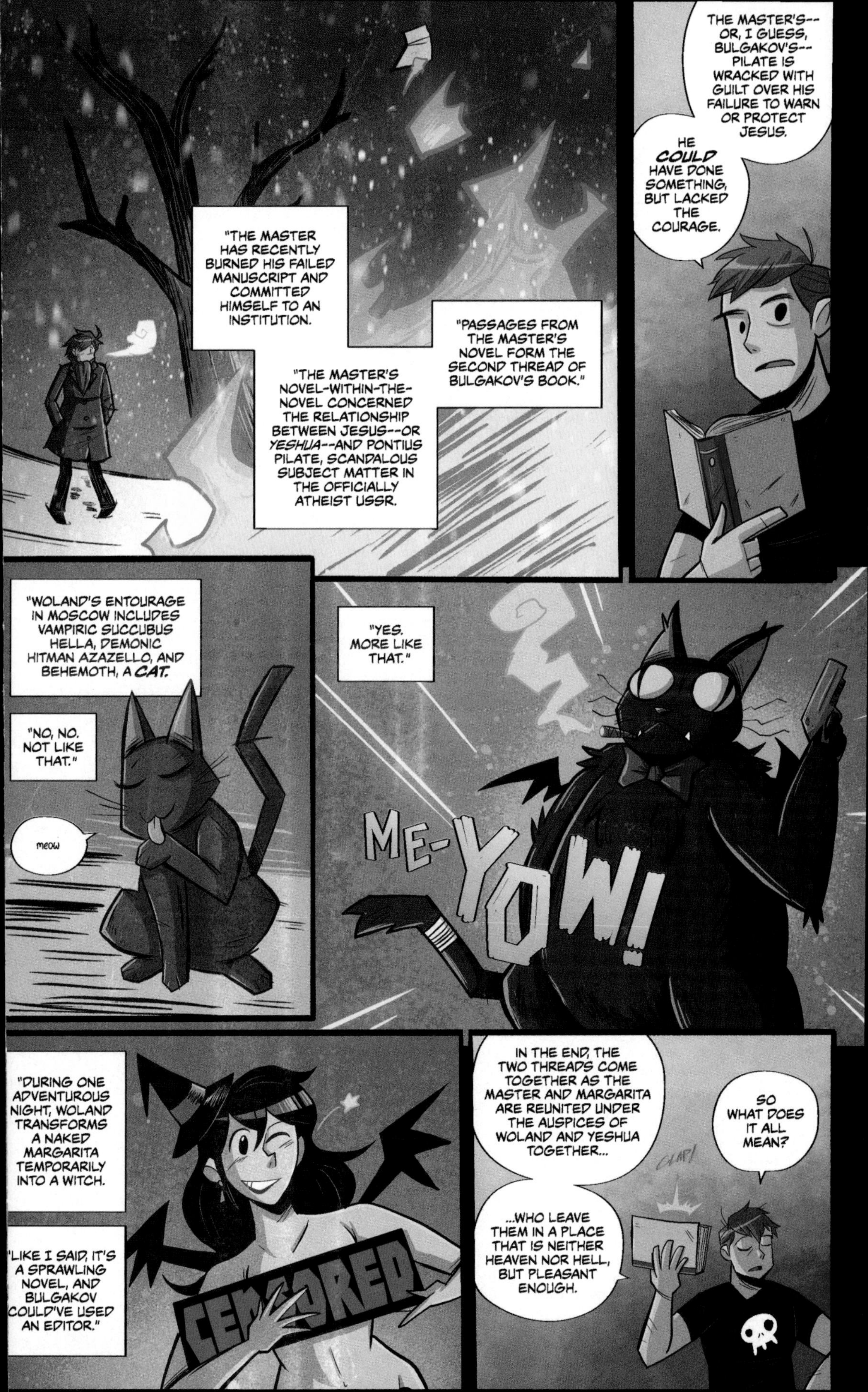
"THE MASTER HAS RECENTLY BURNED HIS FAILED MANUSCRIPT AND COMMITTED HIMSELF TO AN INSTITUTION.
"PASSAGES FROM THE MASTER'S NOVEL FORM THE SECOND THREAD OF BULGAKOV'S BOOK."
"THE MASTER'S NOVEL-WITHIN-THE-NOVEL CONCERNED THE RELATIONSHIP BETWEEN JESUS--OR *YESHUA*--AND PONTIUS PILATE, SCANDALOUS SUBJECT MATTER IN THE OFFICIALLY ATHEIST USSR.
THE MASTER'S--OR, I GUESS, BULGAKOV'S--PILATE IS WRACKED WITH GUILT OVER HIS FAILURE TO WARN OR PROTECT JESUS.
HE ***COULD*** HAVE DONE SOMETHING, BUT LACKED THE COURAGE.
"WOLAND'S ENTOURAGE IN MOSCOW INCLUDES VAMPIRIC SUCCUBUS HELLA, DEMONIC HITMAN AZAZELLO, AND BEHEMOTH, A ***CAT.***
"NO, NO. NOT LIKE THAT."
meow
"YES. MORE LIKE THAT."
ME-YOW!
"DURING ONE ADVENTUROUS NIGHT, WOLAND TRANSFORMS A NAKED MARGARITA TEMPORARILY INTO A WITCH.
"LIKE I SAID, IT'S A SPRAWLING NOVEL, AND BULGAKOV COULD'VE USED AN EDITOR."
CENSORED
IN THE END, THE TWO THREADS COME TOGETHER AS THE MASTER AND MARGARITA ARE REUNITED UNDER THE AUSPICES OF WOLAND AND YESHUA TOGETHER...
SO WHAT DOES IT ALL MEAN?
CLAP!
...WHO LEAVE THEM IN A PLACE THAT IS NEITHER HEAVEN NOR HELL, BUT PLEASANT ENOUGH.

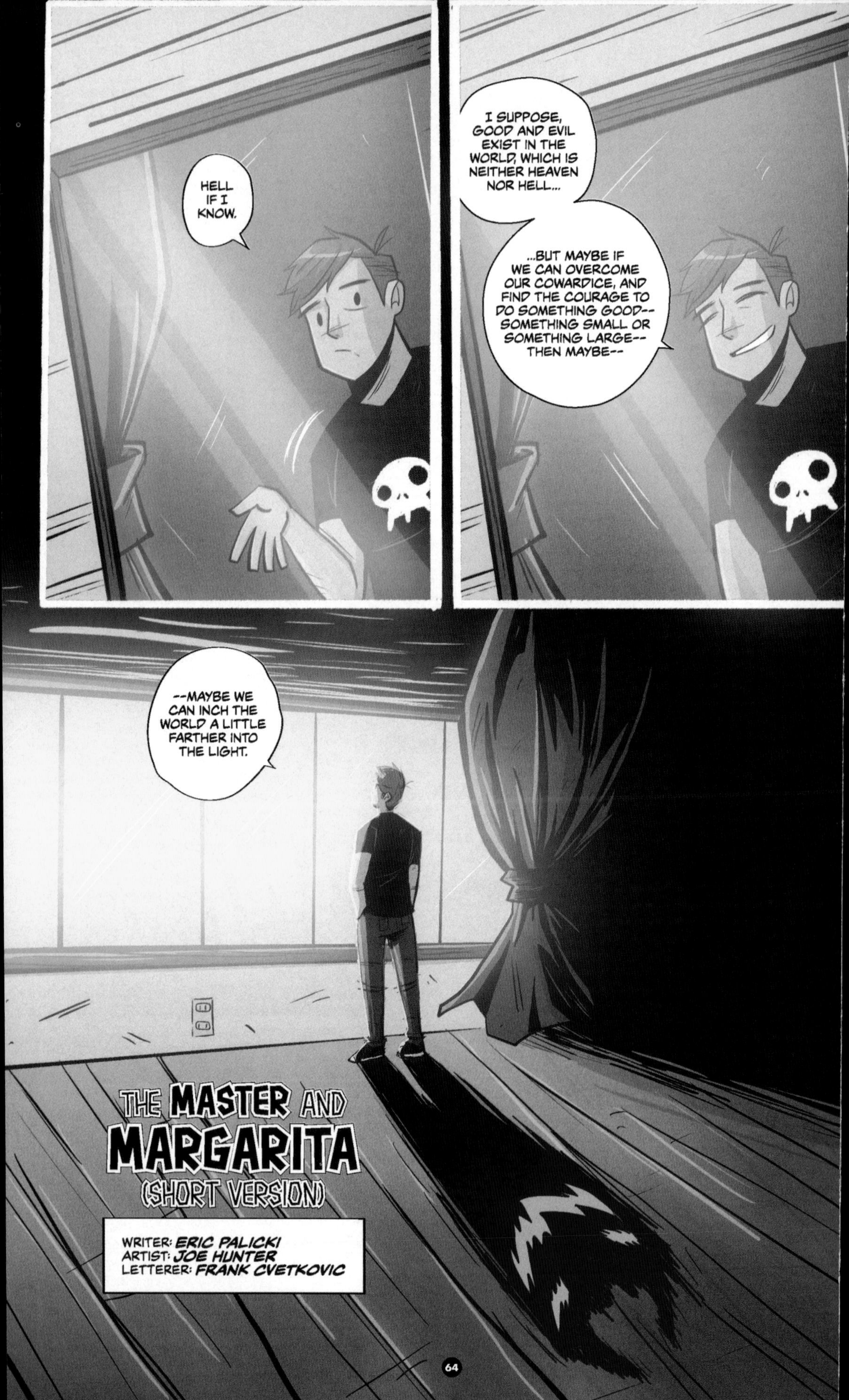
HELL IF I KNOW.
I SUPPOSE, GOOD AND EVIL EXIST IN THE WORLD, WHICH IS NEITHER HEAVEN NOR HELL...
...BUT MAYBE IF WE CAN OVERCOME OUR COWARDICE, AND FIND THE COURAGE TO DO SOMETHING GOOD-- SOMETHING SMALL OR SOMETHING LARGE-- THEN MAYBE--
--MAYBE WE CAN INCH THE WORLD A LITTLE FARTHER INTO THE LIGHT.
THE MASTER AND MARGARITA (SHORT VERSION)
WRITER: ERIC PALICKI
ARTIST: JOE HUNTER
LETTERER: FRANK CVETKOVIC

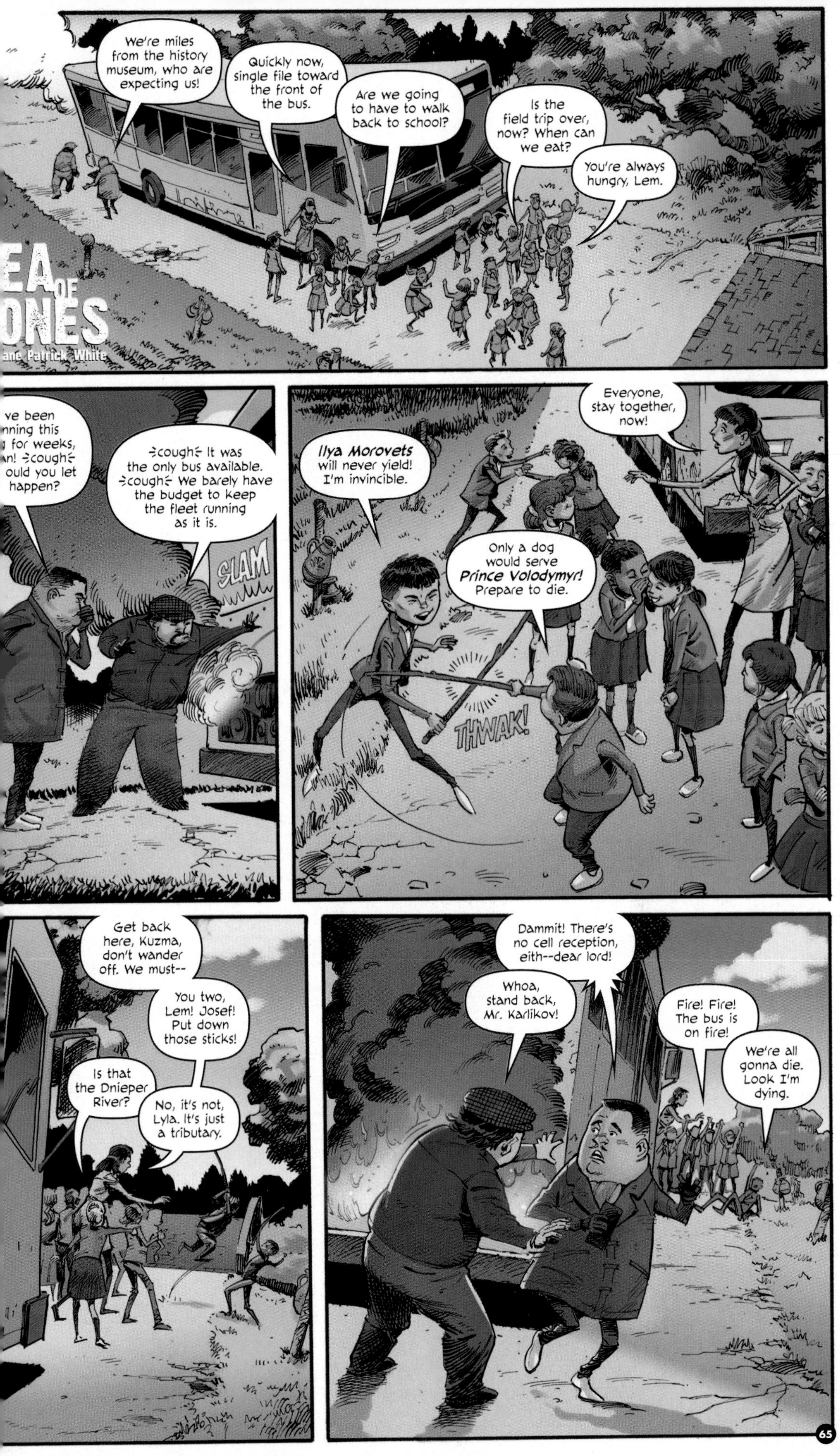
EA OF ONES
ane Patrick White
We're miles from the history museum, who are expecting us!
Quickly now, single file toward the front of the bus.
Are we going to have to walk back to school?
Is the field trip over, now? When can we eat?
You're always hungry, Lem.
ve been nning this for weeks, n! cough ould you let happen?
cough It was the only bus available. cough We barely have the budget to keep the fleet running as it is.
SLAM
Everyone, stay together, now!
Ilya Morovets will never yield! I'm invincible.
Only a dog would serve Prince Volodymyr! Prepare to die.
THWAK!
Get back here, Kuzma, don't wander off. We must--
You two, Lem! Josef! Put down those sticks!
Is that the Dnieper River?
No, it's not, Lyla. It's just a tributary.
Dammit! There's no cell reception, eith--dear lord!
Whoa, stand back, Mr. Karlikov!
Fire! Fire! The bus is on fire!
We're all gonna die. Look I'm dying.

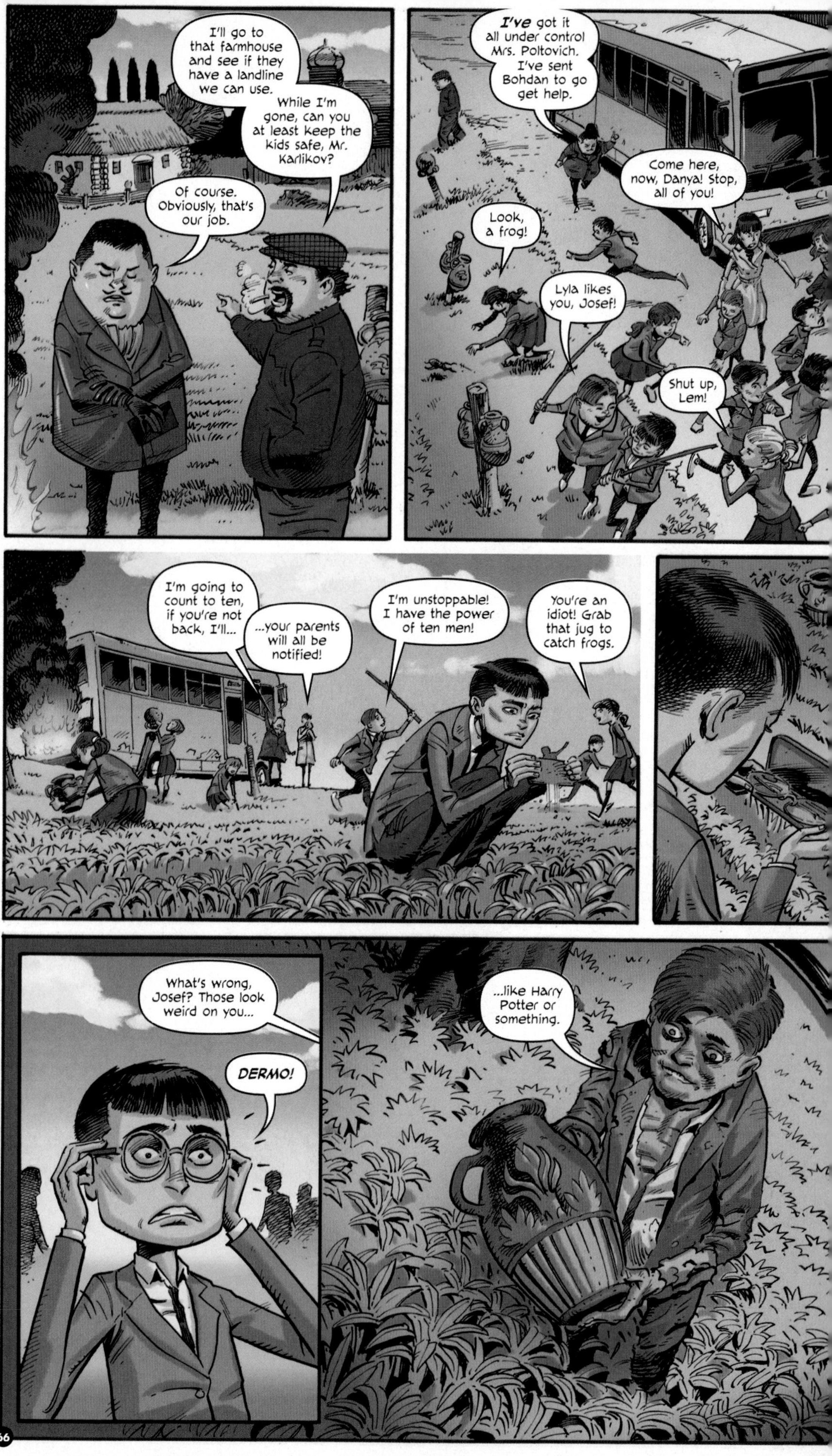
I'll go to that farmhouse and see if they have a landline we can use.
While I'm gone, can you at least keep the kids safe, Mr. Karlikov?
Of course. Obviously, that's our job.
I've got it all under control Mrs. Poltovich. I've sent Bohdan to go get help.
Come here, now, Danya! Stop, all of you!
Look, a frog!
Lyla likes you, Josef!
Shut up, Lem!
I'm going to count to ten, if you're not back, I'll...
...your parents will all be notified!
I'm unstoppable! I have the power of ten men!
You're an idiot! Grab that jug to catch frogs.
What's wrong, Josef? Those look weird on you...
...like Harry Potter or something.
DERMO!

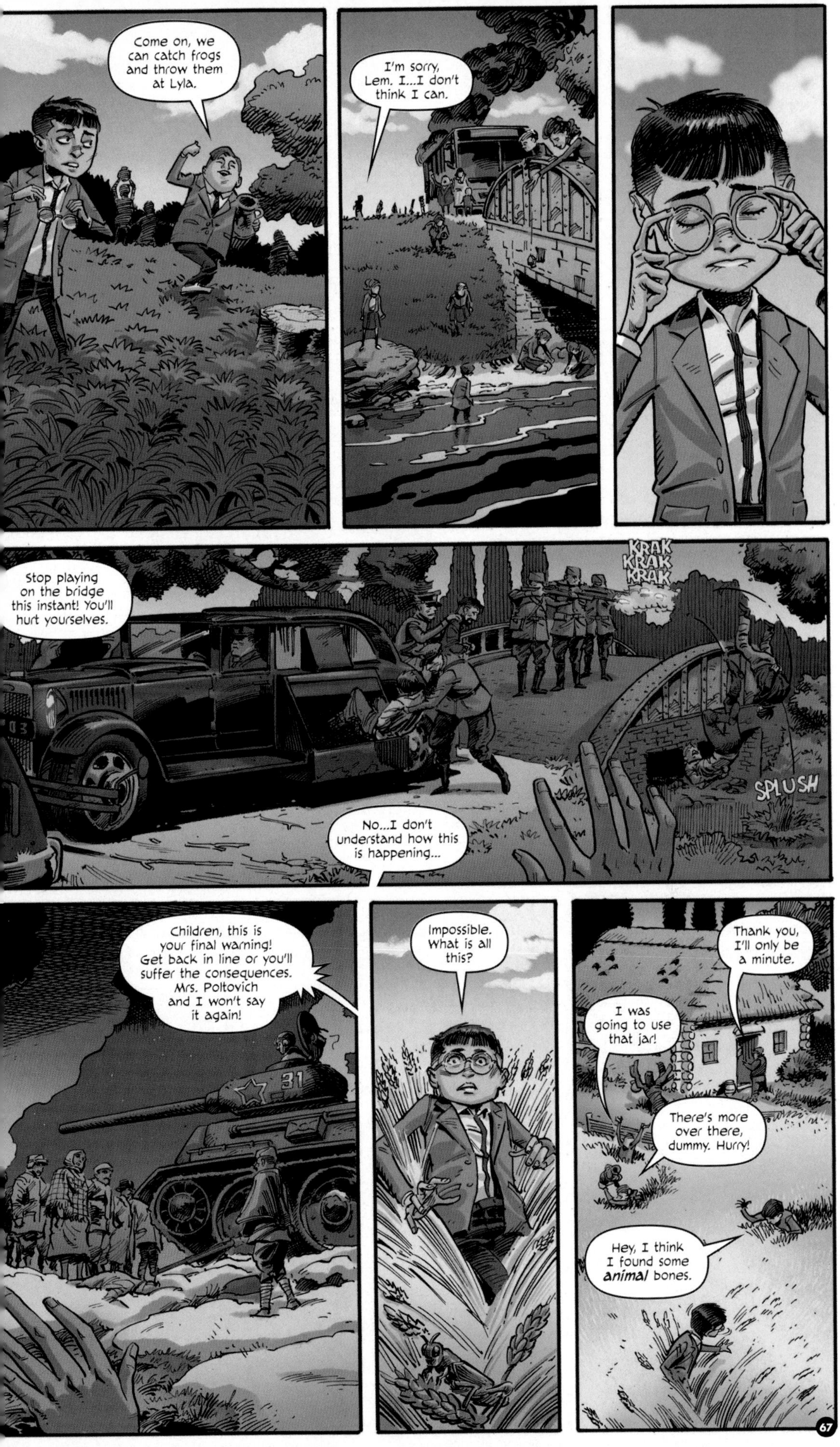
Come on, we can catch frogs and throw them at Lyla.
I'm sorry, Lem. I...I don't think I can.
Stop playing on the bridge this instant! You'll hurt yourselves.
KRAK KRAK KRAK
SPLUSH
No...I don't understand how this is happening...
Children, this is your final warning! Get back in line or you'll suffer the consequences. Mrs. Poltovich and I won't say it again!
Impossible. What is all this?
Thank you, I'll only be a minute.
I was going to use that jar!
There's more over there, dummy. Hurry!
Hey, I think I found some *animal* bones.

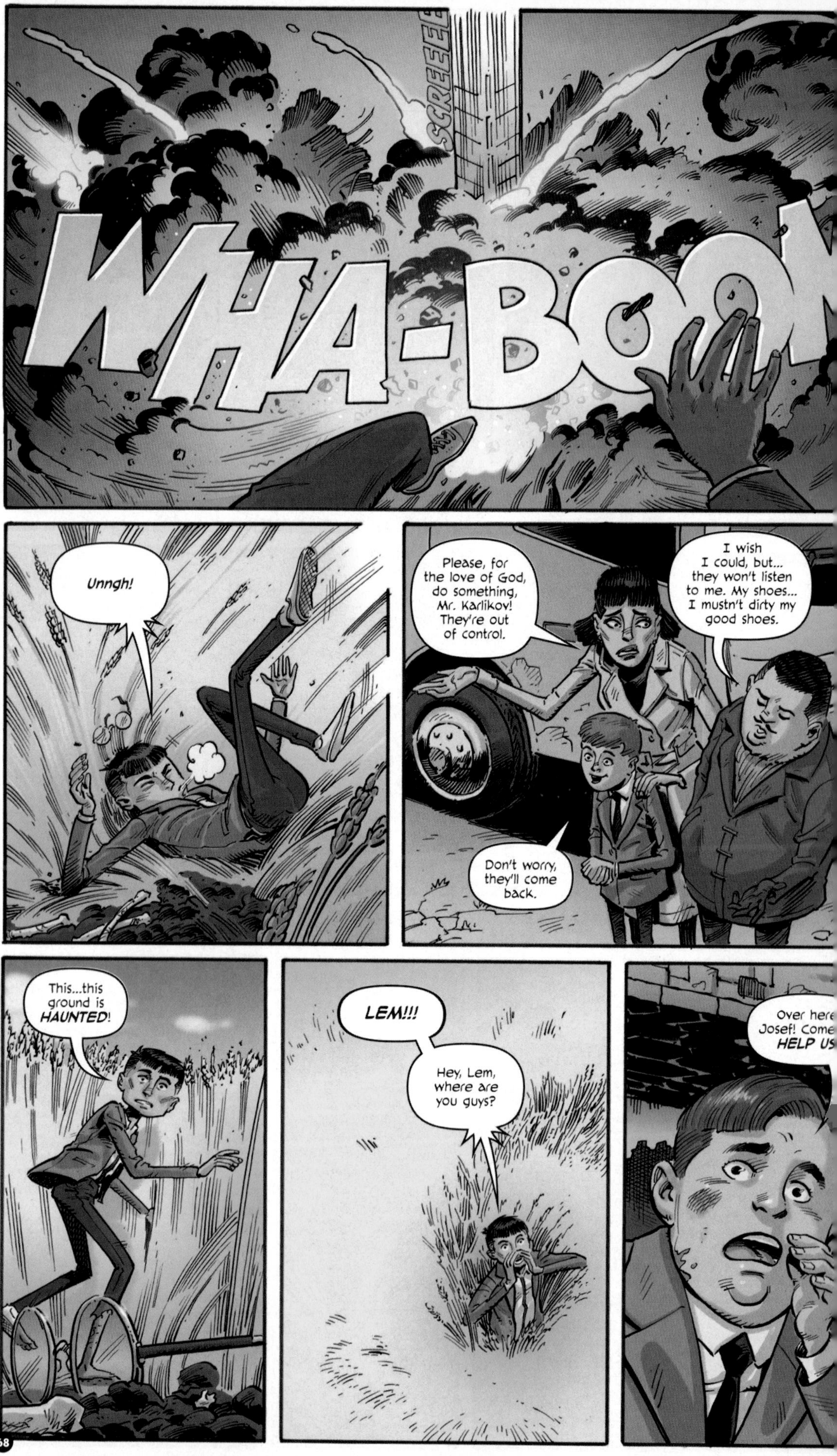

SCREEEEE
WHA-BOO
Unngh!
Please, for the love of God, do something, Mr. Karlikov! They're out of control.
I wish I could, but... they won't listen to me. My shoes... I mustn't dirty my good shoes.
Don't worry, they'll come back.
This...this ground is HAUNTED!
LEM!!!
Hey, Lem, where are you guys?
Over here Josef! Come HELP US

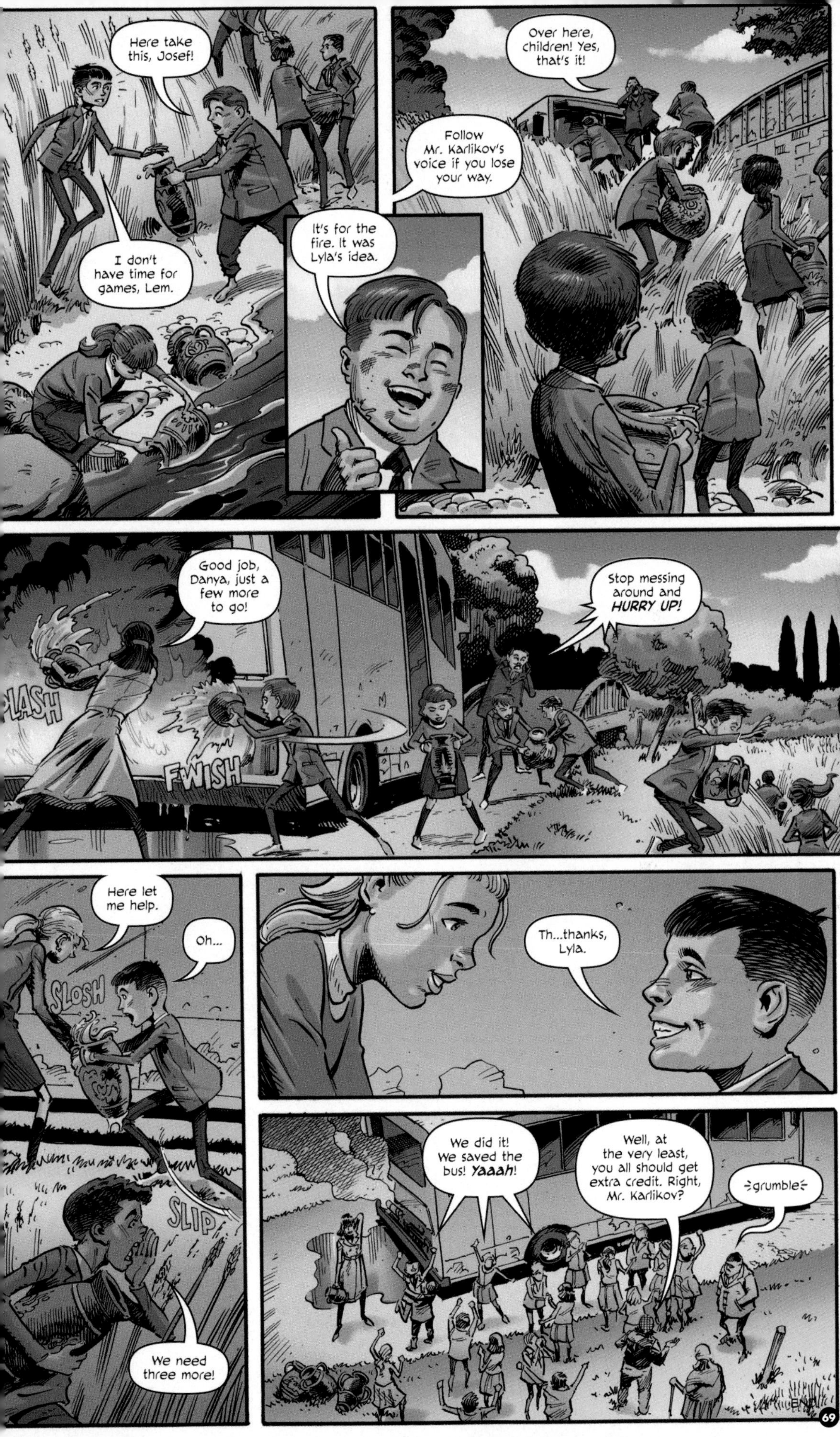
Here take this, Josef!
I don't have time for games, Lem.
It's for the fire. It was Lyla's idea.
Over here, children! Yes, that's it!
Follow Mr. Karlikov's voice if you lose your way.
Good job, Danya, just a few more to go!
LASH
FWISH
Stop messing around and HURRY UP!
Here let me help.
Oh...
SLOSH
SLIP
We need three more!
Th...thanks, Lyla.
We did it! We saved the bus! Yaaah!
Well, at the very least, you all should get extra credit. Right, Mr. Karlikov?
grumble
END

Artist: ***Sean Von Gorman***

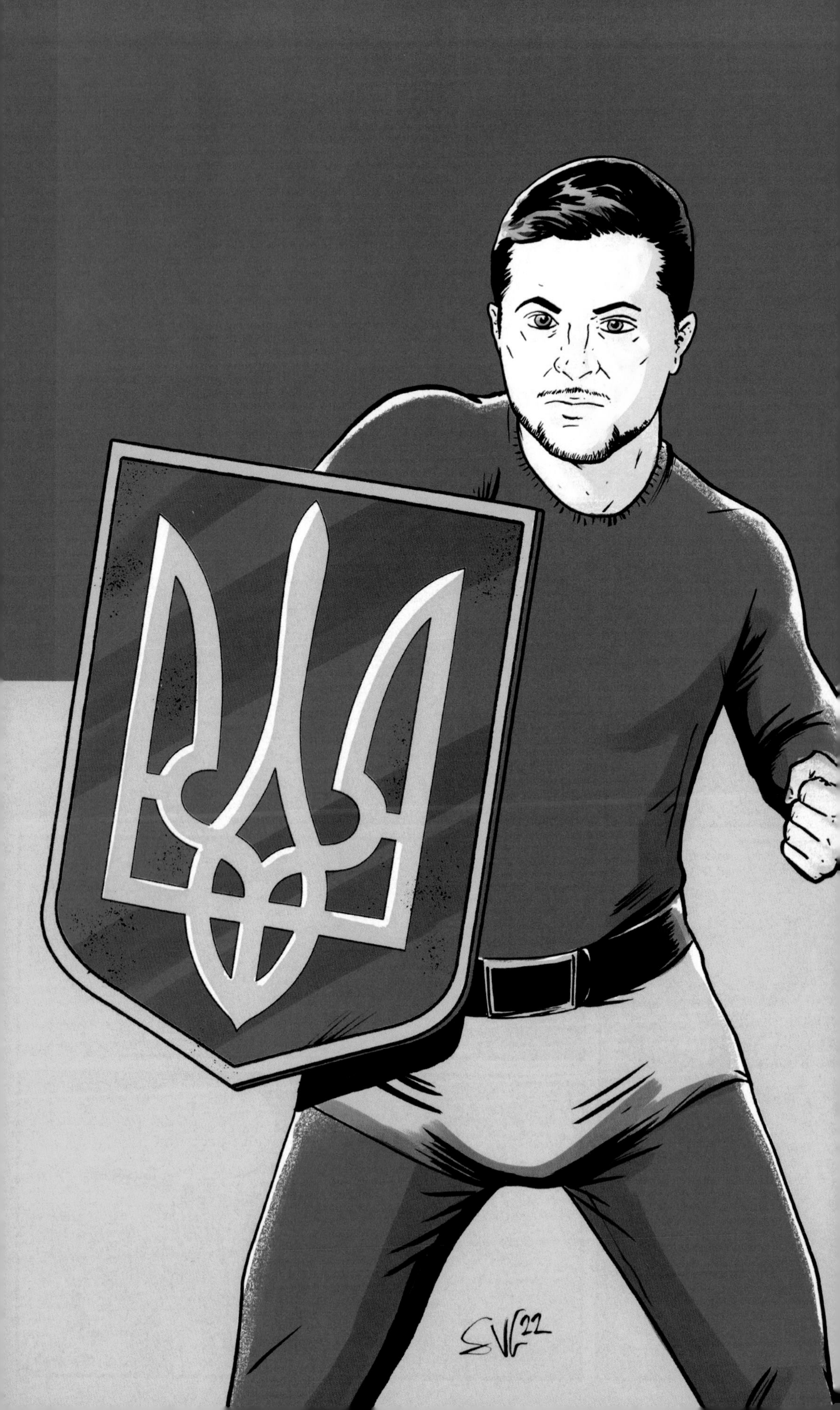

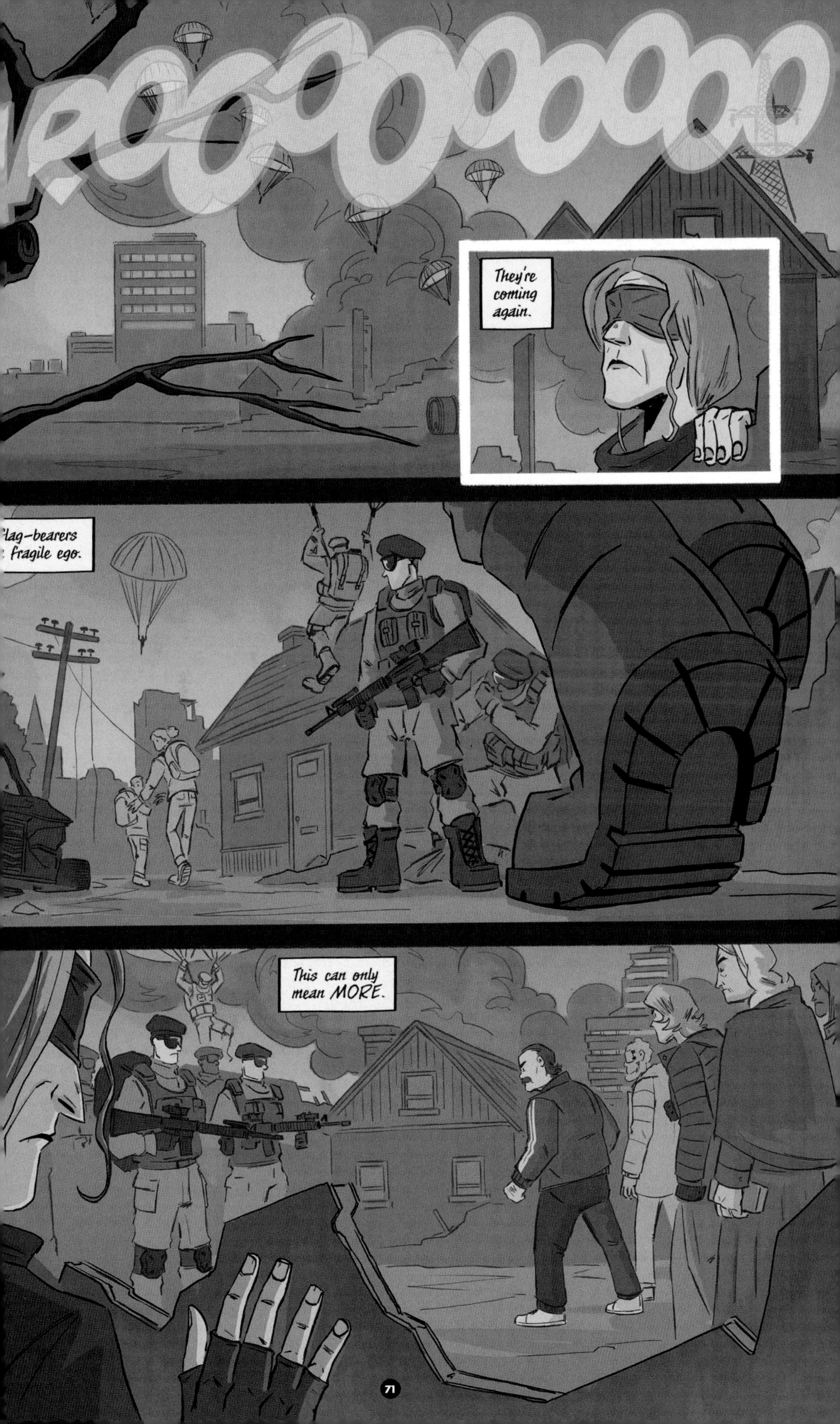
ROOOOOOOOO
They're coming again.
lag-bearers
fragile ego.
This can only mean MORE.

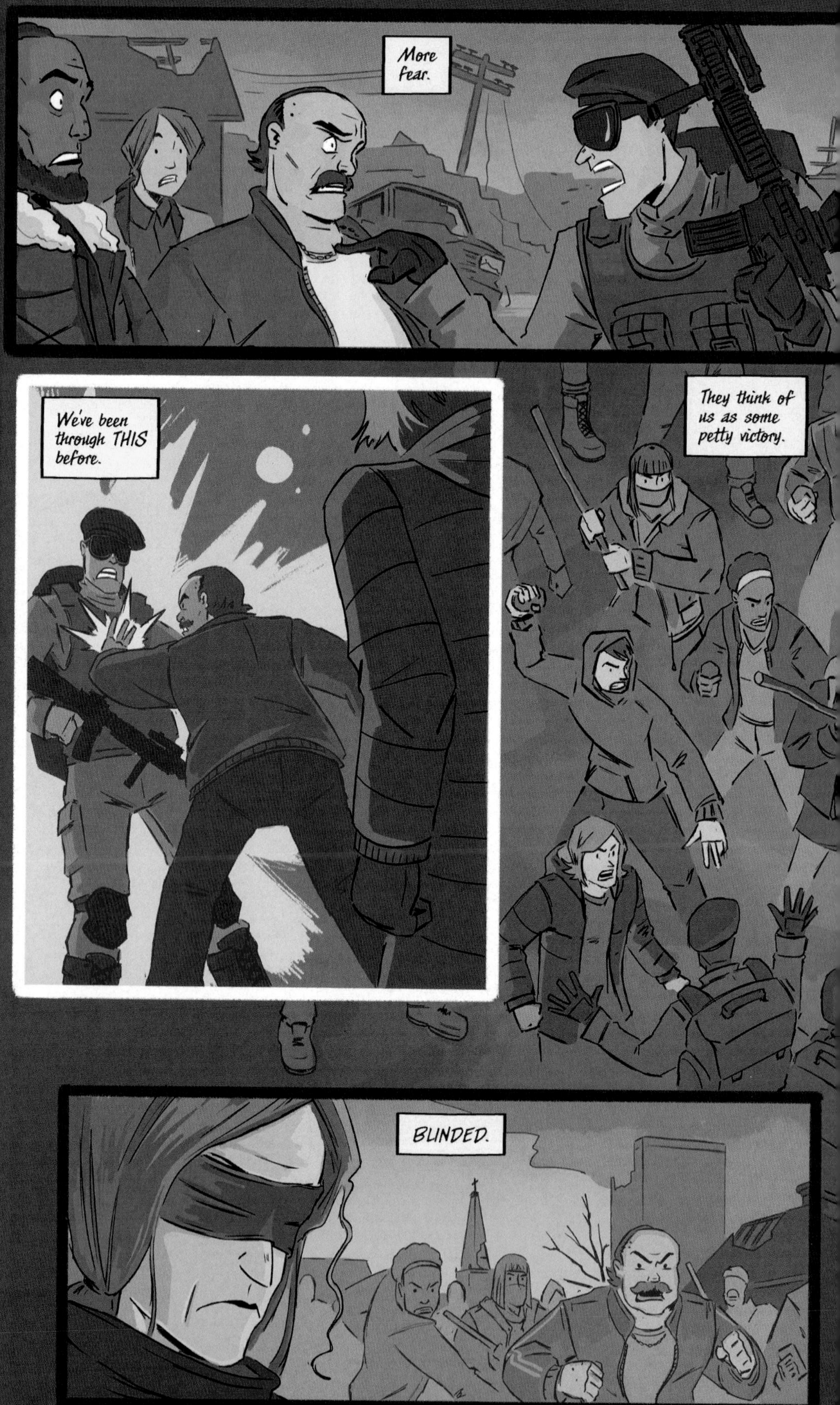

More fear.
We've been through THIS before.
They think of us as some petty victory.
BLINDED.

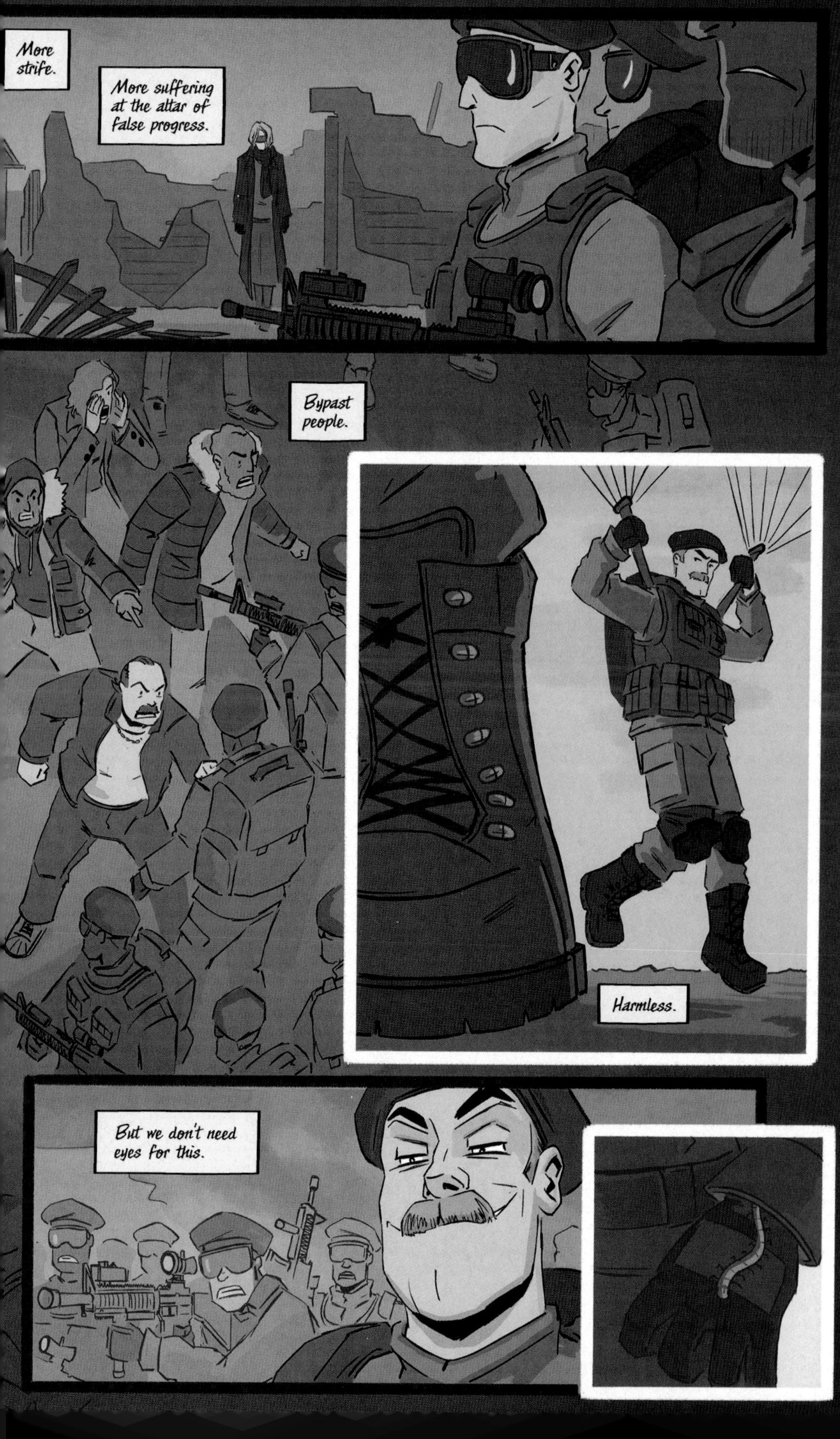
More strife.
More suffering at the altar of false progress.
Bypast people.
Harmless.
But we don't need eyes for this.

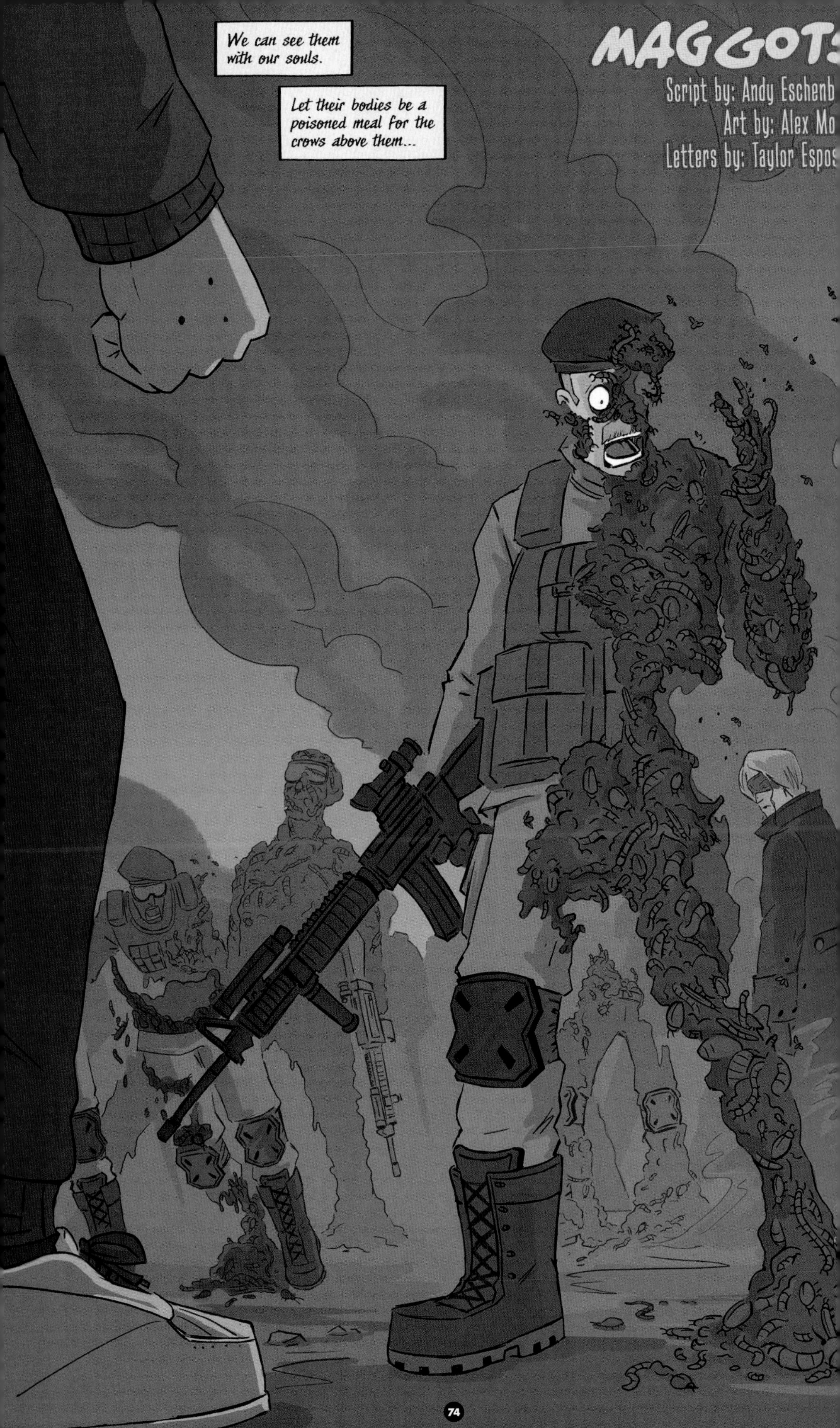

We can see them with our souls.
Let their bodies be a poisoned meal for the crows above them...
MAGGOTS
Script by: Andy Eschenb
Art by: Alex Mo
Letters by: Taylor Espos

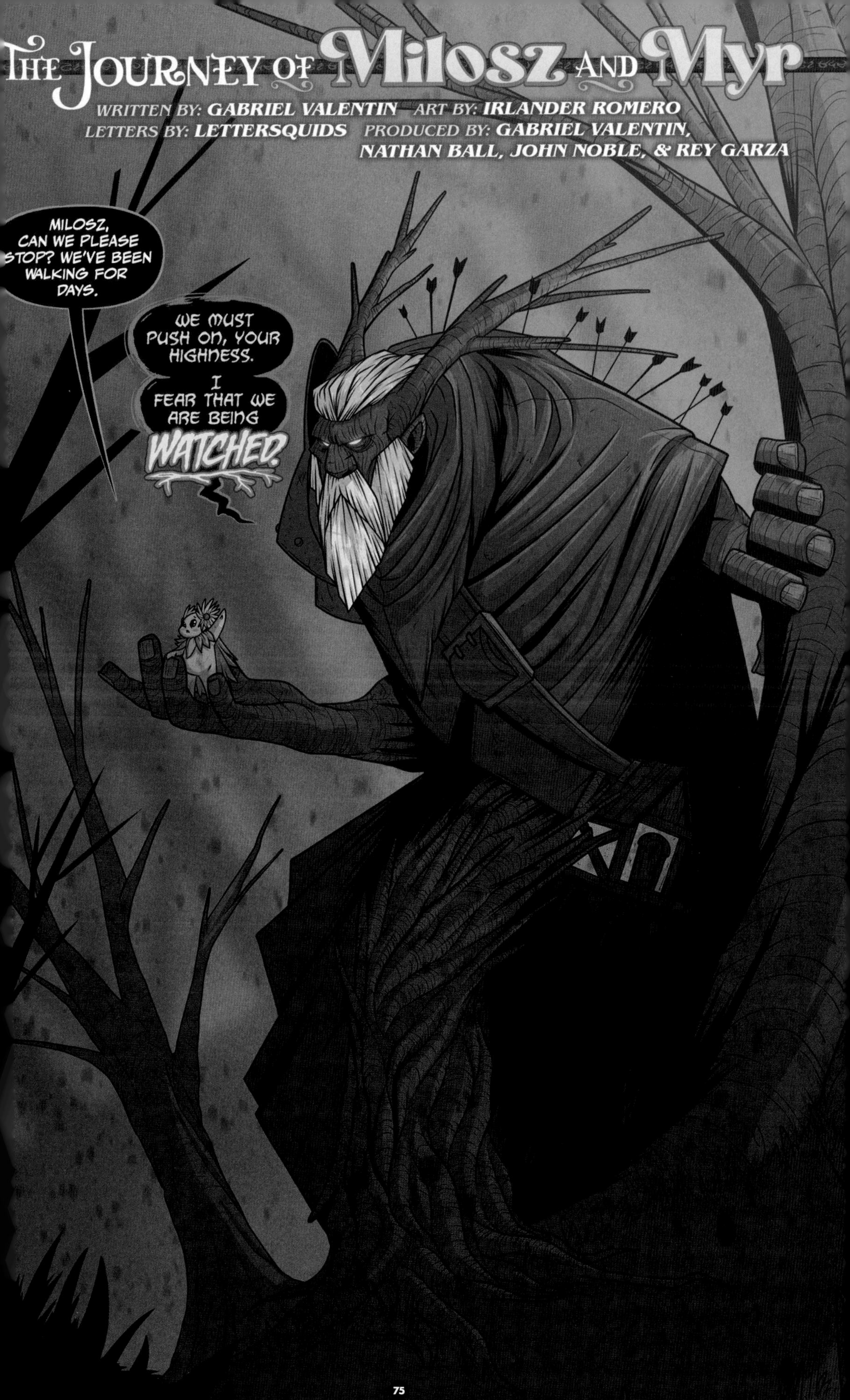
THE JOURNEY OF MILOSZ AND MYR
WRITTEN BY: GABRIEL VALENTIN ART BY: IRLANDER ROMERO
LETTERS BY: LETTERSQUIDS PRODUCED BY: GABRIEL VALENTIN, NATHAN BALL, JOHN NOBLE, & REY GARZA
MILOSZ, CAN WE PLEASE STOP? WE'VE BEEN WALKING FOR DAYS.
WE MUST PUSH ON, YOUR HIGHNESS.
I FEAR THAT WE ARE BEING WATCHED.

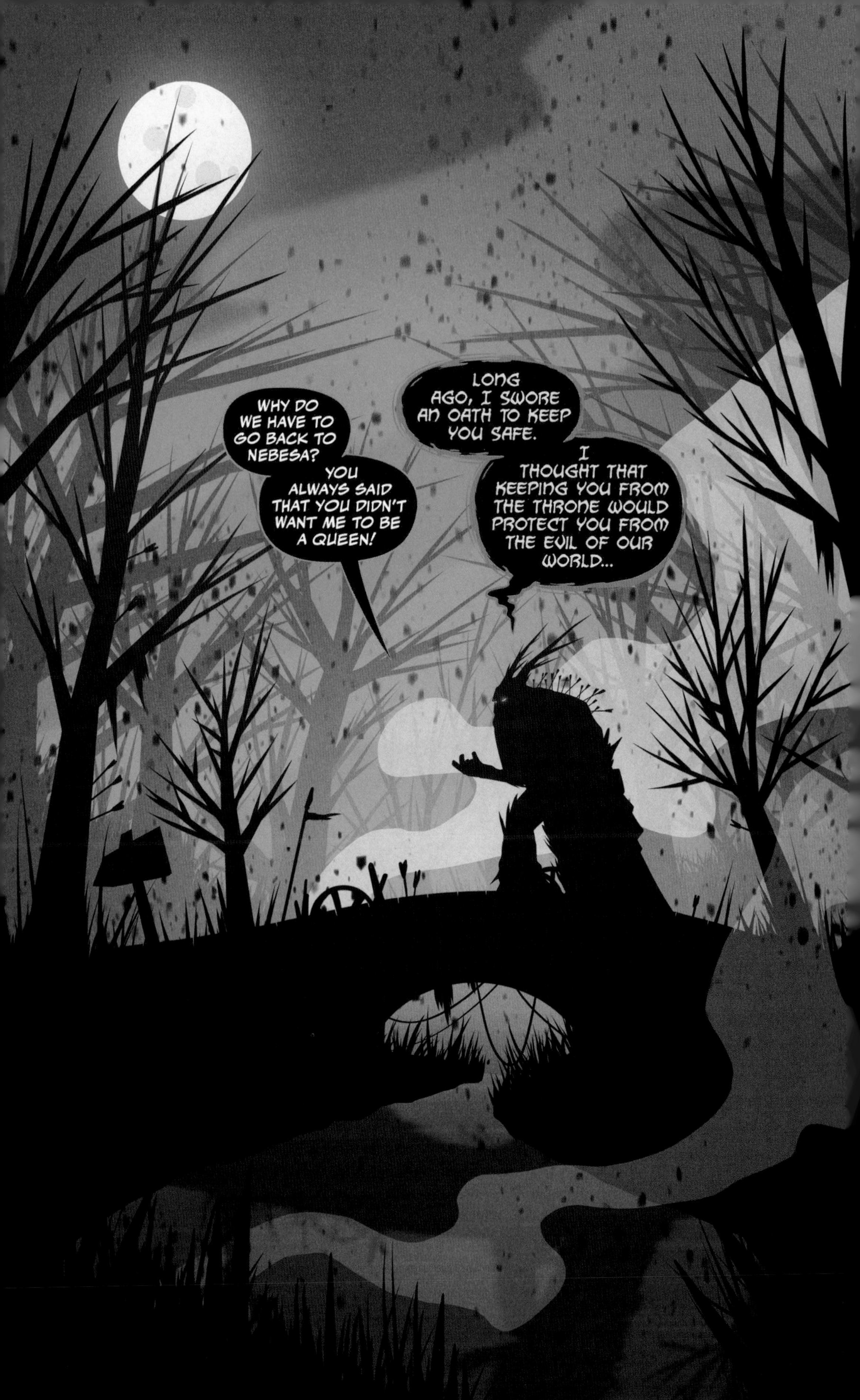
WHY DO WE HAVE TO GO BACK TO NEBESA?
YOU ALWAYS SAID THAT YOU DIDN'T WANT ME TO BE A QUEEN!
LONG AGO, I SWORE AN OATH TO KEEP YOU SAFE.
I THOUGHT THAT KEEPING YOU FROM THE THRONE WOULD PROTECT YOU FROM THE EVIL OF OUR WORLD...

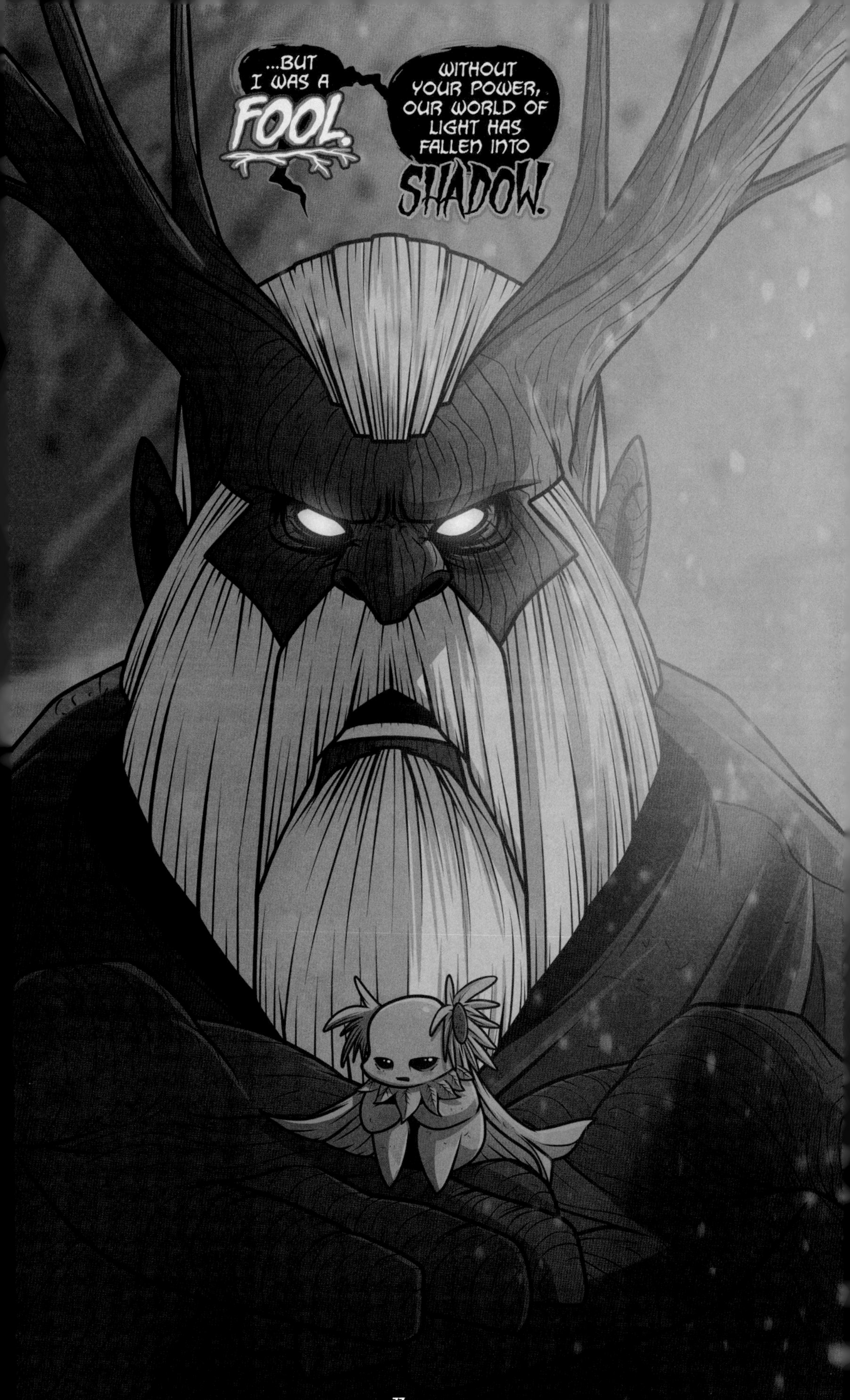
...BUT I WAS A FOOL.
WITHOUT YOUR POWER, OUR WORLD OF LIGHT HAS FALLEN INTO SHADOW!

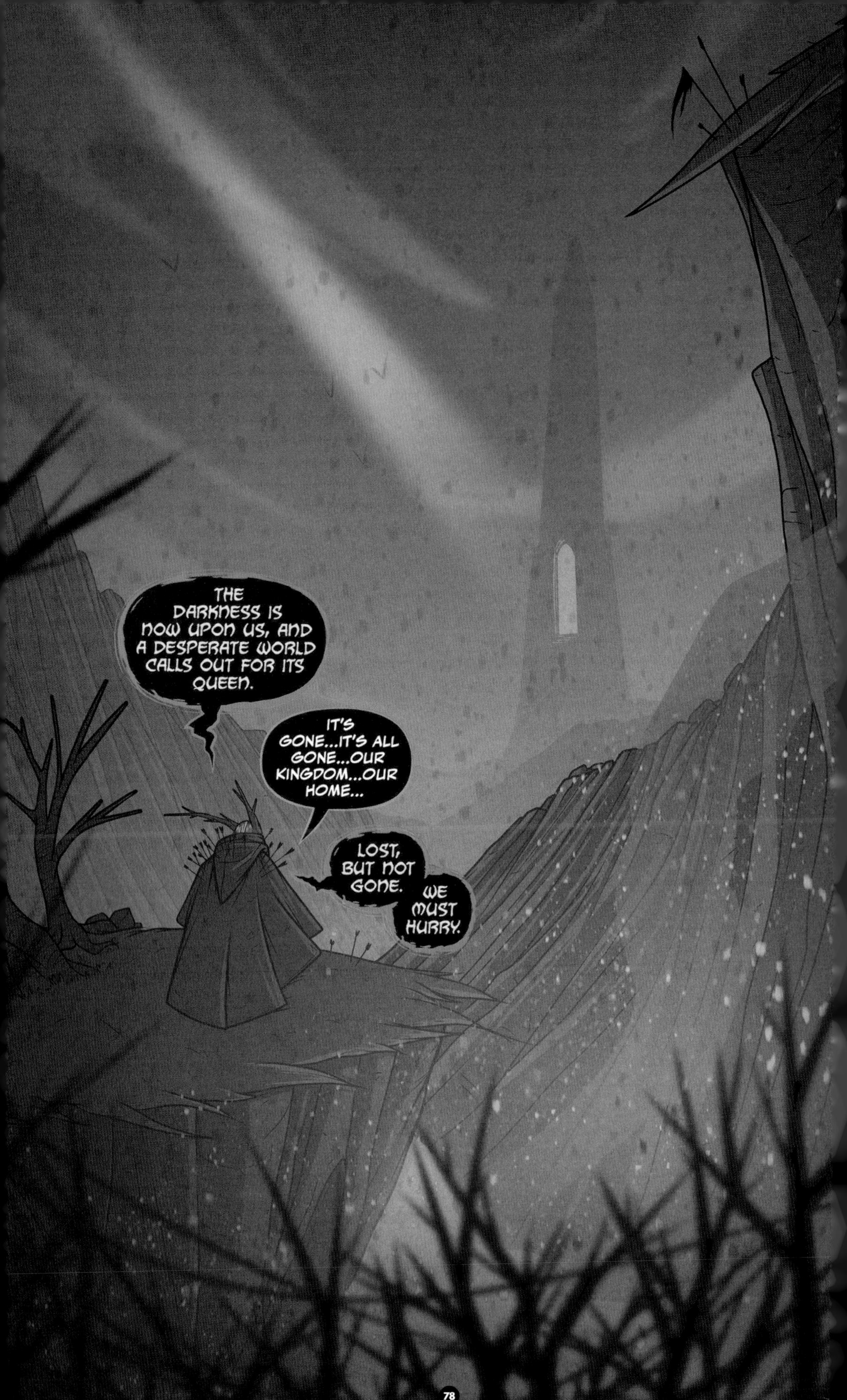
THE DARKNESS IS NOW UPON US, AND A DESPERATE WORLD CALLS OUT FOR ITS QUEEN.
IT'S GONE...IT'S ALL GONE...OUR KINGDOM...OUR HOME...
LOST, BUT NOT GONE.
WE MUST HURRY.

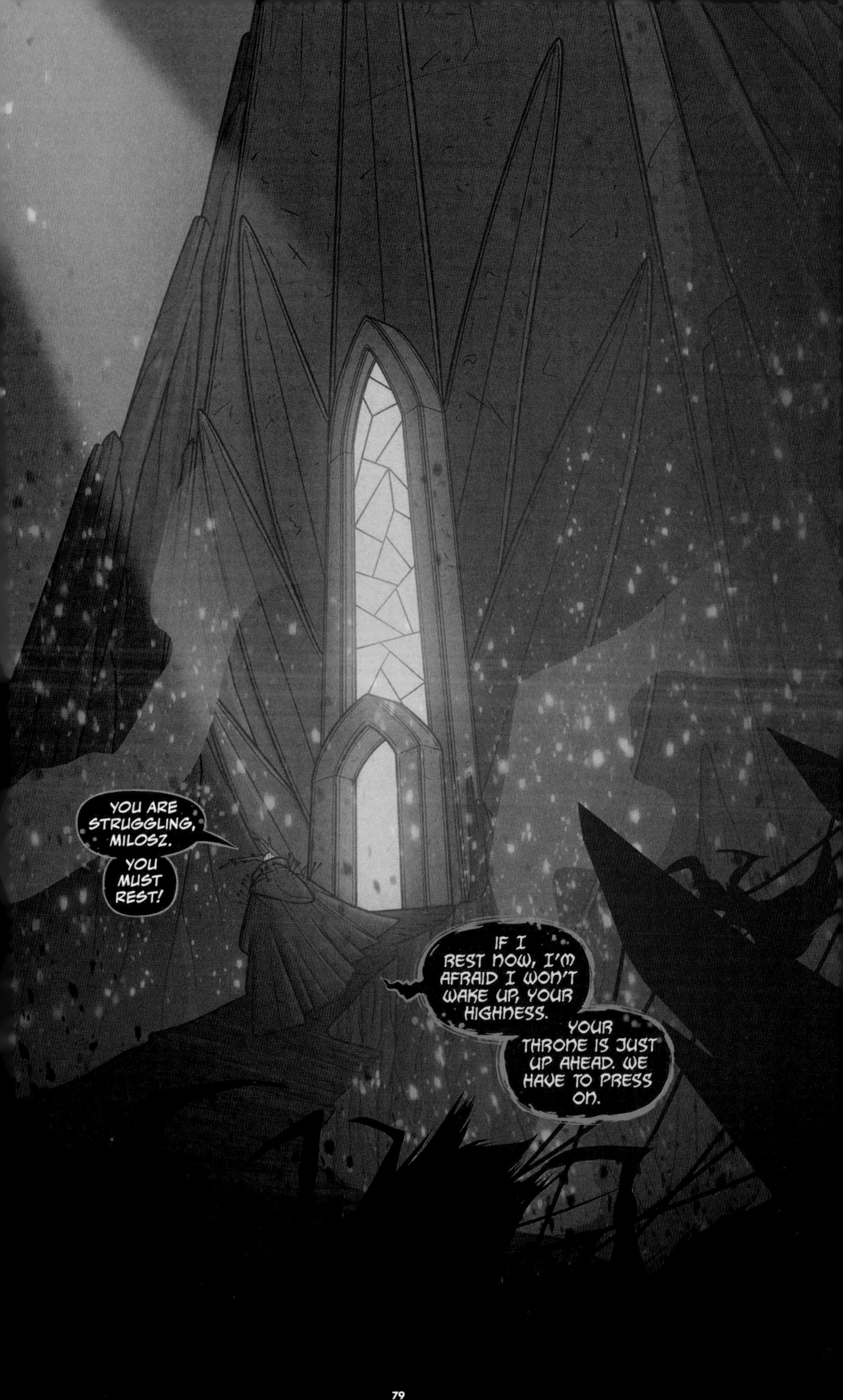
YOU ARE STRUGGLING, MILOSZ.
YOU MUST REST!
IF I REST NOW, I'M AFRAID I WON'T WAKE UP, YOUR HIGHNESS.
YOUR THRONE IS JUST UP AHEAD. WE HAVE TO PRESS ON.

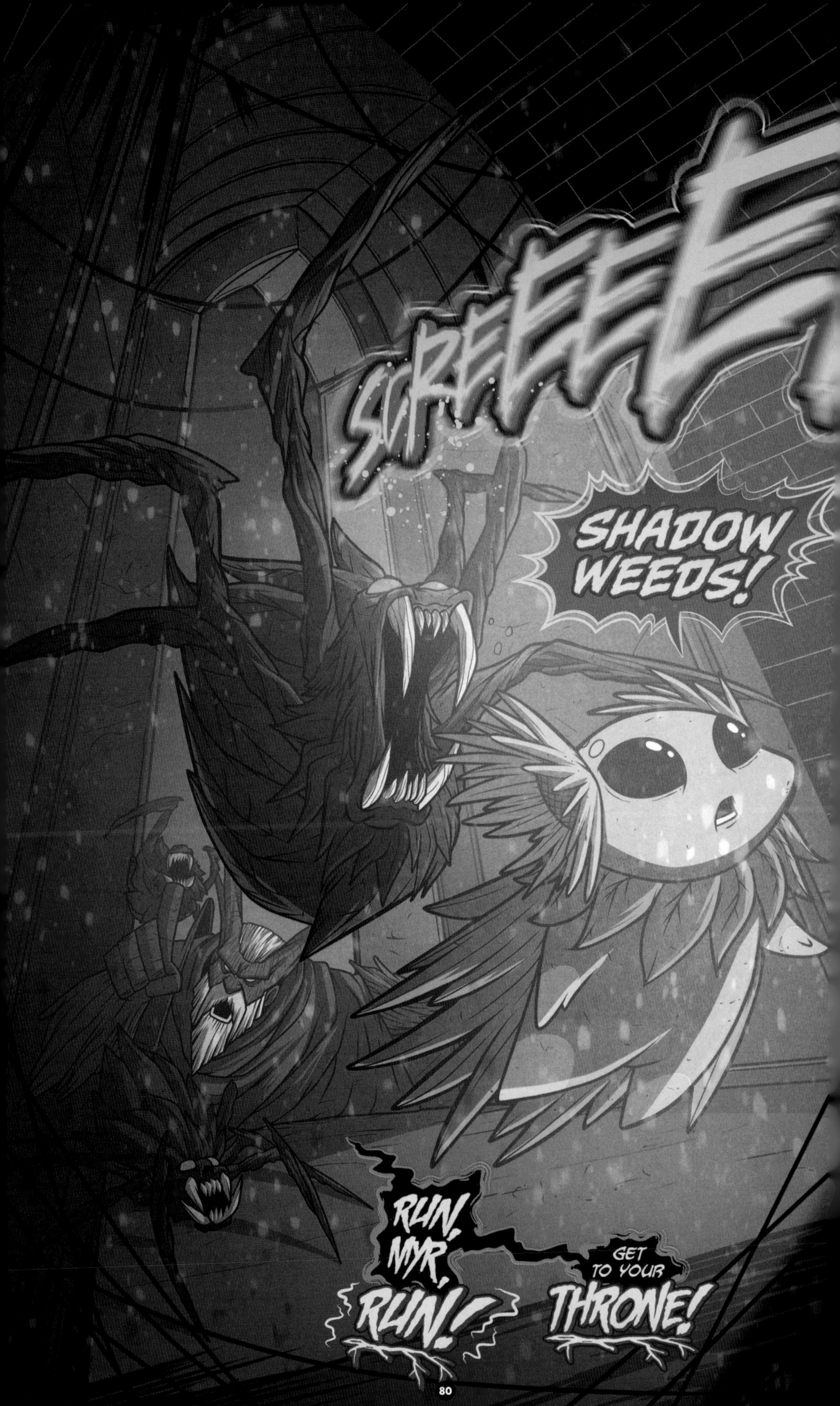
SCREEEE
SHADOW WEEDS!
RUN, MYR, RUN!
GET TO YOUR THRONE!

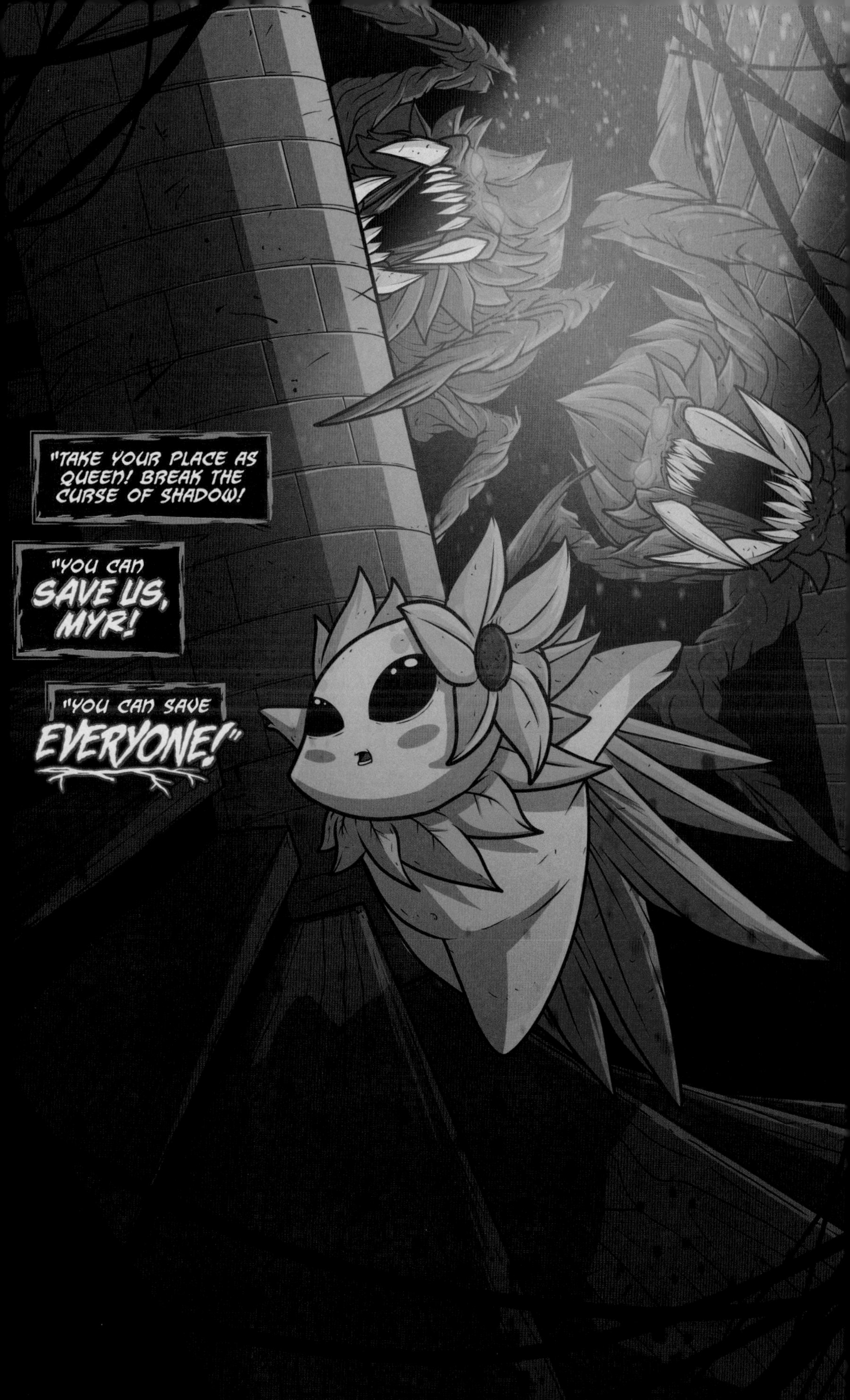
"TAKE YOUR PLACE AS QUEEN! BREAK THE CURSE OF SHADOW!
"YOU CAN SAVE US, MYR!
"YOU CAN SAVE EVERYONE!"

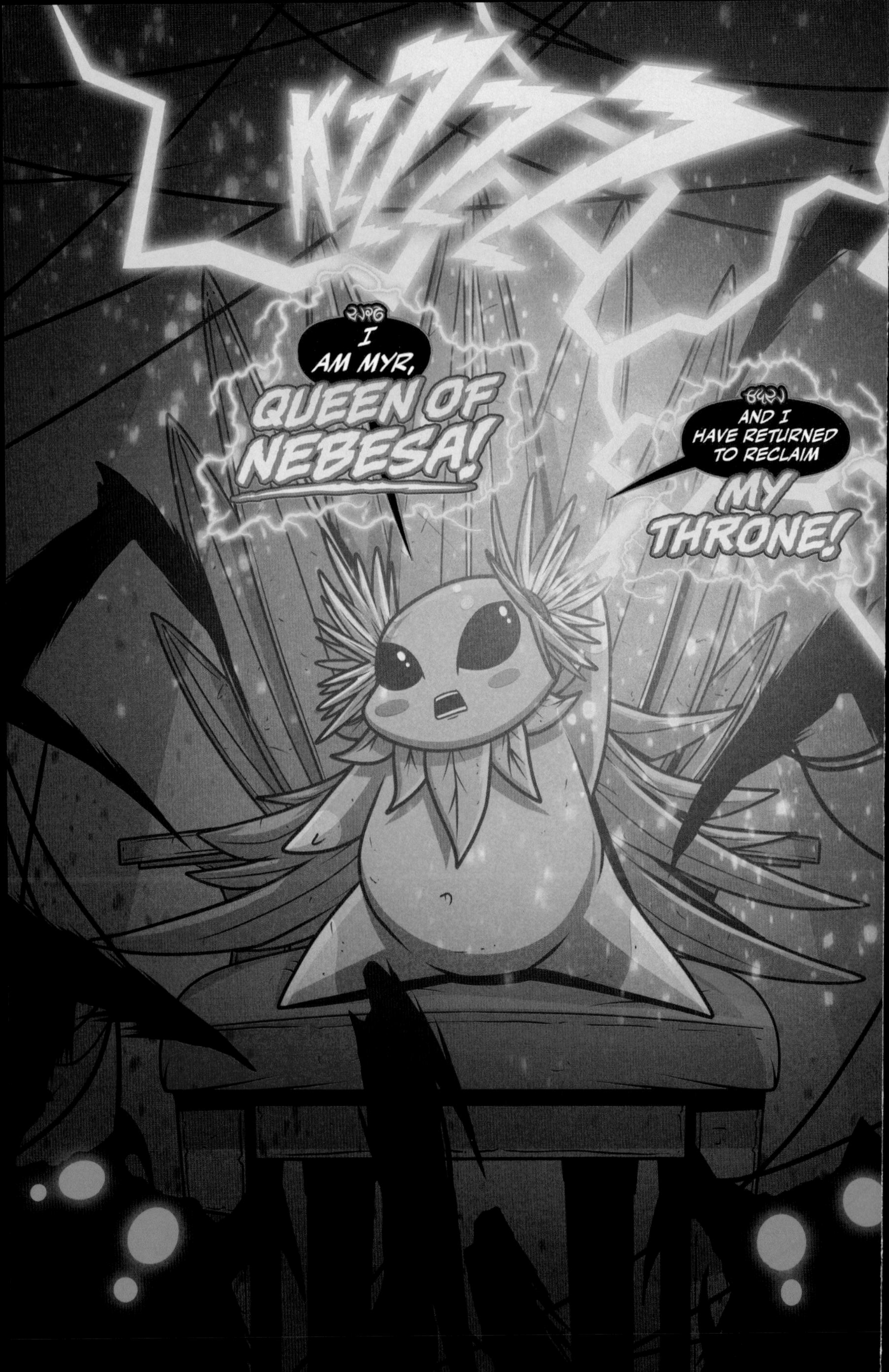
I AM MYR, QUEEN OF NEBESA!
AND I HAVE RETURNED TO RECLAIM MY THRONE!

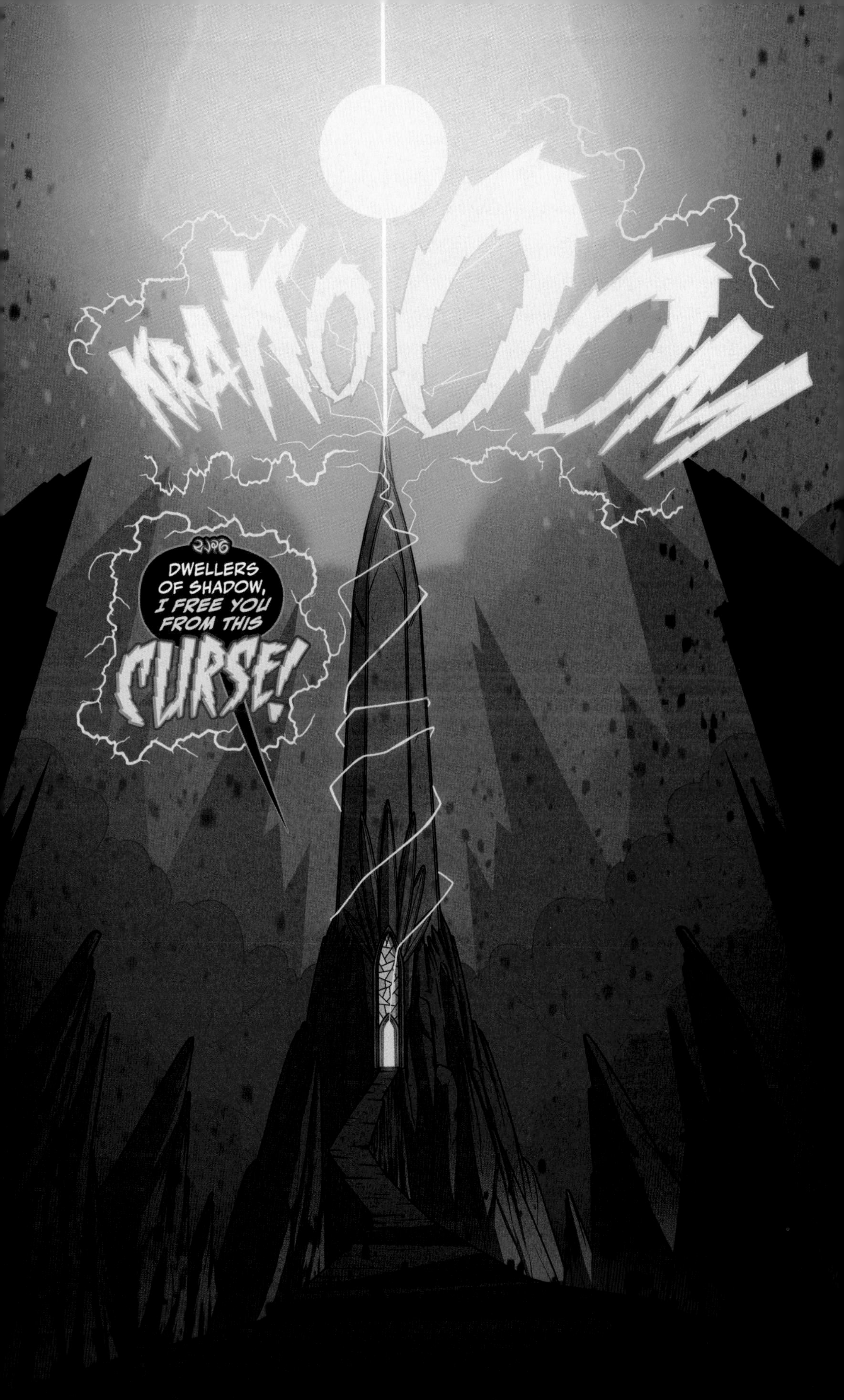
KRAKOOOM
DWELLERS OF SHADOW, I FREE YOU FROM THIS CURSE!

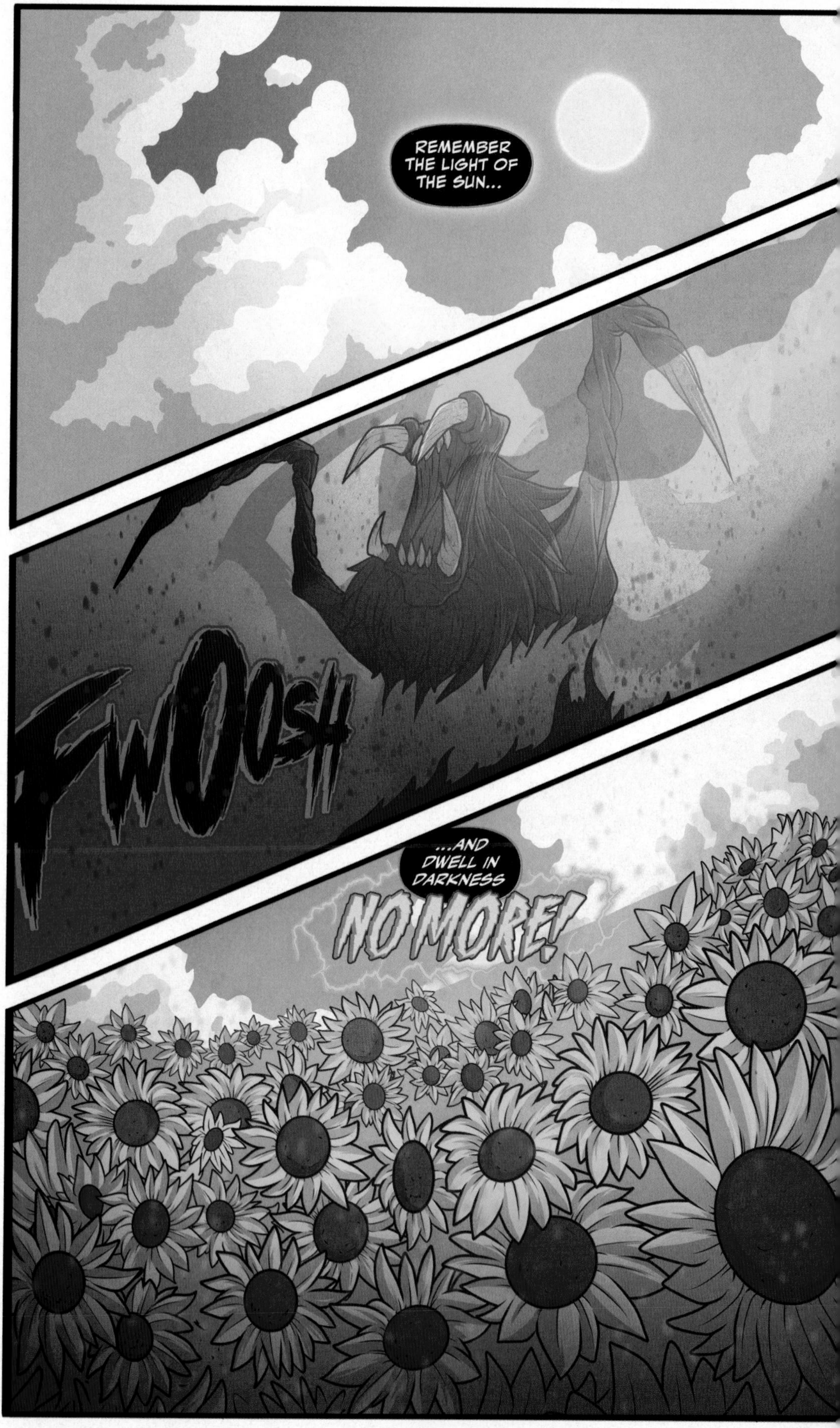
REMEMBER THE LIGHT OF THE SUN...
FWOOSH
...AND DWELL IN DARKNESS
NO MORE!

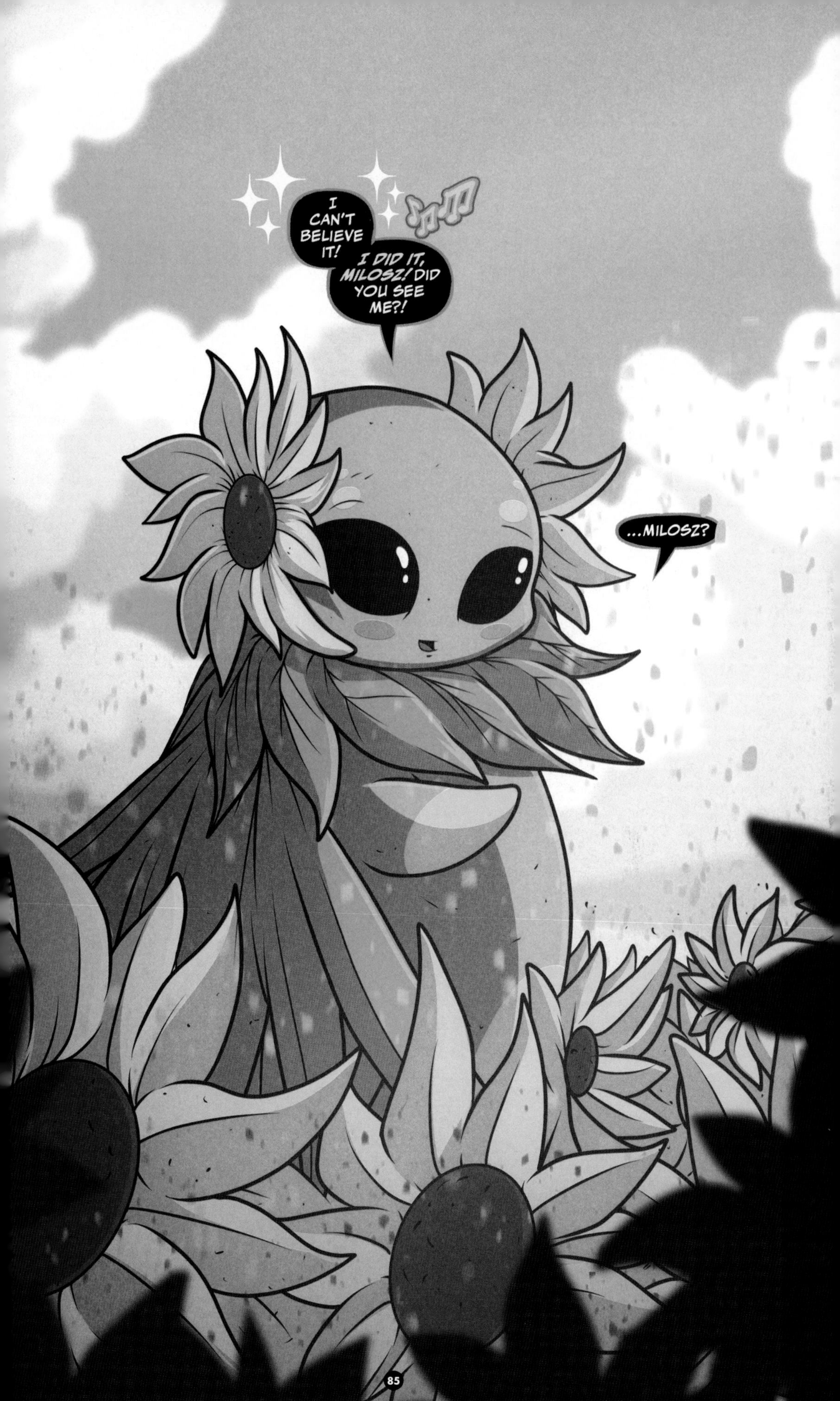
I CAN'T BELIEVE IT!
I DID IT, MILOSZ! DID YOU SEE ME?!
...MILOSZ?

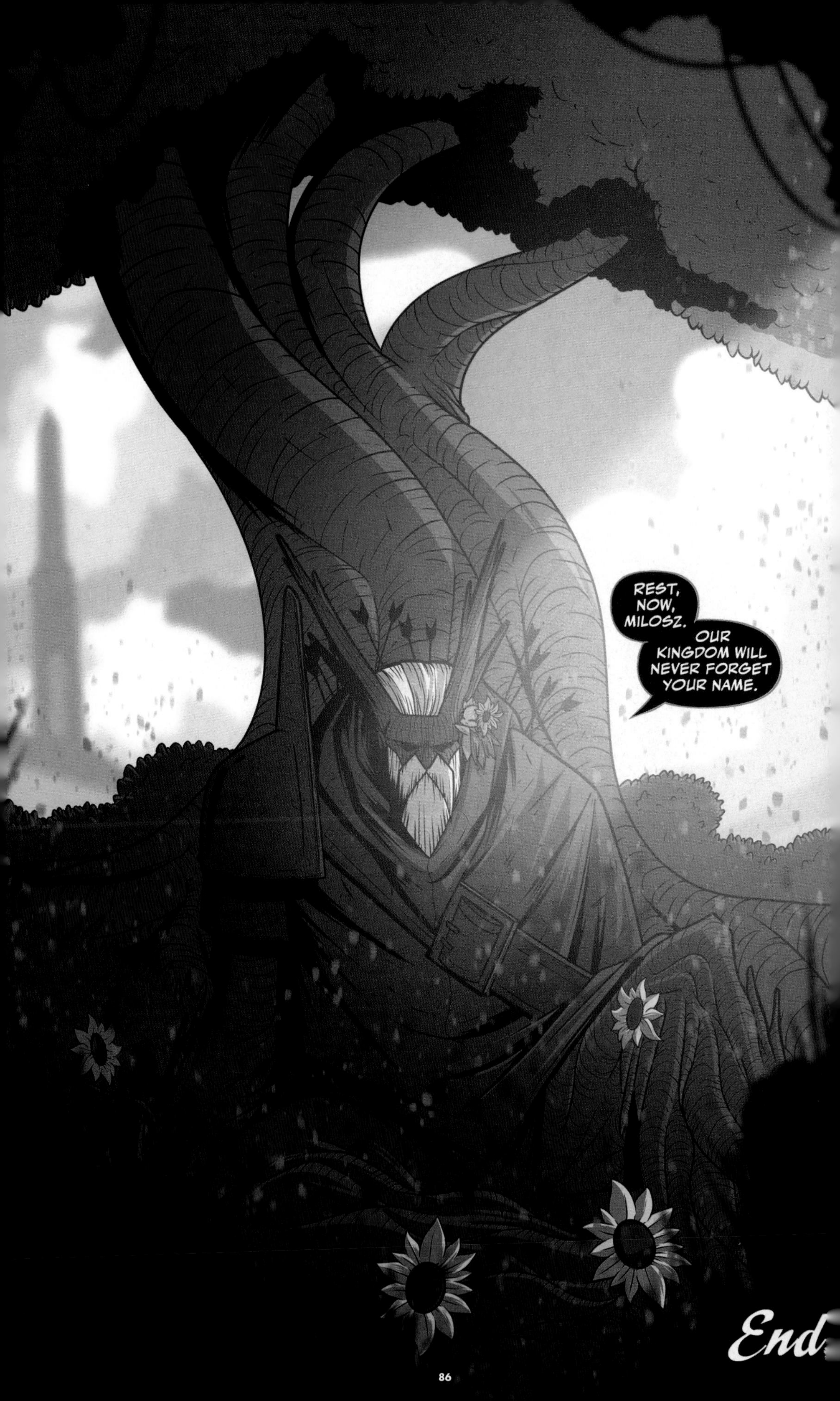
REST, NOW, MILOSZ.
OUR KINGDOM WILL NEVER FORGET YOUR NAME.
End

BREAD MAKING

written by LELA GWENN art by ANDI SANTAGATA

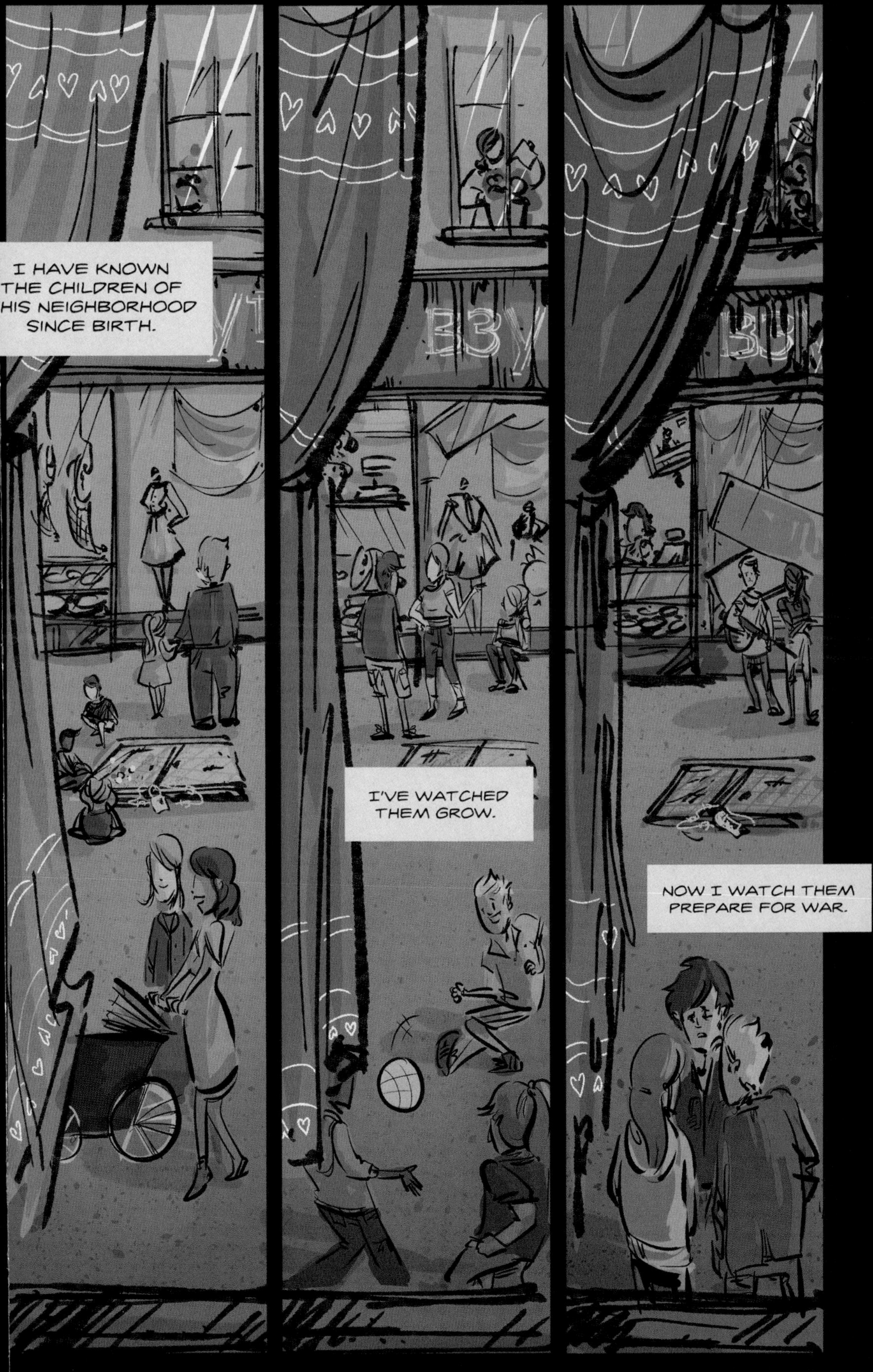
I HAVE KNOWN THE CHILDREN OF HIS NEIGHBORHOOD SINCE BIRTH.
I'VE WATCHED THEM GROW.
NOW I WATCH THEM PREPARE FOR WAR.

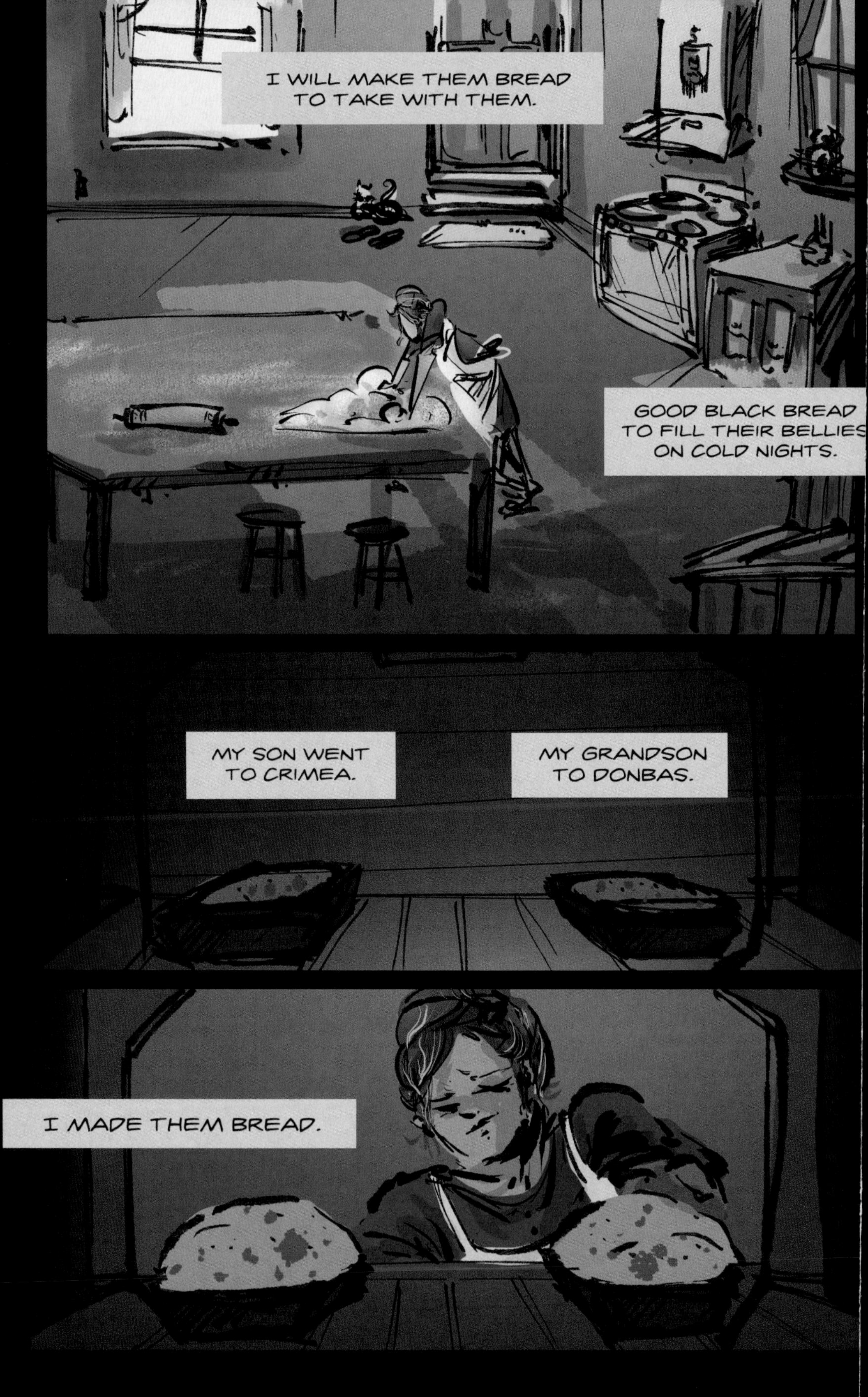
I WILL MAKE THEM BREAD TO TAKE WITH THEM.
GOOD BLACK BREAD TO FILL THEIR BELLIES ON COLD NIGHTS.
MY SON WENT TO CRIMEA.
MY GRANDSON TO DONBAS.
I MADE THEM BREAD.

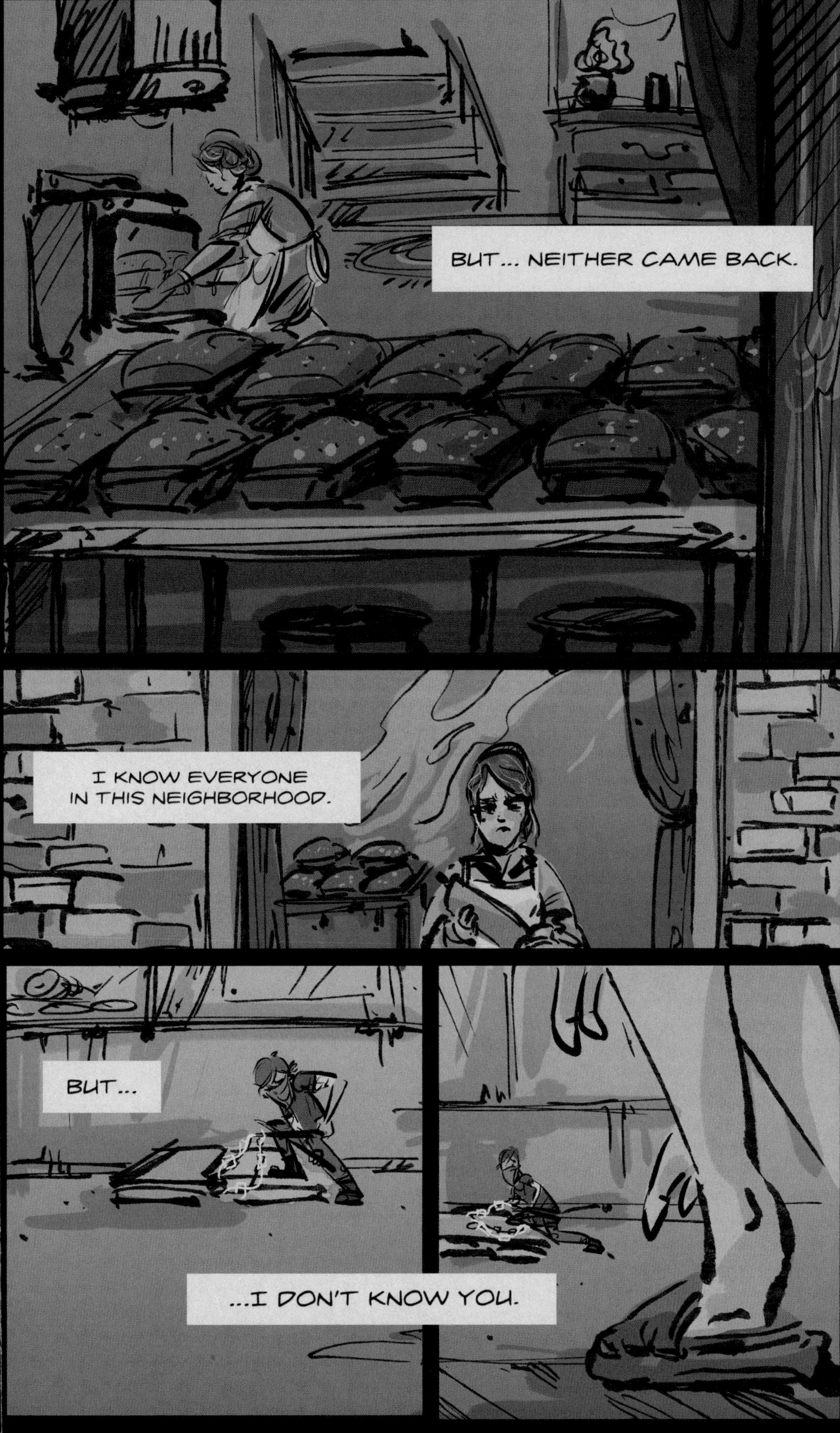
BUT... NEITHER CAME BACK.
I KNOW EVERYONE IN THIS NEIGHBORHOOD.
BUT...
...I DON'T KNOW YOU.

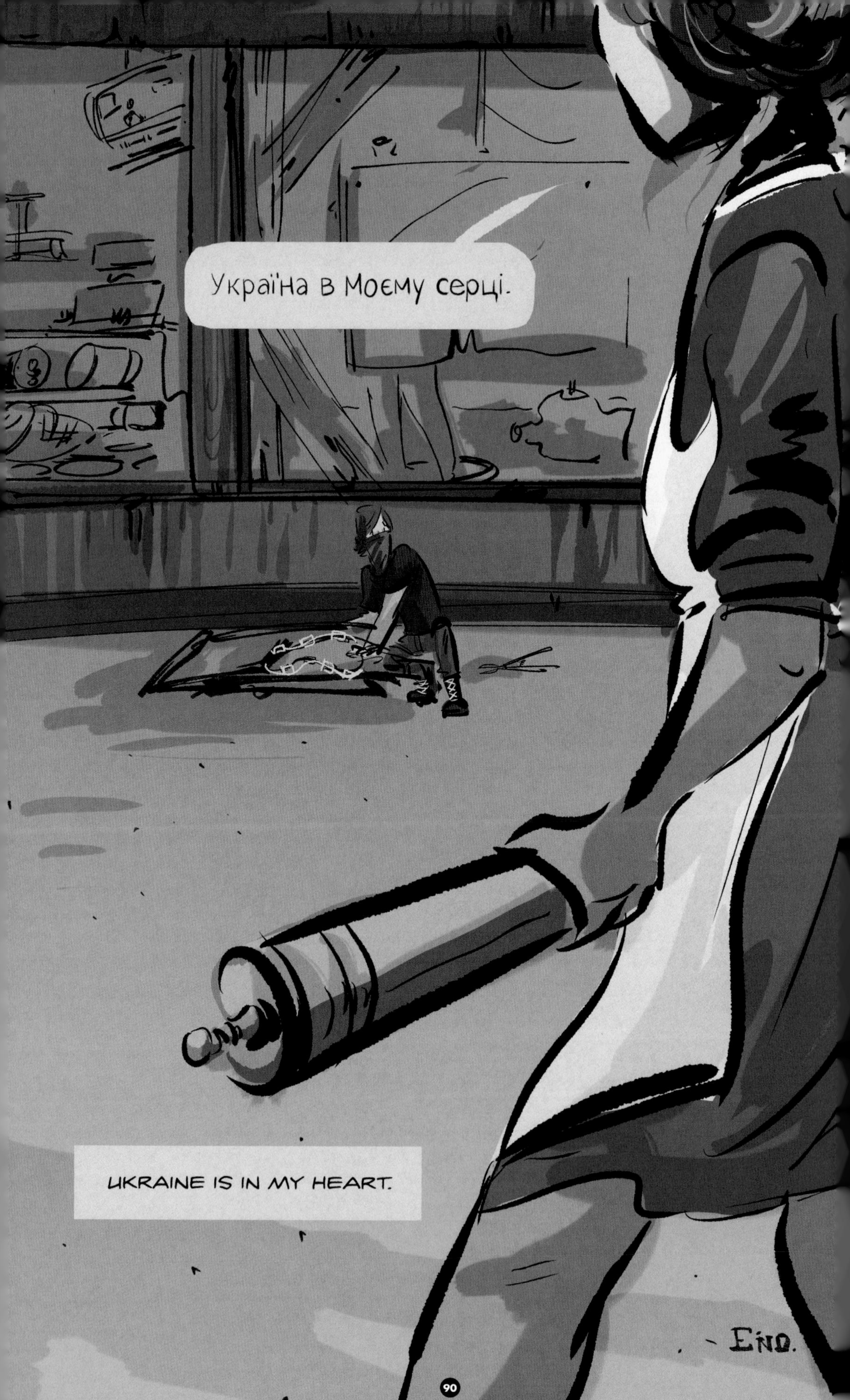
Україна в моєму серці.
UKRAINE IS IN MY HEART.
- END.

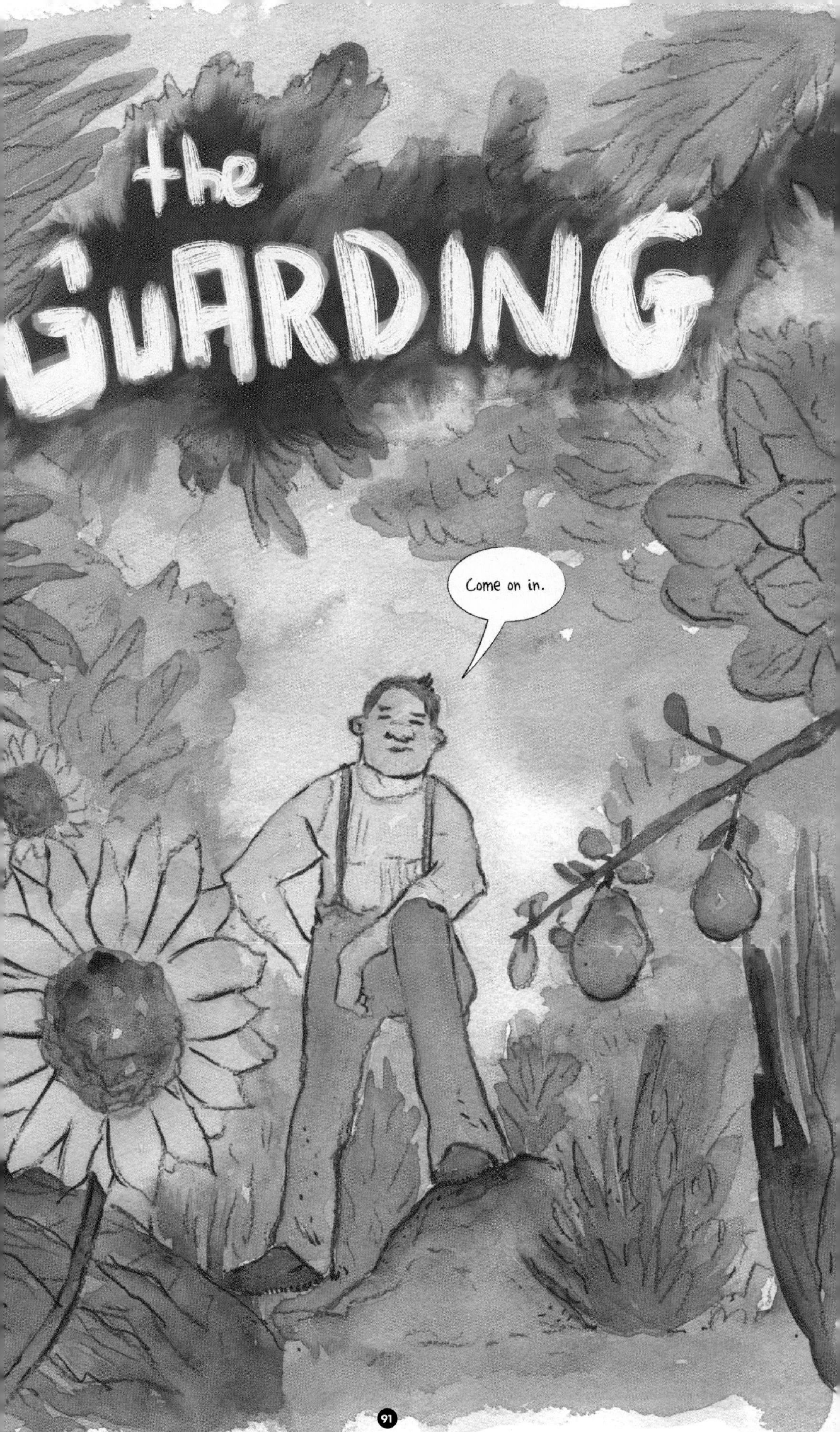
the GUARDING
Come on in.

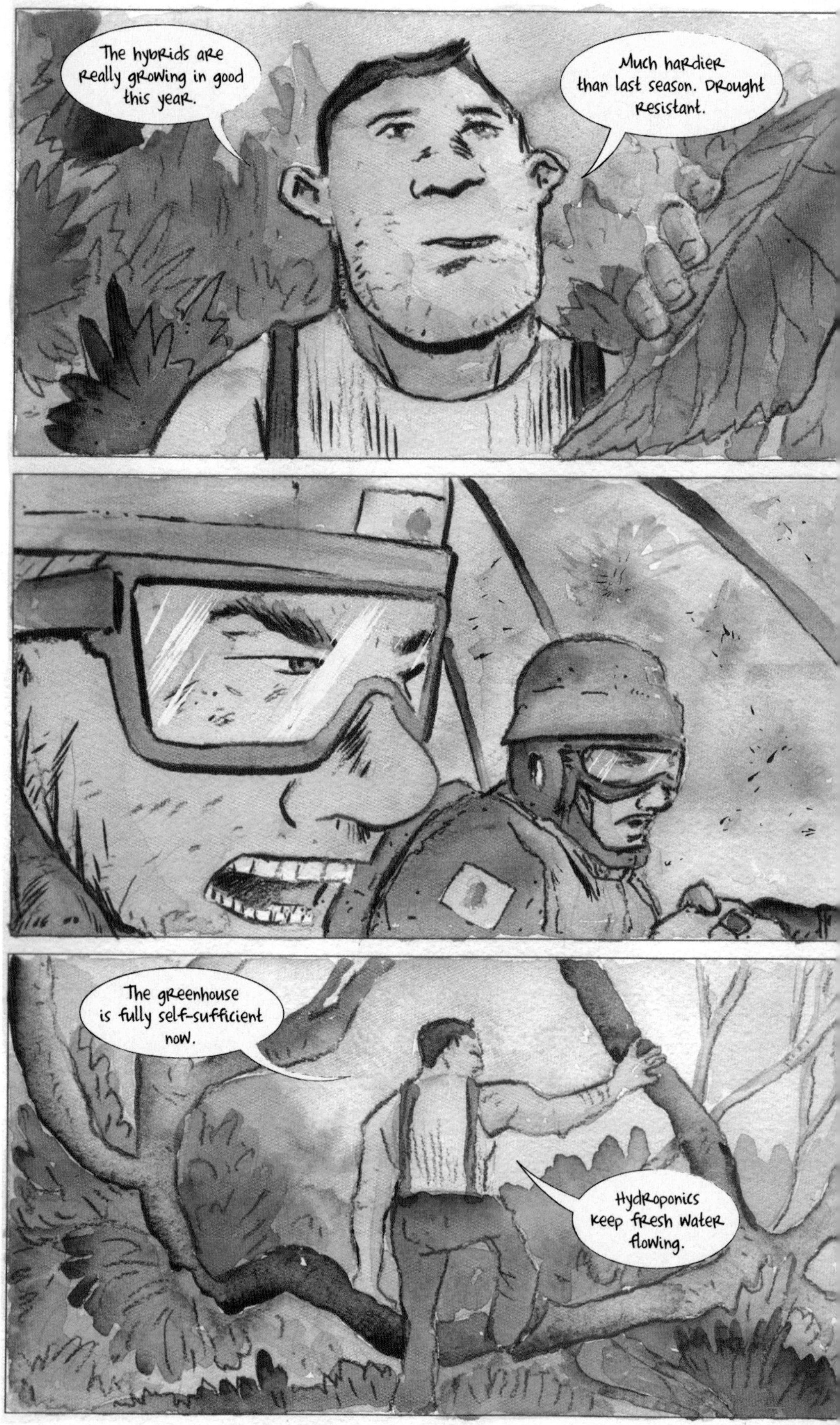
The hybrids are really growing in good this year.
Much hardier than last season. Drought resistant.
The greenhouse is fully self-sufficient now.
Hydroponics keep fresh water flowing.

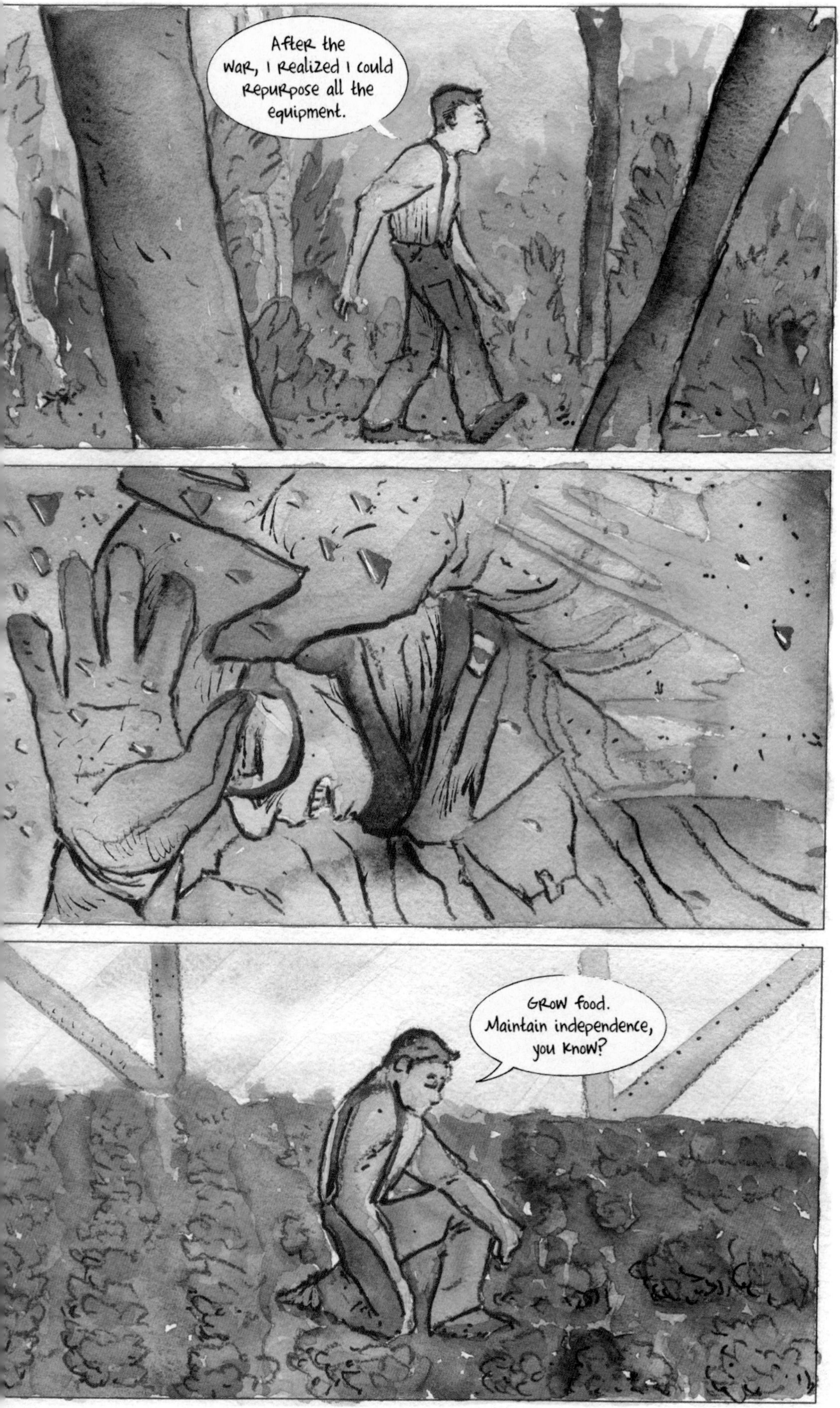
After the war, I realized I could repurpose all the equipment.
Grow food. Maintain independence, you know?

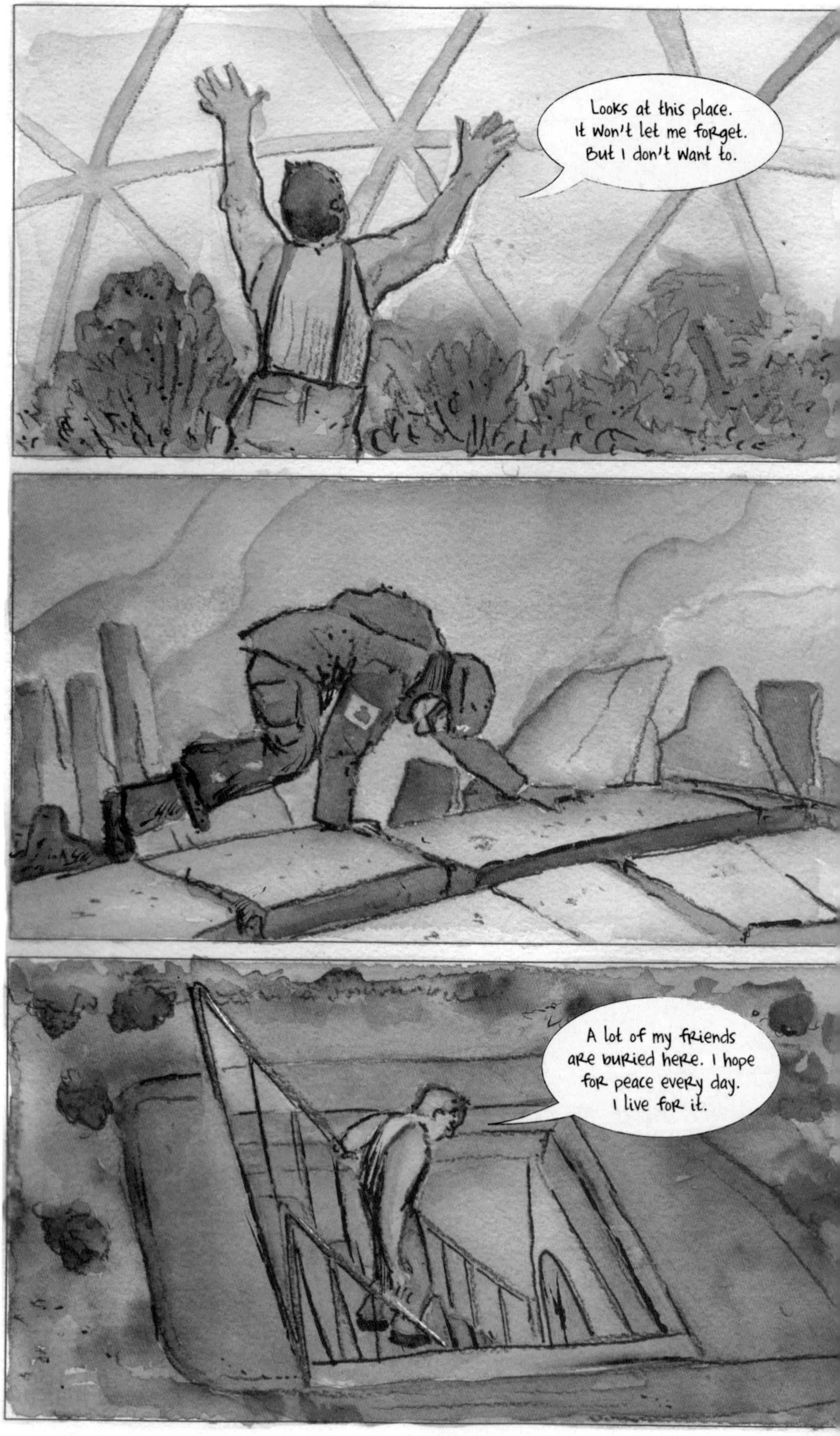
Looks at this place. It won't let me forget. But I don't want to.
A lot of my friends are buried here. I hope for peace every day. I live for it.

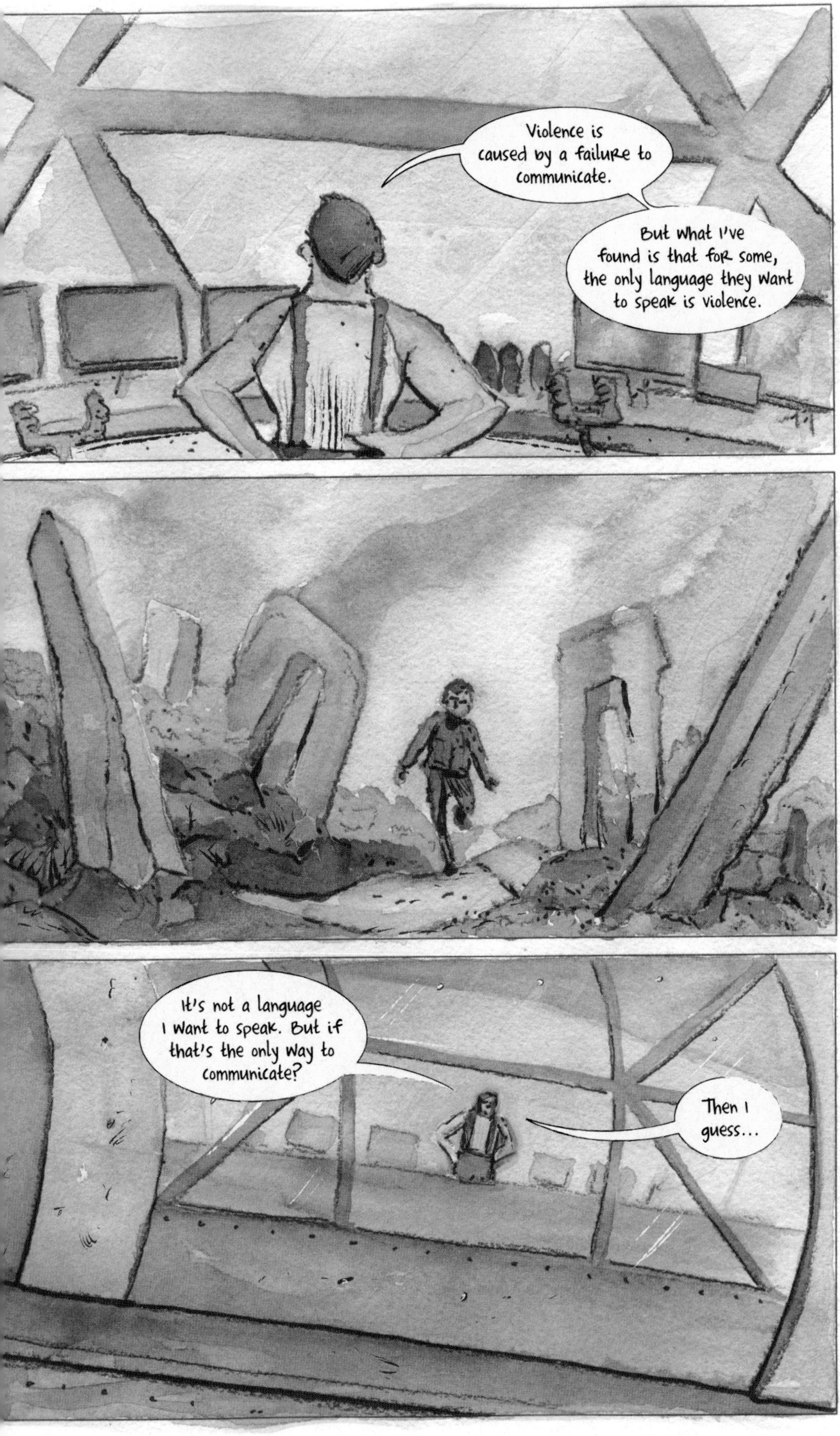
Violence is caused by a failure to communicate.
But what I've found is that for some, the only language they want to speak is violence.
It's not a language I want to speak. But if that's the only way to communicate?
Then I guess...

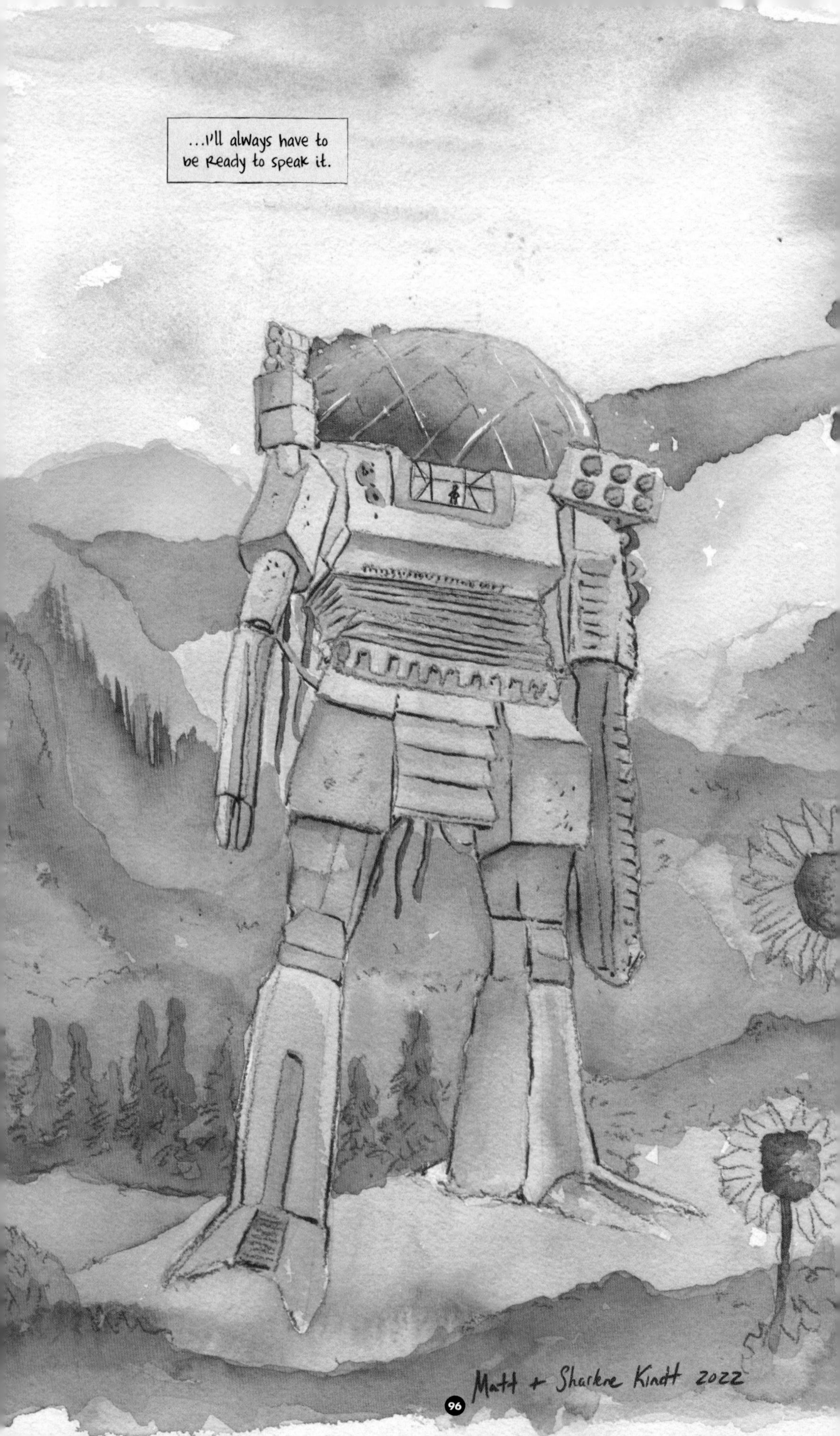
...I'll always have to be ready to speak it.
Matt + Sharlene Kindt 2022

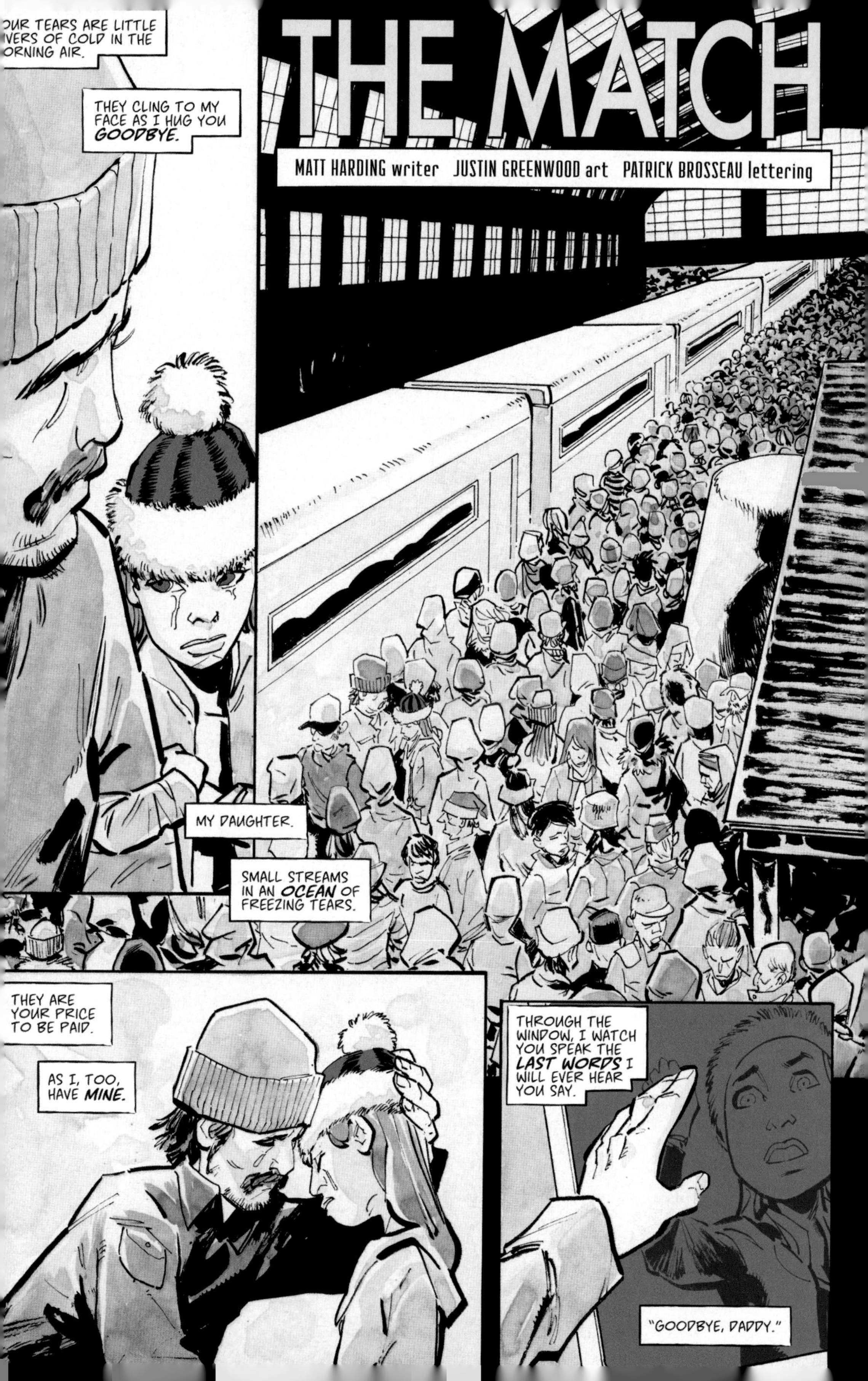
THE MATCH
MATT HARDING writer JUSTIN GREENWOOD art PATRICK BROSSEAU lettering
OUR TEARS ARE LITTLE
VERS OF COLD IN THE
ORNING AIR.
THEY CLING TO MY FACE AS I HUG YOU GOODBYE.
MY DAUGHTER.
SMALL STREAMS IN AN OCEAN OF FREEZING TEARS.
THEY ARE YOUR PRICE TO BE PAID.
AS I, TOO, HAVE MINE.
THROUGH THE WINDOW, I WATCH YOU SPEAK THE LAST WORDS I WILL EVER HEAR YOU SAY.
"GOODBYE, DADDY."

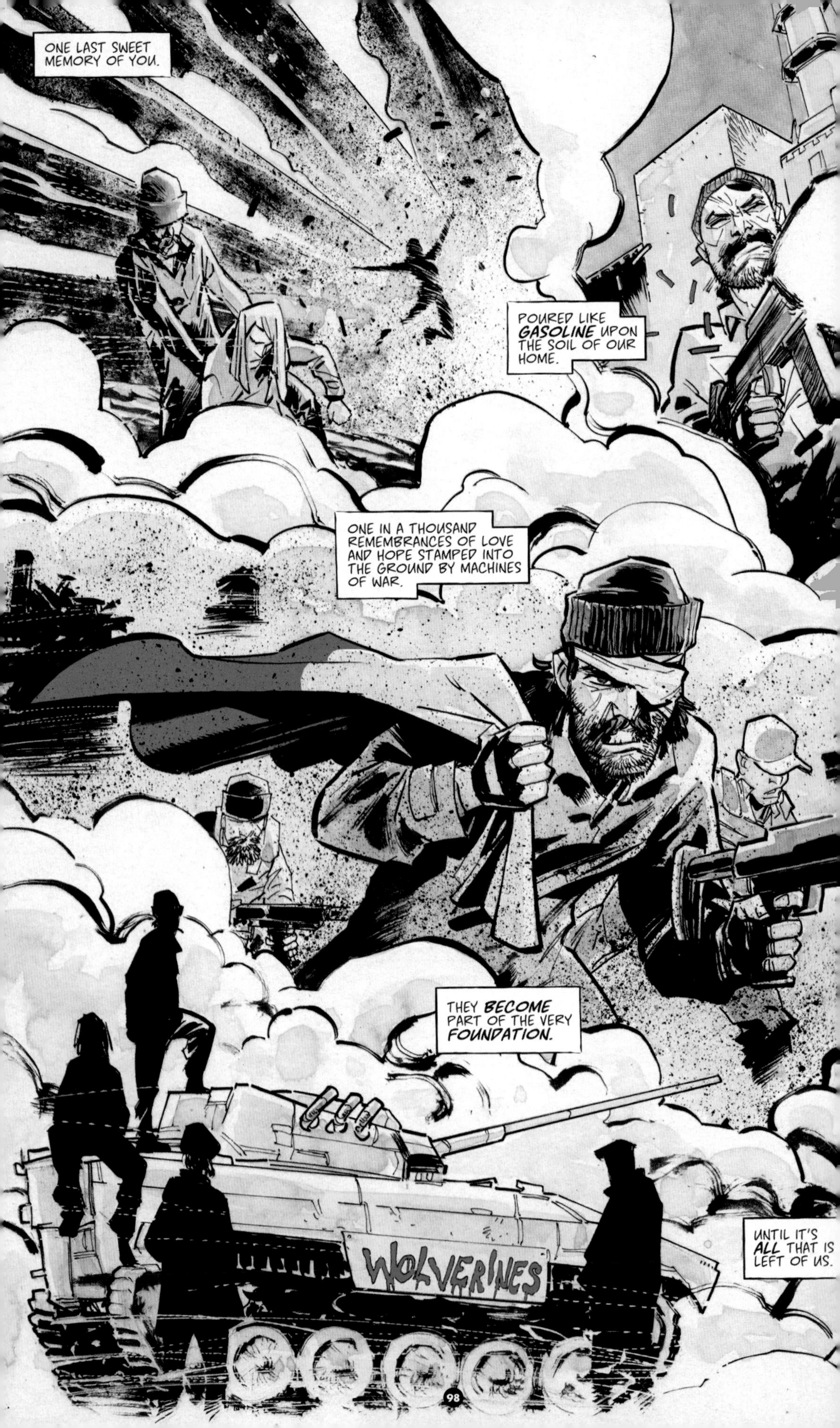

ONE LAST SWEET MEMORY OF YOU.
POURED LIKE GASOLINE UPON THE SOIL OF OUR HOME.
ONE IN A THOUSAND REMEMBRANCES OF LOVE AND HOPE STAMPED INTO THE GROUND BY MACHINES OF WAR.
THEY BECOME PART OF THE VERY FOUNDATION.
WOLVERINES
UNTIL IT'S ALL THAT IS LEFT OF US.

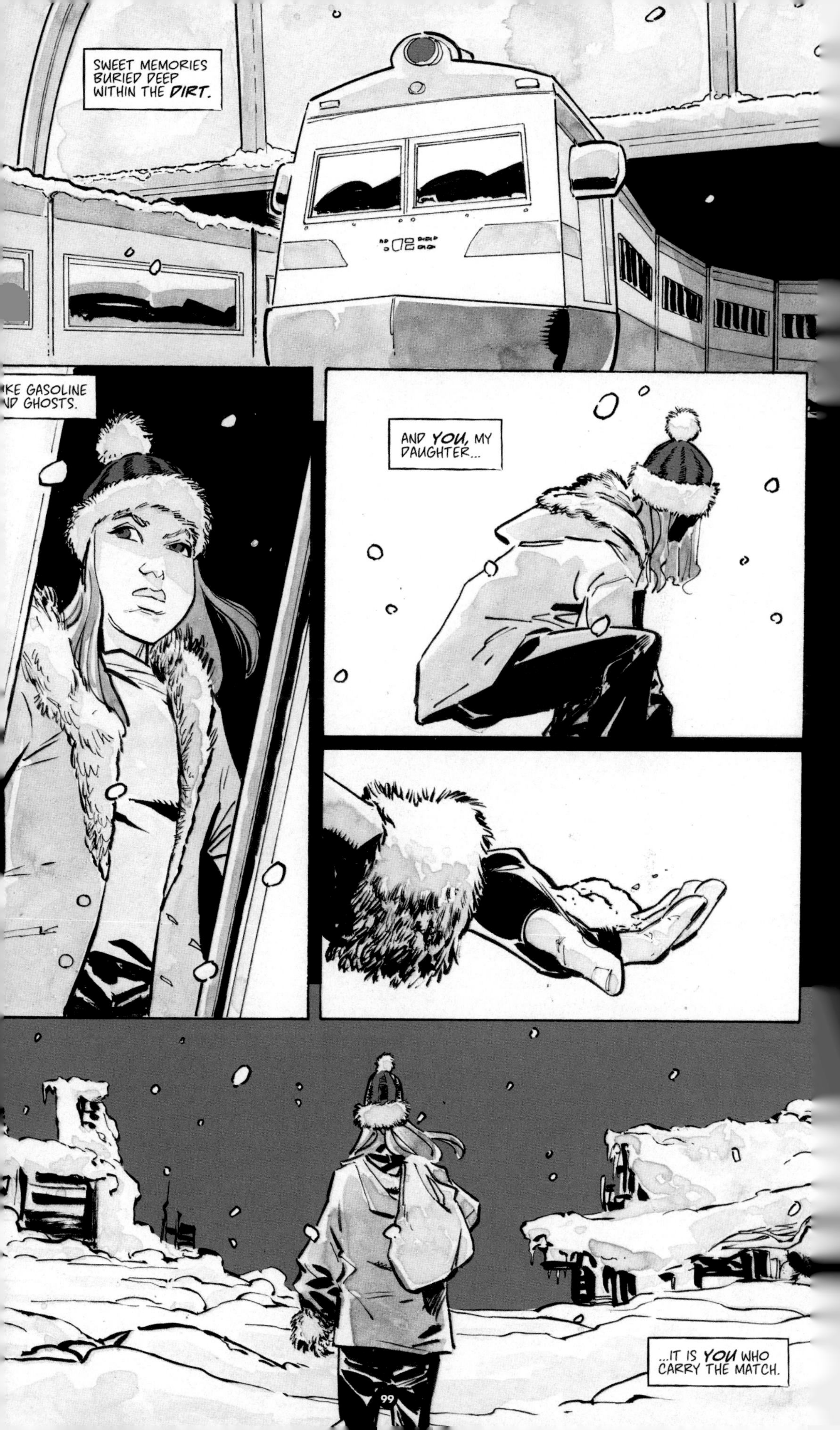
SWEET MEMORIES BURIED DEEP WITHIN THE DIRT.
KE GASOLINE ND GHOSTS.
AND YOU, MY DAUGHTER...
...IT IS YOU WHO CARRY THE MATCH.

Artist: **Ryan Odagawa**

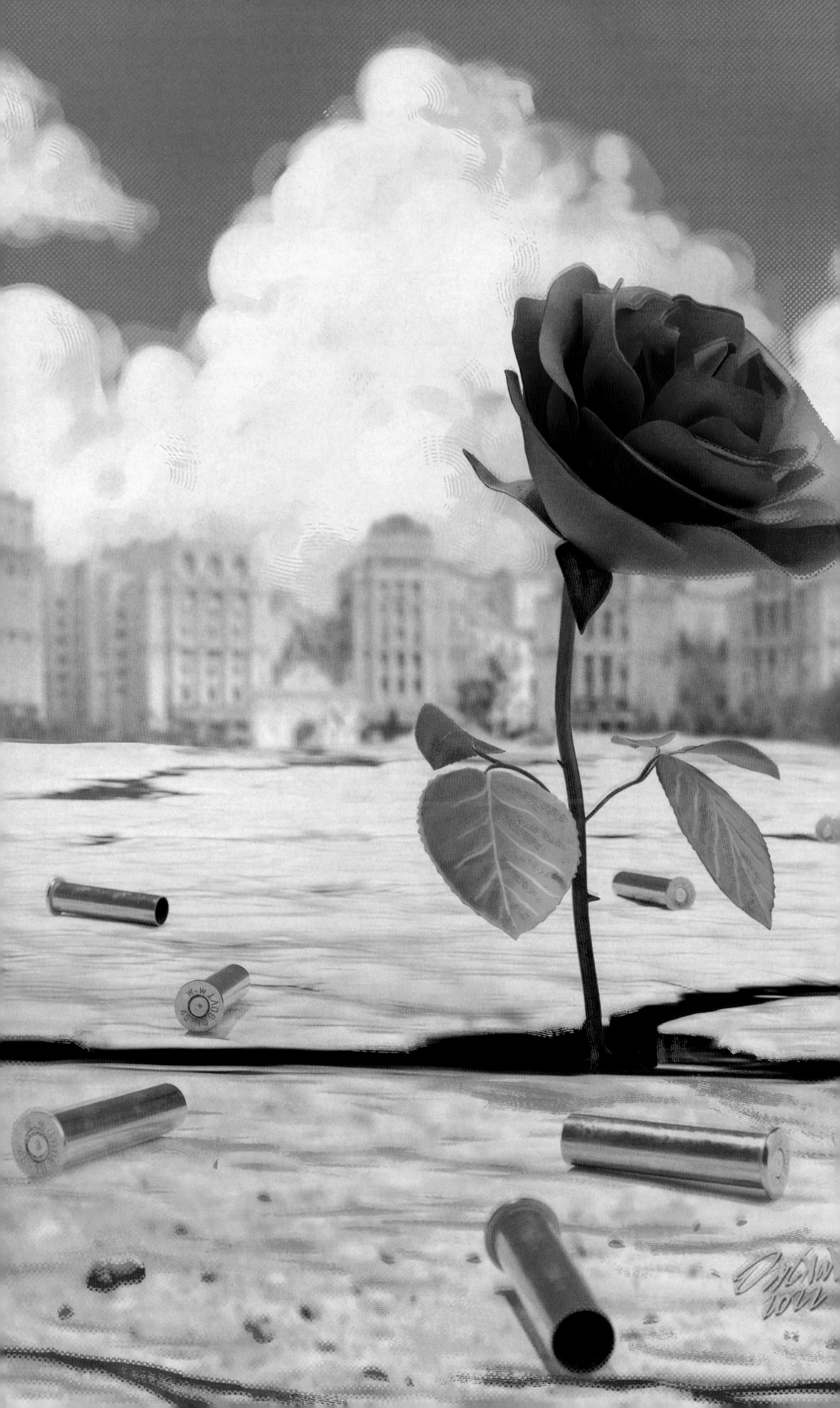

HOMESTEAD

SCRIPT
Jim Zub

ART
Richard Pace

LETTERS
Chas! Pangburn

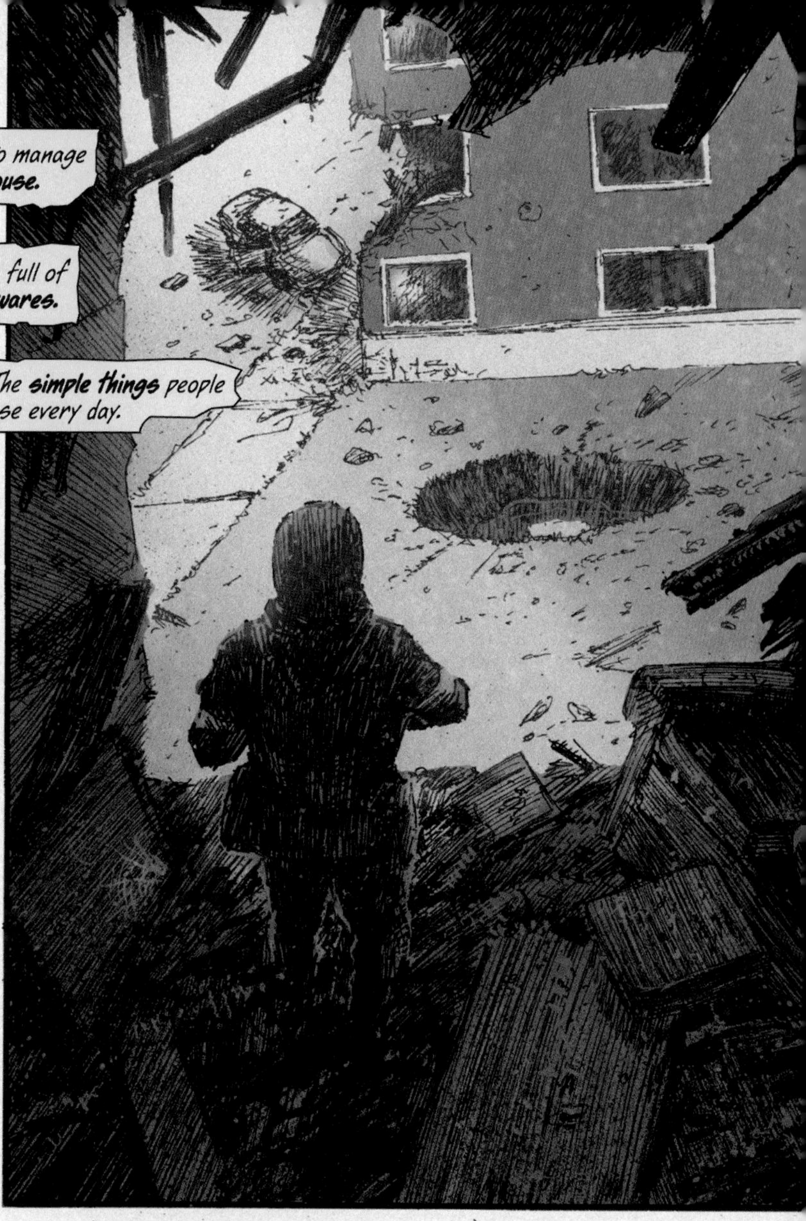

I used to manage a warehouse.
It was full of housewares.
The simple things people use every day.

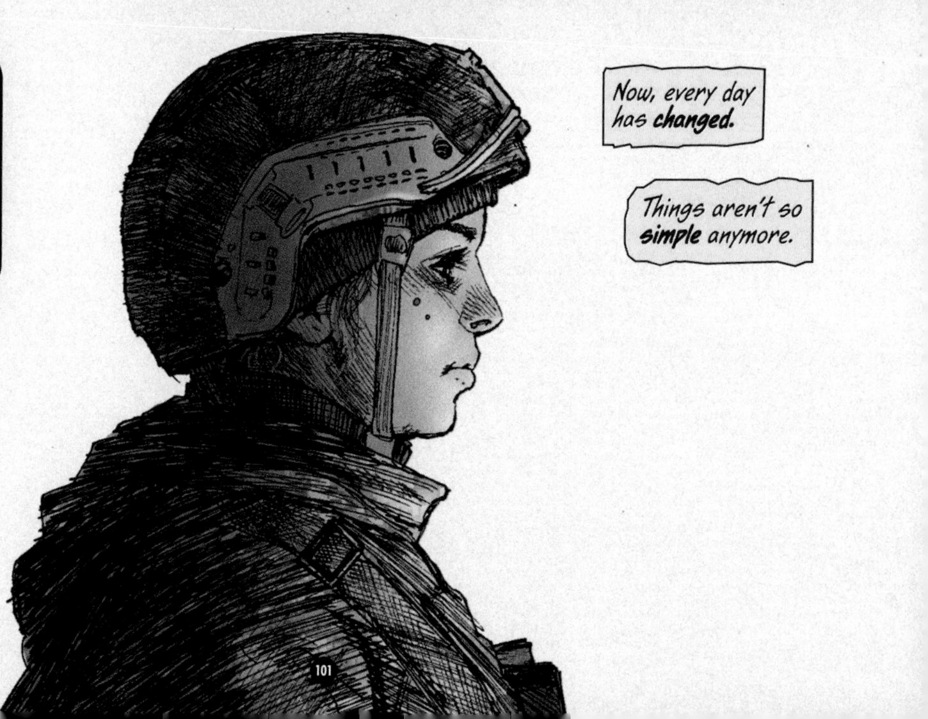

Now, every day has changed.
Things aren't so simple anymore.

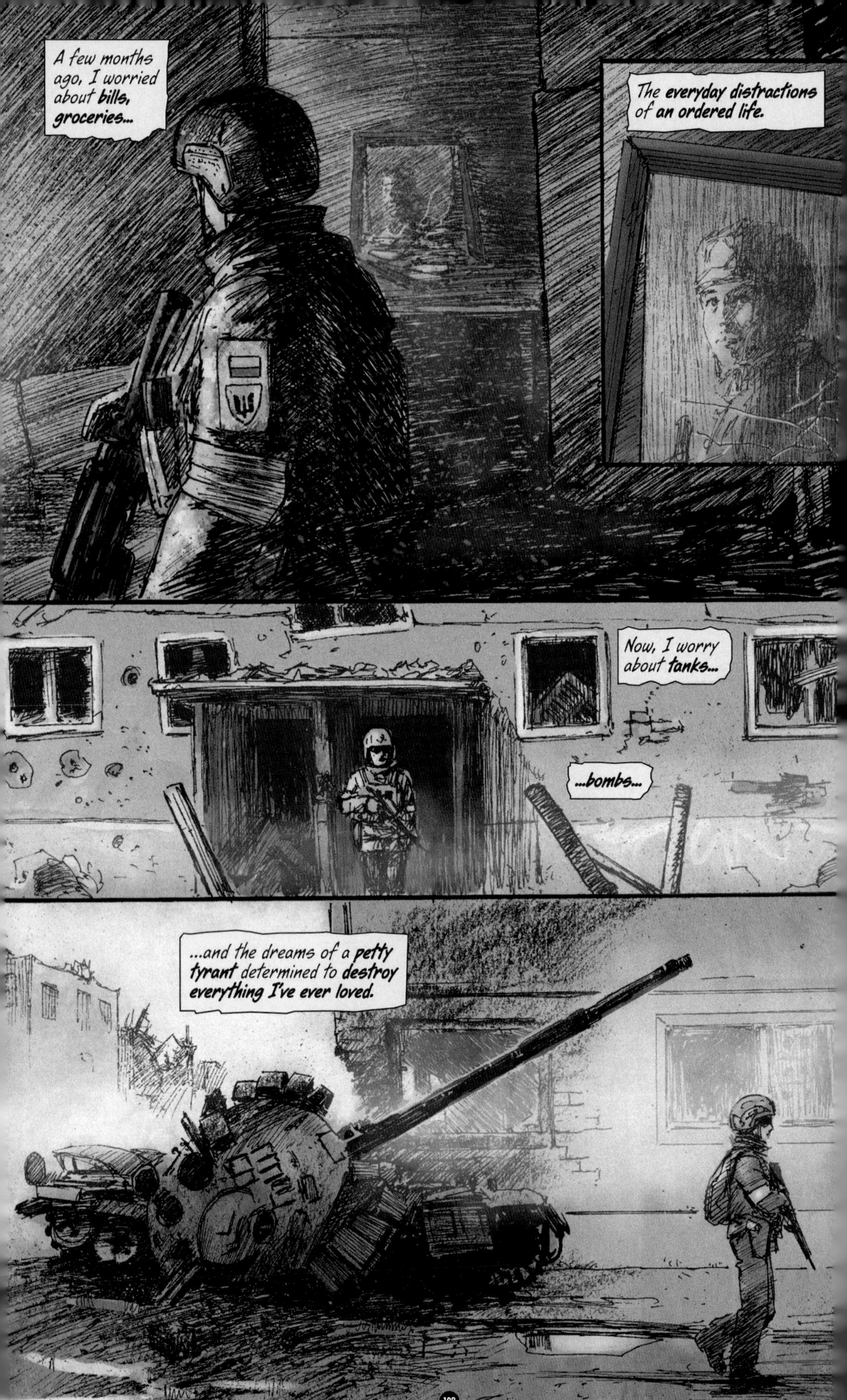
A few months ago, I worried about **bills, groceries...**
The **everyday distractions** of **an ordered life.**
Now, I worry about **tanks...**
...bombs...
...and the dreams of a **petty tyrant** determined to **destroy everything I've ever loved.**

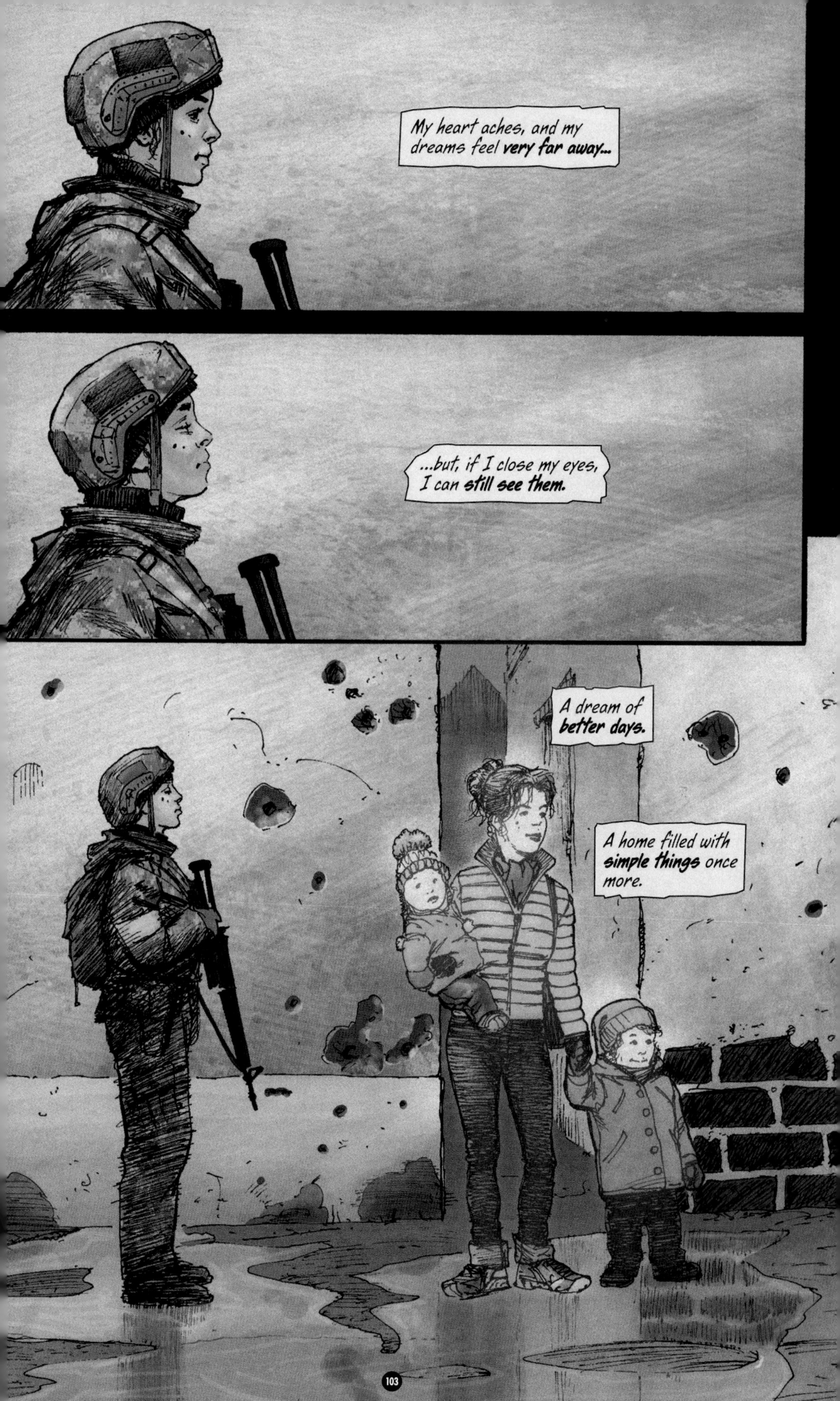
My heart aches, and my dreams feel **very far away...**
...but, if I close my eyes, I can **still see them.**
A dream of **better days.**
A home filled with **simple things** once more.

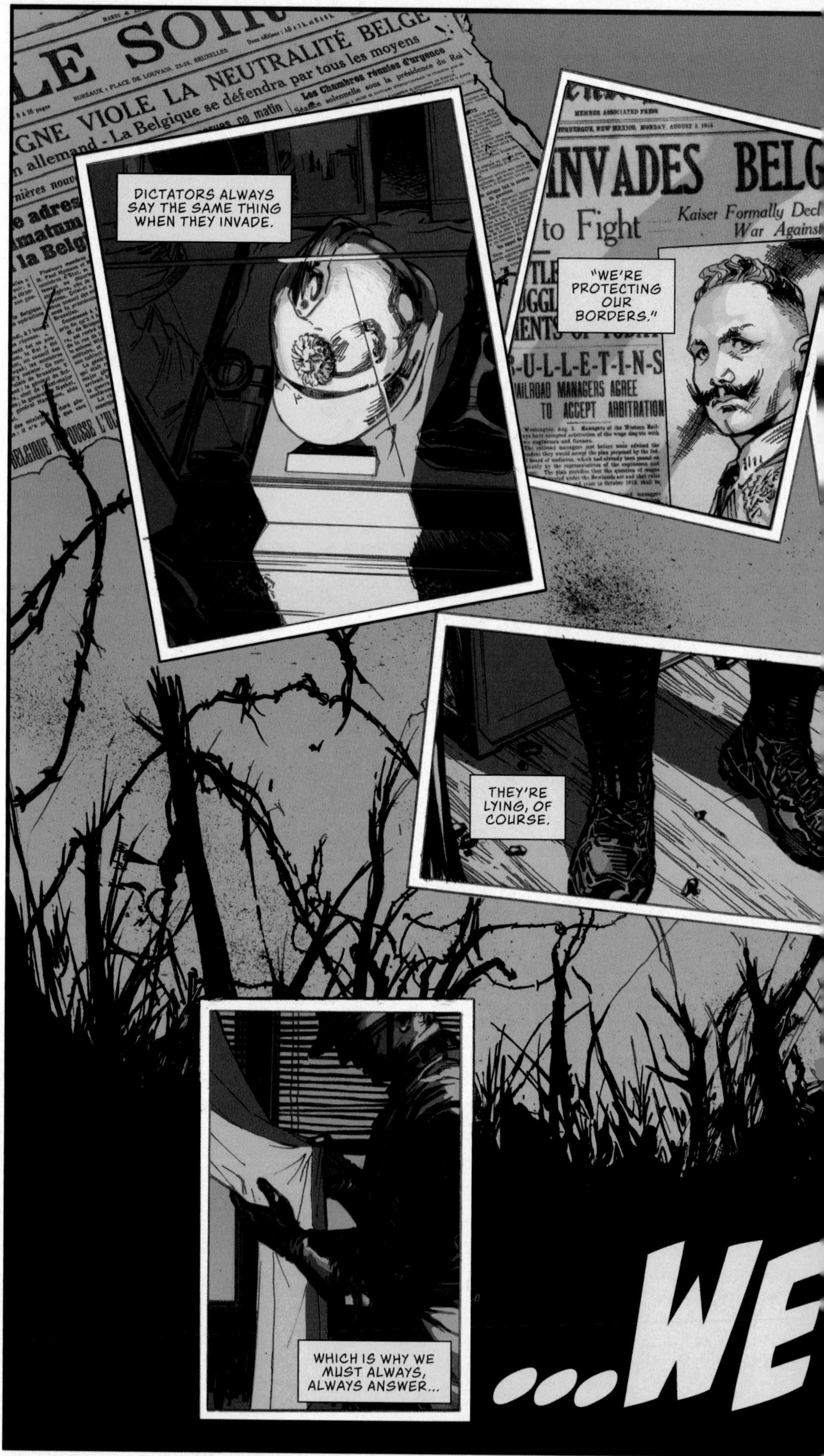

La Belgique se défendra par tous les moyens
Les Chambres réunies d'urgence
DICTATORS ALWAYS SAY THE SAME THING WHEN THEY INVADE.
MEMBER ASSOCIATED PRESS
to Fight
"WE'RE PROTECTING OUR BORDERS."
B-U-L-L-E-T-I-N-S
RAILROAD MANAGERS AGREE TO ACCEPT ARBITRATION
THEY'RE LYING, OF COURSE.
WHICH IS WHY WE MUST ALWAYS, ALWAYS ANSWER...
...WE

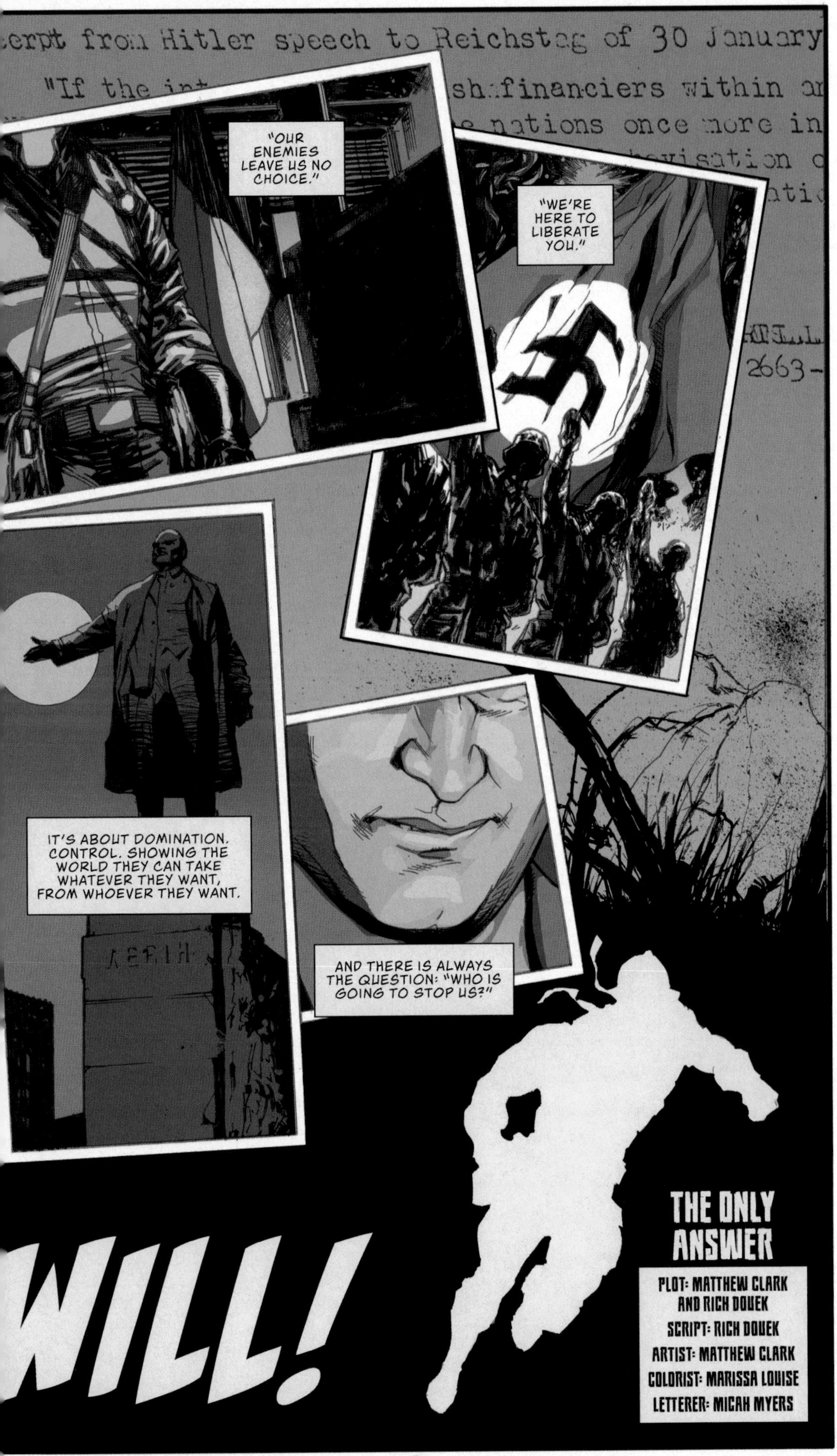
cerpt from Hitler speech to Reichstag of 30 January
"If the int sh financiers within an
e nations once more in
"OUR ENEMIES LEAVE US NO CHOICE."
"WE'RE HERE TO LIBERATE YOU."
IT'S ABOUT DOMINATION. CONTROL. SHOWING THE WORLD THEY CAN TAKE WHATEVER THEY WANT, FROM WHOEVER THEY WANT.
AND THERE IS ALWAYS THE QUESTION: "WHO IS GOING TO STOP US?"
WILL!
THE ONLY ANSWER
PLOT: MATTHEW CLARK AND RICH DOUEK
SCRIPT: RICH DOUEK
ARTIST: MATTHEW CLARK
COLORIST: MARISSA LOUISE
LETTERER: MICAH MYERS

Artist: **J. G. Jones**

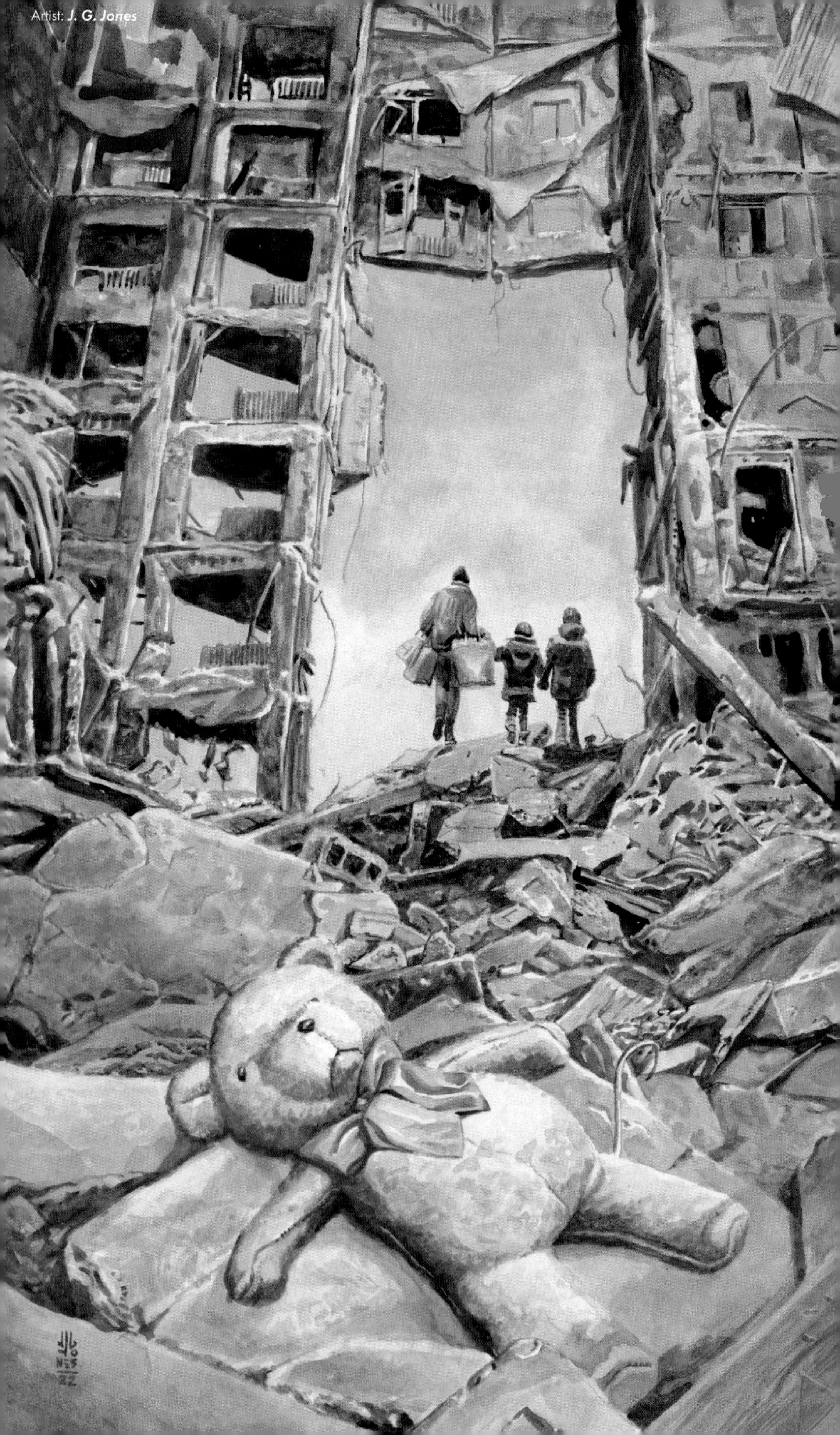

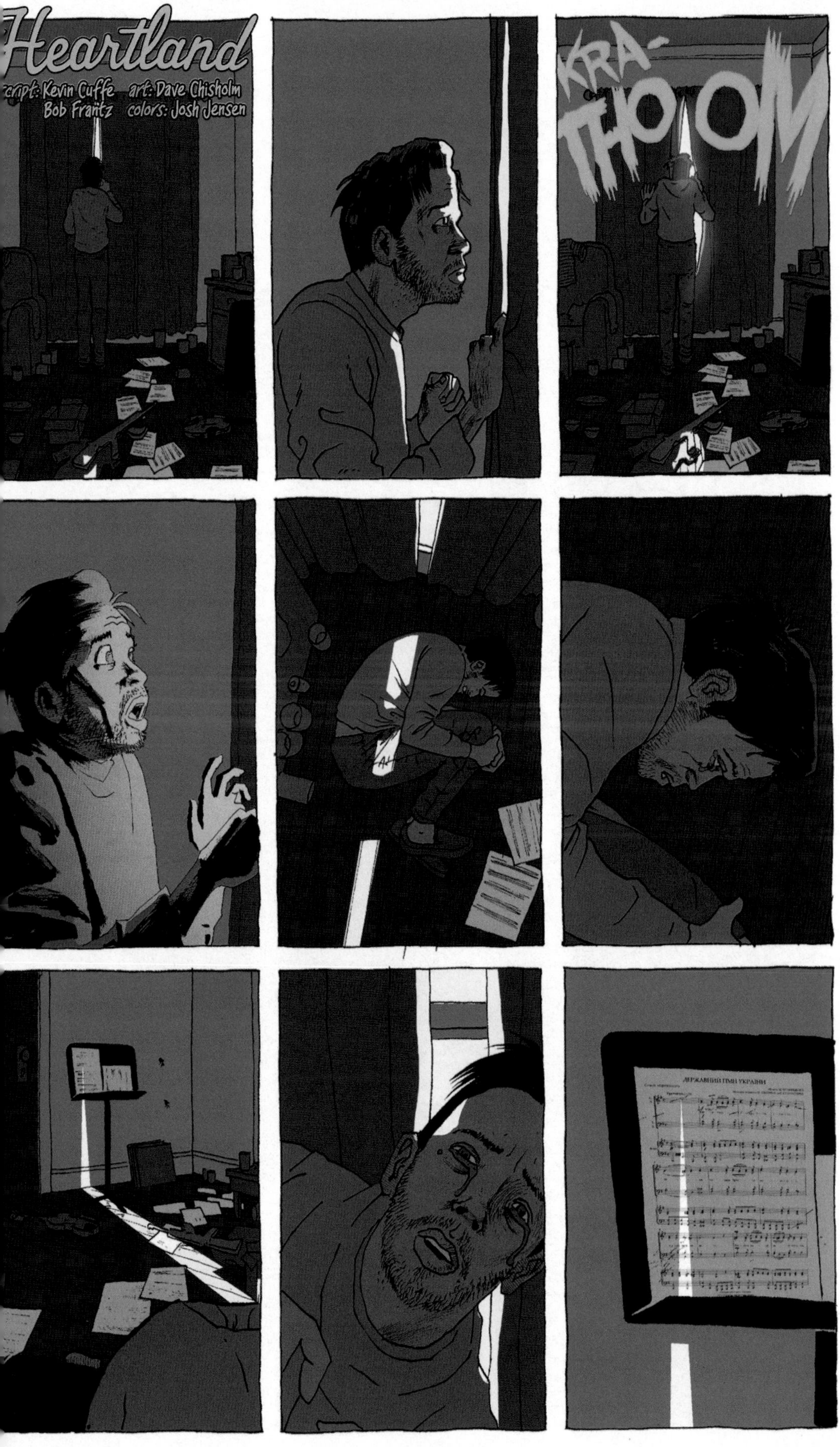
Heartland
cript: Kevin Cuffe
Bob Frantz
art: Dave Chisholm
colors: Josh Jensen
KRA-THOOM
ДЕРЖАВНИЙ ГІМН УКРАЇНИ

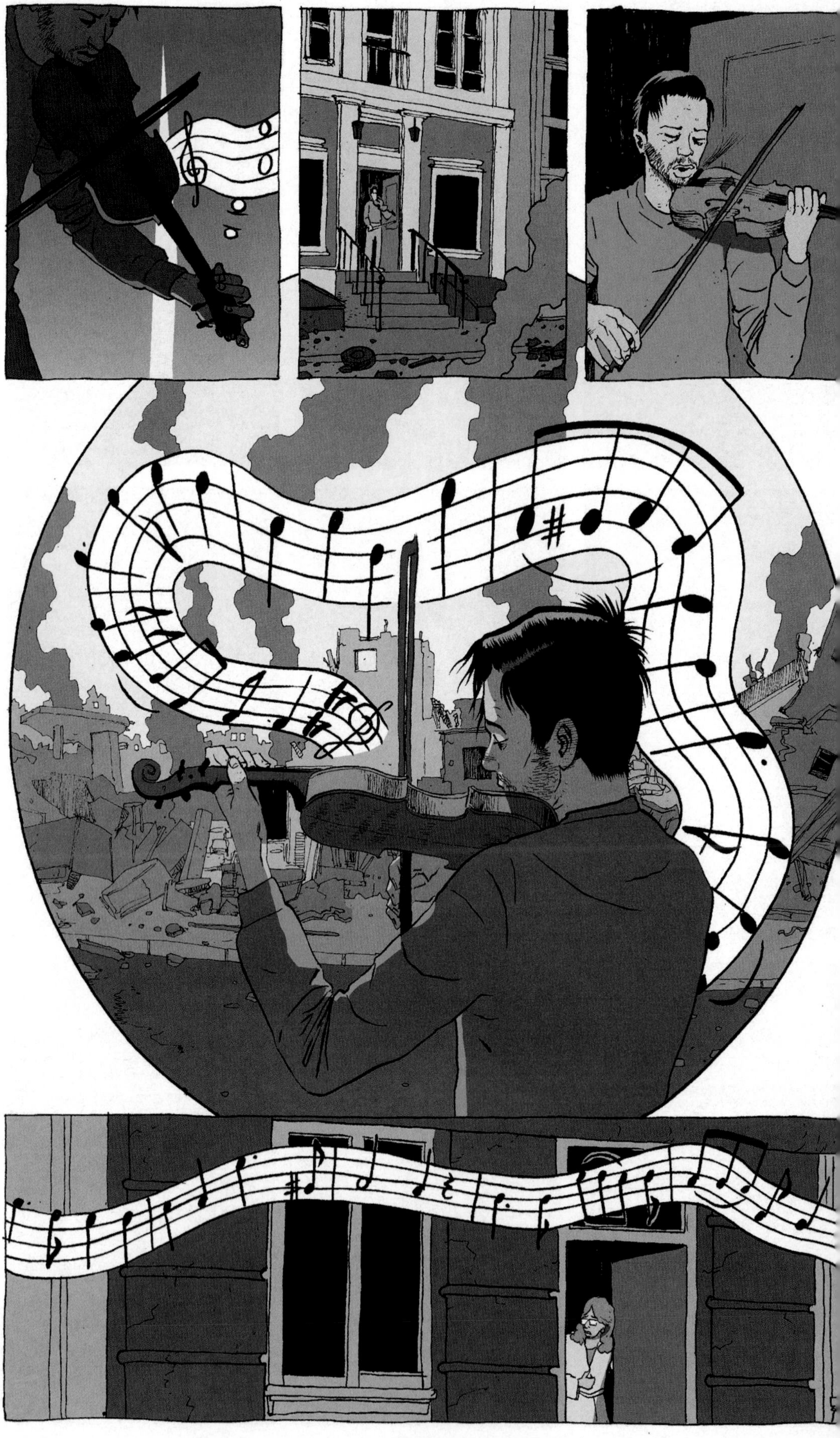

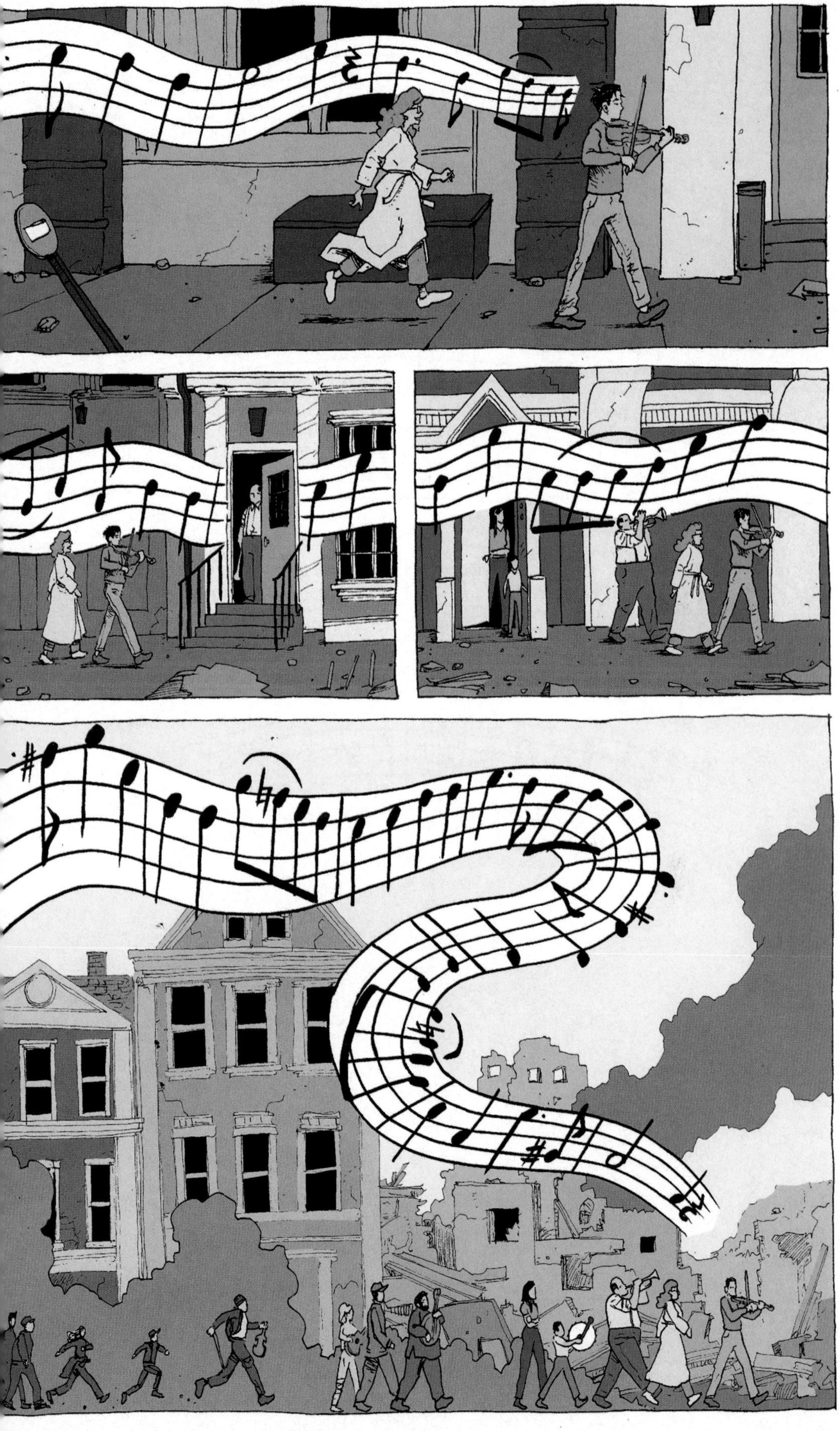

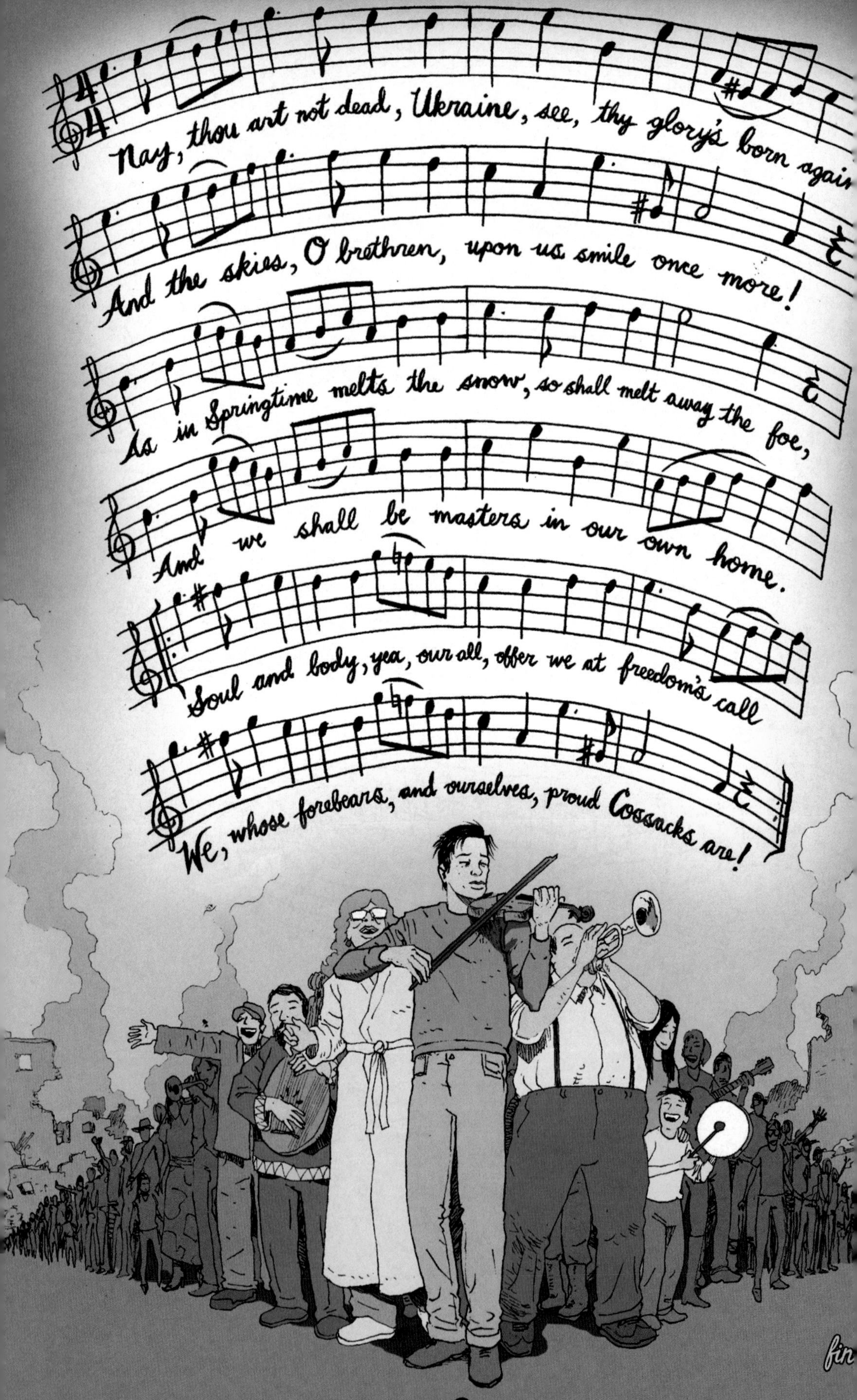

Nay, thou art not dead, Ukraine, see, thy glory's born again
And the skies, O brethren, upon us smile once more!
As in Springtime melts the snow, so shall melt away the foe,
And we shall be masters in our own home.
Soul and body, yea, our all, offer we at freedom's call
We, whose forebears, and ourselves, proud Cossacks are!
fin

: Ryan Sook

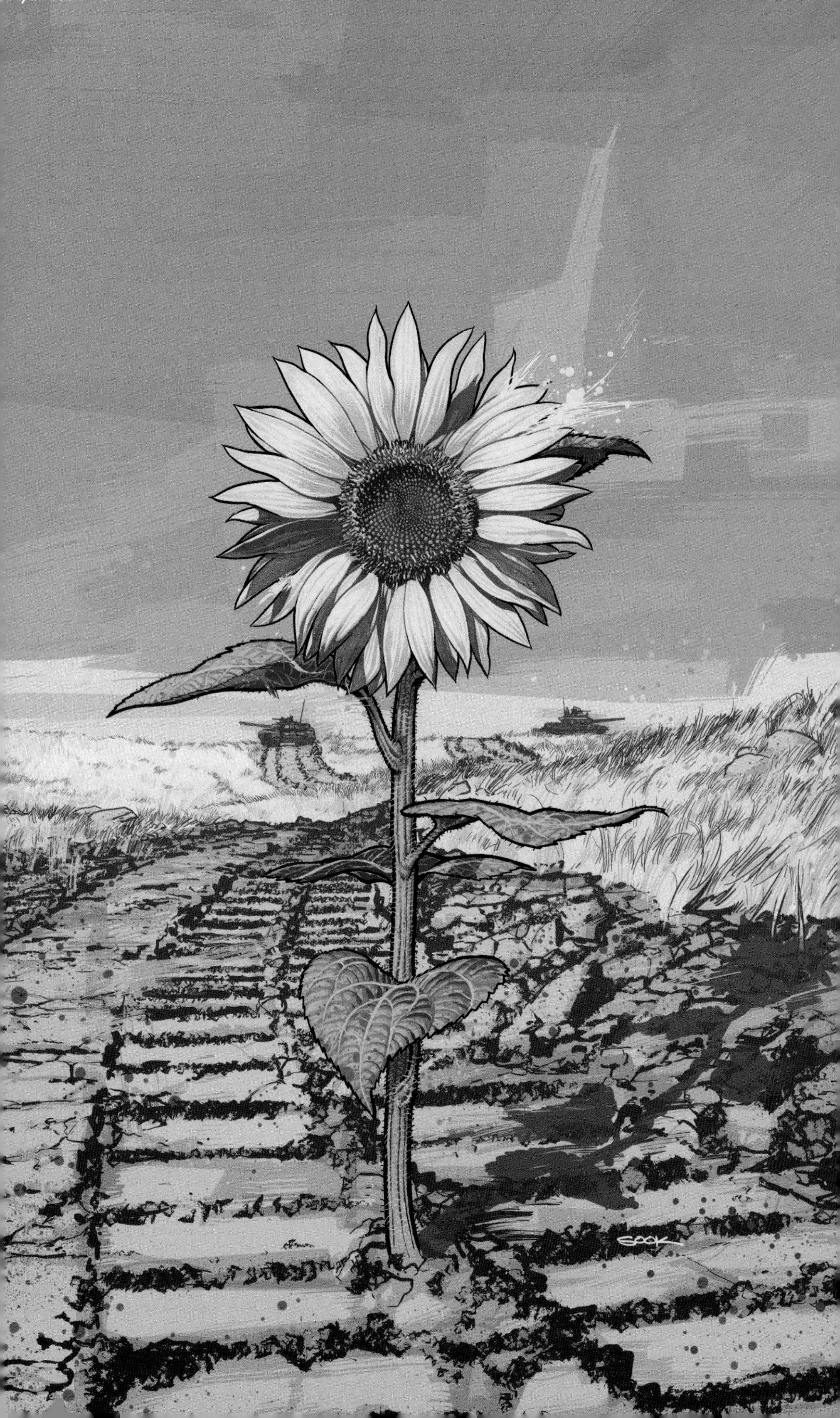
SOOK

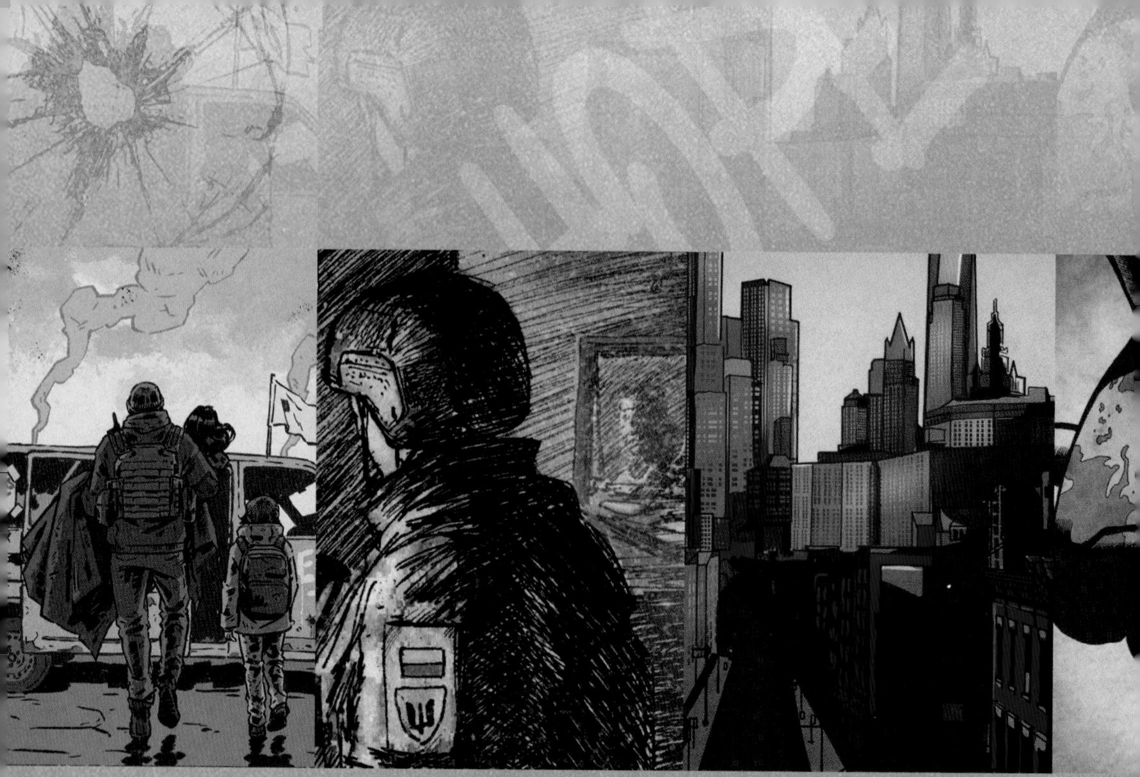

U K R A N

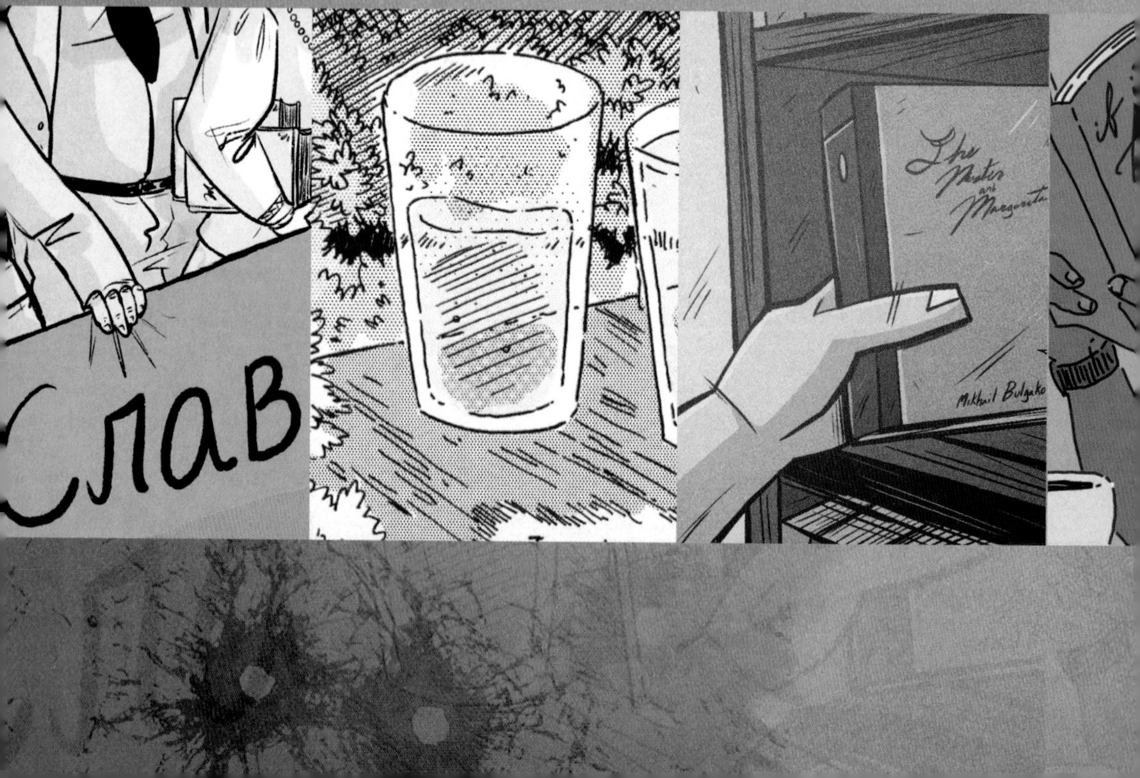
Слав
The Master and Margarita
Mikhail Bulgakov

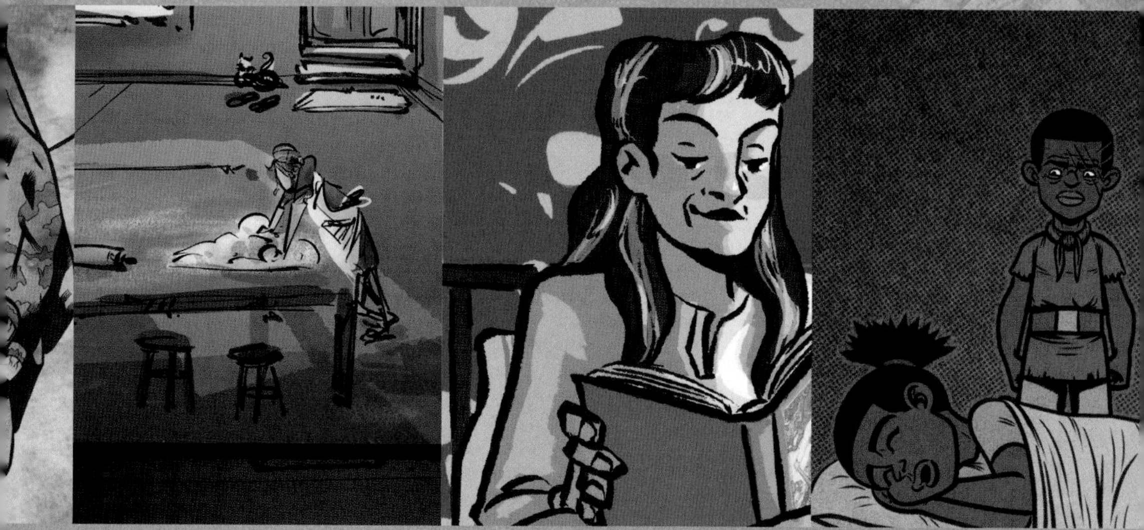

IAN ART

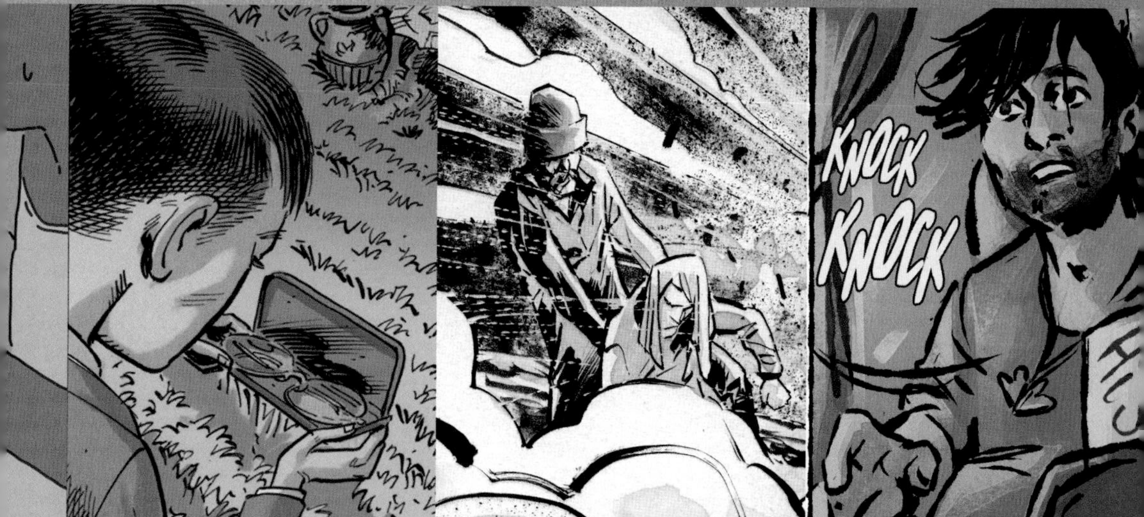
KNOCK
KNOCK

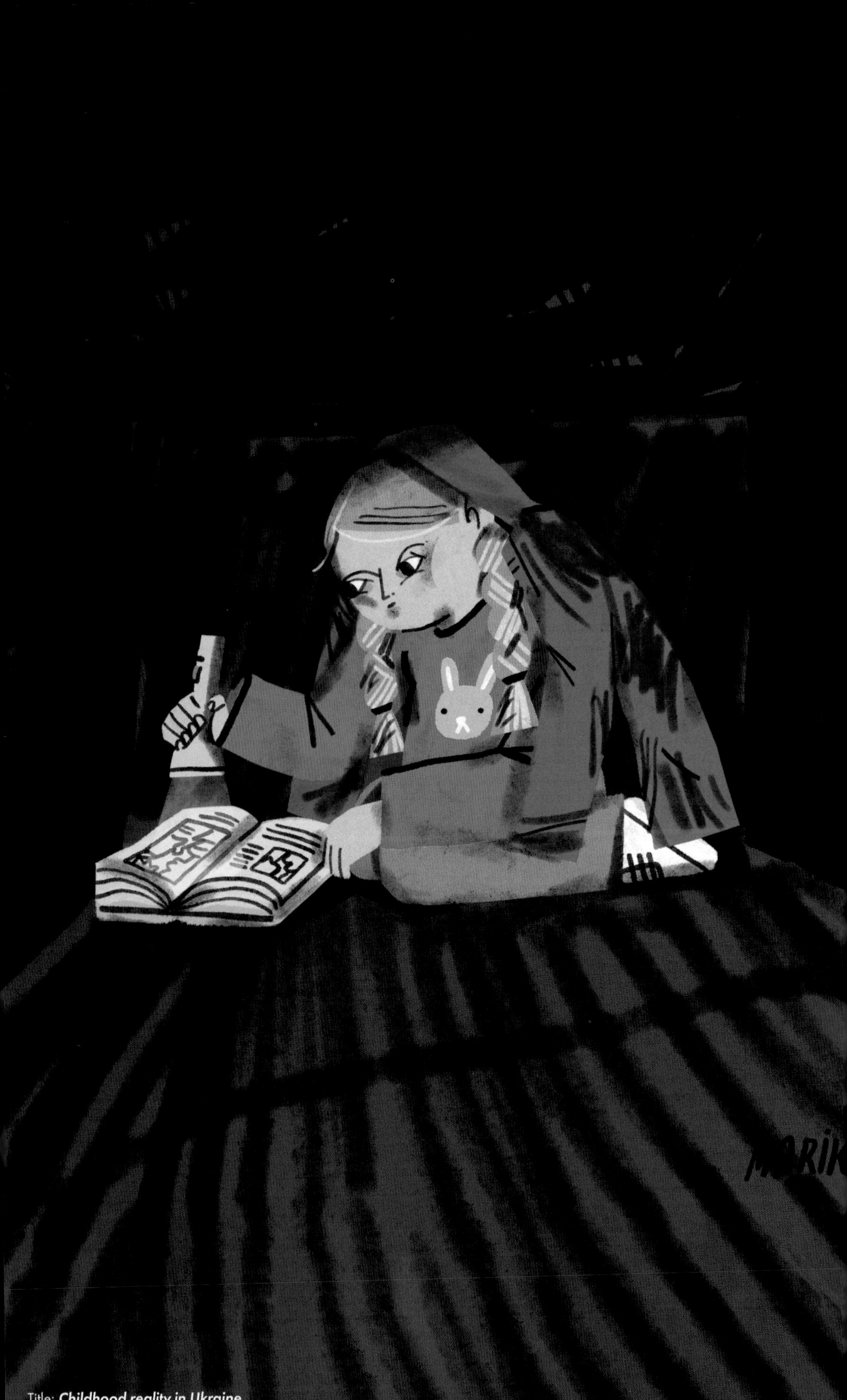

Title: ***Childhood reality in Ukraine***

Mari Kinovych

Instagram: **@marikinoo**

· · · · · · · · · · · · · · · · · · · ·

I don't have children, so I can only imagine what
parents are experiencing now. It's terrible that families
are losing their homes, but Russians are also stealing
many childhoods and opportunities to be appropriately
socialized/educated in schools. The pandemic brought
us difficulties in education, but the war created a further
catastrophe. My only hope is that despite this nightmare,
children will be motivated enough to continue learning

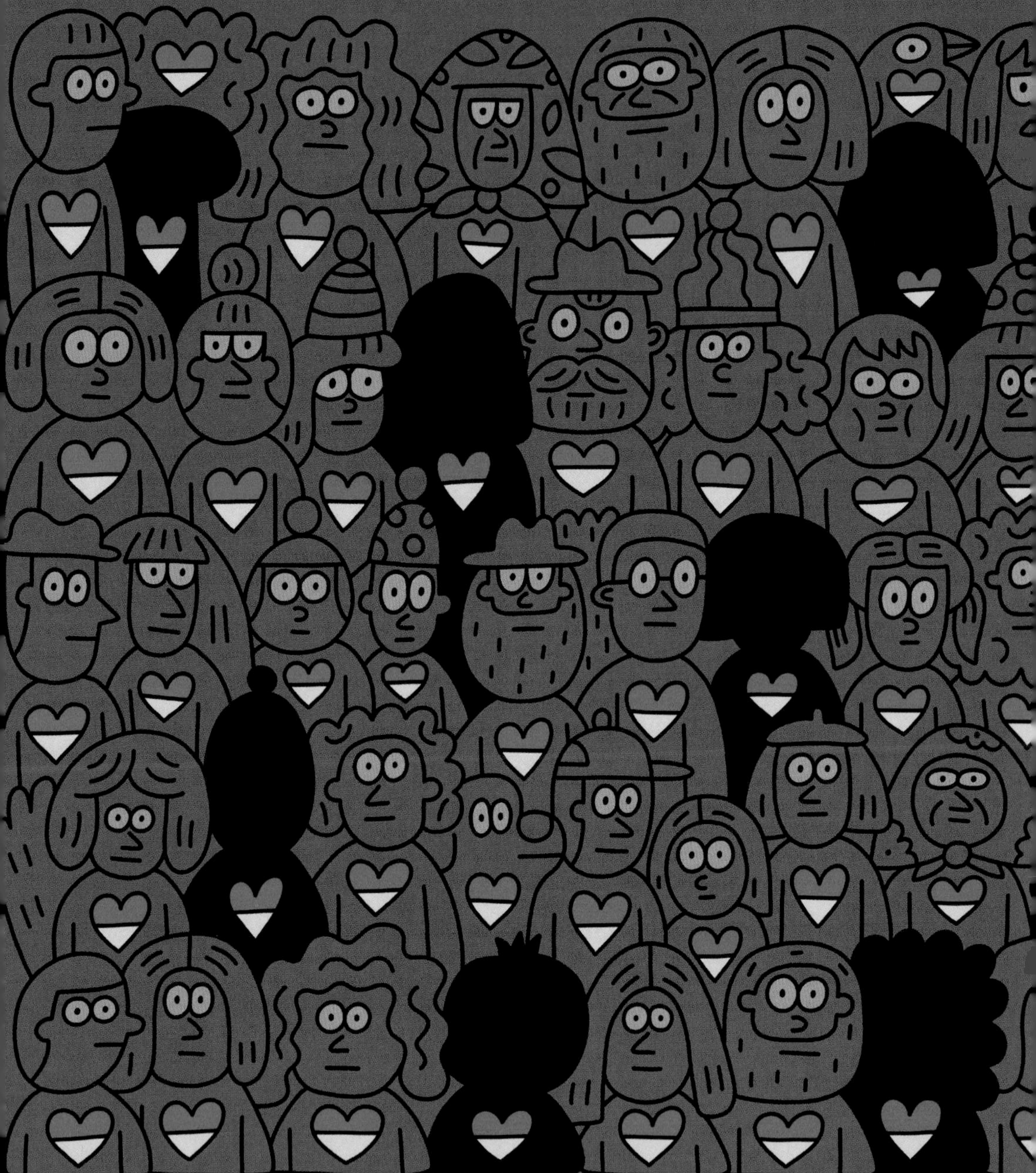

Nina Dzyvulska

Instagram: **@nina_dzyvulska**

. . . .

Pray for Ukraine.

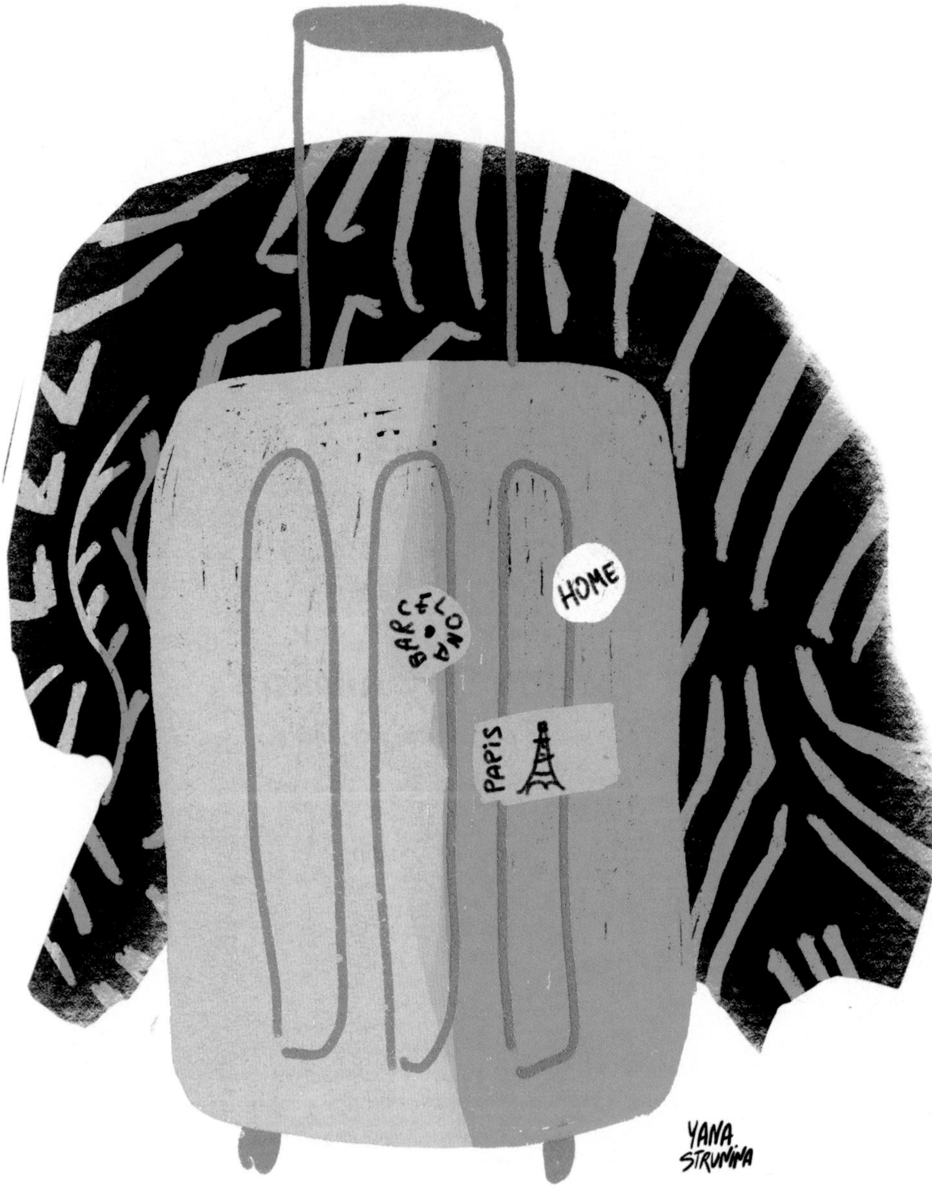
BARCELONA
HOME
PARIS
YANA STRUNINA

Title: *It Just Hurts*

Yana Strunina

Instagram: **@yanastruninaart**

. . . .

I looked at my suitcase and realized that it was happening again. Choosing the "right" things and not taking the "unnecessary" items was physically painful because they are *not* unnecessary.

After 2014, I couldn't imagine that I would again be forced to pack my life into one suitcase. This time, I chose to take my favorite things and not "practical" ones—jewelry, underwear, photographs, pencils, and a sketchbook. I already knew these items would save me from madness away from home and somewhere out there.

Українці, що знаються на зборі тривожних валіз. Ви сонечки

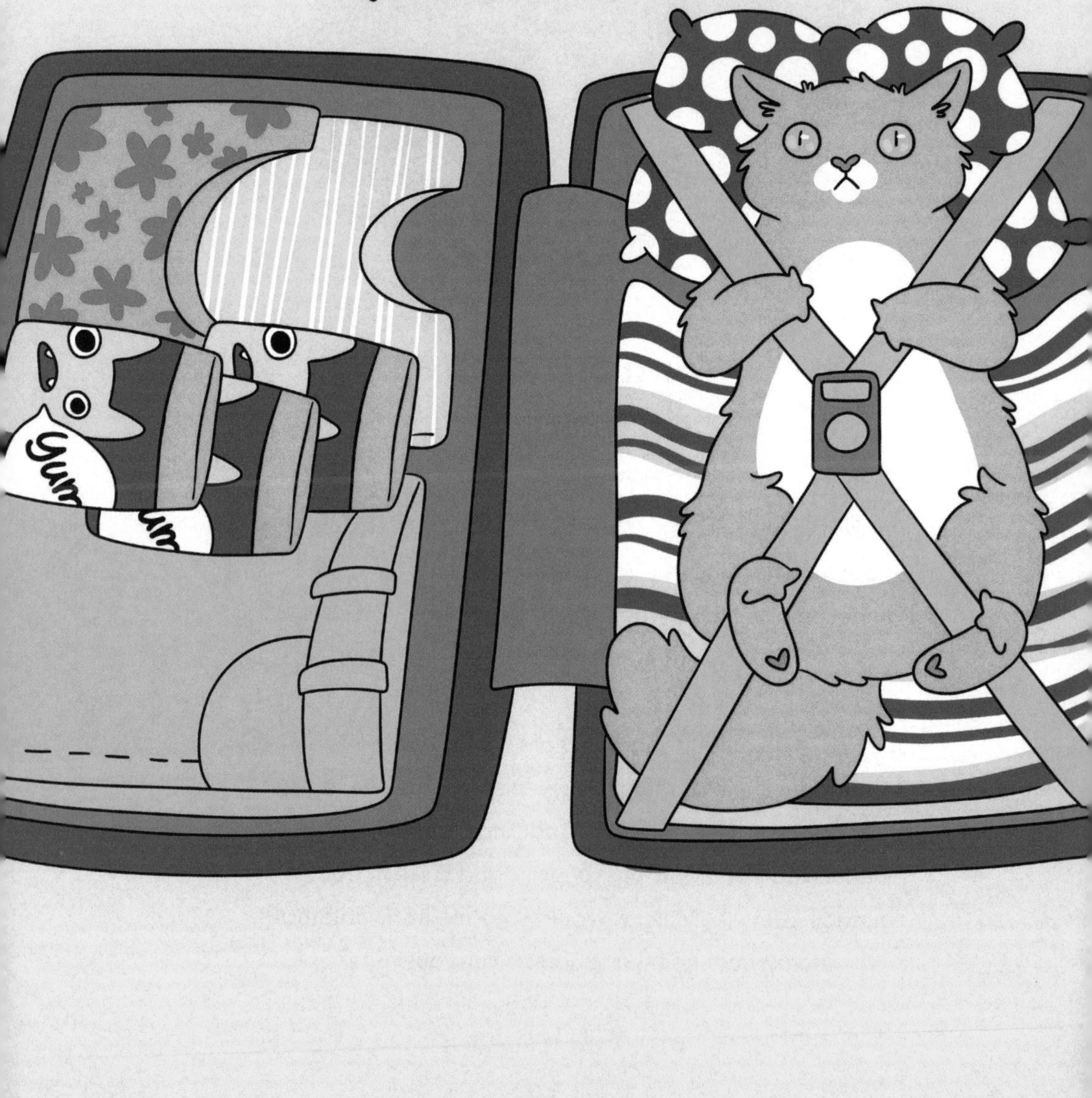

Title: *"Ukrainians, who know how to pack emergency bags, are rays of light."*

Anastacia

Instagram: **@koshisty.pushisty**

· ·

My favorite book is Antoine de Saint-Exupéry's *The Little Prince*. Even those who have never read this book might know of a famous quote from it: "You become responsible, forever, for what you have tamed."

With this art piece, I wanted to cheer up those familiar with this concept and express my condolences to those who couldn`t do so. I have several friends who left their pets at home and asked relatives or volunteers to take care of them.

Contrary to popular belief, this decision sometimes has positive reasons: health, old age, or the nature of the pet. By nature, I mean those who are so afraid of the outside world that they can die on the way from cardiac arrest. Believe me—there were *many* cases like this. I feel pain, anxiety, and guilt when I talk to people who had to leave without their pets.

Ukrainians who had to leave someone behind, please hold on. Hopefully, one day we will meet those we miss so much.

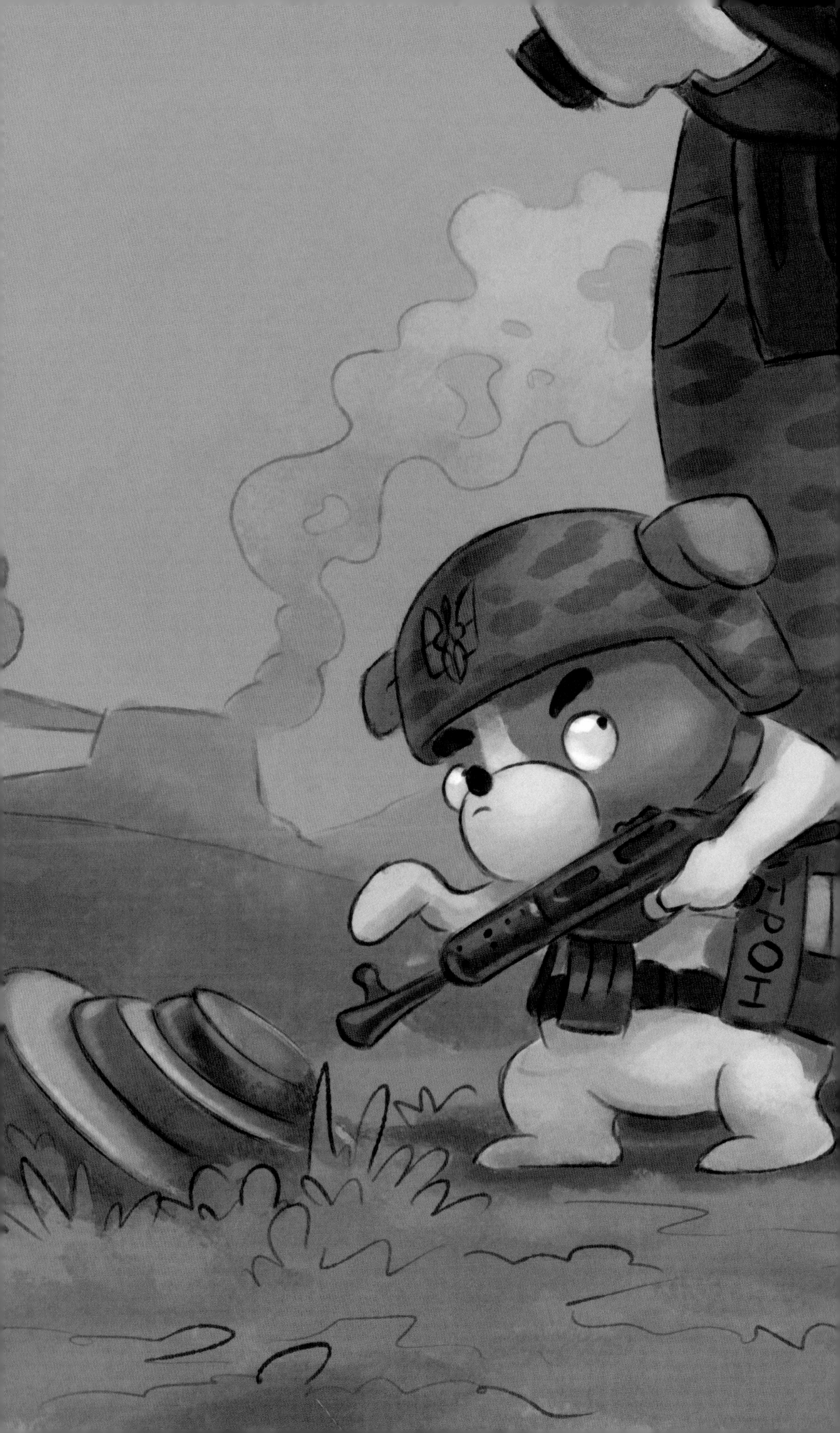

Mikhail Dunakovskiy

Instagram: **@dunakovskiy**

. . . .

This is Patron, probably the most famous dog
in Ukraine. He serves in Chernihiv's Ministry
of Emergency Situations. Since the beginning
of the war, he has helped sappers—combat
engineers—neutralize over 90 mines.

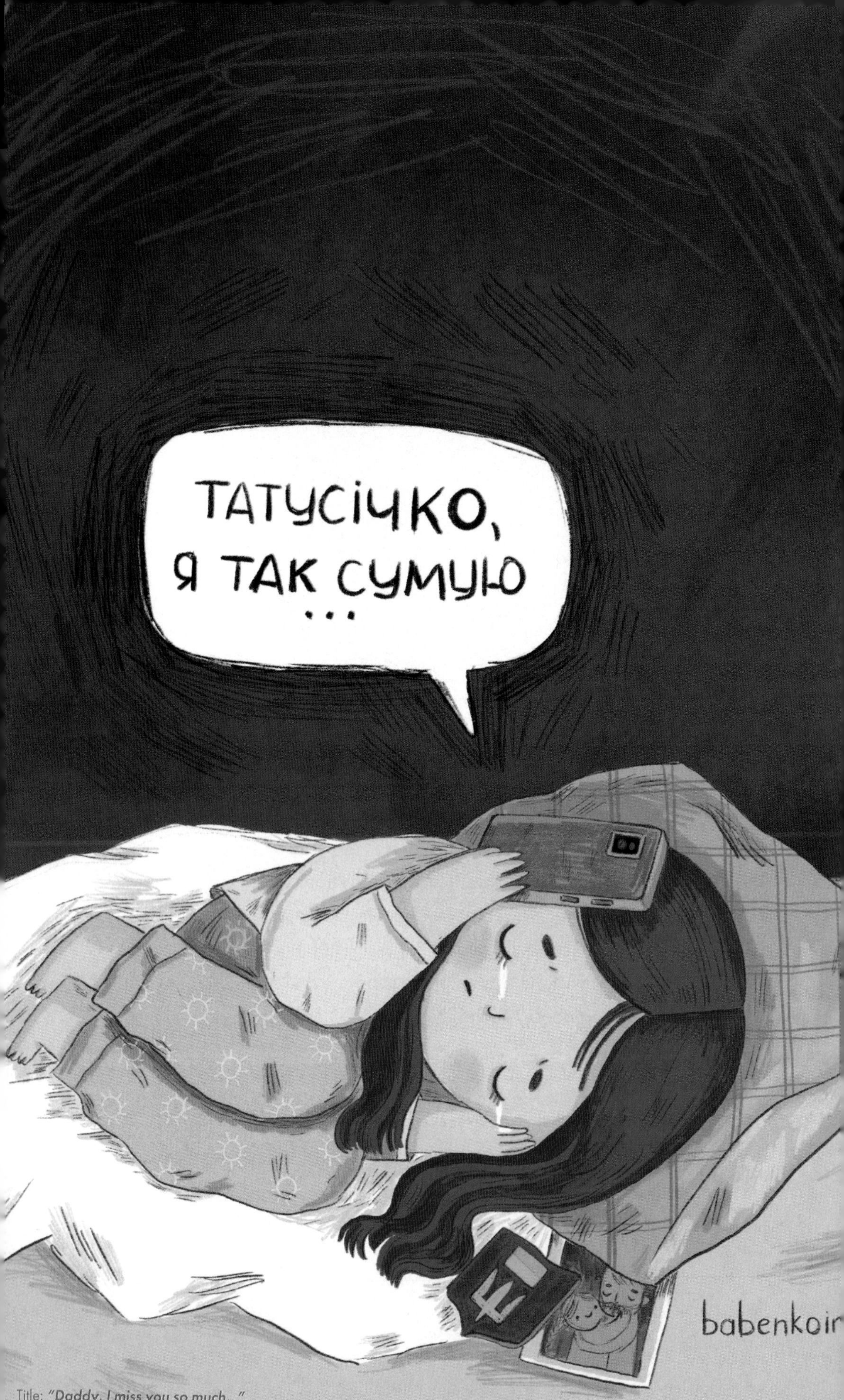
ТАТУСІЧКО, Я ТАК СУМУЮ ...
babenkoir

Title: *"Daddy, I miss you so much..."*

Iryna Babenko

Instagram: **@babenkoirusa**

. . . .

Her father is her best friend.
They have their own rituals: hamburgers in garages, friends/"dudes,"
burpees, rules for the handling of weapons, protection of mom, running
around the apartment, watching "Harry Potter" thousands of times, evening
tickles, gathering treats for Dad on a business trip, waiting for him from
work, etc.

She did not hug her best friend for almost a month.
Like more than half of all Ukrainian children.
Some will never hug...

May God reward everyone."

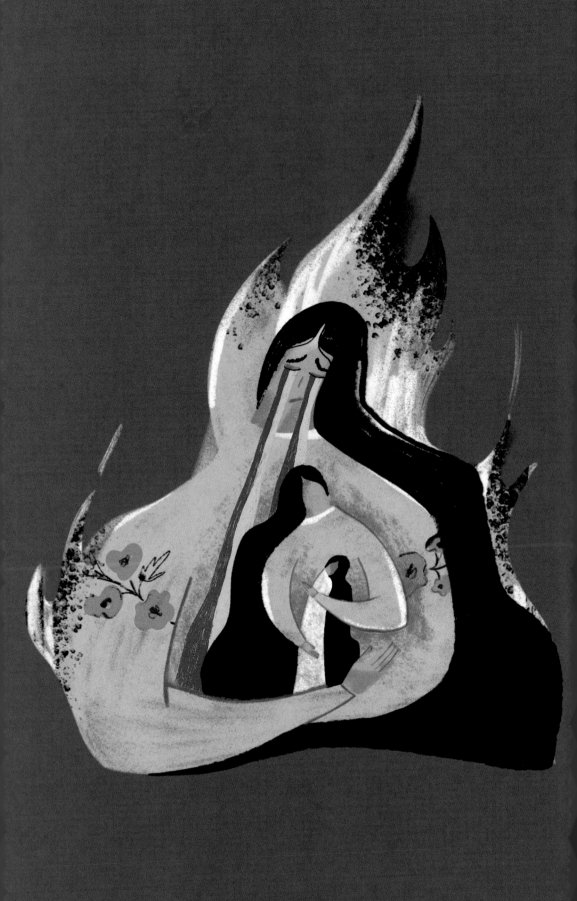

Olena Dziura

Instagram: **@olenadzen**

· · · · · · · · · · · · · · · · · · · ·

My artwork is about the unity of Ukrainians. We are
crying, but we are strong and ready to fight.

This piece depicts a woman in traditional embroidered
clothes as a symbol of Ukraine. This woman is on fire and
suffering, but she is not alone–she has a lot of support.

This piece embodies all of us—victory in our unity.

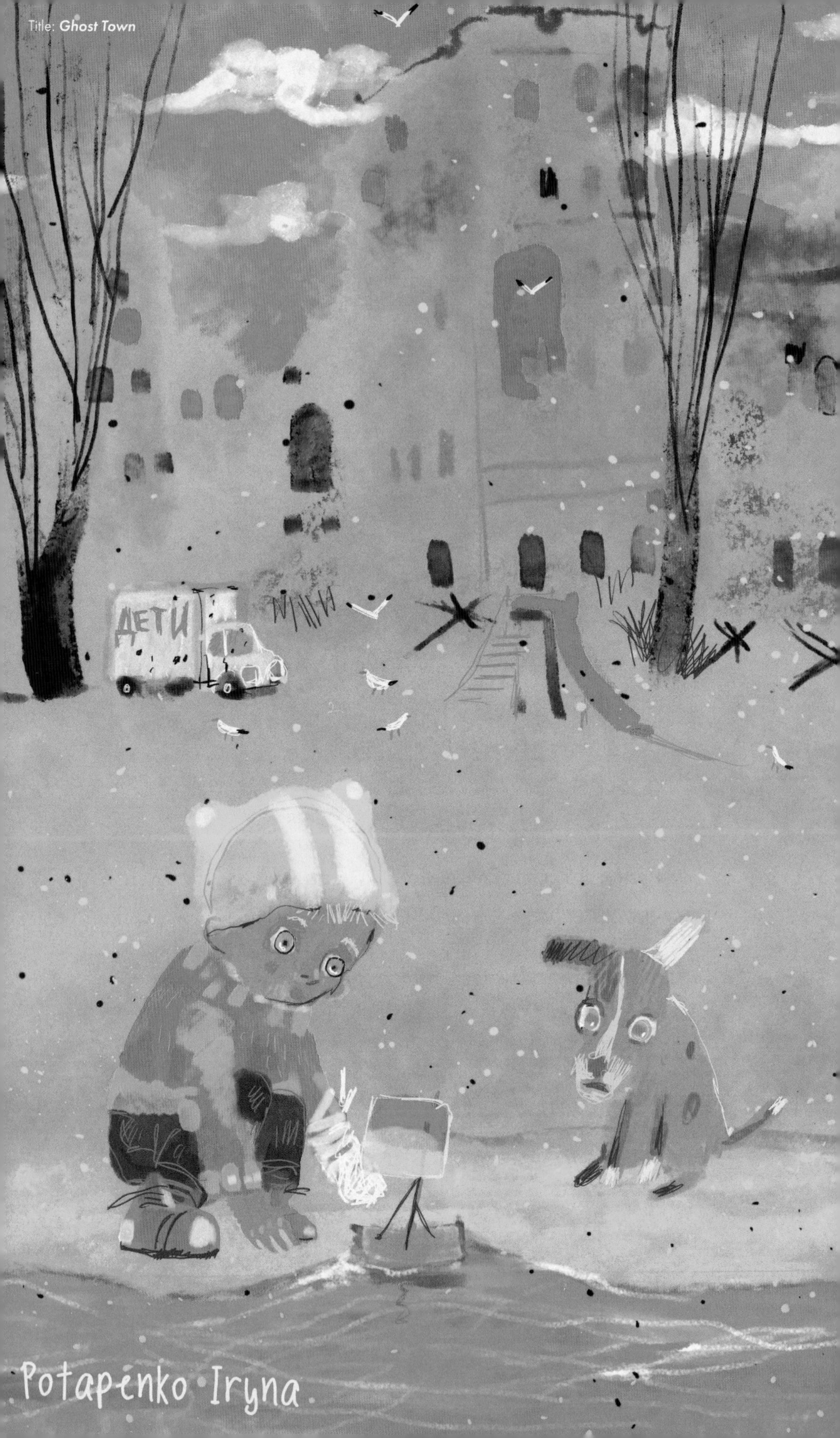
ДЕТИ
Potapenko Iryna

Title: ***Ghost Town***

Iryna Potapenko

Instagram: **@potapenko_iryna_art**

· · · · · · · · · · · · · · · · · · · ·

I look at the annals of the war. Small towns remained after the retreat of the orcs. I won't write how I feel. I will only write that I sincerely believe in the future of these cities.

Title: "Missing Home"

Romana Romanyshyn and Andriy Lesiv, Art Studio Agrafka

Instagram: **@art_studio_agrafka**

. . . .

According to UNICEF, more than 50% of Ukrainian children have become refugees since February, 24, 2022. Millions have moved abroad or to other regions of Ukraine in an attempt to seek shelter. Russia is committing genocide against Ukrainian people.

So we all, children and adults, must remember how strongly we love our home and family, how strongly connected we are with each other, how we suffered, how we cried, how we fought, how we won, how we were hurt, and how we healed. We have to work with our memory to remember who we are.

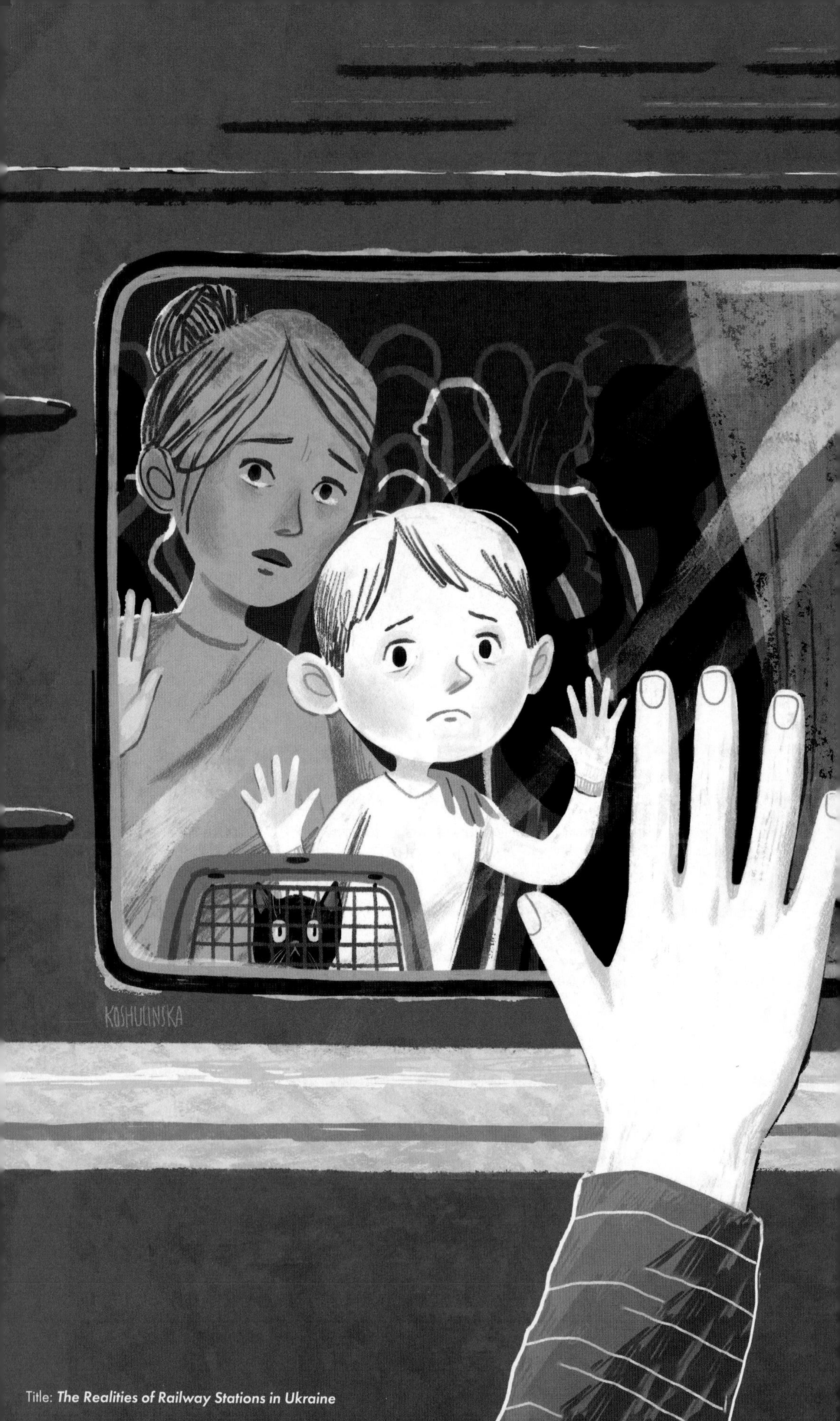
KOSHULINSKA

Title: ***The Realities of Railway Stations in Ukraine***

Marta Koshulinska

Instagram: **@marta_koshulinska**

· · · · · · · · · · · · · · · · · · · ·

Women and children are forced to leave their homes due
to the danger of bombings. They're forced to say goodbye
to their husbands, dads, and brothers...and they don't
know when they'll be able to see each other again.

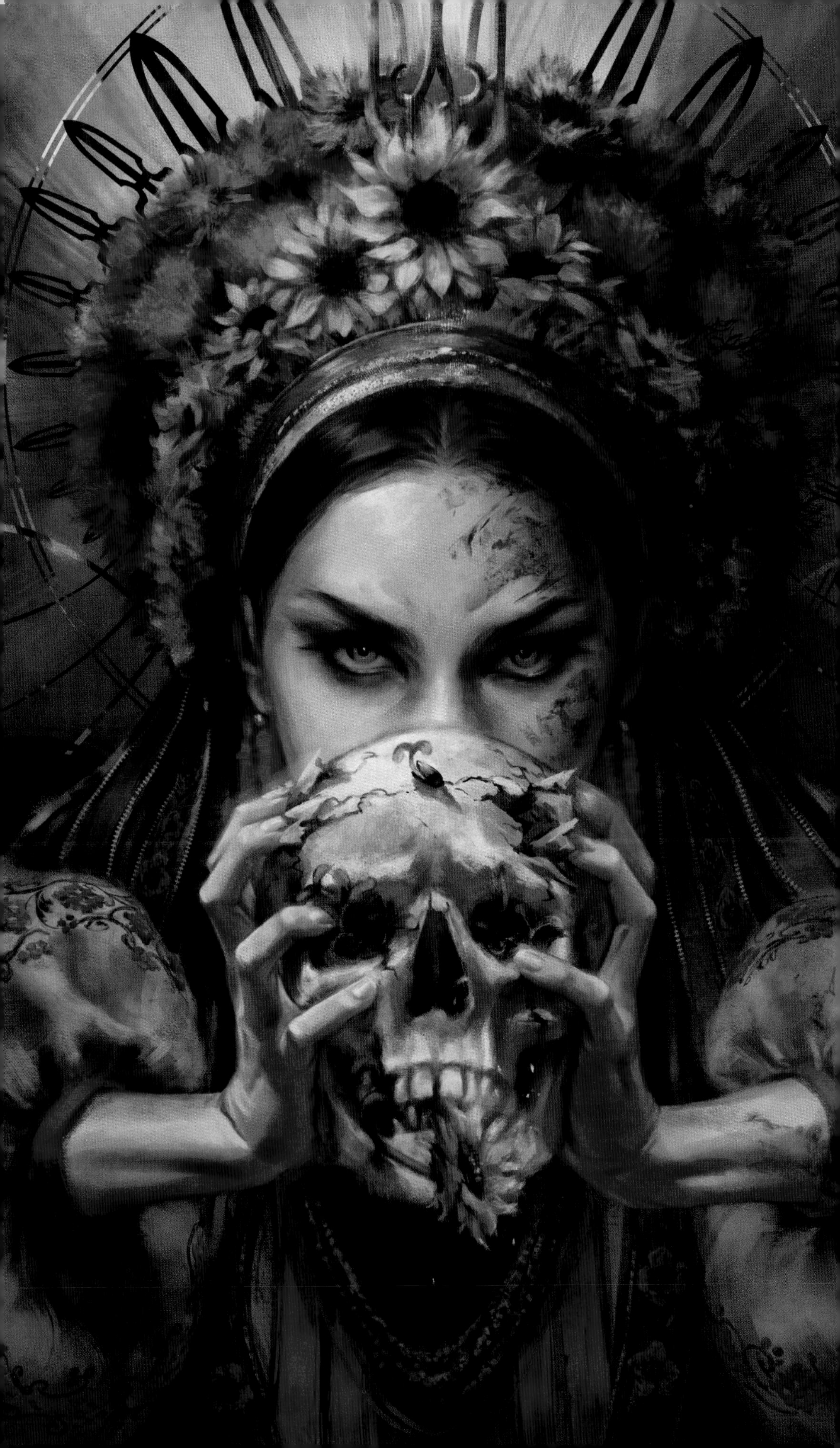

Inna Vjuzhanina

Instagram: **@inna_vjuzhanina**

. . . .

My name is Inna, and I'm an independent artist
and creator based in beautiful Ukraine.

Having grown up watching Xena: Warrior Princess, thrilling adventure movies, and running around the forests of my homeland, I fostered a deep love for nature, strong female characters, and mythology. All of which found their way into my work. I enjoy exploring cultures, myths, legends, and pondering over the bits of real history behind them. I love telling the stories that my mind conjures through the viewpoint of my own characters or the ones that inspire me the most.

With all that in mind, I'm sure you've heard the story about
the "sunflower seeds curse"...

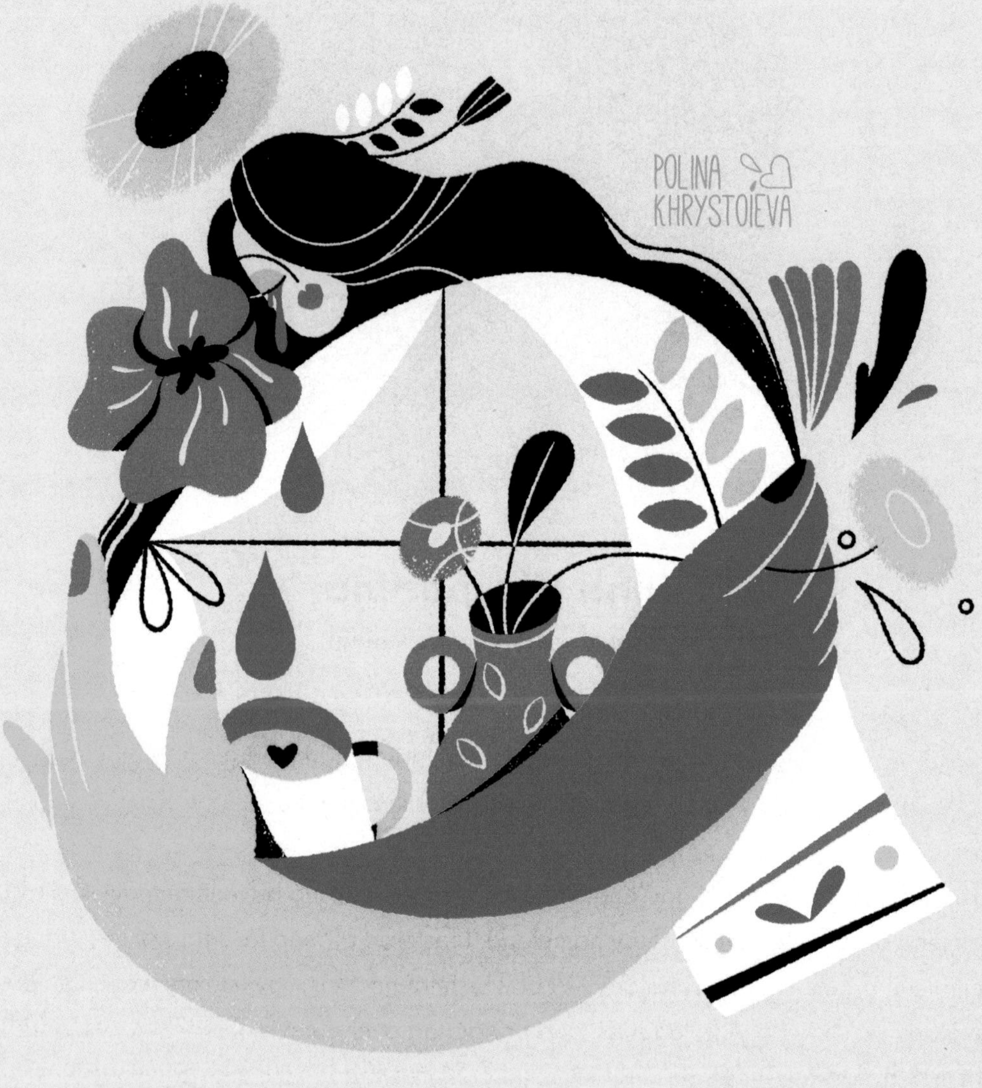
POLINA
KHRYSTOIEVA

Polina Khrystoieva

Instagram: **@polumnart**

· · · · · · · · · · · · · · · · · · · ·

Let me introduce myself. I'm Polina from Kharkiv, Ukraine. Now I'm in a safe place, but Russian forces have almost fully destroyed Kharkiv and many other cities.

Honestly, it's tough for me to be creative these days. I can't believe that these awful things are happening. I feel pain, I'm angry, I'm so confused, and I'm extremely anxious. But I try to keep myself under control. I hope that these rough times will be finished soon.

To quote Albus Dumbledore from Harry Potter: "Happiness can be found, even in the darkest of times, if one only remembers to turn on the light."

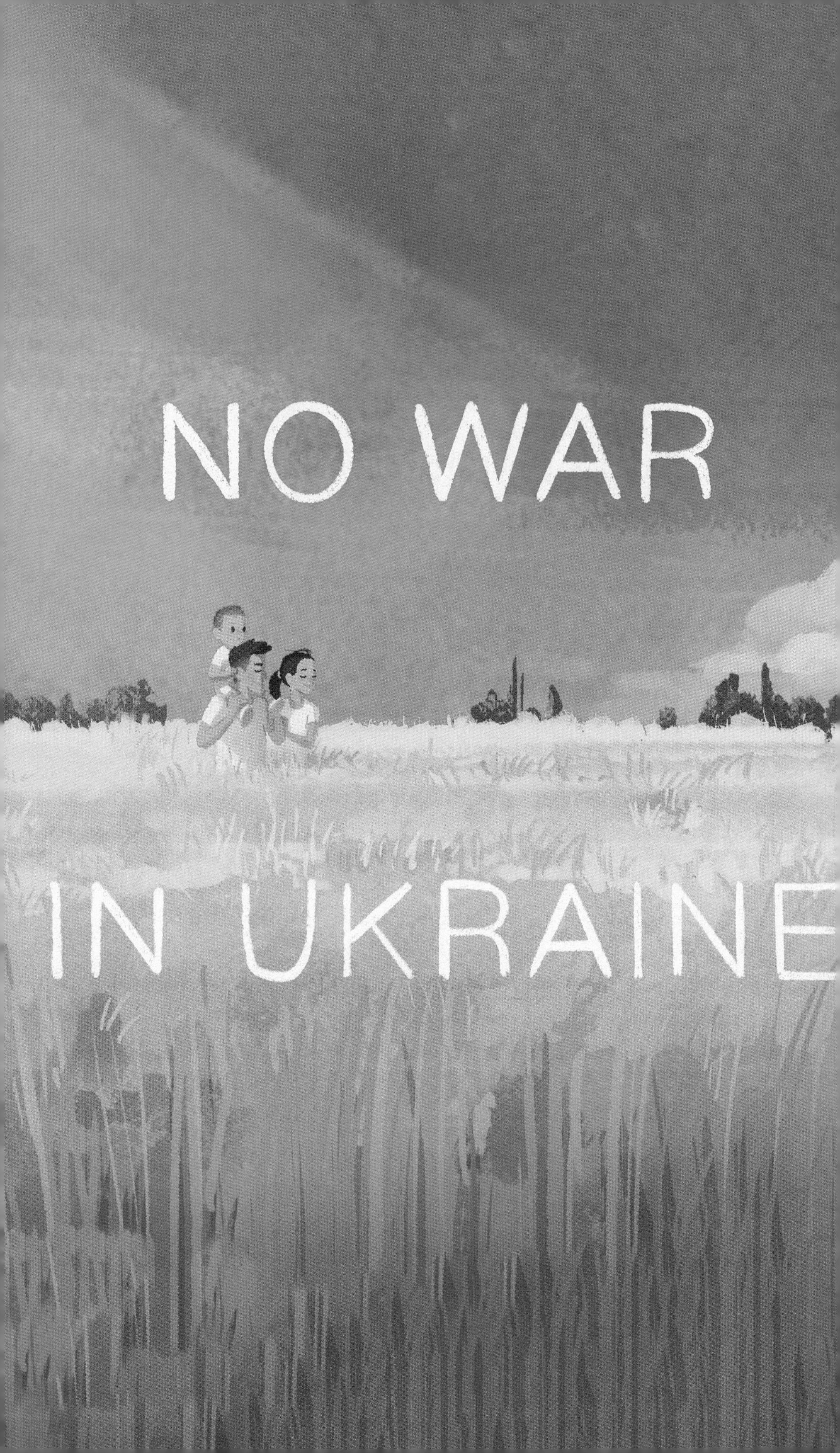
NO WAR
IN UKRAINE

Andy Ivanov

Instagram: **@andivart**

. . . .

On February 22, I decided to draw this art piece.
I wanted to reflect the nature of Ukraine, which would be consonant with the national colors of our flag. My family symbolizes our people's peaceful and benevolent mood.

On February 24, the war began.
The picture received 22672 reposts on Instagram. I hope this piece bolsters the hearts of many Ukrainians in this dark time.

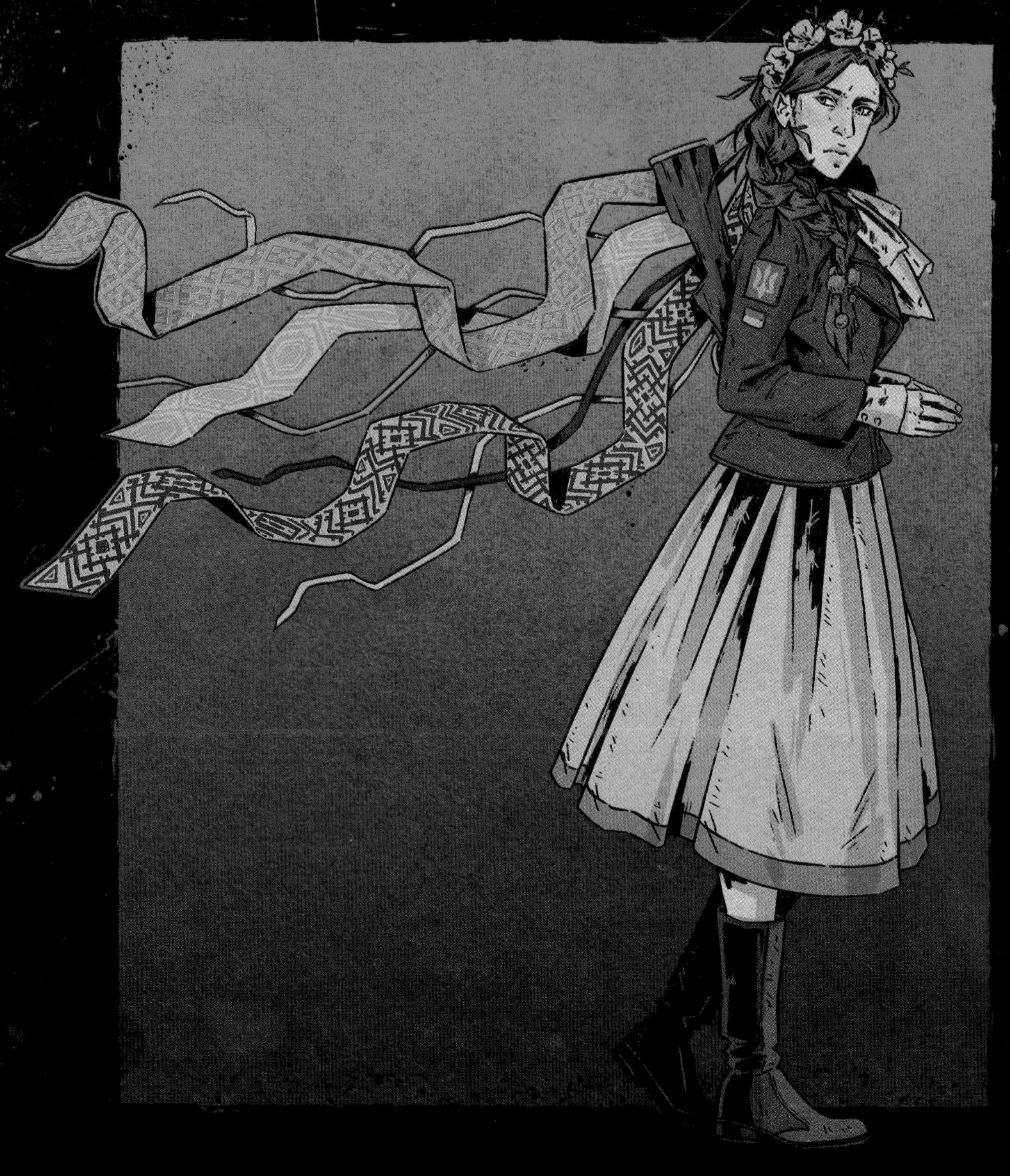

Title: ***"Ribbons"***

Kateryna Kosheleva

Instagram: **@tokkamak**

· · · · · · · · · · · · · · · · · · · ·

The history we've been taught, the history we picked up along the way trying to make sense of "today" through the "yesterday," takes a truer meaning these days. The facts of the past that seemed absurd, like a puzzle with pieces missing, become complete and painfully obvious.

Many facts from Ukraine's history were misinterpreted and perverted to cater to the imperial ambitions of others. Rediscovery and recontextualization are long and painful, just like recovery from any trauma.

There will be a time when the textbook titled *The History of Ukraine* will contain more historical truth than leftovers from our colonial past.

I look forward to that moment.

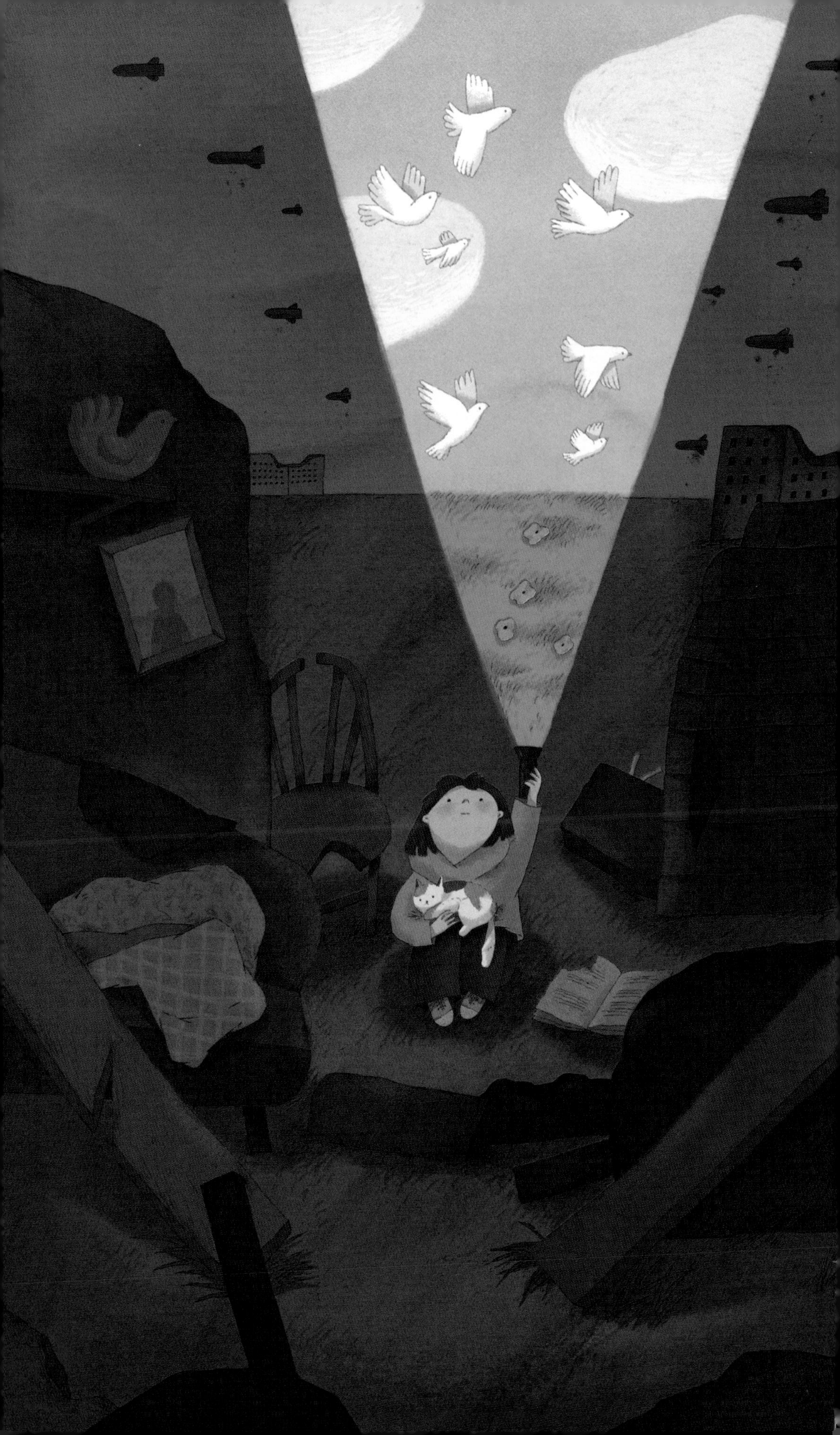

Yev Haidamaka

Instagram: **@yevhaidamaka**

. . . .

Children should be given wings and taught how to fly.

Children shouldn't be killed by missile strikes. Children shouldn't be assaulted by soldiers. They shouldn't be deported or separated from their families and left as orphans. Every time a new wave of Russian war crimes appears, we think, "Nothing can be worse than this." And then...there's news about children witnessing death, forced to stay in basements with bodies of their parents, and/or forced to watch the assault of their mothers. Then there are parents forced to bury their children in their backyard.

I have no words. This is beyond everything I thought I knew.

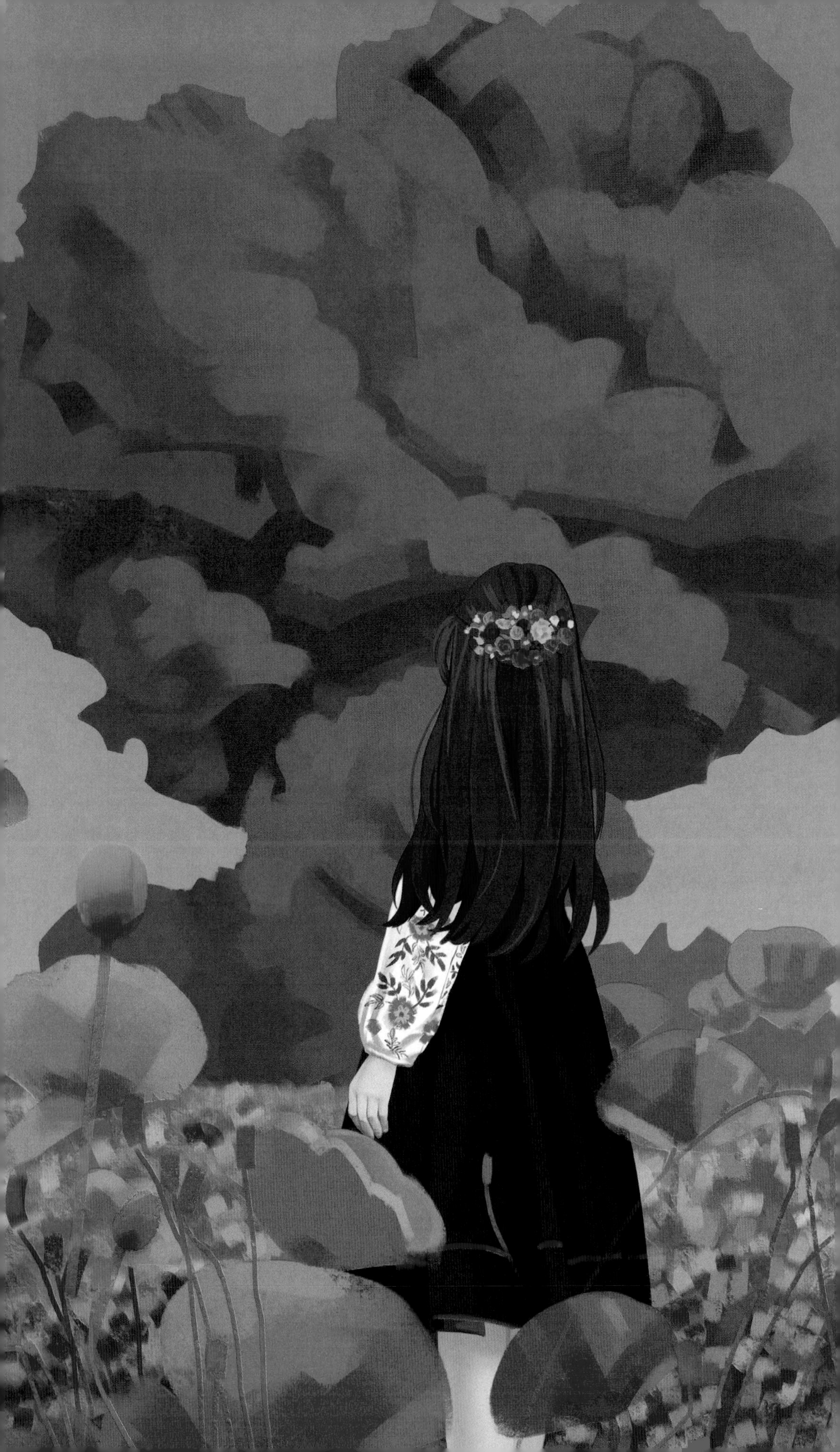

Gexis

Instagram: @_gexis_

. . . .

This girl is watching other cities be bombed. What is she thinking about? Does she regret not being able to help? Does she wait until they come to bomb her city? What is she thinking? What do you think?

I'm proud to be Ukrainian. I'm proud of my people.

After the war, I will rebuild my country. I'll stay here. I'll live here. I know that a bright future is waiting for us, but we have to overcome a lot of struggles. I'm staying here to see that and become a part of it.

Lena Rozvadovska, Co-Founder:

After Russia's full-scale invasion of Ukraine, Voices of Children has been working non-stop to help injured children and families from all over the country, provide temporary psychological assistance, assist in the evacuation of people, provide supplies for relocations, and provide assistance with settlements. When Mad Cave shared the idea of publishing a graphic novel that included Tanya Vovk, we immediately wanted to move forward with a collaboration.

Please meet our seven-year-old illustrator Tanya Vovk.

She's surrounded by her drawings of the Voices of Children team as cats.

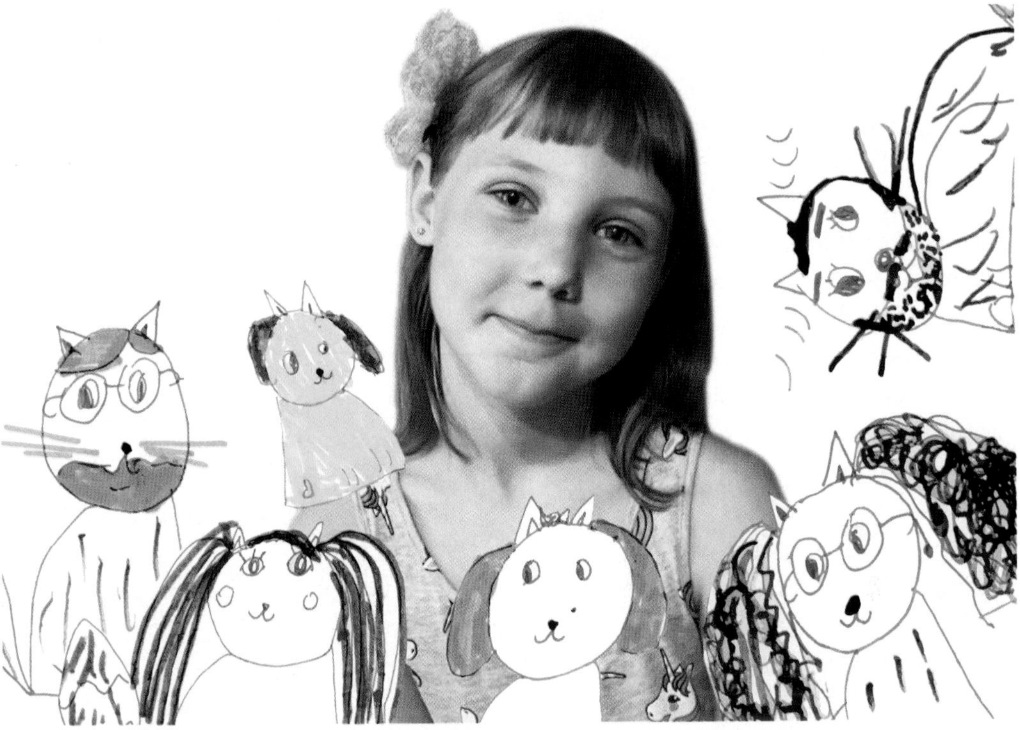

Where do your ideas for drawings come from? They're so unique!

That's how I see the world. The sea, beautiful trees with swings, and colorful flowers—all of it. I once saw some beautiful peacocks and was inspired by their colors, so I now create colorful outfits for everyone. I try to find joy in the world, so I paint everything very bright.

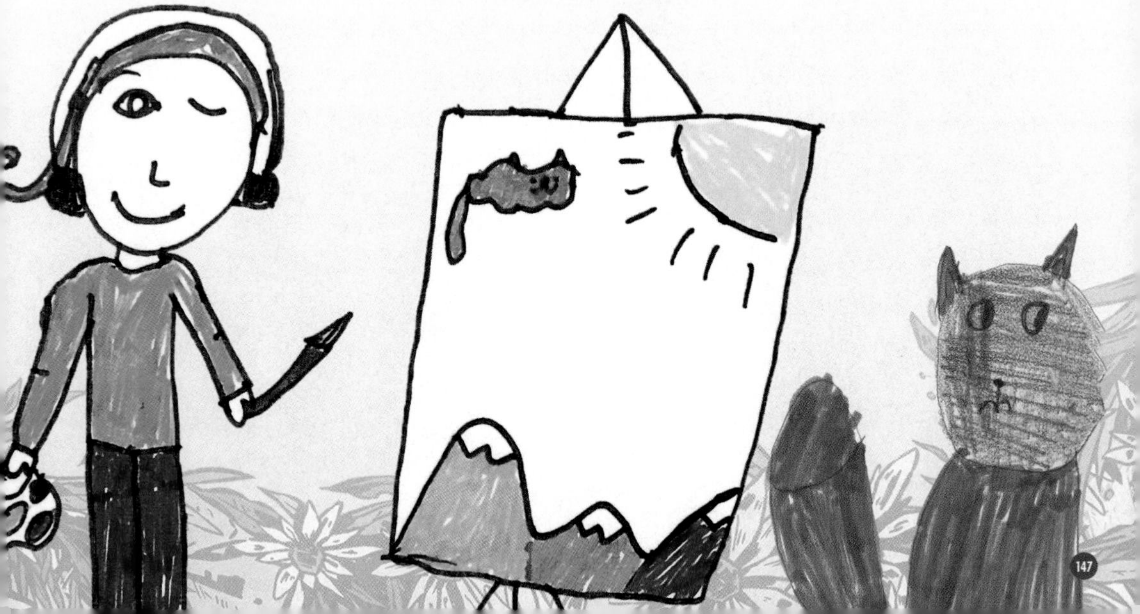

Why do you draw for our foundation?
I want all people to see the stories of children in the war and to help them.

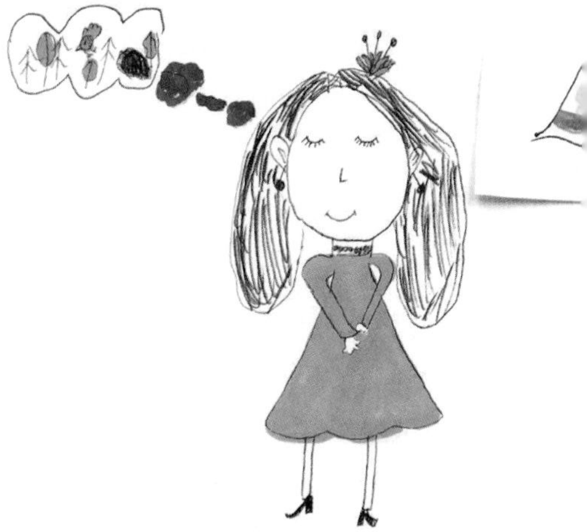

What should be done to create better lives for children in Ukraine?
We should support other children–especially those who are not well.

What sort of things do you dream of?
I have an interesting dream where buses and cars can fly. It wouldn't be scary to see the world from such a great height and be surrounded by birds. But in this dream, there's now peace and children are no longer suffering.

What inspires you?
I'm inspired by my sister, who is extremely cheerful and raises my spirits. I'm also inspired by my mother, who loves me very much.

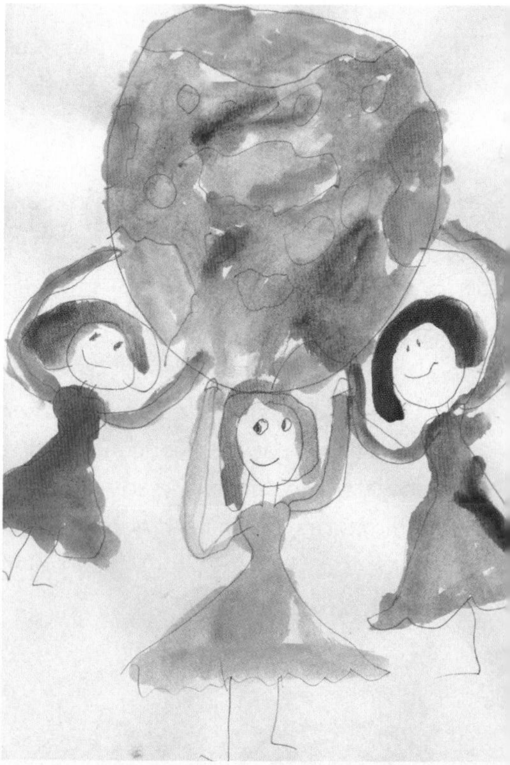

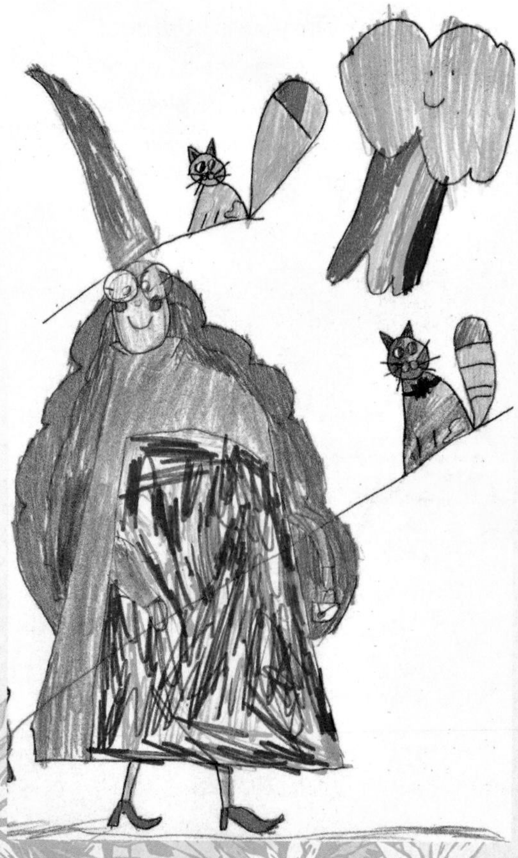

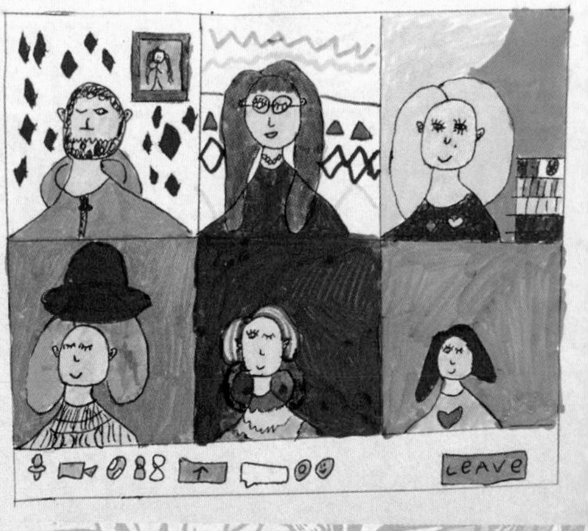
LEAVE

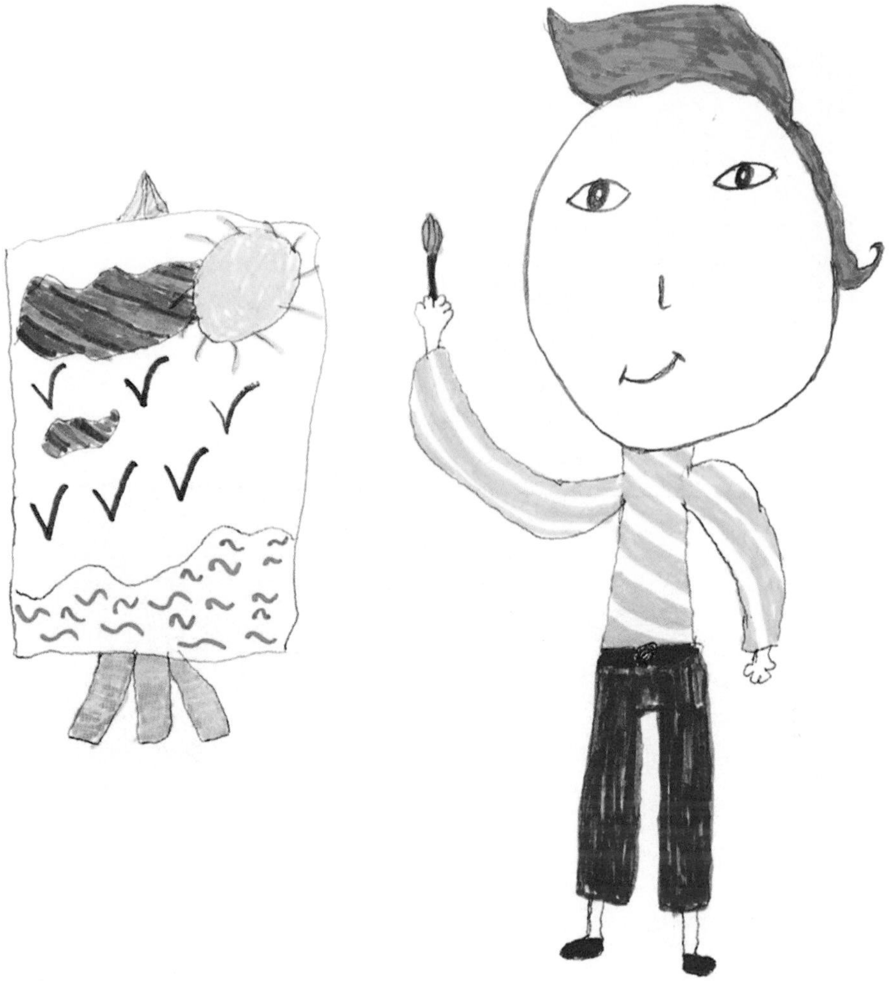

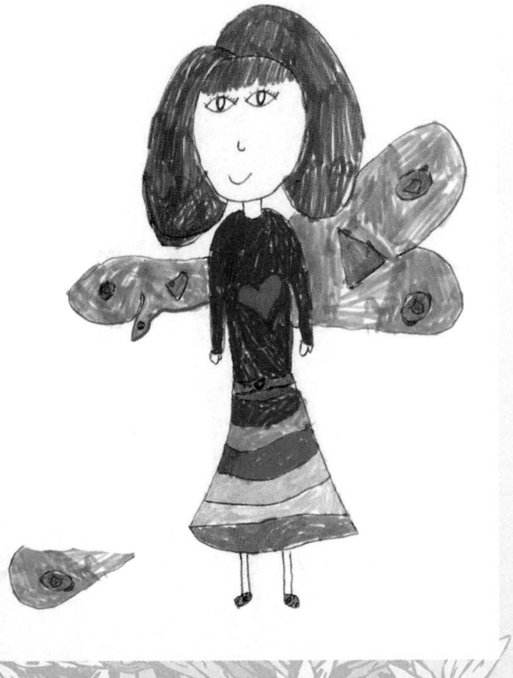

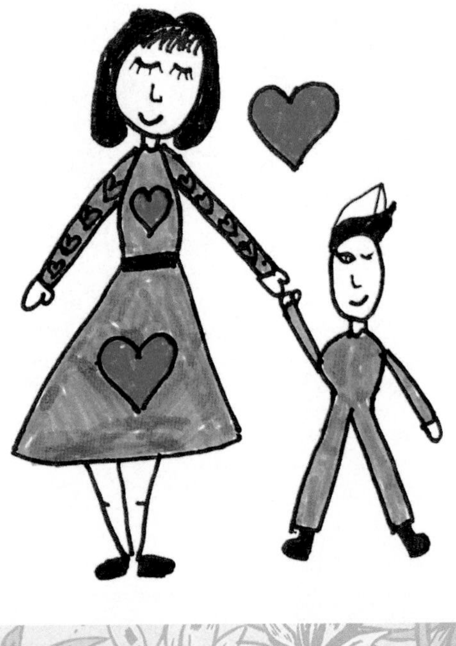

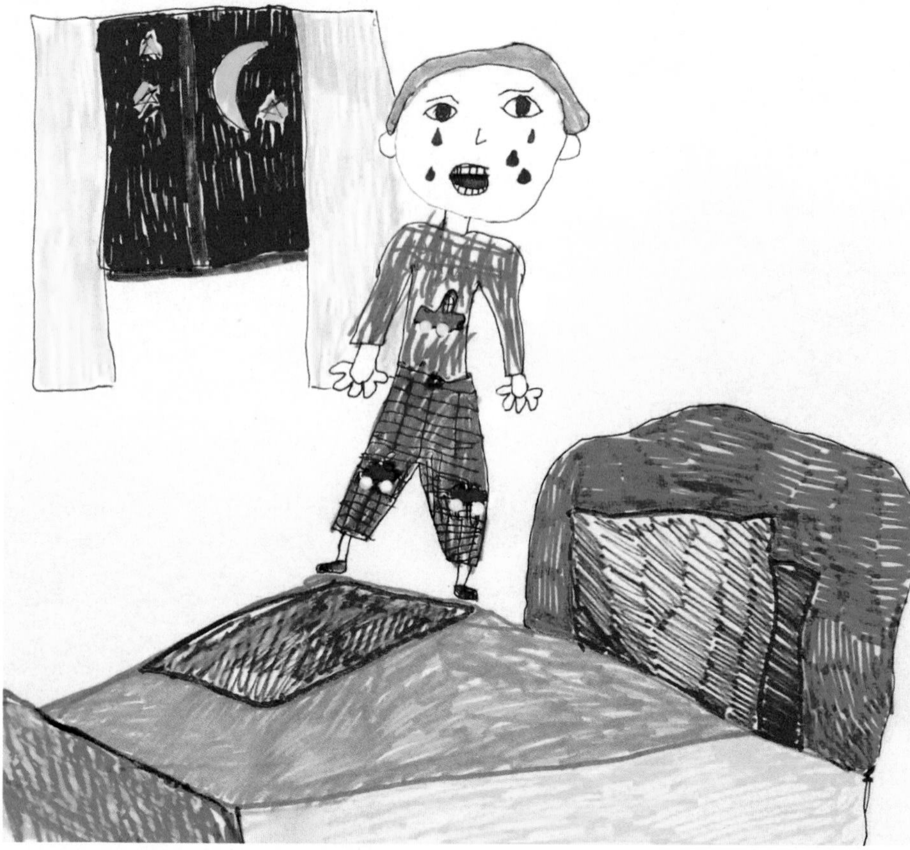

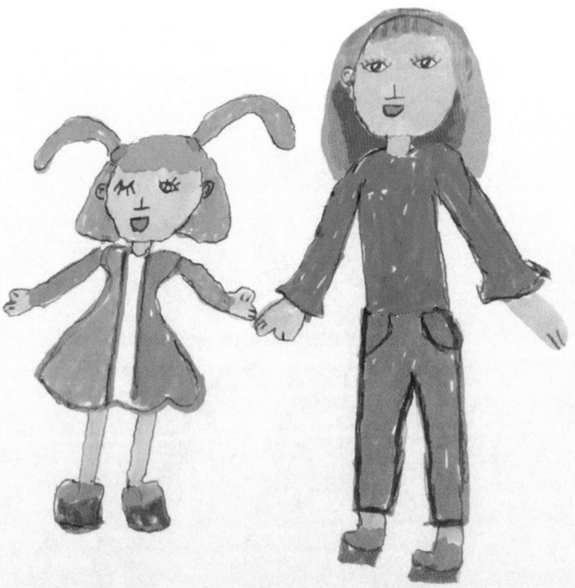

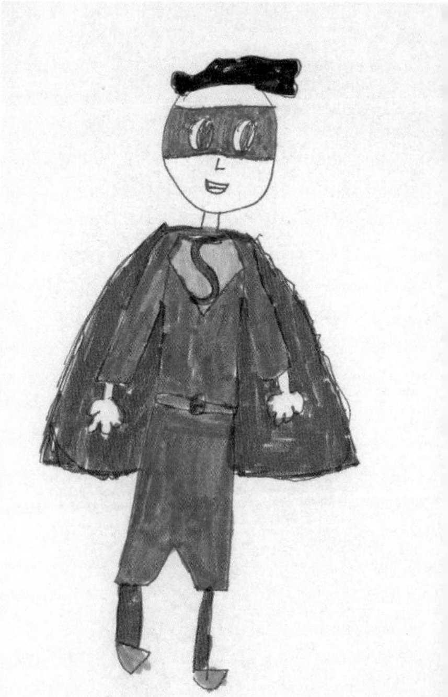

NO CHILD IN UKRAINE SHOULD BE LEFT ALONE WITH THE TRAUMA OF THE WAR

donate

> There is no family in Ukraine left that has not felt the devastating effects of the war. We, the employees of the foundation, also stayed in the basements, left our homes with one backpack, calmed our children while being under shelling. Along with this, we launched new assistance programs, psychological support and tried to reach those who are having the hardest time. Despite the non-stop work, too many children still do not have the basics: food, water, access to medicine, and so on. Thanks to everyone who cares and sends help from all over the world.

Contacts: **voices.org.ua**

Partnership & Collaboration: **partnership@voices.org.ua**

Humanitarian Support: **aid@voices.org.ua**

PR & Press: **press@voices.org.ua**

VOICES
OF CHILDREN
CHARITABLE FOUNDATION

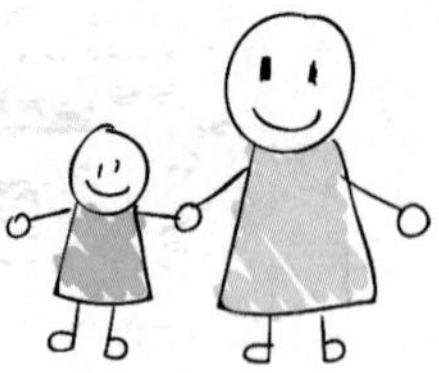

THE FUND PROVIDES PSYCHOLOGICAL AND PSYCHOSOCIAL ASSISTANCE TO THE CHILDREN AFFECTED BY THE MILITARY CONFLICT IN THE UKRAINIAN FRONTLINE CITIES OF THE LUHANSK AND DONETSK REGIONS SINCE 2015.

Currently, the fund has broadened its activity.
We help to evacuate children from the East of Ukraine (territories which are controlled by Ukrainian army), arrange their settlement in the West, giving humanitarian aid, and shelter, providing further psychological help.

The fund activity results during 1st month of the war:

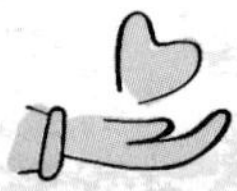

1.5 million UAH in aid to more than **5,000 war victims** and help with the delivery of **20 tons of humanitarian aid** from abroad.

Psychological support:

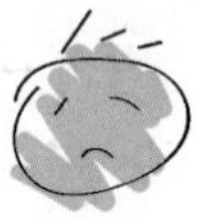

100+ consultations with psychologists from all over the country and abroad. **190 children** relocated from the shelling received psychotherapy sessions.

Evacuation and settlement assistance:

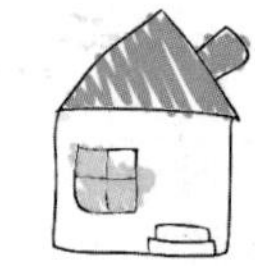

Thanks to **5 tons of fuel** provided, **2,000+ people** were evacuated from the hotspots in the East.

250 families (incl. 850 children) were supported during evacuation and settlement.

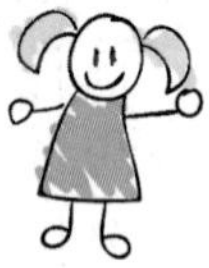

3,000+ families received food and hygiene items after evacuation.

800 women and children were assisted with setting up temporary and permanent shelters in the West.

Assistance to children in orphanages:

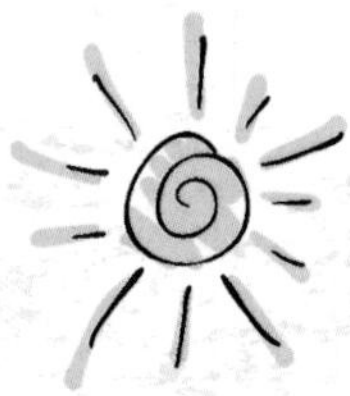

80 students of the Znamyansk boarding school (children with disabilities, difficult to relocate) received medicine, hygiene products, and things to arrange sleeping places in the basement.

Almost 100 children with disabilities of Zhytomyr and Zaporizhia boarding schools received delivery of medicine and hygiene products.

Essentials and clothes were purchased for the **Lysychansk Center for Psychosocial Rehabilitation.**

VOICES OF CHILDRE
CHARITABLE FOUNDATION